LIGHTS OUT

AN INTO DARKNESS NOVEL

LIGHTS OUT

NAVESSA ALLEN

SLOWBURN
A zando IMPRINT
NEW YORK

zando

The characters and events in this book are fictitious. Any similarity to real persons, living or dead, is coincidental and not intended by the author.

Slowburn is an imprint of Zando.
zandoprojects.com

First Edition: August 2024

Design by Neuwirth & Associates, Inc.
Cover design by Christopher Brian King

Library of Congress Control Number: 2024938416

978-1-63893-223-9 (Paperback)
978-1-63893-224-6 (ebook)

10 9 8 7 6 5 4 3 2 1
Manufactured in the United States of America

TRIGGER WARNINGS

Lights Out is a dark, stalker rom-com with heavy themes. Reader discretion is advised as this book contains:

Sexually explicit discussion and scenes (including anal play)

Alcohol consumption

Mention of (off-page) rape

Child abuse (remembered)

Medical content

Blood and gore (in a hospital setting)

Discussion of mental health

Mention of serial killers and their crimes

Limited description of a mass shooting

Stalking

Invasion of privacy

Home invasion

Hidden cameras

Hacking

Theft

Unintentional cannibalism (remembered)

Death

Car accident (remembered)

Description of a violent death (remembered)

Death of a parent

Breath play

Knife play

Gun play

Fear play

Primal play

Mask play

Consensual dubious consent

For everyone brave enough

to ride the handle.

LIGHTS OUT

1

ALY

THE NEW GIRL WASN'T DOING TOO WELL. She was curled up in one of the cheap, uncomfortable plastic chairs when I walked into the breakroom, staring into space. Her scrubs were rumpled, messy bun slipping sideways off her head, blond strands sticking out like she'd been pulling at her hair. Beneath the fluorescent lights, her skin looked waxy and pale.

The two other nurses in the room were giving her a wide berth, casting anxious looks her way as if worried she was going to puke or pass out. Or worse, quit, like so many others had.

Over my dead body.

We needed her. I couldn't keep pulling back-to-back, fifteen-hour shifts, or I would burn out.

I took a deep breath and strode toward her, ducking down by her side so if she did puke, I could dive out of the splash zone. She didn't seem to notice me. Not good.

"Hey, Brinley, right?" I asked, keeping my voice low and calm. It was the same tone I used when speaking to sick children.

She blinked and turned my way, her blue eyes glassy and unfocused like she wasn't really seeing me. This was borderline shock. I would know; I saw it almost every shift in at least one of my patients.

Damn it, she was totally going to quit.

I turned slightly to the side, keeping my eyes trained on Brinley. "Blanket?"

The sound of shuffling feet told me someone was following the request, so I faced forward again and gave the new nurse my full attention. I'd gotten the gossip on her from another of my colleagues. According to them, Brinley had been a nurse for three years and recently transferred from a smaller county ER. This was her first time working in a trauma hospital.

Some people did just fine in normal ERs but cracked when they came here. We were inner city, in a metropolis known for its sky-high crime rates. Not a shift went by where we didn't see the worst of the worst: stabbings, rapes, gunshot wounds, abuse victims, survivors of horrific car accidents, you name it.

Tonight had been especially rough, even for me, and I'd seen so much shit that very little rattled me anymore. It could be scarring for someone new to a trauma center like Brinley, and I cursed her luck that this was her first unsupervised shift.

A blanket appeared in my periphery. I took it without looking and wrapped it around Brinley's shoulders. She moved like an automaton, arms jerky as she clutched the ends together and tugged it tighter.

"His chest," she said, so low I barely caught the words. "The whole middle was just . . . missing."

Ah, so she'd gotten the close-range shotgun wound. It was amazing the man was even alive when he arrived, and terribly sad because there was almost nothing we could do in cases like his. Too much of the heart, lungs, and other vital organs were shredded for someone to live through it. I heard he passed shortly after being rolled in. If Brinley had him, she would have gotten soaked through with blood. No wonder she was wearing different scrubs from earlier, and her hair still looked damp from having to shower it all off.

"There was nothing you could have done," I told her.

She sniffled, and her eyes finally seemed to focus on me. "I know, but . . . *god*. I don't think I'll ever get that sight out of my head."

Don't worry, tomorrow you'll see something equally traumatic, and that will take its place, a dark part of me thought, but I would never say something like that aloud.

"Has anyone told you about the therapists?" I asked her.

She nodded. "Third floor, right?"

"And if you're on a night shift and need to talk to someone, there's a 24/7 call line."

Our hospital might overwork us, but it did an excellent job of prioritizing the mental health of its staff. We saw the same amount of daily trauma soldiers might face on a front line, and the burnout and PTSD rates were sky-high because of it.

I regularly spoke to one of the on-call therapists. It was one of the few things keeping me relatively sane while the healthcare system crumbled around us, and so many people quit the field that we were becoming dangerously understaffed.

"I don't have the number for the call line," Brinley said, a single tear rolling down her cheek.

This was good. Tears I could work with. Tears meant she was already processing, and the risk of her going into shock was passing.

"Which locker did you put your stuff in?" I asked. "I'll grab your phone and add the number."

Twenty minutes later, she was back on her feet with her hands wrapped around a steaming mug of chamomile tea. I'd put the call line in her phone, she'd stopped trembling, and a little color was returning to her cheeks. Only one other nurse was in the room with us now, having replaced the previous, unhelpful two from before. That nurse was Tanya, a trim Black woman in her mid-forties who'd worked in trauma hospitals almost as long as Brinley had been alive. Tanya was my favorite coworker. She was great under pressure, had an excellent bedside manner, and knew more about treating people in emergency situations than most doctors we worked with.

Right now, she was standing with Brinley near the window, talking quietly, one hand gripping the younger woman's shoulder. I tuned in and out as I gathered mine and Brinley's stuff, trusting Tanya to know all the right words to use as she coaxed Brinley back from the brink.

"You did so well," I heard her say. "And I'm not just blowing smoke up your ass to make you feel better. I've seen other nurses with more experience freeze up during nights like this, but you kept your shit together and did what you had to." She turned to me. "Back me up, Aly."

I slung Brinley's bag over my shoulder and joined them. "She's not lying," I said. "You crushed it, from what I saw. And it's totally normal to break down a little afterward. All that adrenaline built up too high, and your cortisol levels probably went bananas. There's no shame in disappearing into a miniature stress coma. I still do it, too, on really bad nights."

Brinley paled. "I thought tonight was really bad."

Whoops. Time to backtrack.

"It was," I said. "I just meant I didn't see the worst this time. I think you and Mallory did."

She let out a shaky breath. "Oh. Okay."

Tanya turned back to her. "Now, Aly's gonna give you a ride home. Her shift is over, too."

Brinley looked between us. "But my car is here."

Tanya nodded. "Yes, but we don't think you should drive right now."

Brinley seemed to see the wisdom in that. "Yeah, you're probably right."

"Don't worry," I said. "I checked your schedule. We're both on shift at the same time tomorrow, so I'll give you a lift back. You parked in the employee lot?"

She nodded.

"Your car should be fine there. Do you need to get anything out of it?"

She frowned. "I don't think so?"

Tanya plucked the tea from her hands. "Then you two should get out of here while you can."

"Thank you," I mouthed at her.

She nodded.

It wasn't uncommon to get roped into a few more hours of work if you loitered too long after your shift ended because someone always needed an extra set of hands or more people were required to help stabilize a patient. Brinley wasn't in any shape for that, and I'd been here four extra hours already. It was time to go.

I steered Brinley toward the exit, and we took the back way out to avoid running into anyone else. She was quiet as we walked but looked much better than when I first saw her, so I took that as a good sign.

"Do you live with anyone?" I asked her.

"My boyfriend," she said.

"Is he home right now?" I didn't love the idea of leaving her alone if he wasn't.

She nodded. "He is. I texted him at the end of my shift before I sat down, and, well. You saw."

"Talking about it helps," I told her. "I'm not sure if your boyfriend is squeamish, but telling him about what you went through tonight could get some of it out of your head."

"I'm not sure," she said, her voice laced with indecision.

"You don't have to go into detail. Just the basics. And I put my number in your phone along with the therapist line, so you can always call me, too."

She shot me a relieved look. "Thank you. I don't think he'd get it. You know?"

I nodded. I did know. Unlike Brinley, I was single . . . ish, but even when I had partners, I didn't talk shop with them. I never dated seriously—I was too career-focused for that right now—and talking about a bad day or how sad it was when I lost a patient felt like the kind of thing you saved for a significant other. Mostly, I spilled my guts to therapists or other nurses, and from the look on Brinley's face, I could tell she would be the same. Civilians, as we called non-healthcare or emergency workers, didn't get it a lot of the time.

We chatted more on the way home about safer topics like the latest TV show everyone was watching to distract ourselves from the night we'd had. By the time I dropped Brinley off at her townhouse, the sun was starting to rise over the city, glinting off the distant high-rises and painting the clouds a macabre ombre that ranged from the deep purple of new bruises to the arterial red of freshly spilled blood.

God, I'm morbid this morning, I thought, pulling my eyes from the sky.

I'd spent so much time trying to help and then distract Brinley that I hadn't processed my own shitshow of a night. There was a guy who'd gotten stabbed three times, a woman with a broken wrist, bloody nose, and a guilty-looking husband who wouldn't let her speak for herself, and a two-year-old with RSV so bad he had to be med-flighted to the children's hospital.

The worst was the homeless man with frostbite. Not because it was an extreme case—his frostbite was relatively mild, and he'd keep all his toes—but because no one else in my rotation wanted to go in his room because he smelled so bad, complaining loudly enough in the hall outside that he probably heard them. It both broke my heart and pissed me off, so I sent the others running and took care of him myself.

Those were the kinds of cases that stuck with me now, not the overly gory ones, but the sad ones. I fixated on them. Where was that man's family? Were they looking for him? What about the woman being abused by her husband? Would she be able to get out before he hurt her again?

My drive home passed in a blur as these thoughts filled my head, and before I knew it, I was pulling into my driveway. The street was dark enough that my house was lit up by twinkling string lights. It was well into the second week of January, but a few of my neighbors still had their holiday decorations up, so I wasn't rushing to take mine down. Seeing those lights flashing merrily in the pre-dawn gloom was precisely the kind of pick-me-up I needed—anything to keep the darkness at bay.

I turned my car off and got out. My house wasn't much, just a small two-bedroom Craftsman-style cottage in a semi-safe neighborhood, but it was all mine, and I was damn proud of the work I'd done fixing it up and putting my unique stamp on the place. The siding was an antique pale blue-green, the trim was a warm white, and the small front deck looked festive and inviting thanks to the holiday-themed welcome sign and the Christmas tree that sparkled with tinsel and decorations.

Inside, it was just as merry. I didn't have any family left that mattered, and decking my house out top to bottom in seasonal décor was how I distracted myself from the depressing fact that I either spent the holidays alone or working every year.

A loud yowl split the air as I closed the door behind me and kicked off my shoes.

Well, I wasn't *entirely* alone. I did have Fred to keep me company. He must have been fast asleep on my bed when I walked in because his yowling started farther away and then rose in pitch and volume as he raced toward me, like an ambulance screaming down a highway.

Man, he's loud when he's angry, I thought. If he kept this up, my nearest neighbors were going to start thinking I hurt him.

"Oh my god, Fred," I said as my long-haired black and white cat raced around the corner. "You're fine. I'm only a few hours late this time."

I scooped him up when he reached me, turning him onto his back so I could bury my face in his fluffy belly. My mom called this "fur therapy" growing up. She'd come home from a long day of work, and before saying hi to Dad or me, she'd head straight to a cat and snuggle them until they started to squirm. It always made her feel better, so I'd done the same thing to Fred since the day after he showed up in my yard, a half-drowned kitten crying to get out of a storm. I didn't know if it was because he was so young when I started doing it to him, but he tolerated fur therapy pretty well, purring and making biscuits in my hair.

I probably would have seemed like a lunatic to non–cat people, but I didn't give a shit. On principle, I didn't trust anyone who didn't like cats, so they'd never be around to judge me anyway.

I set Fred down once I'd gotten my fill, and he trotted behind me as I headed into my room to change. You think I'd be tired after such a long shift, but I was wide awake. Probably because I'd learned how to fall asleep at the drop of a dime, and I found somewhere to take a five-minute power nap whenever there was a lull. The hospital had been weirdly quiet from midnight to one, and I'd slept for a whole hour. Tanya told me one of the floor nurses—someone who worked on a higher floor in a specialty unit—had commented about it being slow when she came to pick up lab work, which jinxed us. ER nurses knew better than to say things like that.

I showered, changed into the coziest pajamas I owned, poured myself an oversized glass of white wine, and snuggled up with Fred on my couch. I had half a mind to turn on the TV and zone out for a while, but I hadn't checked my phone once during my shift, and those social media notifications were calling.

Giving in to the inevitable, I pulled up my favorite app and started scrolling. There were the expected videos of cute animals doing cute things, people acting like idiots and getting themselves into trouble, storytimes about exes, and muscular people posing in gym mirrors. But more than anything else, there were thirst traps. Specifically, thirst traps of men wearing some sort of mask. My obsession with them started at the beginning of autumn when this subgenre of videos rose to the spotlight every year, thanks to horny book lovers and lusty lurkers like me.

With one hand, I scratched behind Fred's ears. The other was busy smashing that like button for videos of men dressed in cosplay, decked out in futuristic military gear, and even a few sporting full horror movie costumes. I saved my favorites for the ghost-like masks, though. The shirtless ones had me drooling. Add in a knife and some fake blood, and that was an instant follow.

My absolute favorite creator was a user with the handle "the.faceless.man" because he had everything I loved most: a custom mask that was unlike anyone else's and was as sensual as it was terrifying, muscles, good lighting, exceptional music selection, and an innate understanding of how to reel the viewer in and keep us begging for more. I had a whole favorite section devoted to his videos, and I routinely went back and rewatched them whenever I needed a distraction after a bad shift.

Like tonight.

I drained the last of my wine—damn, I completely lost track of time when I scrolled—and got up to pour myself another round. Fred jumped down from the couch and curled inside his little felt house by the TV, having reached his snuggle limit. I checked his food and water in the kitchen—both were still mostly full—and emptied the last of the wine into my glass. By the time I finished it, I'd be half a bottle deep.

Yup, I'd be tipsy soon and hopefully tired. I only had ten hours until my next shift started, and I desperately needed to catch up on all the sleep I'd missed during the usual holiday uptick at the hospital.

I tugged a blanket over myself as I sat back down, then pulled up my videos of the Faceless Man, as I'd taken to calling him. It was hard to pick a favorite, but if someone held a gun to my head and told me I had to, it would be the one where he was sprawled out over a couch, shirtless, his head resting on the arm, the scene flooded by red light. He was only visible from the ribs up, his skin covered in tattoos, muscles clenched as his arm moved in a rhythmic motion that suggested he was jerking off but didn't go far enough to get him banned.

I never knew where to look when I watched it. At the way his biceps tensed and flexed with every stroke? Or how his chest heaved like he was on the brink of coming? Or just offscreen, where I could imagine his hand pumping his straining cock?

He started the video staring up at the ceiling. Toward the very end, he turned his head to stare directly into the camera, and even though I *knew* a mask couldn't have an expression, it felt like his did. Like those gaping black eyes stared straight into my soul, and that smirking mouth was calling my name while he came. The video cut off right after he turned his head, and it was embarrassing how many times I'd paused it right before that happened so I could stare into those eyes a few moments longer.

What would it be like to be in the room with him when he filmed it? To be the one he thought of while he got himself off? Or better yet, to come home one day and find him taking up this very couch as he waited for me in the dark, covered in blood, light glinting off the steel of his knife?

That thought made me shudder with a mix of desire and fear. I wanted it in a way that probably wasn't healthy, but after all the ugly shit I'd seen working in the trauma center, and even before that in my fucked-up teen years, it was only natural that my tastes were starting to skew heavily toward the dark side.

Maybe Tyler will wear it for me, I thought.

Right, Tyler. The guy I'd been hooking up with for almost a year now.

I'd nearly forgotten about him. It wasn't that he was forgettable exactly—he was good-looking and a decent lay—but when work got busy, I tended to lose myself in it, and that had been happening a lot because of the hospital's staffing crisis.

When was the last time we hooked up? It must have been before Christmas, at least. Meaning it was far past time for a booty call. Tomorrow was my last shift of the week, and then I had two glorious days off. What better way to spend them than spread out under a man who knew where a clit was?

I drained my wine, feeling high on the possibility of experiencing a masked man in real life. Before I could think better of it, I screenshotted an image of my favorite video and sent it to Tyler along with a text.

I have two days off starting Friday. Wanna come over that night and bring a mask like this? I promise I'll make it interesting for you.

His response didn't come back until a few hours into my shift the next day because he'd been asleep like a normal person when I sent my text.

My heart sank as I read his words.

Damn, girl. You still alive? I thought you ghosted me. It's been two months. Pass on the mask thing. I'm not into it, and I'm seeing someone anyway.

Two months? Had it really been that long? I scrolled up in our text thread, and, shit, it had. Maybe it was time to book another therapy session and ask if they had any tips for balancing a personal life alongside this line of work.

Because clearly, I was failing.

2

JOSH

"You good, man?" I asked my roommate. We'd paused our video game five minutes ago so he could text someone, and I was getting bored.

Tyler flopped onto the couch next to me. "Yeah, just had to break things off with that girl Aly I was hooking up with."

I frowned. "I thought you ended it months ago."

He shook his head and ran a hand through his dark blond hair, flexing his bicep and turning to check his muscles out.

"*Knock it off*" was on the tip of my tongue, but I kept my mouth shut. There wasn't anyone here for Tyler to impress, but he'd been vain as long as I'd known him, and he posed even when he didn't realize he was doing it. It was almost like a nervous tic at this point, so he must have been more bothered by the Aly situation than he was letting on.

"I thought she ghosted me," he said. "But she probably got busy at work again."

I turned toward the TV and tried to act natural. "She's an ER nurse, right?"

I already knew the answer to that, along with several other facts like her address, where she'd gone to nursing school, what kind of grades she got, and what her current work schedule was. You know, normal things people knew about their roommate's ex-hookups.

"Yeah," Tyler said. "I don't hear from her for two months, and then look at the shit she sends me."

He pulled his phone out of his pocket, unlocked it, and tossed it to me. I caught it out of the air and glanced down, freezing the second my eyes landed on the screen.

Oh, fuck.

It was happening. The day I'd dreaded since starting a secret social media account two years ago had finally arrived. My online life was colliding with my real one, and I was about to be found out.

Play it fucking cool, man, I told myself. Tyler was watching me, and I couldn't let him see how freaked out I was. But, fuuuck, Aly had a mask kink, and of all the screenshots she could have sent my roommate, she chose this one.

I cleared my throat. "You never said she was into this kind of thing." Which was weird because Tyler had a habit of telling me every sordid detail of his sex life, even though I'd begged him to keep it to himself.

He snorted. "I didn't know she was, so it's good I'm seeing Sarah because I'm not. I just want to get in, get off, and get the fuck out. I'm not down for playing games."

How unfortunate for the people he slept with.

"I hear that," I lied, tilting the phone toward me as if I were inspecting the picture, and, whoops, there went my thumb. "Shit. I just accidentally deleted the text."

Tyler shrugged. "It's fine. I don't need some shirtless dude on my screen."

Some shirtless dude, I thought as I handed the phone back. So, he hadn't looked at the picture too closely because if he had, he would have recognized the tattoos. My tattoos. A girl he'd slept with had sent him a screenshot from one of my videos, and I would've been laughing if not for the fear of discovery and the adrenaline roaring through my veins.

"You ready?" he asked, lifting his controller.

"Sure."

He unpaused the game, and we went back to shooting at everything that moved. I tried to focus on the split screen before me, but all I could think of was that text. Aly wanted to be fucked by someone wearing a mask.

I'd only met her once, but she'd made an impact. It was over the summer, early one morning after she'd spent the night in Tyler's bed, *not* sleeping. I'd been awake, too, cursing the weird acoustics of our apartment until I found my noise-canceling headphones and drowned them out with music.

I'd always slept like shit, so I didn't expect anyone else to be up when I finally threw in the towel and went to make coffee several hours later. Tyler's door cracked open right after the machine beeped to tell me it had finished brewing. I'd half turned, expecting my roommate, only to see a woman instead. A tall woman, which was unfortunate because she was wearing one of Tyler's shirts, and it barely covered her crotch. My eyes had immediately fallen, taking in her long legs. Tyler met her at his gym, and she looked like someone who regularly hit the weights: thick thighs, toned calves, and from what I could see of her arms, they were just as muscular.

I'd lifted my gaze, realizing I was staring, and instantly regretted it. Aly was hot. Not that I'd expected otherwise; Tyler always dated attractive people. But she was more striking than beautiful, with a pointed chin, full lips that looked like they'd been well-used the night before, a nose my mother would have said was distinctively Italian, and large dark eyes. Her brown hair was a mess, falling to her elbows in loops and snarls.

The smile she'd given me when our gazes locked was nearly blinding. "Please tell me you made enough for two."

I'd grunted an affirmative and put my back to her.

She'd tried to make small talk with me, and I hadn't been outright rude or anything, but I'd kept my distance and my face turned away while giving her monosyllabic answers, and she'd fallen quiet pretty fast. To make up for it, I poured her coffee first and set the mug on the counter where she could reach it. Then I'd splashed some into my cup and hightailed it out of there.

Tyler hadn't told her who I was. He knew better than that, but I couldn't risk her seeing my face for too long and starting to wonder who I reminded her of. I looked too much like my goddamn father, and that Netflix documentary had just come out about him. It would have been my luck that Aly had seen it.

The whole summer was rough, thanks to that documentary, and I'd barely left the apartment because of it. Whenever Daddy Dearest was in the news, I'd have someone stop me on the street or in the supermarket and say, "I don't know if anyone has ever told you this, but you look just like a guy I read about the other day." Or they'd listened to a podcast about him. Or watched a true crime episode that focused on his many misdeeds.

With the documentary came a fresh wave of interest, and I'd been working overtime for months to keep people from finding me or my mom and stepdad. Everyone wanted the exclusive interview from George Marshall Secliff's surviving family members, and sometimes they went to illegal lengths to track us down. It was why I'd gotten into hacking when I was still in high school. I'd wanted to help the three of us disappear from the internet, and I'd learned everything I could in pursuit of making that happen.

Those skills had paid off in the long run. Now, I worked for an exclusive cybersecurity firm writing code that kept other hackers from infiltrating Fortune 500 companies and stealing all their clients' money. It allowed me to work from home, with flexible hours, leaving enough time to pursue other hobbies.

Like making thirst traps for all the other mask enthusiasts out there.

The same reason I stayed inside was why I didn't date much. Even though my hair was darker than my dad's, and I wore it shorter than his, we looked damn near identical. It wasn't so bad when I was younger, and my face hadn't filled out yet. Being a scrawny kid had saved me. Now that I'd grown into my man body and was nearing the age Dad was when he got caught, I was a carbon copy of his mugshot.

One of the first questions I asked the women I matched with on dating apps was whether or not they were into true crime. If they said yes, I blocked them and moved on. I only ever took a chance on the ones who said they hated "all that gross stuff." On the rare occasions I did meet and hook up with women, it only lasted a few weeks at most. I broke things off when it felt like they were catching feelings or they got that look in their eyes that said they were trying to puzzle out where they knew me from.

Even mirrors were a problem nowadays because I couldn't look at one without picturing my own face contorted in rage as fists rained down on me. I'd seen other documentaries about violent men, and it always baffled me when their family members swore they had no idea what their father/husband/uncle had been doing in their free time.

My dad was a fucking monster, and there was no disguising it. He'd only gotten away with his crimes for so long because he targeted marginalized women, was handsome, and could put on a good show for short periods. Just long enough to convince the sex workers he frequented to get in the car with him.

A lot like his idol, Ted Bundy.

The only communal mirror left in our apartment was the one in the half bath, and I turned my head down every time I was in there to avoid it. So, yeah, my face was a problem, which was why the thought of wearing a mask was so appealing. I'd been fixated on it for years and finally found an excuse to don one after a story popped up on my news feed about the rise of thirst trap accounts with people wearing masks. It was a lofty think piece about the psychology behind the trend, but I ignored all that bullshit and zeroed in on the videos embedded into the article.

I could do that, I realized, the thought striking like lightning. Here was a way to finally join social media, show off the body I worked so hard for, and fulfill every human's desire to interact with others. Plus, I'd inherited some shit from my father, and one of those traits was wanting to be admired. I'd suppressed it for most of my life, but lately, my therapist had been trying to convince me how normal it was to chase after fame and acclaim. Our primitive brains craved it because back when we were still bashing each other's heads in with mammoth bones, to be popular was to be safe and protected inside the cave.

Deciding it was okay to indulge my desires for once, I'd placed an online order for some high-end videography equipment, spent hours designing and 3-D printing a custom mask, and watched far too many YouTube videos on filmmaking before I even created a social media account.

And I'd told absolutely no one about it. Not even Tyler, who'd been my best friend for as long as I could remember.

"Dude, you're fucking trash today," he said as we both died onscreen. Again.

"Shit, sorry. Thinking about work," I lied.

He tossed his controller onto the coffee table harder than was necessary. "Whatever. I'm over it. I need to get to the gym before it gets crazy."

He stood from the couch and strode into his room.

Tyler could be a dick and was absolutely a fuckboy, but he was also the only person who hadn't immediately abandoned me when my dad got arrested. He was a good friend beneath the douchey exterior and loyal almost to a fault. It was his idea to move to this city and start over when people at college figured out who I was. His exact quote was, "Fuck 'em. Let's bounce," so I didn't think he was serious at first, not until he filed transfer paperwork to switch schools and started sending me listings for off-campus housing.

I'd dropped out instead of switching with him. It felt like my time at school had run its course by then, and none of my professors could teach me anything else about hacking. The rest of my education lay online, and I studied endlessly until I felt ready to enter the job market. I'd applied for only one position—the one I currently held—by hacking into a huge media conglomerate and showing the company I now worked for how I'd gotten past their defenses.

They paid me a king's ransom to keep one step ahead of emerging cyber threats, enough that I bought the most expensive amateur camera on the market without blinking, and our rent was paid off for the next two years.

I heard a drawer slam shut in Tyler's room, and I took that as my sign to stand. My phone was on my work desk, and I was itching to get it within my grasp. I needed to pull up the video Aly sent and see if I could find her in the comment section. She had a mask kink. Or, at the very least, she was into it enough that she wanted someone to wear one for her.

So far, I'd ignored every single DM asking me to meet with people IRL and play out their fantasies. They were strangers online. They could be anyone, and I didn't want to show up at some octogenarian's house when I'd been expecting a hot twentysomething.

Aly wasn't a stranger. I knew her. Better than I should have, sure, but thanks to Dad's genetic contributions, boundaries were hard for me.

She had been in my house, the one sanctuary I had left. The need to protect my identity and keep Tyler and me safe was strong enough that I did FBI-level research into anyone Tyler invited over. Thankfully, he understood my compulsion and told me ahead of time when he planned to have company. Usually, I stopped caring when I realized people weren't a threat to either of us, but my interest in Aly had remained long past the point it probably should have.

I snagged my phone off the desk and sat on my bed as I pulled up my account. The video Aly screenshotted was one of my most popular, with over 3.4 million views. The downside was that I had thousands of comments to look through if I had any hope of finding her in them, and even that was a crapshoot. Most people were pretty anonymous online. It'd be just my luck that Aly was one of them. I wished I could write a code to look for her, but this part of the job required manual intervention, so I settled back against my headboard and started scrolling, glancing at names and avatars for any sign of her.

An hour passed before I sat bolt upright, thumb hovering over the username "aly.aly.oxen.free." Holy shit, was it her? I clicked on her profile, and, of course, it was private. I leaned in, squinting. The avatar was a close-up photo of a dark-haired woman. I screenshotted it, then used the AI software I had loaded onto my phone to blow it up and fix the resolution issues until I was staring at a crystal-clear picture of Aly, sure that it was her.

Just to be a hundred percent certain, I logged into my computer and hacked her account, using every trick in the book to cover my tracks and keep her from being flagged. The IP address she used to create her account was local, and when I did some more digging, I discovered that it originated from the block she lived on.

I'd found her. Aly not only had a mask kink, but she'd liked one of my videos enough to leave the comment, "*Sir, I'm at work. How dare you?*"

Had she left any others?

I logged into my account on my computer and created a few lines of code that would search for her in my comment sections. There were so many returns my head started to spin. She'd liked and saved and commented on almost every single one.

All the blood in my body went straight to my dick, tenting my sweatpants. This wasn't good. I shouldn't be sitting here lusting after my roommate's ex . . . whatever she was. Not his girlfriend. They'd never been serious enough to define their relationship, and Tyler had seen other people at the same time as Aly. That meant this wasn't breaking any bro code, right? Only several privacy laws and a whole bunch of societal norms, but I'd never really cared much about that. Tyler was the only friend I had. I didn't want to risk losing him over a woman, even if that woman had been plaguing my dreams since I'd first laid eyes on her.

What he doesn't know won't hurt him, I thought. And it wasn't like I'd done anything yet anyway. What was the harm in a little light online stalking? She'd done the same to me.

My eyes landed on the first comment that my search returned.

"Is this video why I randomly woke up at 2 am? Was I summoned here?"

I grinned, shaking my head. Of course she was funny, too. It wasn't like it was bad enough that she was hot and probably off-limits.

I kept reading. Her comments ranged from lighthearted to downright lascivious.

"I would like to thank the algorithm for bringing me here."

"I'm on season six of this video."

"Well, this has me feeling feral far too early in the morning."

"The way I would CRAWL to him."

"Boom. There went my ovaries."

"This is the horror movie I would die in. Everyone else would be running away while I sprinted straight toward the danger instead."

I pushed back from my computer desk. Oh, this was bad. Because that last comment hit me harder than the rest, and now all I could picture was chasing her down and fucking her when I finally caught her.

Was this how it started? Just a quasi-innocent fantasy about ravaging a woman somewhere that no one could hear her scream? Would it get worse from here, and my desires would progress past that to fucking her and choking her a little at the same time? And after that, squeezing even harder until I watched the life blink out from her eyes while I pounded into her?

My dick instantly deflated, which I took as a good sign. I wasn't turned on by the idea of seriously hurting Aly, so maybe I wasn't as far gone as I'd always feared.

I rolled my chair back to my desk and read through the rest of what she'd written, which took a while because there were over a hundred search returns.

Less than a minute passed before my dick was standing straight for her again. So many of her comments revolved around coming home and finding me waiting for her, and soon, my mind began to fill with thoughts of feeding into her fantasy.

What would happen if I actually broke into her house?

In reality, she'd either shoot my dumb ass or run away and call the cops, and then my entire life would blow up when I got arrested and the headlines started screaming that I was just like my dad.

But I wasn't living in reality right now. My thoughts were pure fantasy, and I couldn't stop picturing myself breaking in and Aly responding exactly like she said she would. Crawling to me. Begging me to fuck her while I held a knife to her throat.

"This man is always coming onto my FYP and never on me, and that is a tragedy," was probably my new favorite quote of all time.

I groaned and palmed my dick through my sweatpants. The things I would do to this woman if she let me. I'd play into every lustful dark thought she'd ever had. And I wouldn't have to worry about her desire turning to terror beneath me because, with my face hidden, there wasn't any risk of that. For once in my life, I could be free of the fear of discovery or recognition.

That thought turned me on almost as much as Aly did.

I leaned back in my chair and slid my hand into my boxers, gripping the base of my dick. What would it be like to break into her house? I knew I could do it. Along with hacking, I was pretty good at skulking around at night. I'd always been a night owl, which was especially true lately when there was less risk of anyone seeing me in the darkness than in daylight. I did my shopping at a twenty-four-hour grocery store. My workouts were saved for 2 a.m. when there wasn't anyone in our apartment's gym.

I stroked my hand up my dick as I imagined picking Aly's lock. I'd learned how to do it as a teen so I could sneak into my therapist's office and see what he'd written about me—a mistake because I wasn't ready for what I'd found, but at least I'd learned a new skill in the process. I could dust it off now and put it to better use, slipping into Aly's house in the dead of night while she was on shift at the hospital.

I rubbed my thumb over the head of my dick when I reached the top, coating it in precum before sliding my hand back down to grip my base again. My lids fell shut as I pictured Aly standing in her doorway, looking rumpled and tired after a long night, her eyes flashing wide with fear when she realized she wasn't alone.

"Who's there? What do you want?" I heard her call out in a quavering voice.

In my head, I pointed the knife at her in answer.

You.

She put her hands up. "Just take what you want and get out. Please don't hurt me."

I shook my head and tilted the knife tip toward the floor in an explicit command. She dropped to her knees like a good little girl. I strode toward her, watching her chest rise and fall as I approached. Her eyes moved from the knife to my shirtless torso, covered in blood, the black of her pupils inching out brown as her fear started to shift into lust.

I stopped above her, staring down at her upturned face, reveling in the vulnerability of her position. Oh so carefully, I placed the tip of the knife beneath her chin and tilted her face up as I unzipped my fly and let my dick spring free. Her gaze lifted to the dark eye sockets of my mask for one breathless moment, and then her lips popped open, and she leaned forward, suctioning that luscious mouth around the head of my dick, and—

Oh, fuck, I was about to come.

I yanked a few tissues from the nearby box and got them down my pants just in time to soak them. The sight of Aly before me, afraid and horny at the same time? I wanted it. Bad. More than I'd wanted anything in a long time.

All I had to do was figure out a way to make it happen that didn't end with my arrest.

■ ■ ■

Aly's neighborhood was still lit up like Christmas, and that was, surprisingly, the biggest hurdle I had to face while planning my little stunt. A week had passed since I saw her text to Tyler. Seven days of trying to talk myself out of this insanity while practicing my lock picking, researching whether or not Aly had a home security system—she didn't, which was unacceptable—and driving through this neighborhood at night doing recon.

Clearly, the still-rational part of my brain had failed to get the rest of me to see reason because here I stood in the shadows by Aly's back door, trying to catch my breath after triggering a mini street-wide blackout and sprinting behind her house to unscrew her rear floodlights before the power kicked back on.

I leaned my head against the vinyl siding and closed my eyes. I was going to get caught. I was going to get caught and make international news, and because of who my father was, there was no way a jury would ever think this was my first break-in. They'd think I planned something far more nefarious, and I'd get sent to jail for the rest of my life for this stupid shit.

All because I wanted to fuck a pretty girl while wearing a mask.

I should have gone home. Pushed off the wall, got in my car, drove away, and forgot all about Aly's mask kink. A normal guy would have. A sane guy. But I must not have been either of those things because the second thoughts of leaving swirled through my head, a resounding "NO!" cut them off.

Maybe it was time to accept the fact that I wasn't normal, and I never would be. I wanted things most people didn't, craved darkness and depravity instead of light and love. I'd been fighting my nature for as long as I could remember, and I was tired of it.

So fucking tired.

It'd be much easier to give in for once. A relief, really. I'd worked so hard to fix and suppress the things that I'd been taught were abnormal, but after over a decade of therapy and drugs, the thoughts and desires that most of society deemed problematic remained.

Here was my chance to finally live them out. I'd done as much preparing as I possibly could. My skin was covered head to toe, so there'd be no trace epithelial cells for a forensics team to find. Only one of Aly's direct neighbors had a security system, and I'd hacked into their network to see if any of their cameras overlooked her backyard. They didn't. Just in case I'd missed something, I wore a balaclava to hide my face. The boots I'd shoved my feet into were a size larger than I normally wore, and I'd plastered over the soles so there wouldn't be any distinguishable tread marks left behind. All that was left to do was get in, do what I had to do, and get out.

I took a deep breath and turned toward the door. The moon was only half full, but between it and the nearby Christmas lights, I was able to make out the doorknob. I tugged my backpack off and pulled my mini lockpicking kit free. The steel tools gleamed in the moonlight as I slipped them out and got to work.

My personality sometimes skewed toward obsessive behavior, and I'd practiced this so much that it only took a minute to get the door unlocked. I turned the handle, praying it wouldn't be this easy, and let out a relieved breath when the door wouldn't budge because of a deadbolt. It still wouldn't be enough to keep me or a serious burglar out, and Aly needed better security than this.

I made a mental note to place an anonymous order for her as I put the lockpicking kit away and pulled out the expensive magnets I'd purchased online. Getting the deadbolt open would take a lot longer than the lock. I could have easily kicked the door in or used another destructive method to gain entry, but I didn't want to damage Aly's property or make it easier for anyone else to follow in my footsteps, so that meant doing things the slower, harder way.

Sweat beaded along my brow as the minutes ticked by. Every time a noise sounded too close, I froze, my heart hammering in my chest as I wondered if I was about to get caught. I nearly bolted when I heard the sudden wail of a siren, but instead of coming closer, it moved parallel to Aly's street and then away.

I lost an entire minute afterward as I relearned how to breathe.

This was fucking crazy. Full-blown batshit. And yet, I couldn't seem to stop myself as I lifted the magnets and got back to work on her deadbolt.

After what felt like a small eternity, the magnets caught, and the lock slid open. I leaned my forehead against the door and let out a shaky breath, so much adrenaline sluicing through my veins that my whole body shook with the need to expel it. I was still half afraid this would end in disaster, but the sheer thrill of doing something so dangerous and illegal was more exhilarating than anything I'd ever experienced, including skydiving.

Was this what it had been like for my dad? Did this same thrill drive him on as much as his more sadistic desires?

I shook my head and straightened. I could wonder about that shit later. Right now, I needed to get inside.

I turned the handle and cautiously pushed the door open. The one thing I couldn't find online was whether or not Aly had any pets. I hadn't heard barking while I jimmied the locks, but that didn't mean there wasn't an attack dog waiting for me inside that had been trained to be quiet. Sure, I could have assuaged my worry by asking my roommate—Tyler had been here a few times, so he would know the answer—but I didn't want him to think I was interested in any of his exes, especially Aly.

The rear of the house was dark, with only a soft glow emanating from the front room, where Aly's Christmas tree stood proud and fully lit in a window. It was enough illumination to make out my surroundings and realize there were no dogs waiting to pounce.

I quickly shut the door behind me and locked it.

An unholy yowl split the air.

Fuck! Aly had some sort of demonically possessed canine after all, and it would probably rip through my pant leg and splash my blood all over the goddamn house for the cops to find.

I grabbed the doorknob and was about to tear out of there when a small, fluffy shape darted into the room and stopped short.

A cat. Aly had a cat.

We eyed each other in the darkness. It was pretty runty despite the long black and white hair. If push came to shove, I could take it.

"Don't fuck with me," I warned.

In response, it turned sideways and stood on its tiptoes, fluffing up like a skunk.

Despite myself, I grinned. The cat might be small, but it looked like a fighter, and that, I could appreciate.

I'd never had a pet. Serial killers were well known for getting their start on small animals, and I didn't want the temptation in case I was more like Dad than I realized. I worried that if I adopted one, I either wouldn't feel anything for it—meaning none of the protective instincts or cute aggression most pet owners seemed overwhelmed with—or I'd have all my greatest fears confirmed and take one look at it and think "prey."

As the seconds ticked by, I stood glued to the doormat, waiting for some violent urge to overtake me. All I felt was slight trepidation. Cats had claws, right? What if it lunged at me and scratched deep enough to draw blood? Even a drop was enough to identify someone.

Without warning, the cat deflated and sauntered forward.

Oh, fuck. What was it doing?

I stepped back and flattened myself against the door, weirdly mesmerized by how its eyes glowed in the darkness. This small, fluffy creature would be so easy to kill, yet I had no desire to harm it. That had to be a good sign, right? Or was this such a new experience that whatever horrible response I might normally have was muted?

"No scratching," I told the cat.

There was still a chance that some monstrous craving for blood was stirring beneath the surface, undetected, and if it attacked me, those murderous instincts might roar to the forefront of my psyche and cause me to do something terrible. I'd been taught not to trust myself, and this seemed like the perfect setup for learning just how alike Dad and I really were, once and for all.

The cat strode right up to my feet, unperturbed. I remained frozen in place, waiting for the proverbial other shoe to drop, but instead of biting me, it sniffed my pant leg and butted its forehead into my shin, purring so loud that it sounded like an engine turning over.

I let out a relieved breath and half fell to a squat to get a closer look at it. The thing was kind of . . . cute, with white patches above its eyes that made it look like it had eyebrows. Right now, they were drawn together as the cat half-lidded its eyes and butted against my leg again as if looking to be petted. Had I ever thought anything was cute before? Maybe the better question was, had I ever let myself?

"Sorry if I fuck this up," I said, lifting a hand to scratch the cat between the ears and then stroke down its back like I'd seen other people do on TV. This was the first time I'd ever pet an animal, and my fingers shook. Thankfully, it was from unspent adrenaline and not the rising desire to strangle Aly's furbaby.

Crisis averted. For now, at least.

So far, I'd learned two crucial things about myself this week: I didn't want to hurt Aly or her cat. Maybe I wasn't a psychopath after all. They cared about no one and nothing but themselves. But that didn't rule out sociopathy. Most sociopaths were capable of caring for a few select people. They were their rare exceptions, developing intense love and devotion for them while feeling absolutely nothing for anyone else. I cared about my mom, stepdad, and Tyler. They were my people, and I barely thought of others. But was that because of a personality disorder or because they were the only ones who had *earned* my trust?

I shook my head and stood, ignoring the cat's annoyed meow of protest when I stopped petting it. I wasn't here to bond with an animal. My time was limited, and the longer I lingered, the higher the risk of detection. I could puzzle out my mental health later.

I had a video to film and a camera to place.

It was time to find out just how serious Aly was about wanting to walk into her house and find a masked man waiting for her in the darkness.

3

ALY

EVERYONE IN THE GODDAMN CITY had lost their minds. Or at least that's what it felt like tonight. We saw our fair share of accidents during a regular shift, but this one was different. I'd lost count of the number of patients I'd seen over the last seven hours who had hurt themselves or gotten hurt by someone else doing some dumb shit even a child should know better than to attempt.

Was there some dangerous new social media trend I hadn't seen yet? Or a revamp of that old show with dudes crashing shopping carts into things? Something had to explain this level of stupidity. It couldn't all be coincidental.

We were in the middle of a mini lull, not uncommon so late at night, and I was curled up in a breakroom chair, trying to get comfortable as I downed another cup of coffee. My shift was only halfway over, and if the second leg of my night progressed like the first, I'd need all the caffeine I could get to keep me going.

Tanya swept into the room and strode right to the window, so focused as she stared into the night sky that I didn't think she'd noticed me. "And it isn't even a goddamn full moon," she said under her breath.

I straightened in my chair. "So, it's not just my patients?"

She turned my way and shook her head, her long braids falling over her shoulder. "No. Something's gotten into this city tonight."

We shared a troubled glance and then looked away from each other. Things like this happened sometimes, odd patterns emerging that made me think humans were more connected than we realized. One week, we might see a spike in car crash victims without anything like bad weather or traffic to explain the uptick. The next, we could get more domestic assault victims than usual, and the one after that, more gunshot wounds.

Tanya and I had talked about it a couple of times, wondering if humans shared some kind of hive mind, or if it had something to do with magnetic currents or our subconsciouses all picking up the same subtle signals from the world around us.

I'd even mentioned it to one of the cops who regularly got stationed here, and instead of thinking I was a weirdo, he'd agreed with me, telling me he and his coworkers saw something similar. They'd get a slew of people who had almost no traceable connection to each other committing virtually the same crime one week. The next, it would be a new group doing something else.

I'd told Tanya about it afterward, and we'd both been so freaked out that now we avoided the subject altogether, as if bringing it up might trigger a new wave of weirdness.

"How was Brinley?" I asked. Tanya had worked with her the night before, keeping an eye on her like I had the night before that.

Tanya pushed away from the window and went to the coffee maker. "Good. Thank god. I think you're right, and she'll be able to stick it out. That first bad night just threw her."

"Nothing like a baptism by fire to test someone's mettle," I said.

Tanya finished pouring her coffee and turned toward me, leaning her hip against the counter as she took her first sip. "It wouldn't have been so bad if we had more people to split patients between."

I perked up at that. "Speaking of, are you going to that job fair next month?" The hospital regularly put up booths at high school job fairs and local recruitment events in an effort to lure more people into nursing fields. Few would end up working here, but we saw any increase in numbers as a win.

Tanya nodded. "Wanna come with? It counts as a shift, and you might see some daylight for once." She eyed me over the rim of her mug, one brow rising. "You're looking pretty pasty lately."

I rolled my eyes. "I hope your sales pitch at the fair is better than that."

She snorted. "You in or not? Don't make me take someone like Donna."

We both grimaced. Donna was one of the nurses who'd been in here with Brinley last week. She had a terrible bedside manner and no natural instincts for caretaker work. Bringing her to a recruitment fair was more likely to drive people away from our career field than toward it.

"Yeah, I'll go," I said.

Tanya let out a relieved breath and took another sip of coffee.

Silence fell between us, but it was a comfortable one we both settled into. Some nights, we'd sit and chat between patients, sharing gossip. Others were like this, both of us stuck in our heads, just trying to catch our breath in the middle of a rough shift.

Tanya's pager beeped on her hip, and she swore under her breath as she checked it. "Lab results," she said, downing the dregs of her coffee before striding out of the room.

I checked my pager as she left. I was waiting on bloodwork for two patients myself, and it was surprising mine hadn't beeped at me yet. Maybe I could bribe my lab tech friend, Vern, to bump me up in her queue.

The date at the top of my pager caught my eye, and I straightened in my seat. Today was Thursday. That meant a new video from the Faceless Man. He posted every Tuesday, Thursday, and Saturday like clockwork. How the fuck had I forgotten?

I dove out of my chair toward my locker. To have the breakroom to myself was a minor miracle, and I wouldn't miss my chance to watch the new video in peace.

"Come on," I muttered as I turned the dial on my lock with impatient fingers. The door could open at any second, and then this opportunity would be over, and I'd have to wait until the next lull or the end of my shift to watch it.

I opened the lock and grabbed my phone out of my purse. My fingers flew as I pulled it close, tapping my favorite social media icon and going straight to the search bar. His creator page filled my screen a heartbeat later, and warmth flooded my body as I saw the familiar video covers of him in various poses and stages of undress.

Damn, the man was fine.

My breathing picked up as I stared down at my phone, nipples peaking beneath my scrubs. I was like a Pavlovian dog for him, but instead of drooling over the anticipation of food, I got wet somewhere else over the expectation of pleasure. This couldn't be normal—my knee-jerk reaction to him, like I was primed and ready to go after the merest glimpse at his page. I needed to stop masturbating to his videos because being this turned on this quickly was starting to be a problem. Especially right now, when there was no time to relieve my sudden need, and I'd be left aching with thoughts of him for the rest of the night.

I probably should have put the phone down and watched the thirst trap later, preferably in the solitude of my bedroom where I had easy access to a vibrator, but there went my finger, opening the latest video as if it had a mind of its own. It must be a good one because it had only been posted a few hours ago and already had over a hundred thousand views.

I pulled the phone closer and watched as a haunting song started to play. All I saw was darkness until the camera panned upward, revealing the Faceless Man's mask lying flat on something. The camera panned more, and—holy shit! It was lying on a bed, and I had that same comforter!

I hit pause and let out a tortured groan. Oh, no. No, no, no. I should not have started watching this here. My pussy clenched at the sight of that mask lying on what could have been my bed, spasming in a way that only my biggest vibrator or a long hard fuck could ease.

Quit now while you're ahead, I thought. Watching the rest of the video could only end in torture, but despite knowing how uncomfortably aroused I'd be for the rest of the night, I couldn't help but lift the phone back up and hit unpause.

The music started playing again, and a masculine hand slid into view, nails clipped short, tattoos whorling down the back of it right onto each finger. The camera panned out a little more. I released a shaky exhale as a muscular forearm was revealed, covered in tattoos and veins, and, oh, god, what was it about forearms that had such a chokehold on me? Was it because I could picture those muscles flexing as that big hand held both of mine over my head? Or better yet, bunching with barely restrained strength as long fingers wrapped around my throat?

The hand slid over the mask, curling into the eye sockets before dragging it slowly out of view as a painfully low male voice sang about doing unholy things in the bedroom. The Faceless Man's music selection was always perfect, able to turn even a simple video like this into a clit tease. It was even worse this time because I couldn't stop picturing him filming it in *my* bedroom.

Suddenly, the camera snapped up, and I sucked in a sharp breath. There he was, framed in a mirror in all his shirtless glory, phone in one hand as he filmed himself, the other slowly undoing his belt. I hit the pause button again to take it all in. He was perfection—maybe not for everyone, but he was for me—with heavy muscles gained from what must have been hours in the gym, toned and trim in all the right places, wide and dense in others.

I wanted to trace my tongue through the valley between his pecs, worship his abs, and spend an ungodly amount of time memorizing the deep V of his hip flexors.

More than anything, I wanted to replace his hands with mine, undo his belt, pull out what looked like a sizable dick, if the bulge in his pants was anything to go by, and spend the rest of the night doing things with him that would make the Devil blush.

A noise sounded in the hall, reminding me that my time was limited. I unpaused the video and watched the last few seconds, reveling in the slow, measured way he slid his belt loose and wrapped it around his fist while taking deep, labored breaths, his chest heaving. Why was that so goddamn sexy?

Probably because you're picturing him breathing like that while wrapping his belt around your wrists to restrain you, you horny little bitch.

Damn, I had it for this man, and I'd never even met him, had no idea what he looked like beneath that mask or what he even sounded like. He'd never spoken in his videos.

That was probably the allure. Kinky sex with a hot, faceless man who didn't speak? Sign me the hell up. I'd had about enough of men's voices lately.

Something in the corner of the mirror caught my eye, and I hit pause again right before the video ended. The backgrounds of his videos were always dark and out of focus, but I could have sworn I was staring at the edge of my dresser, complete with what might have been the clutter of my makeup containers and hastily discarded hair clips.

I must have had it bad if I was so far gone that I saw a few blurry shapes and supplanted them with my furniture and belongings.

Either way, this was officially my new favorite thirst trap. Because whether it was a coincidence or my mind was playing tricks on me, it was far too easy to imagine it being filmed in my bedroom. God, the things I would do to myself while watching this in the coming days and weeks. I wondered if this guy had any idea of the effect he had on people. Would he be freaked out if he learned how hard I lusted after him? Or into it?

My beeper went off, jarring me out of my thoughts so badly that I almost dropped my phone. Before shoving it back in my locker, I saved the video to my favorites and typed out a hurried "*I have that comforter. This could have been filmed in my bedroom. Let's goooo, bitches!*" knowing all the other people I'd interacted with countless times before in the Faceless Man's comments would see it and be dying of jealousy by the time I logged back in.

■ ■ ■

Nine excruciatingly long hours later, I pulled into my driveway and cut the car's engine, leaning my forehead against the steering wheel.

Tonight was shit. Complete and utter shit. Capped off by losing a heart attack patient we thought had been stable. She'd been so young, too, barely fifty, her husband and teenage kids crowded around the bed when the second heart attack hit, watching in horror as we shoved them out of there and tried and failed to save her life.

It was nights like this that made me want to quit. I'd gotten into nursing to save people, and every single death felt like a personal failure. Like it was my fault they hadn't made it because of some sign I'd missed or test I hadn't thought to perform.

Logically, I knew that couldn't be true. It wasn't like I was alone in treating them. I worked with countless nurses and specialists and doctors, and these feelings were likely caused by my lingering grief over Mom, but it didn't make it any better or lessen the guilt that wracked me every time we lost a patient.

I made a mental note to bring this up in my next therapy session and got out of the car. Fred came yowling toward me once I was inside, and I scooped him up and smushed him for longer than usual, trying to ground myself in him and trick my brain into thinking happier thoughts.

I put him down when he started squirming, then went straight to the kitchen. Wine was calling my name. I'd held off on drinking since sending that regrettable text to Tyler, but if ever I needed alcohol, it was tonight.

The clock on my stove was blinking, reading 12:00, and it stopped me short. We must have lost power sometime during the night. My house was toasty warm, and the utility company hadn't sent a message about it like they usually did when it went out, so it must have been a weird blip or something that didn't last long enough to trigger a notification.

I shrugged and went to the fridge, Fred winding between my legs like he was hell-bent on tripping me. He stayed glued to my shins, extra clingy for some reason, as I pulled out a fresh bottle of white and poured myself a large glass. I suppose I had been gone longer than expected again, my scheduled twelve-hour shift turning into sixteen instead. Tomorrow was an off day, so I'd make it up to him then.

Right now, I needed wine and alone time with my phone and vibrator.

You'd think all the blood and trauma I'd seen tonight would distract me from my desire, but I was so used to it that it only did so in the moment. As soon as I had a second to myself again, images of that mask lying on what could have been my comforter swirled to the forefront of my mind. Lust was a natural response to traumatic events, the body wanting a reminder of being alive after skirting so close to death, and I'd long since stopped fighting it.

"I know, buddy," I said, leaning down to scratch Fred behind the ears. "Just give me, like, ten minutes." That's all it would take at this point.

I shut him out of my room, flicked the light on, and froze.

There was something on my bed.

There was something on my bed that I hadn't left there.

The wine started trembling in the glass as my fingers shook, but I couldn't force myself to put it down because I couldn't move. I was completely immobile, held in place by my rising fear. Had someone been in my house? Were they still here? Fuck, was that why Fred had been so insistent? He'd been trying to warn me?

I will not be a victim, I thought, forcing myself to move, to step forward, set the glass and my phone down on my dresser, and drop to a squat as I quietly slid open the bottom drawer and pulled out the gun I kept there.

Living alone in a big city and seeing the worst of what it could do to women on a nightly basis made me paranoid. I had a gun in my car and one more besides the one I now held hidden nearby. I slept with a baseball bat beside my bed and mace and throwing knives on my nightstand within easy reach. Two days a week, I took a hand-to-hand combat course taught by an ex-marine who didn't go easy on me because I was the only woman in his class. If someone else was in my house right now, they'd be leaving it in a body bag.

I strained my ears as I straightened and slowly approached the bed. I didn't hear anyone else, but that didn't mean someone wasn't standing in my closet or waiting beneath my bed, ready to grab my ankle when I got close. With that in mind, I stopped out of arm's reach and leaned forward, freezing in place for the second time in less than a minute. There was a mask on my bed.

And not just any mask.

His mask.

I'd stared at it so much over the past several months that I would recognize it anywhere.

I hadn't lost my mind and imagined my things in his video. That was really my dresser in the corner of the mirror, because he'd filmed the thirst trap I'd been lusting over all night in my actual goddamn bedroom.

Holy shit. What was happening? And what the hell did I do now? Call the cops? Check to see if he was still here?

My vision swam in and out of focus for a heartbeat. What if . . . what if all the blood in his videos wasn't fake? What if none of this was a fun little kink for him like it was for the rest of us? What if he was some sort of serial killer hiding in plain sight, and he used his platform to lure his victims to him?

Was I about to be next? Was this the beginning of some twisted game of cat and mouse?

I shook my head. If that were the case, wouldn't I have noticed all the different bedrooms he filmed in as he taunted his victims? I hadn't. Aside from the one he shot tonight in here, all his videos had one of three backgrounds—a couch, a wall with red lighting, and a massive bed with black sheets—making this the one exception to the rule.

Why me? And why now?

And why was I so fucking turned on by it when I knew I should run screaming from my house instead?

4

JOSH

OH, I'D FUCKED UP. I'd fucked up *bad*.

The camera I'd discreetly placed in Aly's room showed her standing several feet from her bed. Her light blue scrubs were rumpled after her marathon shift at the hospital, and strands of hair had slipped free from her braid to frame her face in loose waves. Her dark eyes were huge, an expression of pure disbelief on her face as she stared at the mask I'd left for her.

She lifted the gun she held, bracing it with both hands as she looked around the room. "Is anyone in here?" she called out, loud and clear.

I'd never been so attracted to someone in my life. She looked ready to shoot anything that moved. Thank fuck I hadn't stayed, or I'd probably be bleeding out on her floor right now.

I quickly went over the entire night in my head, searching for any trace evidence I might have left behind. I'd been so careful while there that I didn't think there was anything for the cops to find when Aly eventually snapped out of it and called them. Even when I took off my shirt to film the video, I'd left the balaclava on the whole time, so there wouldn't be so much as a stray hair to give me away. I'd even taken the time to relock her back door and cover my footsteps in the melting snow.

I didn't put the camera in her room to watch her change or sleep like some sick fuck, though, now that I thought about it . . .

Wait, no. I needed to stop right the hell there. That road led nowhere good. This invasion of privacy was bad enough without adding sexual predator to my list of crimes.

The reason I put the camera in her room was to gauge her reaction and learn whether or not she meant what she said in all her comments. Was she actually into the same dark shit that I was, or was she just a tourist?

Judging from her open look of horror, she was the latter. Which meant I needed to start implementing my exit strategy. I had orders to cancel, plans to scrap, and cover-up work to do. I'd taken every safety precaution I could think of to obscure my digital footprint, and knew of only three hackers in the US capable of tracing my steps and, maybe, if they were lucky and avoided all the traps I'd left in my wake, finding me. Two of them worked for the NSA, and another one was currently in jail, so I felt safe in my work for now. Plus, I doubted the local cops would go so far as to call in the feds over a run-of-the-mill home invasion in which nothing got destroyed or stolen.

Even my social media account was secure, or as secure as it could be. Anyone who hacked it would be led straight to a mid-thirtysomething dad in Utah with a secret mask kink. He was a real guy named Carl with an actual mask fetish and a matching clandestine thirst trap account his wife didn't even know about. Our tattoos weren't the same, and he filmed different content, but the amount of work it would take for cops to figure all that out would give me ample time to cover the rest of my tracks and disappear offline.

Sorry, Carl, but sacrifices had to be made.

I should probably feel worse for the guy than I did, but, like boundaries, empathy was hard for me. Maybe that's where I'd gone wrong with Aly. I'd been so excited about the prospect of living out our shared fantasy that I hadn't stopped to consider things from her perspective. What would it be like for a woman living alone to realize a stranger had invaded her home?

I popped up a second tab and split my screen, watching Aly duck down and look under her bed, gun leading the way while I typed in a quick internet search.

The results were not good. Yup, this was where I'd fucked up. According to Google, Aly was probably terrified, angry, and felt like her home was compromised, violated even, turning from a sanctuary to yet another place where she felt unsafe.

How did I make up for such a colossal misstep? Roses? Men in movies and TV were always sending roses. That didn't seem like enough, though. Maybe if I sent a lot of them?

I popped open another tab, pausing to watch Aly clear the rest of her room like a woman who knew what she was doing. It was hot. Despite her apparent fear, she moved confidently and competently, like she had formal training. And maybe she did. Maybe that self-defense course she took taught her how to do this.

I made a mental note to hack into their cameras and check as I bought out a local floral shop using someone else's money. Theft, I didn't feel so bad about—especially when my victim was a wealthy criminal who'd recently tried to steal millions of dollars from one of my company's clients. I'd rebuffed their infantile attempt and slid right into their own system unseen, learning all sorts of interesting things about them, including their credit card information.

Onscreen, Aly finished clearing her bedroom and en suite and then strode out the door. I cranked my speakers as loud as they would go, hoping to hear if she called the cops while out of sight. Several minutes passed in near silence, with only the soft sounds of movement to tell me she was working her way through the rest of the small house.

I cursed myself for only placing one camera instead of two. What was she doing? How was she feeling? Was there any way to come back from this, or had I lost my chance with her already?

"Are you okay, Fred?" I heard her ask, and I immediately perked up, wondering who the fuck she was talking to.

Anger roared through me out of nowhere as I waited for Fred's response. There was already another guy in her place? Had she planned to meet him there after work? I didn't hear any doors open or shut, and—

"He didn't hurt you while he was here, did he?" she asked.

A soft meow echoed out of my speakers.

"You were trying to warn me when I came home, weren't you?"

Another meow.

Oh. Fred was her *cat*. My jealousy deflated, and I unclenched my hands from where they had a death grip on the arms of my computer chair. Wow, okay. This knee-jerk rage was new. And probably not a good thing. I'd have to keep an eye on it. I might not want to hurt Aly or her cat, but the thought of another guy in there with her had sent me straight to *kill-him-with-knives*.

My speakers went quiet, and I sat straining my ears as I waited for some sign that Aly was, I don't know, okay? Or pissed? Or scared? Anything, really. Not seeing her was a problem after all the nights I'd watched her through the hospital's cameras this week. She wore every emotion on her face, and I'd spent my sleepless hours learning each one.

Finally, she walked back into view carrying Fred in one arm and a dining room chair in the other, sporting a look of sheer determination. She set Fred on her bed and shut the bedroom door, bracing the chair beneath the knob and barricading herself inside.

I wouldn't be canceling that anonymous purchase after all if a chair was what she resorted to in order to protect herself. She needed all the home defense equipment I'd bought her. Why didn't she already have it? Her neighborhood had a relatively low crime rate compared to other parts of the city, and she could clearly defend herself, but hadn't I just proven how easy it was for someone truly determined to break into her house?

I knew it wasn't about money. Her mother's life insurance policy had paid for nursing school and most of the down payment on her home, and she made a respectable income thanks to her salary and all the overtime she pulled at the hospital. Had she merely grown complacent?

Maybe I'd done her a favor by breaking in and showing her the error of her ways.

I grimaced. Yikes. No to any more thoughts like that. I was obviously trying to rationalize what I'd done and lessen my guilt over it, which I shouldn't, because if Google had taught me anything tonight, it was that I'd royally fucked up.

That revelation was confirmed when Aly strode to her dresser and swapped her gun for the wine she'd left there earlier, chugging it like a beer at a frat party. The glass shook in her fingers as she set it back down, and I cringed. Because, *fuck*. Her fear turned me on. I'd been avoiding acknowledging how aroused I was, but the way my dick strained against my gym shorts as Aly visibly trembled was impossible to ignore.

Okay, so I didn't want to hurt her, but I did want to scare her. Potentially troubling but far from the worst-case scenario. And really, didn't that confirm something I'd already known about myself? For fuck's sake, I regularly covered my chest in stage blood and held a butcher knife while sitting in the dark and staring into a camera like I just got done slaughtering an entire family.

I got off on all the comments from people telling me they were both turned on and slightly terrified by my content. Those comments stirred something inside me, making me feel powerful, feral, and dangerous, like the world was mine for the taking. The fact that there were so many others into my specific kinks also normalized my desires. I didn't feel wrong for liking mask play or like I toed the line of dangerous territory that skirted too close to what my dad had done.

This felt like it was all for me. And that's why I wanted Aly to be all for me. Not just because she was a beautiful woman with a mask kink who regularly propositioned my alter ego, but because, technically, she'd stalked me first. Or she'd tried to if the search history I'd discovered when I hacked into her laptop was anything to go by.

How do I find someone from social media?

Who is the faceless man from TikTok?

The faceless man's other social media accounts.

Is there AI software to find people based on their tattoos?

See? She'd started it. And yes, I was aware that argument wouldn't hold up in a court of law, but this was the hill I chose to die on—the belief that Aly was a little fucked up, too. Just enough that she might hesitate before reporting me. And if I were really lucky, enough to play along with all the things I had planned for her.

My attention returned to the video feed as she scooped her phone up and sat on the edge of her bed. The camera I'd installed was a genius little device. It mimicked her phone charger, with a working USB port and everything. While the blank white space above it looked innocuous enough, it was actually a film screen with a wide-angle camera hidden behind it that was damn near imperceptible without a specialty device detector. I'd swapped her charger out for it right before leaving, checking on my phone to see if it was up and running before I slipped into the night and triggered another blackout to hide my escape.

I tapped a few buttons and zoomed in on Aly's phone. She was on my social media page, probably getting ready to either block me or read me the riot act through a DM.

"I knew it," she said as she scrolled. "Bed. Couch. Wall."

I started to frown before I realized she was talking about the backgrounds in my videos. I filmed them all in my bedroom while Tyler was either fast asleep or out of the apartment, and those were the three locations I used. Until Aly's bedroom. Had she noticed the difference?

She ran a hand over her face and turned to look at Fred, who sat by her side purring so loud I could hear it over the speakers. "So, he's probably not a serial killer who uses the app to lure his victims."

I reared back. Was that what she'd thought? Fuck. That was the absolute last thing I wanted. How did I fix this? I was half tempted to send her a DM explaining myself, but how would that work? *Hey, Aly, it's me, the man who broke into your house. I was just watching you through the camera I hid in your room, and I wanted to let you know that you are correct. I am not, in fact, a serial killer.*

Jesus Christ.

I knew I should have argued with my therapist when she said it was time to wean me off the anti-psychotics. Clearly, they'd been necessary if one of the first things I did once they were out of my system was start stalking someone.

I lifted my hand and was about to kill the video feed when Aly turned on her bed and finally looked at the mask. My finger hovered over the button as her expression shifted into something I hadn't seen before. Her eyes fluttered half shut, and she bit her full bottom lip in a way that had me leaning forward in my chair. A pretty flush stained her cheeks pink. Was she about to cry?

She glanced sideways at her cat. "Only one way to find out."

Before I could zoom back in on what she was doing, she tapped something out on her phone, fingers flying over the screen before hitting a final key. A *swoosh* sound followed, like she'd just sent an email or a text.

My phone chimed on my desk.

I froze.

Oh, shit. Had she DM'd me?

Carefully, like it might rear up and bite me, I lifted my phone. A notification flashed across it, reading, *User aly.aly.oxen.free would like to send you a message.* My heart pounded against my ribs as I unlocked the screen and opened her message.

This might sound completely insane, but did you break into my house tonight, film a video in my bedroom, and leave a mask behind?

Fuck. How did I respond? If I said yes, it could eventually get held against me in a court of law. If I said no, I'd be gaslighting her. Was there some way to play it cool? Answer her question with a question that neither confirmed nor denied her suspicions?

What would you do if I said yes? I asked. There. That seemed safe enough.

Onscreen, her app pinged, and I had a front-row seat as she read and reacted to my reply. She bit her lower lip again, sucking in a breath as she pulled her phone close. A few loose strands of hair fell over her shoulder, obscuring her profile from my sight.

"Holy fucking shit, he answered," she said, her voice barely above a whisper. "He never answers anyone. Ever."

Turn right a little so I can see you better, I almost demanded, but that would give the camera away, and now that I had her talking, I wasn't ready to have the feed cut off.

She started typing again, and a second later, my phone chimed.

That depends, she said.

On what, Aly? I typed back.

She sucked in another breath, and I grinned. So she liked it when I used her name. Did it make her feel special, knowing that the man she'd openly lusted after online, who notoriously never responded to comments or DMs, had finally chosen to speak to someone, and that someone was her? If so, I'd type and say her name every chance she gave me.

On what your intentions are, she said.

I sat back in my chair. My intentions. How to respond? There were so many options, so many fantasies I'd played out in my mind with her already. There was the one of waking her up in the middle of the night with a knife to her throat, but instead of turning the blade on her, I slid the handle between her legs and used it to edge her to the brink of insanity, teasing her but never giving her what she wanted despite how much she begged and sobbed for release. Or the one where I kidnapped her in the hospital parking garage, drove her into the middle of the woods, and told her to run as far as she could because what I planned to do when I caught her would make even the Devil weep.

But she probably wasn't ready for any of that right now, and she might still be thinking about calling the cops, so I settled for taunting her instead.

My intentions? Oh, Aly. Why would I tell you what they are when your previous comments have led me to believe that fear is half the fun for you?

I lifted my eyes just in time to watch Aly drop her phone on the comforter and place her head in her hands. "I need so much more therapy than I'm currently getting."

I grinned, because same.

Fred meowed and butted his head against her arm.

"Fur therapy isn't going to cut it this time, buddy," she said, scooping him up. "And I'm sorry for this, but I need to do grown-up human things right now, and you can't be in here."

As I watched, she strode to her bathroom and set Fred on the tile floor, apologizing again as she shut him inside. I waited with bated breath as she returned to the bed and picked up her phone.

How can I trust that you wouldn't hurt me? she asked.

You can't, Aly. I'm a stranger on the internet.

She let out a sharp exhale and shook her phone. "Don't you think I know that? I just need some sort of reassurance that I'm not about to be headline news."

I should have felt bad for her, but, just like her fear, her obvious aggravation only turned me on. It had been a long time since I'd made a woman this frustrated. Usually, I preferred their frustration to be sexual, winding them higher and higher until they finally snapped, but with Aly, I got a thrill from even this benign form of antagonism. There was something about seeing such a beautiful woman turn feisty that got me going. Maybe it was the challenge. I liked women with some fight in them. Ones who didn't put up with bullshit, spoke their minds, and could take care of themselves.

Not that I had anything against meeker women; they just weren't for me. In fact, they downright terrified me because they'd been Dad's preferred prey. I'd never even dated one, let alone slept with one, on the off chance that I shared his proclivities. I stuck to strong, borderline-aggressive women instead. Ones who had a better chance of fighting me off if I ever . . . well, I'd rather not think about that while Aly still filled my computer screen.

Seeing her all riled up made me feel like rewarding her, despite my instincts screaming at me to be careful. I pulled up the second half of the video I'd shot in her room, the half that would get me banned from social media if I ever posted it, and before I could question myself, I uploaded it into our message thread and hit send, acting on instinct alone.

Aly clapped a hand over her mouth when she opened it, her voice muffled when she groaned out, "Oh my fucking god."

I leaned back in my chair and waited, wondering what she'd do with the video. It was another test. Most likely, she was about to call the cops, but on the off chance she didn't, she was about to take the first step toward becoming *mine*.

"Is his . . . ?" she said.

Hand sliding into his pants? Yes, it was, and I was absolutely going to hell for taking a video of myself stroking my dick to full arousal in her bedroom.

Her head fell forward, and a low moan slipped from her lips. Her eyes were half-lidded again when she raised them, cheeks pink, and suddenly, I realized what this expression was: lust.

Aly was fucked up, too. Hallelujah.

She reached out with her free hand and propped my mask against her pillows. Once it was settled, she stood and double-checked the chair braced against her door, ensuring it was secure before she went to her dresser, opened the top drawer, and pulled out a vibrator.

Oh, fuck.

I needed to kill the video feed.

Not ten minutes ago, I'd told myself the line in the sand was watching Aly sleep or change. Spying on her while she masturbated was way over it, wrong on so many levels that I—holy shit, there went her pants. I caught the briefest glimpse of a well-manicured triangle of hair before she turned and—

Look. At. Her. Ass.

I wanted to slap it. Hard enough to leave a mark. And then I wanted to bite it. Turn her around in my lap and watch it bounce as I fucked her from behind. God bless whatever glute exercises she did at the gym because they were paying off.

No. This was wrong. I wasn't going to watch Aly pleasure herself to a video I'd sent her. And I definitely wasn't snaking a hand into my shorts and choking the base of my dick.

Stop that. Bad hand. We're not doing this.

Onscreen, Aly laid back on her bed with her spread legs facing my mask, her phone held aloft with one hand. She clicked the vibrator on with her other one and, without any foreplay whatsoever, positioned it at the apex of her thighs and slammed it all the way home, her back arching, a half-tortured, half-pleasured cry ringing out over my speakers.

I slapped the button to cut the video feed, and my screen went black. For good measure, I shoved my computer chair back and strode away from my desk, stopping in front of my bedroom windows. My hands shook, and I clasped them behind my head as I stared out at the rising sun. Fucking hell, that was close. The sight of Aly's arched back was burned into my retinas, and her tortured cry had been far too sweet to my ears. If I'd watched for even a second longer, I never would have found the willpower to stop.

It was slightly reassuring that I still had some morals. Aly might be masturbating to a video I'd sent her, but she hadn't consented to me watching her do it. And sure, she hadn't consented to me breaking into her house, filming a thirst trap inside her bedroom, sending her a sexually suggestive video, or watching her since she'd gotten home, but the line had to be somewhere, and sexual predation seemed like a pretty good place to draw it—no matter how much the darkest parts of my mind protested that what she didn't know wouldn't hurt her.

I was already becoming unhealthily obsessed with Aly. There was no way this would end well for either of us if I didn't hold myself in check, but now that I had her within my sight, I couldn't seem to stop myself, and all my carefully laid plans of taking it slow and easing her into things were going up in flames.

I needed her, and whether she was ready or not, I was about to put her to the ultimate test.

I just hoped it didn't end with either of us traumatized or dead.

5

ALY

THE FACELESS MAN HAD BEEN HERE. Here, in my bedroom, *on my bed* with his hand in his pants as he filmed himself. I should have been scared out of my fucking mind that a stranger from the internet had broken into my house. And I was. Truly. But I was also more turned on than I'd ever been in my life, and at this rate, it was only going to take a few more brutal thrusts of my vibrator before I came screaming.

I turned the vibration up and pumped the sex toy into myself with one hand while I held my phone aloft with the other, watching as the man I'd lusted after for months pleasured himself on this very comforter. Look at those goddamn muscles. At the knife he held in his free hand. The way his forearm bunched and flexed as he stroked himself. He was the hottest thing I'd ever seen, and he'd somehow noticed all the thirsty comments I left him out of the thousands he must get on a daily basis.

It made me feel special. Seen. Chosen.

Until tonight, I honestly thought my obsession was just a phase. That I *was* all talk, and my recently awakened kink was purely driven by the overwhelming abundance of masked men on my social media feed. I was convinced that a new trend would gain traction online, and I'd be into bondage by the end of the month instead.

Silly me.

I knew better now. This wasn't just a passing fancy for me. It was my ride-or-die fantasy, and the fact that I might be living it out made me feel more alive than anything else had in months.

But I wasn't stupid. My years working as a trauma nurse had taught me that this was much more likely to end in tragedy than anything else. I'd checked my entire house, top to bottom, and knew he wasn't inside. I'd also braced chairs against both my front and back doors, as well as my bedroom. I was as safe as I could be for now, and as soon as I got this overwhelming *need* out of my system, I'd go back to being terrified and angry.

The video started over, and I pulled my phone in for a close-up view as the Faceless Man flattened a big hand over his abs and then slid it torturously slow into his unbuttoned jeans. He stroked downward first, tugging his dick from base to tip. I moaned and imagined the feel of it in my hand, so wide I could barely wrap my fingers around it, hard as steel, soft as silk, and warm enough to set my blood on fire.

I wasn't lying in my comments; I wanted to crawl to this man. Give him the most toe-curling, leg-shaking, dick-throbbing, sheet-gripping, soul-sucking, ball-draining head of his life. I was close just thinking about it, so I let the fantasy play out in my mind as I inserted myself into the video, joining him on the bed and replacing his hand with my mouth, choking down that dick until my eyes watered and my pussy clenched. I wanted his hands in my hair, gripping so hard it hurt as he fucked my mouth.

I craned my head up to stare at the mask, *his mask*, that he'd left for me like some macabre memento. It was all too easy to imagine him staring out of it, watching me while I shoved the vibrator deep and held it in place.

I was done teasing myself, needed to come like I needed to breathe. The small nub at the base of the device thrummed against my clit in a way that had my spine arching off the bed. My phone fell from numb fingers, and I slammed my eyes shut as my entire being spiraled down into the sensitive bundle of nerves between my thighs.

Oh, god, I was going to—

"Fuck!" I half-yelled/half-moaned as light exploded behind my closed lids, and an orgasm tore through me with as much violence as pleasure.

I lay there panting afterward, half dazed and still aroused. Shit. This wasn't good. A man had broken into my house, and instead of calling the cops, I'd masturbated on top of whatever evidence might remain. No way could I call them now. How the hell would I explain myself?

"And why didn't you call us immediately?" they would ask.

"Sorry, Officer. I was too busy diddling myself instead."

Ugh. And also? I'd asked for this. I wasn't victim-blaming myself; I had literally begged for it to happen. At one point, I'd even left a comment offering him money to break in and wait for me in the dark. How would that hold up in court? His defense could probably argue that all their client had done was take me at my word. I should ask the hospital's lawyers about it. Technically, I was one of their clients as an employee. That meant they couldn't tell all my coworkers about the freaky shit I was into outside of work, right? Client privilege and all that?

I got up and cleaned myself off. I was soaked. Wetter than I'd been in a long time. Regular sex was fine, cathartic even, but at this point, it'd become less exciting than it used to be and more about stress relief and the need for physical intimacy with another person—a reminder that people could give each other pleasure instead of pain.

My job was truly starting to impact my life. I'd known it was a possibility going in. School had tried to prepare me. Back when I'd first entered the career field, my on-the-job trainer and other coworkers had told me how much of a toll trauma nursing could take on someone, detailing the sky-high divorce rates at the hospital, PTSD diagnoses, and addiction issues, but I hadn't listened. I'd been too naïve and headstrong. No one had been there when my mom needed it, and I couldn't let what happened to her happen to anyone else if there was something I could do about it.

Now, I was starting to become numb. I'd seen so much shit that my faith in humanity was at rock bottom, and I'd lost contact with everyone but my nursing and other first responder friends because no one else understood what I faced day in and day out. Even sex had lost its thrill. Or at least, vanilla sex had. What I had just done proved that I needed something spicier to get me off. Something darker with a sharp edge of danger.

A soft *meow* pulled me from my thoughts. Right. I'd locked Fred in the bathroom. It made me feel like a bad parent after the night he'd had. He'd probably hidden under my bed and only came out when I got home. He didn't like or trust most people, especially men (who could blame him?), and he'd run from or hissed at every guy I'd ever invited over. A stranger being in his space when I wasn't even here must have scared him shitless.

I got changed into pajamas and then let Fred out. He zoomed into my room and went straight to the door. Poor guy probably had to pee.

My nerves returning, I scooped my gun off the dresser and carefully slid the chair from beneath the knob, half afraid that someone was waiting to bust inside. I flicked open the lock and then cracked the door, gun aimed. No one stood in the short hall separating the bedrooms—thank god—and I'd left so many lights on that I didn't see anyone anywhere else when I craned my head around the corner and looked into my open-concept living area.

Still, my paranoia had reached an all-time high, and while Fred raced toward his litter box, I cleared my house for the second time. A chime had me turning back toward my bedroom when I was done. I'd left my phone in there. Had completely forgotten to respond to the video the Faceless Man sent me.

A blush stole up my cheeks. If only he knew the reason why. He'd probably be even more convinced that I approved of what he'd done and was hopeful for a repeat, preferably while I was home.

I scooped my phone off the dresser and froze. Was I hopeful for a repeat? I shook my head. No. Absolutely not. That would be crazy, right? But there was no denying the heat blooming in my core or how my heart tripped in response to the thought.

My phone chimed again, and I glanced down at it. I saw two new social media notifications. The Faceless Man had sent me more messages.

My fingers shook as I unlocked the screen. What had he said? Did he send another video? And why was I so desperate to find out when I should be blocking and reporting his ass?

It wasn't another video. Just two simple, heart-stopping messages.

Sleep tight.

Alyssa.

I blinked. Not Aly. Alyssa. My full name. That I hadn't used in my profile, comments, or anywhere else on this goddamn app. I wasn't even surprised. He'd broken into my house, so he must have learned my full name, and god only knew how much else about me before he came here. Still, having him type it out felt even more intrusive for some reason, and not in an entirely bad way, either.

What the hell did I say back to him? Thank you? Go fuck yourself, you creep? Try something like this again, and I'll shoot you? Get your ass back here right now, you monster, you can't leave me this turned on?

It felt like my brain was splitting in half. On the one hand, this was the hottest thing that had ever happened to me. On the other, it was also the most fucked up.

This truly was the horror movie I would die in, wasn't it?

■ ■ ■

Somehow, despite how horny and afraid I'd been, I managed to fall asleep. I'd barricaded myself in my room with Fred, moving his litter box into my bathroom and his food and water bowl by my dresser. I also fell asleep clutching a baseball bat, my gun within easy reach.

I was convinced I'd have nightmares, or worse, sex dreams, but I'd slept like the dead for a solid ten hours, waking only when Fred got bored with his imprisonment and started running laps around my bed.

Now, I sat at my small dining table, clutching a huge mug of coffee while my mind worked on overdrive. Part of me couldn't believe what had happened. The Faceless Man broke into my house last night. Even thinking it felt surreal. Like I'd detached from reality and resided in a dark matrix glitch of my own making.

He could have hidden in here and murdered me the second I walked through the door, but he didn't. I was still whole and hale, if more than a little rattled, and that had to mean something, didn't it? That he didn't want to kill me?

Don't be a dumbass, I told myself.

Right. For all I knew, this was foreplay to him. He could be like a cat toying with its prey, relishing the chase, watching mercilessly while I flailed around, waiting for the opportune moment to strike. He might really be a killer and did this with all his victims. Lured them to him online, flirted, broke into their houses, maybe even fucked them a few times without hurting them. I could see it now, how easily someone could fall for that trap, dropping their guard only for him to serial murder them in some spectacularly messy way.

Well, I'd be his next victim over my dead—whoops, wrong phrase for right now. I *wouldn't* be his next victim. Later today, I'd add the gun store to my long list of errands. They sold more than weapons. In addition to personal defense items, they carried home defense supplies. I'd get cameras. An alarm. That motherfucker wouldn't be getting back in here without one hell of a fight.

I shifted in my seat, trying to ignore the fact that despite my new-found resolve, I was still turned on and had been since last night, my panties damp and my nipples shooting little shivers of pleasure through me every time they brushed against the inside of my sweatshirt.

Stupid kink making me lust after a man who probably wanted to carve my skin off and make himself a pair of gloves out of it.

I grimaced at that image and took another sip of coffee. This whole situation was beyond frustrating. Did he want to hurt me, or didn't he? And why had he chosen me, out of all the people in his comment sections, to single out? Did he live somewhere nearby? Had I met him offline somehow? Bumped into him in my favorite coffee shop or lifted weights next to him at the gym?

Even if I had, how had he found me online? He must have known my name and what I looked like if he was able to pick me out of his comments because I'd told no one, absolutely *no one*, about my mask kink IRL, and I wasn't friends or following anyone I knew personally on my account either.

What happened after he found me? How had he gone from figuring out who I was to learning where I lived?

Most importantly, how did he get in here last night? None of my windows were broken or unlocked, I didn't have a chimney for him to slither down, and my back door had a deadbolt that I kept locked from the inside. As far as I knew, he would have had to break it to get in. I'd checked last night, and there were no signs of forced entry. So that left the front door.

The power had cut off sometime during the night. Had he somehow triggered it and used the cover of darkness to sneak inside? No. It must have been a coincidence. He'd have to be a top-notch hacker to pull something like that off.

And to figure out everything else he had about me, now that I thought about it.

My phone was sitting face up on the table beside me. I eyed it warily. Was he somehow watching me through it even now? I shoved it behind my napkin holder, out of sight, just to be safe. I was in way over my head. I'd taken a few programming courses in high school and college. Enough to realize that a job in one of the computer science fields wasn't for me. I had no idea what skills were needed to hack my phone or if it was even possible.

Wait a minute. Wasn't Tyler's roommate a computer genius? Could he answer my questions? Things might have been over between me and Tyler, but it wasn't like it was ever serious between us or ended badly. I'd seen him at the gym the other afternoon, and he'd been nice enough, waving to me across the weight room and giving me a thumbs-up when I hit a new max on my deadlift. Would it be weird to ask him if he would talk to his roommate for me? How would I even explain what I needed?

Hey, Tyler. It's Aly. Don't worry, I'm not still into you or anything. I just need your roommate to track down the man from that thirst trap I sent you.

I rolled my eyes. Yeah. That would go over well.

Maybe I'd be okay if I kept it vague and offered to pay the guy. I'd only met Josh once, so it wasn't like he'd have any reason to do it out of friendship or the goodness of his heart.

My thoughts wandered back to that one meeting. The only details Tyler had told me about Josh were that he was a recluse with a fancy cybersecurity job. I'd expected him to be some reed-thin short guy with glasses, and yes, I was aware that meant I'd fallen for the Hollywood stereotype of what a "geek" looked like.

Josh taught me better. Because he was huge, at least six-four, and though he'd been wearing baggy gym pants and a sweatshirt the morning I bumped into him in their kitchen, there was no hiding the fact that the man was yoked. I'd only caught a glance at his profile—strong jaw, aquiline nose, the kind of thick, long lashes most women would kill for—but that one glimpse was enough to tell me Josh had heartbreaker-level good looks. He must have had Mediterranean blood in him because his skin had some olive in it, and his hair was just as dark as mine. Mom would have taken one look at him and said something inappropriate about him being a man who could give her strong Italian grandchildren.

He'd made me stand up straighter, instantly aware of the fact that I was wearing his roommate's T-shirt, and he'd probably heard me fucking Tyler just a few hours earlier because we hadn't been as quiet as we should have after splitting a bottle of wine over dinner.

None of that mattered because I didn't need Josh for his looks; I needed him for his brain. Would paying him be enough incentive to get him to help? And how much would I have to tell him about what I needed? Could I simply ask him to find someone for me without going into too much detail?

I needed Google to answer all these questions.

My fingers strayed toward my phone, but I hesitated, not trusting myself not to pull up my DMs again and obsess over the video the Faceless Man had sent me. Instead, I set my coffee down and went in search of my laptop.

6

JOSH

Aly was Googling what information a hacker needed to find someone for her.

This could be a problem.

I watched her through her laptop camera as she read the article, her dark eyes filled with focus, a small divot appearing between her brows as she started to frown. Her hair was in a messy bun, she had no makeup on, and her clothes were rumpled like she'd just rolled out of bed. Something inside me softened at the sight. I'd been so fixated on playing out a fantasy with her that I hadn't stopped to consider what reality might look like.

I closed my eyes and pictured myself sitting across from her at the dining table, watching her sip coffee as she woke up, her hair wild and lips bruised from what I'd done to them the night before. I nearly groaned at the thought. It'd been so long since I'd shared a bed with someone for more than just a quick hookup. When was the last time I'd woken to a woman splayed across my chest as she slept, using me for body heat? The fact that I couldn't remember probably wasn't a good thing.

Tyler regularly called me a recluse, but up until now, I hadn't given it a second thought. So what if I was one? My aversion to leaving the apartment building was warranted, considering my past and the fallout of being recognized. But picturing myself inside a simple slice-of-life scene with Aly had me questioning my choices. How much was I missing out on by locking myself away from the rest of the world? Was it still necessary to guard myself from people and vice versa? I was twenty-six years old, and so far, I'd gone all this time without hurting anyone.

Did that mean I might never hurt someone?

Dad had committed his first assault as a young teen. The podcasts that examined his case loved talking about how an early childhood filled with abuse and a couple of head wounds had started him down his dark path. He'd passed the pain on to me before Mom managed to get us away from him for good, but at least I'd been lucky enough to escape suffering a traumatic brain injury.

The MacDonald triad was an outdated but sometimes eerily accurate prediction of violent tendencies in a person. The first point of the triangle was fire-starting. Burning shit down had never appealed to me. The second was bed-wetting. I'd had an iron bladder even from an early age, and I'd never pissed the sheets. The third was the one I'd always worried about because I'd never wanted to test myself—animal cruelty—but since I hadn't hurt Fred the other night or was even tempted to, I was starting to feel more confident than I had in a long time that I wasn't going to snap one day and turn into my father.

Bro, you are literally stalking Aly right now, I reminded myself.

Yeah, there was that. Okay, so I might not be a danger to the public, but I had some traits most people—my therapist included, if I ever confessed what I was doing to Aly—would call problematic. At least I wasn't watching Aly because I wanted to chain her up in my hypothetical basement or anything. I just needed to figure out whether or not she was into what I'd done, and then I'd stop.

I rolled my eyes. Unfortunately, I was too self-aware to believe my own bullshit.

I wasn't going to fucking stop.

Aly sat forward in her seat and started typing.

Can someone watch me through my laptop camera?

Uh-oh.

Her eyes flashed wide as she read the results, then jerked to the top of the screen, looking straight at me.

"Hello, gorgeous," I said, wishing she could hear me so I could watch the blood drain from her face in fear.

Yup. Definitely problematic. I'd circle back around to analyze that later.

"Shit," Aly bit out, pushing away from the table.

She turned and strode out of view, and I watched her ass the entire time. The things I wanted to do to that ass. I'd always thought of myself as a tit man, but Aly was proving me wrong.

I heard her rustling around somewhere nearby before she marched back into the feed carrying duct tape and scissors. She was about to cover the camera.

Fuck.

Disappointment and frustration sank straight into my gut, and I couldn't stop myself from pulling my phone out and typing a one-word message to her.

Don't.

Her phone pinged onscreen, and she paused in the middle of tearing off a piece of tape to look at it. Fear flashed across her face—sweet, delicious fear—before being quickly replaced by anger.

"Listen, motherfucker," she said, setting her phone down and planting her hands on the table as she leaned in close. God, she was beautiful when she was mad, her dark eyes almost black as she narrowed them at me. "I am going to find you, and then we'll see how much you like it when you come home to discover someone waiting for you in the dark."

A thrill shot through me, zooming straight to my dick. Apparently, I'd like that a lot. I might not even try to block whatever two-bit hacker she might end up hiring if it meant the result was her waiting for me with a gun or a knife. I'd be her willing victim. Or maybe I'd test her to see how far she'd go.

I didn't have a death wish. It's not like I wanted her to shoot me or anything, but I was curious about how much darkness hid beneath her beautiful façade. If she wanted to rough me up a little, I might just let her.

Actually, no. Scratch that. Instead, I'd rather put up a good defense, push Aly to her limit, and see how much she'd learned in her self-defense classes. She looked like a woman who didn't pull her punches, and with all the muscle on her frame and how well she must know her body after all her workouts, she could probably do some real damage, even to someone like me who outweighed her by at least seventy pounds.

I grinned. Unfortunately for Aly, I'd been studying various martial arts since I was eleven. Mom enrolled both herself and me in our first class after we'd left my dad, wanting us to be able to defend ourselves if he ever tried to hurt us again. Even now, I practiced once a week with Tyler, who'd taken them with me starting in high school.

I'd let Aly get a few punches in, make her feel like she had a chance before pinning her to the ground and finding some way to convince her she'd rather fuck than fight.

I sat back and watched her while she tore a piece of duct tape free. I didn't miss the way her mind had gone straight to revenge. She could have threatened to report me, ordered me not to break in again, or told me she was calling the cops. But she didn't do any of those things. Did that mean some part of her enjoyed this as much as I did? After all, a "normal" person would go to the police. They'd let the professionals try to find me instead of searching for me themselves.

Not only had Aly not done any of those things, but she hadn't even told me to stop spying on her.

I palmed my erection through my shorts. She was into it. She might still be trying to convince herself she wasn't or shouldn't be, but she was. I just knew it. Somehow, I'd find a way to get her to accept it about herself.

She leaned in again and sent me a wink through the camera that had me gripping the base of my dick so hard it almost hurt. "See you soon," she threatened before lifting the tape.

Sooner than you think, baby, I thought as the screen went dark. Last night, I'd formulated another plan for breaking into her house, but now I had a better idea, where she'd have just as much control as I would.

I slid my hand beneath my waistband and idly stroked my dick, tipping back in my chair. Aly might have temporarily blocked me from looking at her, but I still had a window open that mirrored her computer screen. Her next Google search was for how to turn off her camera entirely. I followed along as she went through the steps, letting out an exhale when she was finished. She'd killed the video feed but hadn't disabled the microphone. I heard rustling through it, wondering what she was doing before the quiet sound of a phone ringing hit my ears.

Who was she calling?

An all too familiar voice picked up. "Aly?"

I yanked my hand away from my dick. She'd called *Tyler*? What the fuck?

And why did I suddenly want to drive to his office and punch him in the face?

Get ahold of yourself, I thought. *He's your best friend.*

"Tyler, hi," Aly said. "Sorry for calling you out of nowhere. I'm not about to beg you to reconsider breaking things off or anything, but I have sort of a weird favor, and if this is crossing a line, feel free to tell me to fuck off."

"Okaaay?" Tyler said. I recognized that tone of voice. He didn't believe her. He totally thought she was about to proposition him.

Aly took a deep breath. "I feel like I remember you saying your roommate was good with computers?"

Oh.

Fuck.

No.

She wasn't about to . . .

She couldn't really be . . .

Tyler blew out a laugh, sounding relieved. "He is. Why?"

"Could he find someone for me? Online? I have a bit of a situation here."

Fuck!

I was a danger, after all. To Tyler. Because I was going to kill him for telling her that much about me.

The humor was gone from my roommate's voice when he responded. "What kind of situation? Are you okay?"

"Uh . . ." Aly said, and I wished I could see her face. "I think so? Actually, I'd know for sure if your roommate could find this person."

I jerked to my feet and threaded my hands behind my head. This was bad. This was sooo bad.

"Aly. Seriously," Tyler said. "If someone threatened you or something, you should go to the cops, not my roommate."

"I haven't been threatened." A long pause. "I don't think."

Goddamnit. If I knew Tyler, he was about to offer to handle things himself.

Right on cue, he said, "Just tell me what you need, and Josh and I will take care of it. Between the two of us, we'll make whoever it is regret being born."

"I can handle this," Aly said, a hint of annoyance creeping into her tone. "I just need to find the person. That's all. Can Josh help me or not? I'll pay him."

There went my dick, tenting up my shorts again the second she said my name.

"Save your money," Tyler said. "I'm sure he'll do it for free."

I nearly flipped my fucking desk. Great. There was no getting out of helping Aly now. At least not without seeming like a monumental asshole and making Tyler question why I'd turn her down. It would look suspicious as fuck if I said no.

Aly let out a sigh. "Thank you. Just let me know a good time to come over."

Come over? Come over here?

I whipped my head to the left, toward the distinctive couch along the far wall that I heavily featured in my videos, then to my bed and the stupid fucking custom headboard I just had to commission because I couldn't go to IKEA like everyone else on the goddamn planet. No, I had to be special. Unique.

Aly was smart. She'd probably worked out that I lived nearby. The second she stepped inside my room, I'd be fucked.

"I'll talk to him after work and let you know," Tyler said.

"Okay. Thank you for this."

They got off the phone, and I started pacing, feeling like a caged animal. No need to panic. I could figure this out. For starters, Aly couldn't come in here. That much was obvious. Nor could she get a good look at my hands. My tattoos were just as distinctive as my furniture choices, and they crawled all the way down to my knuckles. Thankfully, I had a pair of fingerless gloves. I'd chuck them on before she arrived, and if she asked why I was wearing them, I'd tell her I was cold.

I paused in my pacing and grabbed my phone to start planning everything I'd need to do to avoid detection.

I'd have to turn the thermostat down to sell the lie about being chilly. I'd need to move my laptop into the living room and work from there instead of on my desktop. And I'd definitely need to swap the Utah dad I'd framed for someone within driving distance if I was going to pretend to track myself down.

My fingers flew over my phone as I made a list in the note app. I was nothing if not organized.

By the time I had it all written out in front of me, I felt marginally better. This wasn't a total disaster, and on the plus side, I'd have a reason to spend time with Aly, learn more about her, and get a better read on what she thought about the situation I'd dragged her into.

I slipped my phone into my pocket when I was done, still feeling jittery. I had to get out of there and clear my head.

A glance at my computer showed me the sound monitor tied to Aly's laptop was still measuring noise, so she hadn't closed it. I sent the feed to my tablet, grabbed that along with my keys and wallet, pulled on sweatpants and a jacket, and headed out.

I connected the tablet to my car speakers through Bluetooth as the engine roared to life and I waited for the heat to kick on, listening in as Aly moved about her house. Just in case she walked into her bedroom, I set my phone in its dashboard holder and pulled up the feed for the hidden camera.

Mobile stalking unit: activated.

I felt proud of myself for all of a second before I realized what a creep this probably made me. Despite knowing I should feel guilty and wrong for what I was doing, I didn't. All I could drum up was a slight hint of regret, but even that didn't make me want to stop. At this point, only law enforcement or Aly telling me to fuck off would be enough to put an end to my behavior.

I hoped.

Twenty minutes later, I was driving past Aly's house for the second time, laughing to myself as she spammed my DMs. My first present had arrived, and she was not amused.

Flowers? she asked. *You bought me fucking flowers after breaking into my house?*

Also, what the hell am I supposed to do with an entire floral shop???

These delivery men are telling me that it's against policy for them to take them back since they've been paid for.

If you meant this as an apology, you failed.

I'm madder at you now than I was last night.

That last statement piqued my interest. She was more annoyed by flowers than a home invasion? Yup, Aly was fucked up, and she probably didn't even realize how much her comments revealed because she was still trying to convince herself she didn't want this.

I longed to say something back to her, but I wasn't responding to anything because it might come too close to an admission of guilt.

"I don't have anywhere else to put these," Aly said, loud enough that both the microphone on her laptop and the one attached to the camera in her bedroom picked it up.

The delivery man's response was muffled.

"No, I know that's not your problem, but come on," she said.

My amusement faded. Was he being rude to her?

Keep driving, stupid, I told myself. I couldn't pull over and teach him a lesson about politeness right now. That would ruin everything. But maybe I could figure out who these guys were and find some digital way to show them the error of their ways.

"How about this," Aly said. "Take them to the nurses' station at Prescott Memorial."

The response was muffled again.

"Fifty bucks to drive them ten minutes away?" she said. "Are you serious?"

I grimaced. Well, this was backfiring.

A heavy sigh came through the speakers as I parked a street away from hers. "Let me get my wallet," I heard her say.

I yanked my phone from its dock just in time to watch her stomp into her bedroom, looking pissed. Fred was lying curled up in a ball on her comforter, nonplussed at all the noise.

Aly grabbed her wallet from her handbag and paused long enough to scratch Fred between the ears. "I hope you bit the Faceless Man."

Fred made a little chirruping noise in response. I chose to interpret that as him defending my character. Weren't pets supposed to have some sixth sense and could always tell the good people from the bad? He hadn't so much as hissed at me. In fact, he wouldn't leave me alone the whole time I was there, and I eventually had to shut him out of Aly's room so I could film in peace. I took that as a sign that I wasn't as damned as I thought, and a little light, okay, heavy stalking wasn't enough to condemn me.

Aly paid the delivery driver and shut her front door hard enough that my speakers rattled.

Great, she typed a minute later. *On top of being a pain in the ass and way over the top, your gift just cost me fifty bucks.*

I slid down in my seat, wishing I could apologize but knowing I shouldn't. Oh, wait. Didn't Aly have a payment app? I pulled one of my anonymous accounts up on the tablet and found her on the app, sending her fifty bucks via the same stolen credit card I'd used to buy the flowers.

Seriously? she asked. *You think that makes up for all this hassle?*

I drummed my fingers against the dashboard, frustrated about my inability to communicate with her. I almost brought my burner phone, but I'd left it behind, telling myself it was too early to text her from it.

A loud *ding-dong* came from my speakers. Her doorbell? I pulled up my tracking app, and sure enough, my other gifts had just arrived.

I heard a door open and then, "Can I help you?"

"I'm here to deliver a package to Alyssa Cappellucci?" a man said, mangling her last name.

She didn't bother to correct him. "I'm she."

"Sign here?" he said.

"But I didn't order anything."

"So, you're refusing delivery?"

"Uh . . . no?" she said.

"Then please sign here."

"Who sent this?"

"No idea," was the response. "We don't get that information. Do you want the package or not?"

"Fine, yeah."

It got quiet for a minute, and I assumed she was signing.

"Here you go," the man said. "Have a good day."

The front door closed again, and I heard more muffled sounds.

My phone pinged a second later.

Did you send me something?

Several somethings, but she'd figure that out soon enough.

It better not be a bomb, or I'm coming back as a poltergeist and finding some way to ghost-murder you.

I grinned. Aly was just as snarky as her thirsty comments made her out to be, and I was here for it.

Suddenly, she appeared on my phone screen as she entered her room. She went straight to Fred, scooped him up, and put him in her bathroom.

"Sorry, bud," she said. "But you have to stay here. Mom is about to do something stupid, and I don't want you to get hurt if this goes sideways."

She shut the door on his protesting meow and left her room.

I tried to drum up some remorse as I leaned forward in my seat and listened to her open the packages, but I was too excited. Plus, I knew it wasn't a bomb. Obviously.

"What the—" she said. "What is all this? Oh, you have got to be fucking kidding me."

My phone pinged, and I immediately opened her messages.

You sent me home defense tools?

After breaking into my house?

Are you serious right now???

Keep going, I wanted to tell her. On top of buying her burglar-proof wedges with built-in alarms that could be shoved beneath her doors, I'd gotten her titanium bars that braced against knobs way better than a chair could, extra locks that couldn't be manipulated with magnets, and an entire in-home security system complete with cameras for her front and back doors.

Lastly, because some small part of me believed in fairness and wanted to even the playing field, I got her a high-tech camera detector. Watching her had been fun and was fulfilling a surveillance kink I didn't even know I had until now, but it'd be even more fun if Aly decided she *wanted* to be watched.

I heard more rustling and then, "This motherfucker."

Why did you get me these things? she demanded. *To make it harder for yourself the next time you try to break in?*

Are you some sort of sick fuck who likes the challenge?

Also, you saved me the trouble of having to buy them for myself later today, like planned, but if you're waiting for a thank you, you're shit out of luck, buddy.

A solid minute of silence passed.

"Answer me, goddamnit!" her voice echoed through my car.

I know you're reading these messages, you bastard. I can see the read receipts.

Before I could stop myself, I sent her a kissy-face emoji. One day, I would learn to stop being such a smartass, but today was not that day.

The growl that rumbled out of my speakers in response was adorable.

"That's it," she said. "I change my mind. I'm calling the cops on his ass."

Don't, I typed back, the same single word from before.

This couldn't be traced to anything she'd written, and if we ever ended up in court, it would be her word against mine that my response was to something she said. I really hoped it didn't come to that. I was having way too much fun with her.

"What the fuck?" she said. "Are you listening to me somehow? How the hell do I disable the microphone on a laptop?"

Well, I'm certainly not telling you, I sent back.

"I hope you're enjoying yourself, you son of a bitch," she snarled.

Immensely, I responded, adding a smiley face emoji for good measure.

"I am going to find you, and I am going to make you regret this."

Sounds kinky.

A strangled laugh came through my speakers, and the grin that split my face in response felt evil. Got her. She was enjoying this on some level, too. Now, I just needed to keep pulling her strings until I found the one that unraveled her enough that she stopped fighting against her nature and joined me on my descent into darkness.

"Do not misconstrue the sound that just came out of my mouth," she said. "It was hysterical laughter only. Brought on by stress and a murderous rage."

Hot, I replied.

She choked on another laugh. "Goddamn it. That's it. I'm turning off my computer."

I sent a crying face emoji.

"You're not funny," she said.

Then why do you keep laughing?

"I am *not* laughing. Not really."

I pulled up my photo app, double-checked that the background of the video I needed was blurry enough that her room wasn't identifiable, and then sent her an outtake from last night, just to keep her talking.

She went quiet as she watched a shirtless me trying to film myself in her mirror, only for Fred to suddenly leap onto the bed and start meowing at me at the top of his lungs, rubbing against my hand when I wasn't fast enough to pet him.

This was a huge risk. The room might be blurry, but me pictured alongside a black and white cat could prove harder to defend. I was operating on instinct alone at this point. Aly hadn't reported me yet, and if my gut was right, there was a good chance she never would.

"No," Aly said. "There is absolutely no way. What did you do? Cover yourself in catnip? He hates men."

Now, why did that little piece of information suddenly make me feel so special?

He just has exacting taste, I said.

I sent her another outtake, this one of Fred stalking up behind me before pouncing at my dangling fingers, slapping at them without using his claws, and then bounding offscreen, where he yowled like he wanted me to play chase with him.

Aly chuckled, but it turned muffled after a clapping sound, like she'd clamped a hand over her mouth to stifle it.

"This means nothing," she said. "Cats are sociopaths by nature. Fred simply recognized a similar creature."

If I'm the cat, what does that make you? I asked. *The mouse?*

"I'm a motherfucking wolf," Aly said, and then her computer cut off as she killed the power.

Damn it. Well, at least I still had her bedroom camera for a few more minutes. I locked the tablet and switched my phone to Bluetooth to hear her better over the speakers.

"What the hell is this thing?"

My phone started rapid-fire chiming.

A CAMERA FINDER???

NO.

DUDE.

NO.

YOU BETTER NOT HAVE.

She marched straight into her bedroom with the device aimed.

Welp, here goes my last way to monitor her in her house, I thought.

It took less than a minute for her to find the camera I planted, and when she did, she just stood in front of it, staring for so long that I started to get nervous.

Unable to stand it any longer, I picked up my phone.

Say something, I typed.

She glanced at her phone screen and then back at the camera. "The other night, after you sent me that video. Did you—" She snapped her mouth shut like she couldn't bring herself to finish the sentence.

Aly, no, I said, feeling desperate. I wanted her to be afraid of me, but not like this. *I stopped.*

"I don't believe you," she said, so low I barely heard it.

Fuck, I was starting to lose her, wasn't I?

And you don't have any reason to, I typed. *But I'm still telling you I stopped.*

"Have you been watching me change and sleep and . . ."

No. My moral compass might not point north, but it's not that fucked up.

"Why should I believe you?"

I sighed, wanting to convince her but knowing that wasn't the right move. As far as she knew, I was a stranger on the internet.

You shouldn't, Aly.

She let out a low noise of frustration and shook her head. "Fuck."

As I watched, she yanked the camera from the socket, and even though I knew it was coming, I wasn't ready for the sense of loss that punched through me.

I don't want to hurt you, I told her, knowing I might regret it when this all went to shit, and she finally reported me.

Didn't you just imply I'd be an idiot to believe you? she responded.

I suppose I had.

Her "online" notification cut off as she logged out of the app.

This was fine. I'd expected Aly to be pissed about the camera for a little while. She had every right to be.

But if everything went to plan, I was going to prove that I didn't intend to hurt her, and she could trust me.

7

ALY

I NEED TO STOP CHECKING MY PHONE, I thought as I pushed open the breakroom door.

Every time I had five seconds to myself, I dashed inside to look at it. I'd installed my security system yesterday, placing the little sensors on all my windows and setting up the doorbell cameras. It also came with interior cameras, but there was no way in hell they were getting installed. Not when the Faceless Man could use them to keep spying on me.

The bastard.

I couldn't fucking believe he'd put a camera in my bedroom. Breaking in was bad enough, and even though I shouldn't have been, I was halfway to forgiving him for it yesterday. I mean, I had asked him to do it. But watching me without my consent crossed the line, and after everything he'd done, I'd be foolish to believe his "Aly, I stopped" bullshit, despite my weird gut reaction telling me I could trust him.

What kind of stalker had that moral fortitude? How was *that* his line in the sand? Maybe it made me a bad person, but if our roles were reversed and I'd gotten the chance to watch him masturbate, I wouldn't have stopped. I would have slid a hand into my underwear and joined in on the fun.

Two notifications were waiting for me from the security system when I grabbed my phone from my locker. One showed a tubby little raccoon ambling past my back door, and I saved it to my photos to rewatch it later because even though I knew they were wild animals and carriers of the rabies virus, every time I saw a trash panda, I wanted to pick it up and smoosh it.

The second video was of my weird neighbor Steve from down the street, who ran late at night, even in winter. He was an ultramarathoner and competed in some of the most extreme environments on the planet, and the harsher the conditions, the better, according to him. I knew far too much about the man because he was also chatty as fuck, and he'd cornered me at the last neighborhood block party and talked for a solid twenty minutes about his training regimen and how ultramarathons were more about being mentally tough than physically tough. I'd avoided him since. His intensity was unnerving.

That was it. Just two videos. I'd watched a dozen others over the last six hours, and all of them were cars driving past my house. I needed to find some way to turn the camera sensitivity down, or I'd get spammed with notifications during the day as my diurnal neighbors went about their lives.

I kept expecting to come into the breakroom and see the Faceless Man in full masked glory, trying to get back into my house while I was at work, but there was no sign of him. The disturbing thing was I couldn't tell if I was more relieved or disappointed. On the one hand, a stranger had broken into my house and filmed me; on the other, he was fulfilling the dark fantasy that had haunted both my waking and sleeping self for the past three months.

The biggest reason I longed to believe him when he said he didn't want to hurt me was the potential to play out my mask kink. How often had I dreamt about putting that muscular body through its paces? I wanted his fingers wrapped around my neck while he fucked me so I could stare at the veins popping out along his forearms as he held me in place. I wanted him behind me, my hands gripping a headboard while he pressed a knife to my throat and told me not to move.

Damn it, I needed to stop getting this turned on at work.

My gaze refocused on my phone.

Don't do it, I told myself, my finger hovering over my social media app. It was Saturday night, which meant a new video from the Faceless Man. He was punctual to a fault, and I doubted that stalking me would interfere with his posting schedule. So far, I'd managed to hold out, but my willpower was cracking.

"You are a weak, weak woman," I said as I opened the app and navigated to his profile. Sure enough, there was a new video.

"You don't have to watch it," I told myself. But my thumb was already moving of its own volition, and a heartbeat later, a low, drugging melody came from the phone speakers. The Faceless Man was back in one of his usual filming locations, and I let out a heavy breath of relief that it wasn't more content from my bedroom. He lay on his couch, clad in a black Henley with the sleeves pushed to his elbows, revealing tattoos and the corded, veiny forearms I obsessed over. Like usual, he held a knife, toying with it as he stared up at the ceiling while a tortured male voice sang about getting his heart broken.

The scene changed, showing him sitting up in bed against a heavy-duty headboard that looked made to take a pounding. It spoke of vigorous, athletic sex, complete with what looked like hook holes designed to tie people to it. He was shirtless now, big body leaning against his pillows, head turned to the side like he was staring into space.

The scene changed again, to a locale I'd never seen before. He stood in front of a large picture window, still shirtless, his arms lifted overhead as he leaned against the top part of the frame. I hit pause, taking a minute to let the sight of him sink in. His body was a goddamn masterpiece. Pretty privilege was real because looking at him made me want to forgive him for all manner of sins.

Right until I glanced down and noticed that he'd added a caption to one of his videos for the first time ever. It read: *When she's mad at you.*

Oh, hell no. This motherfucker better not have been talking about me.

I hit unpause, and the video lasted a few more seconds before it looped back to the beginning. My eyes narrowed as I listened to lyrics filled with regret and remorse for past actions. Was this his way of saying sorry? He'd have to do a hell of a lot better than this.

I scanned through the comments. People were losing it.

Who hurt you like this???

Give me a name and address, and I'll take care of it.

No. I refuse to believe anyone could be mad at him.

Ladies, we ride at dawn.

When I say I would forgive this man for literally anything.

"Ha," I said, my tone humorless. "You say that now, but just wait until he murders me and comes after you next."

I jerked my head up, relieved to see I was still alone. I really needed to stop talking to myself so much.

I dropped my gaze back down and read a few more comments defending his nonexistent honor before my anger got the better of me, and I typed, *When she has good reason to be mad at you, did you mean to say?*

I had barely hit enter when my phone pinged. He'd already seen and liked my comment. Oh, fuck. He never liked comments. Would people notice?

Another notification popped up. *User the.faceless.man has started following you.*

I nearly dropped my phone. No, he didn't.

Another chime came through. Someone, not him, had responded to my comment.

UM, MA'AM, HE LIKED YOUR COMMENT???

Someone else wrote, *OMG, SHE IS THE ONLY PERSON HE FOLLOWS.*

I reared back from my phone as the responses started pouring in. Uh-oh. What had I done? And what had he just done by singling me out like this?

My phone started pinging so fast that it sounded like the beginning of an EDM song.

Forgive him, you monster.

What is he like in real life?

Are you dating him???

So this is what jealous rage feels like.

How's it feel to be the most hated woman on the internet right now?

If you don't want him, I'll take him.

I quickly exited the app and muted it through my settings. Nope. Not dealing with this shitshow right now. I still had the second half of my shift to get through, and tonight was already bad enough because we currently had both a rape victim and her attacker in the hospital after he'd gotten caught in the act. The woman's family found out he was here, and we were having a hell of a time keeping them from killing him.

Not that I could blame them.

It was good that I wasn't the woman's nurse because, despite all my training and the ethics agreements I'd signed, I'd be tempted to slip her husband the man's room number. Only the thought of going to jail might stop me, but I'd learned so much about myself in the past twenty-four hours that I wondered if even that would be enough.

Was I more like the Faceless Man than I realized? Between contemplating whether or not to act as an accomplice to homicide and choosing to go the vigilante justice route instead of reporting my newfound stalker to the police, I was heading down a dark path. Maybe it was time to take a few weeks off work and clear my head. I hadn't taken so much as a sick day in . . . two years? No, that couldn't be right.

I frowned, thinking back. Holy shit, it was. The last time I missed a shift was thanks to that bout of food poisoning from a local deli that had since, unsurprisingly, closed down.

Two fucking years of trauma nursing without a vacation. Yikes. Yeah, I needed to fix that. No wonder my head was so messed up lately.

Well, that was also partly thanks to the Faceless Man. Was he watching me even now through the hospital security cameras? Probably not, but just in case he was, I flipped the bird at the one in the corner of the breakroom.

My phone chimed with a text message.

I pulled it up to see an unknown number and a single word: *Rude.*

I nearly choked. He'd hacked into the hospital cameras. How good did someone have to be to pull that off? How obsessed did someone have to be to go this far?

And why, for the love of god, did that make me feel special instead of freaked out?

I shouldn't have responded. I really shouldn't have, but I couldn't stop myself from typing, *Are you watching me right now?*

Maaaybe, he said, followed by a wink emoji.

I ground my teeth, trying to ignore the fact that, for a stalker, he seemed more cute than creepy in our exchanges so far.

You are breaking so many laws, I wrote back.

And you don't even know the half of what I'm up to, he replied.

Listen, you, UGH, I don't even know what to call you!

How about boo? he wrote back. *You know, because of the*—this was followed by three little ghost emojis meant to represent his mask.

Damn it, I was not going to smile right now. Not when he could see me do it. It was bad enough that he'd made me laugh yesterday. Curse Dad for passing his dark sense of humor on to me. The urge to laugh always overwhelmed me at the absolute worst moments.

I am NOT calling you boo, I said. *I'll stick with "asshole" TYVM. And don't you have anything better to do than spy on me at work?*

Not really, he said. *Insomnia is kicking my ass this week.*

I blinked, feeling bad for him for a second before I checked myself. He deserved insomnia for his behavior.

I saw your comment on my video, he added. *Looks like everyone else did, too. You're real popular right now.* He tacked on a laughing emoji to, I assumed, provoke me.

I swiped back into my app and cringed. So far, there were over a hundred responses, and people were out for blood tonight.

I blame you for this, I told him.

You're the one who left the comment, Aly.

Oh, no. You're not pinning this on me. I made a bad choice by leaving it, but it would have gone unnoticed without your interference. You knew damn well what would happen when you liked it and followed me.

I have no regrets about publicly claiming you.

Claiming me?

Oh, god. No, vagina, do not quiver at that. Damn it. Not you, too, ovaries.

Conscious that I was still being watched, I went completely still and fought the urge to squirm. His declaration was oddly reassuring. Here was a digital record that tied me to him, so if he did wind up murdering me, there would be a hundred thousand witnesses online who could point to him and say, "The boyfriend did it." He might not have actually been my boyfriend, but they didn't know that. For all intents and purposes, he'd just insinuated he was.

Was this his way of showing me he didn't pose a threat?

I shook my head. No, I was not going to be softened by this. He'd filmed me. He was watching me even now. He could have lied about how much he saw the other night. Hell, he might have recorded me. There could already be a video of me fucking myself with a vibrator on a revenge porn site.

I didn't know this man, and I'd be an idiot to trust him.

I still don't forgive you, I said.

I'm not asking you to yet, he responded. Meaning, he would later?

I lifted my head and stared at the camera, my thoughts churning like an angry tide. I needed to end this. Tell him to fuck off to space. So why couldn't I bring myself to do it? Was some deranged part of me actually enjoying this?

My torment must have shown on my face because he texted me.

Just tell me to stop, Aly, and I will.

My thumbs hovered over the screen. I needed to do this. It was the healthy thing. The right thing. Sure, the idea of a man breaking into my house to fuck me was an appealing fantasy, but it was just a fantasy. Real life had shown me there was only one logical conclusion to this madness, and that was my eventual assault or murder.

I managed to type the letter S before my pager went off. I looked down, and all thoughts of the Faceless Man fled from my mind.

Ambulances were pulling up with multiple gunshot victims. There'd been a mass shooting at a nightclub.

I threw my phone into my locker, slammed it shut, and raced into the hall.

Brinley lurched out of the bathroom door as I passed it, and we nearly collided. I slowed down enough to steady her before we took off toward the ambulance bay together.

"On your left!" Tanya yelled, sprinting past us.

"Jesus, she's fast," Brinley wheezed as we hauled ass after her.

"She's a cardio queen," I told her. "Does three marathons a year."

"How bad is this going to be?" Brinley asked.

I sent her a sideways look. "The truth?"

She nodded.

"As bad as it gets," I said.

■ ■ ■

Twenty hours later, I stumbled out of the hospital. Nearly the entire nursing staff was called in to help with the shooting, and many of my coworkers showed up before we even got to their numbers. When tragedy struck, we knew to come here.

We'd only taken a fraction of the victims. The rest had gone to other ERs and trauma units across the city. Six people were dead, another fifteen had been shot, and twenty more were wounded during the stampede to the club's exits.

According to one of the cops collecting witness statements, the shooter had been killed by a heroic bartender. She'd popped up from behind the bar not long after he opened fire, hit him with a baseball bat, and kept hitting him until his head looked like a pulped pumpkin.

She'd saved a lot of lives, but we had at least three people who might still succumb to their injuries. Sadly, this wasn't even the worst mass shooting I'd seen. Last year, a man had gone to his ex-wife's place of employment, killed eight people, and injured countless others before a SWAT sniper took him out.

I managed to sleep an hour or two here and there between rushing from one room to another, but it wasn't enough to combat the fact that I'd been awake for almost forty. This was why I left Fred with so much food and water. My vet kept telling me not to open feed him, that he was starting to get chubby, but I'd rather Fred be overweight than starving every time I got stuck at work like this.

I took the elevator up to the third floor of the parking garage, tugging my heavy winter coat tight when the doors opened, and an arctic blast rushed in. A glance to my right stopped me in my tracks. It was snowing again, coming down in big, fat flakes that the wind blew sideways. Great. Hopefully, the roads weren't too bad.

I was tempted to turn around and go sleep in one of the bunk rooms reserved for long-shift work, but if I did that, I'd probably only get another hour or two before someone woke me up looking for help. Saying no in those situations was a problem for me, and I knew myself well enough to know that I needed to go home to avoid self-sabotaging, even if that meant taking a taxi or car service.

I just needed to get a few things out of my car first, and then I'd go back inside and order an Uber. It was stupid of me to think I could drive right now. The last thing anyone needed was for me to fall asleep behind the wheel and cause another emergency.

I pulled my gaze from the snow and ambled toward the corner of the parking garage where I'd left my car.

It was running when I got to it.

I stopped fifteen feet away, staring in confusion. I didn't have an automatic starter that might explain this. Was I so tired I was hallucinating?

I glanced around, looking for someone else so I could ask if they were seeing what I was, but there was no one nearby. It was three in the morning, and this level was the employee lot. Everyone else was hunkered inside the hospital, trying to save lives.

I blinked several times in quick succession. Nope. Not hallucinating. My goddamn car was running. I couldn't have left it on—the keys were in my bag—so what the fuck was happening?

My groggy brain finally started to wake up. Was this somehow *his* doing?

I grabbed my mace from my purse and walked parallel to the car, looking around for anyone waiting to ambush me. The garage was brightly lit, and I didn't see another soul, but wasn't taking any chances. I kept my finger on the spray button until the driver's side came into view. Someone was sitting in the driver's seat. A large someone. Wearing a hoodie that hid their face.

No. No fucking way.

Without warning, they turned, and I jumped back, hitting the car behind me. The Faceless Man stared out of my window.

Well, I was wide awake now. And not in the mood to be messed with. The gall of this man to pull a stunt like this after the night and day and night I'd had.

He raised a hand and waved at me, then held up a finger like he was asking me to wait before it disappeared, and he looked down. My phone beeped in my purse. I kept my eyes trained on him while I dug around for it.

It took me a long time to read his text because I kept looking down at the phone and back up just as quickly to scan my surroundings. I didn't trust him not to have an accomplice somewhere nearby, waiting for me to be distracted so they could catch me off guard.

I thought I'd give you a ride home. The weather is shit, and you must be exhausted. It's not safe for you to drive right now.

I glared daggers at him and twirled a finger, indicating he should roll the window down.

He turned away to type again.

Don't mace me.

"You are in no position to give me orders," I called out. He cracked my window the barest slice to hear me better. "There are twenty cops inside that hospital right now, and I know most of them by first name. One phone call, and you're fucked."

He turned and started typing.

"Seriously?" I said. "You're not going to speak to me?"

He shook his head and kept going.

I must know him well enough to recognize his voice if he was going to such an extreme. Who was he? One of the cops I'd just threatened him with? I could think of several who were about his size, and it would explain how easily he'd found me if he'd used government equipment to do it.

I'm just giving you a ride, he said. *I saw what you went through, saw how dead on your feet you were as you started to pack your things, and I thought I should come.*

I pinched the bridge of my nose and debated screaming for help. "Why would you think that?"

You didn't tell me to stop, Aly.

I dropped my hand and glared at him. "Because I was interrupted by a goddamn tragedy."

Say it now, then, he typed, then raised his head to look at me through those soul-sucking black eye holes.

I opened my mouth, but nothing came out.

Say it, Aly, I thought. *Say it, goddamn it. Just fucking tell him to stop like the mentally healthy, rational person you used to be before his videos took over your social media feed.*

I tried to force the words out and felt like I was choking. Fuck. I couldn't do it. What the hell did that say about me? What did it mean? Was I actually into this?

It's the exhaustion, I tried to tell myself, but the lie fell flat. The ugly truth was that I'd felt more alive in the past few days than I had in years. Sure, I'd spent half that time terrified, but at this point, fear was preferable to numbness. Until he broke into my house, I'd been living in a world of grays, going about my life like a robot. Work, gym, home, repeat. The brief flashes of feeling that bled through the haze all revolved around this man and his videos.

I let my gaze roam over his mask, and even though he looked out at me from a frozen plastic façade, I swear it looked like the corners of the lips had tipped up in the slight hint of a grin.

I pointed my mace at the cracked window. "Just because I've gone stupid enough that I can't say it right now doesn't mean I'm getting in the car with the man who broke into my house and filmed me without my consent."

I hoped the parking garage cameras were recording all this and he hadn't found some way to freeze or loop them. If someone did jump out and manage to overpower me, it'd be the only visual evidence of what had happened to my dumb ass.

He typed something else, and I was already over this communication style.

Just speak! I wanted to yell.

My phone pinged, and I did the same glance-up-and-glance-down dance I'd been doing the past five minutes.

Look in the passenger seat, he said. *You'll have all the power.*

"If someone is waiting to jump me over there, I'm going to murder both of you," I told him. "I'm not feeling very friendly toward men tonight."

He nodded like he expected no less and motioned at me to get on with it.

I ground my teeth and cautiously rounded the bumper toward the other side of the car. He must have sensed my reluctance to get too close because he leaned over and pushed the passenger door open. My gun and a wicked-looking knife sat next to each other on the seat. He leaned back, pointed to them, and then at me.

Another frigid gust of wind tore through the parking garage with a howl, and a full-body shiver wracked my body. I might be wearing a heavy coat, but my scrub pants were thin, and I'd been so out of it when I stumbled out of the hospital that I hadn't thought to pull on gloves.

I stepped toward the open door and the warmth pouring out of it, waiting for the other shoe to drop. He made no move to lunge at me, merely leaned back and slowly raised his gloved hands to show he was unarmed. I dove forward and scooped up the gun, then leaped back again and quickly checked to see if it was still loaded. It was.

Its weight in my hand felt like a security blanket. He didn't have a weapon on him that I could see, and at this distance, I could easily shoot him before he could reach for one. I did have all the power, and it felt good to have the upper hand with him for once.

This was the part where I should order him out of my car and call the cops, but I was starting to crash again as my adrenaline faded, and I was so cold that my teeth were chattering. I didn't want to take an Uber and have to find a ride back for my next shift. I didn't want to call the cops either. There was no rational explanation for my reticence about involving them—I worked with them daily and knew they'd have my back—but something was stopping me.

Maybe it was that I'd met a lot of bad men in my line of work. Murderers, rapists, gang members, drug dealers, burglars, pedophiles, you name it. My gut instincts had been honed over the years, and I had developed almost a sixth sense for recognizing danger. Those instincts were silent right now. It was only my mind telling me to involve the police. And not for nothing, but Fred liked him. Fred didn't like anyone. He hissed or ran and hid. That was his MO with anyone who came over. The fact that he'd actually played with the Faceless Man still blew my mind.

My gut told me to get in the car and see where this went. It wasn't like I'd be helpless if I climbed into the passenger seat. I'd have a gun and a knife, and I could hold them both on him while he drove. The second he took a wrong turn or tried to hurt me, *blamo!* Being a nurse meant I knew right where to aim to do the most damage possible.

And, god help me, I was curious. On some level, I wanted to see how this played out. Despite the potentially catastrophic consequences. Despite the fact that no rational person would do it.

Fine. I wasn't rational. It was time to accept that about myself. Sometime in the past year or two, I'd waded into darkness, and now I was swan-diving into the deep end. I was a sex-craved, sleep-deprived woman more interested in a kinky fuck than safety and comfort.

It was oddly freeing to admit that. Now that I'd stopped fighting myself, I could look back at the past few days and see what I'd been trying to ignore: I wanted this. I'd been lonely as hell my entire adult life. The men I met on dating apps or social media didn't seem to mind when I flaked on them or forgot to text them back for weeks on end. They just moved on to someone else, like Tyler had.

My entire life was devoted to caring for others. I wanted someone to take care of me for once. I wanted someone to want me. No, *need* me. I wanted a man so obsessed that he hacked into cameras to watch me when he couldn't sleep. I wanted him to monitor my location data, order me a home security system so no one else could break into my house, and threaten to murder anyone who hurt me.

I didn't want him morally gray. I wanted someone with a soul as black as night. Someone who would burn the world down for me and not lose a single minute of sleep over it.

The Faceless Man lowered his hands and beckoned me into the car.

I dragged in a fortifying breath of frigid air, got inside, and shut the door behind me, sealing my fate.

8

JOSH

ALY WAS GETTING IN THE CAR. I watched her slide into the passenger seat beside me, gun aimed at my middle, eyes trained on my mask while she slowly pulled the seatbelt across her chest and buckled in.

She reached out and blindly closed the door behind herself, as unwilling to look away from me as I was her, if for a different reason. I let out the breath I knew damn well I'd been holding—I didn't want to so much as breathe, let alone move in case I scared her off.

There was a woman with a mask kink within arm's distance of me. A woman who had recently masturbated to one of my videos, and I couldn't get that one brief image out of my head of her thrusting her vibrator into herself.

Was that how she liked it? Raw and rough? A hint of pain to heighten her pleasure?

Fuck, I wanted her. Here. Now. It was so tempting to turn and pin her to her seat so I could—

She shoved the barrel of the gun into my side. "Drive. And lord help us if we get pulled over on the way. Between your horror movie getup and my weapons, we'd probably make headline news."

Right. About that.

I grabbed my phone off the dash. I wished I could talk to her, but I'd have to do it again soon as Josh, and I couldn't risk her recognizing my voice. The fancy modulator I ordered was getting delivered tomorrow, and then I could be done with this typing nonsense.

I'm going to take the back way there, I typed. *I put the directions into my map, so you know I'm not lying.*

I showed her the text instead of sending it.

She cocked her head sideways and eyed the edge of my mask like she was considering ripping it off. "Or you could just show me who you are and drive my car like a normal person. I already know we've met before, and it can't be easy to see in that thing."

My heart thudded inside my chest. Aly was at the top of her class when she graduated nursing school. Maybe I should be worried that she was smart enough to figure out who I was, but it only excited me. It felt like a game we played, with me constantly staying three steps ahead of her to avoid getting caught. The challenge was thrilling. And despite her concern, I could see just fine in my mask. The black material covering the wide eye sockets was made from a kind of high-tech nanofiber that was opaque from one side and transparent from the other. It was no different than looking out of a pair of glasses.

I can see fine. And do you really want to ruin the fantasy? I typed, showing her the phone and praying she wanted this as much as I did.

She blew out a shaky breath and looked away, the gun slipping an inch, and I took her silence as confirmation.

A glance at the gun showed me her finger was nowhere near the trigger. Not that anything would happen if she pulled it. I'd replaced her bullets with blanks. I was horny, not suicidal. And yes, I planned to switch them again. The thought of her unarmed in this city made me want to both rage and puke at the same time, which would probably be messy, so the real bullets were going back in as soon as we got to her house. I'd just have to find a way to be sneaky about it so she didn't get mad at me again.

Her eyes were guarded when they came back to mine, but there was a hint of a flush in her cheeks that hadn't been there before, driving the point home that Aly would rather have me masked and anonymous as well.

I buckled my seatbelt and put the car in reverse, using the rearview camera to guide me out of the parking space.

"You put my seat heater on for me," she said.

I nodded. For whatever reason, empathy was starting to come easy for me with her. Watching her through the hospital cameras showed me a woman who would do anything to help others, even to the detriment of herself. I figured she must have been sore after being on her feet for so long, and even though the orthopedic shoes she wore looked comfortable, I was betting her legs and back still hurt.

She was probably hungry, too—I hadn't seen her eat much in the past day and a half. Luckily, I had a solution for that. I put the car in drive but kept my foot on the brake.

Lifting my hands, I slowly rotated in my seat. The gun bumped over my abs as I turned her way, and her gaze drifted down like she felt it happen. I reached behind us and grabbed a small lunch bag from the rear seat.

"Woah, buddy," she said, leaning away as I turned back around with it. "Is that a bomb or something?"

I almost forgot myself and swore. Why hadn't I realized Aly might jump to a conclusion like that after the shift she'd had? It was a dumb mistake, and I wouldn't make one like it again. I'd be better for her going forward. She deserved someone at the top of their game.

I shook my head and set the bag in my lap. Moving slowly so she wouldn't freak out, I unzipped it and showed her the contents.

She frowned and leaned forward for a better look, glancing up at me afterward with one brow arched. "You brought me snacks?"

I nodded and put the bag on the center console for her.

She made no move to take it, her expression turning exasperated. "I'm not eating any of that. You could have drugged it."

Fair point. I snagged the sandwich bag filled with apple slices. My gloves were thin enough that it was easy to lift one out. I tugged my mask away from my face just enough to get the slice inside it without revealing more than the edge of my jaw and slid the apple into my mouth.

I made a "See?" motion as I started to chew, but Aly was too busy staring at where my jaw was hidden again to pay much attention to my hands.

My mouth went dry. Did she feel it, too? This undeniable pull between us? I was trying to be a gentleman, had promised myself that tonight and this ride home was about reassuring her that she could trust me with her safety—after all, it was a big ask to get someone to agree to sex with a knife-wielding stranger—but if she kept looking at me like that, I didn't know if I could keep myself in check for much longer.

She licked her lips as her eyes slid from my face to take in the rest of me. I went still in my seat, telling my dick not to react, but it had a mind of its own when it came to her, so there it went, shoving against the restriction of my jeans, demanding to be let out.

Aly took her sweet time looking me over. There wasn't much on display—I wore jeans and a hoodie—but I'd left the sweatshirt unzipped, and Aly's gaze went straight to the way my fitted Henley flattened against my stomach.

"Is that the shirt you wore in your latest video?" she asked, her voice hoarse.

I nodded.

She shook her head as if trying to clear her thoughts. Dirty thoughts? "Did you think you were being funny by posting such a sappy thirst trap after what you did to me?"

I nodded vigorously this time, glad she couldn't see my shit-eating grin.

She huffed out a breath and looked away, but not before I caught the edge of her lips tilting up.

A car horn honked behind us, and we both jumped.

Right. I was supposed to be driving Aly home, not contemplating whether or not she'd like to get ravaged in the back of her car.

I waved to the impatient person behind me and took my foot off the brake. They pulled into the open space I'd just vacated, and I slowed again, just long enough to tilt my phone away from Aly, kill the loop

I'd placed on all the cameras on this level of the parking garage, and hit go on my map so she would know I wasn't blowing smoke up her ass about following directions. That done, I headed toward the exit ramp while a soothing British woman's voice told me where to go next.

The sound of crunching came from the passenger seat. I glanced over and saw Aly helping herself to the apple slices with one hand, the other still pointing the gun in my direction. A frisson of warmth wound through me at the sight. Why did it feel so good to care for her, even on such a micro level? Was it because I'd never had anyone to call my own before? Or was this some inborn instinct all men had that, up until now, was suppressed by the cocktail of prescription drugs I'd been on since puberty?

Either way, I wasn't questioning it. Taking care of her felt good. It was clear to me from what I'd seen that someone needed to, and I'd be damned if I let another man do it. My roommate was a goddamn moron. Didn't he realize what he'd had when he was with her? How was he foolish enough to let such a perfect creature slip through his fingers? How were all of her past partners equally blind? She should be wifed up by now, spoiled and cherished like the queen she was.

Men were idiots. That was the only explanation.

Aly finished the apples as I pulled out of the parking garage. She tugged the lunch bag toward her and started poking around in it. I'd packed a variety of other options: a squeezable yogurt, carrot sticks, an orange, and trail mix I made myself. There was even a water bottle in there to wash everything down.

"You first," she said, passing the trail mix over.

I stopped at the end of the exit ramp and took the bag from her. Our fingers slid against each other.

Curse these fucking gloves and the need for them.

That was the first time we'd touched, and I hated that it hadn't been skin-to-skin. I craved the feel of her against me, even if it was just a fleeting brush.

I hefted my phone and typed, *You just want to get another look at my jaw.*

"It's a nice jaw," she said, unapologetic. "Now quit stalling. I'm hungry."

I set my phone down to keep from typing something potentially offensive about how hungry I was, too. For her. Then I scooped out a handful of the mix and turned away because I needed to pull the mask up a little further to manage this, and I didn't want her to see more than I was ready for her to.

"Spoilsport," she said as I shoved the trail mix into my mouth and tugged the mask back down.

I gave her a thumbs-up as I chewed and then eased my foot off the brake. The snow was really coming down. I'd checked the weather several times over the past few hours, and the accumulation predictions kept climbing. Storm totals were hard to forecast in our area because cells habitually stalled over us and dumped more snow than expected. At this rate, I wouldn't have been surprised if we had a foot on the ground by sun up.

Even though the plows were out, they couldn't keep up, and the roads were shit. My Uber driver had a hell of a time getting me to the hospital earlier, and her vehicle was an SUV with four-wheel drive. Aly's car was a small sedan, and it might not have had four-wheel, but at least it came with traction control. I hoped I wouldn't need it as I pulled onto the slush-covered road.

"You're gonna have to do better than one sappy video if you want me to forgive you for watching me without my consent," Aly said between bites.

I nodded to show I understood. Was I sorry for what I'd done? No, not at all, but I wouldn't deny her right to be angry, and if there was a chance she'd forgive me for it, I'd find a million ways to apologize for upsetting her until she gave in.

"Thank you for driving me home," she added in a softer tone. "I didn't want to call an Uber or try to sleep in the hospital."

I smiled and started to reach out to pat her knee as a way to say, "You're welcome," but the gun jammed back into my ribs, and I stalled out halfway there.

"No touchy. Still angry."

I held my hand up, fingers spread until the gun eased off me. My dick chose that moment to remind me how turned on I was by making another bid to break through my zipper. Feisty Aly was hot. I couldn't wait until she forgave me so I could start finding ways to piss her off again. Masochistic? Maybe. But for some reason, our bickering felt more like foreplay than an actual argument, and I was into it. I could only imagine how good the makeup sex would be.

The city was quiet so early in the morning. I'd driven through it a lot around this time, thanks to my insomnia, and I never got over how eerie it was. It felt like I was on the set of a post-apocalyptic movie, one of the only humans left after a terrible plague or zombie virus swept over the planet.

Tonight was less creepy and more cozy thanks to the storm, the sidewalks covered in snowbanks, everything bright and fresh like the city had been washed clean of all its sins. I knew it wouldn't last, that it would only take a couple of hours once the snow stopped falling for life to resume and the banks to turn black from the dirt and grime splashed onto them by passing cars.

Aly leaned forward and turned the heat up another level. I shifted in my seat as I stopped at a red light, shrugging off my hoodie. My blood was up from being so close to her. I was on the verge of perspiring, and there was nothing to kill a mood like clammy skin.

I pushed my sleeves up to my elbows and turned left when the light changed, heading toward the city's outskirts and a smaller road where there was less chance of passing anyone.

There, that was better. Sweat crisis averted.

It took me a moment to notice how motionless Aly had become. I glanced over as we passed under a streetlight and caught her staring at my forearm, the gun resting forgotten against her thigh.

Well, well, well. I'd spent so much time thinking up ways to soften her toward me that I'd missed the most obvious ally I had: her body and the way it betrayed her after all the time she'd devoted to my videos. I'd downloaded her user data off the app, and she'd spent a staggering two hundred hours staring at me. When you looked at it that way, I seemed like a saint. I'd watched her less than forty so far.

She might be mad at me, but her lizard brain was probably triggered by being so close to someone she'd pleasured herself to. I knew it had happened at least once, but I prayed it wasn't the only time and that she'd gotten off to me so often that my proximity alone was enough to soak her panties.

What was it she'd said about my forearms in that one comment? That she wanted to trace each vein with her tongue?

Testing my hypothesis, I gripped the steering wheel tighter, making them pop. Aly made a small, helpless sound and yanked her gaze away, dropping it back to her dwindling baggie of trail mix. I tried to stifle my smugness and failed spectacularly. She wanted me. Bad. Maybe more than I wanted her, which was saying something.

I wished I could turn and watch her, memorize the way her cheeks warmed and her breath picked up, but as we headed farther from the city center, the driving conditions got worse, and I had precious cargo with me. I needed to focus on getting her home safely before I gave in to my darker needs.

"Turn left at the next light," my phone told me. I dutifully slowed to another stop a few minutes later and threw on my blinker. A lifted truck pulled up next to us, and I heard a man's voice call out, muffled by the windows.

"Assholes," Aly said, flipping the other vehicle off as she turned my way, effectively hiding her face from the driver's sight.

Did they just say something rude to her?

The truck honked, and I heard the obvious sound of a catcall.

Oh, hell no.

I shifted into park, scooped the forgotten knife off the floor by Aly's feet, and got out of the car to stare down the other driver over the roof.

The middle-aged white dude took one look at my mask and reared back in his seat.

His buddy on the passenger side started shoving his shoulder. "Dude, what the fuck?"

I lifted the knife with one hand and twiddled my fingers hello with the other.

Boo, motherfuckers.

The driver gunned the gas, running the red light as he took off into the night.

I grinned and got back in the car, flipping the knife and catching it by the tip before offering it to Aly hilt-first.

She eyed me for a long moment before setting the gun down to take it. "You're deranged. You know that?"

I shrugged. Deranged. Protective. Same thing.

"I thought this was fake," she said, pressing the pad of her pointer finger to the knife tip. "Jesus, that's sharp."

I jerked my gaze down, worried she'd cut herself, but I didn't see any blood, so she must not have pressed too hard. I kept that thing sharp enough to slice into bone.

The light turned, bathing us in green, and reluctantly, I turned away from her and started driving again. She closed the trail mix and set it back into the lunch bag, zipping it up like she was done eating. Then she turned to put it in the back, and I caught a whiff of her floral-scented shampoo. Unable to help myself, I dragged in a deep breath. I couldn't wait to bury my face into all that hair while I fucked her, the sound of her ragged cries filling my ears, her legs thrown over my shoulders as I bent her in half and dicked her to within an inch of her life.

I shifted in my seat, trying to ease the pressure in my jeans. Had Aly caught sight of my erection when I got out of the car? Christ, I would have been standing in the open door with it right at eye level while I scared those guys off. Whoops. Probably should have paused to consider my "situation" before my anger got the better of me, but the rage had taken hold too fast for rational thought to stand a chance.

I glanced over at Aly. The street I'd turned onto had fewer overhead lights, but it was still bright enough to see that she was staring straight at my crotch. She'd seen, all right, and from the way her brows crept up her forehead, she was either impressed or concerned. Hopefully, a bit of both.

An apology was on the tip of my tongue, but something in her expression stopped me. Slowly, she lifted her eyes to my mask and bit her lower lip. She needed to quit doing that if she knew what was good for her.

"I want to see it," she said.

No, she didn't, fuckwit, I told myself.

Surely, I'd hallucinated that declaration. I wanted Aly so badly that I'd slipped out of reality and was now living in a make-believe world where the woman I lusted after asked me to whip my dick out while driving.

"Please," she added.

I jerked my head sideways to look at her, disbelieving, and the car slid a little on a patch of ice. I whipped forward again and straightened us out. I'd grown up in the frigid north, and driving in shitty conditions was second nature, but I hated that my distraction had almost cost us.

"I can do it for you," she said, and something cold pressed into my side.

I glanced down. Aly still had the knife, and she was using the tip of it to drag the hem of my shirt up.

Oh, shit. Why was that so hot?

"All this time, you've been trying to reassure me that I'm safe with you," she said, sliding the blunted side of the blade higher. "But did you ever stop to consider whether or not *you* were safe with *me*?"

I nearly groaned. Aly in her villain era? I would bankrupt myself for front-row tickets to that show.

And yes, I had considered what she asked, which was why I'd taken the bullets out of the gun. I couldn't bring myself to replace the knife with a fake, though, and maybe that would be my downfall. If so, I'd probably die with a dopey smile on my face while she carved me up.

But I didn't think it would come to that. There was nothing in her therapist's notes to indicate that Aly suffered from homicidal tendencies. I didn't doubt that she was angry but angry enough to hurt me? Nah. Scare me a little, maybe, and I was now, because if she turned that blade around, my skin would part like a tide for Moses.

I carefully reached around the knife and hauled my shirt up so she could get a better look at my rig. Sitting down wasn't the ideal way to show my body off, but I'd take any attention from her that I could get, so I leaned back in my seat a little and let her take her fill of me.

She giggled.

Not the response I was hoping for.

"Sorry," she said. "But I was just thinking, what if one of these storefronts has CCTV?"

I glanced out the windshield at the narrow street around us and all the mom-and-pop stores crowded next to each other along it.

"Imagine checking your camera in the morning and seeing a masked man driving with his shirt hiked to his nipples and a woman holding a knife to his stomach?"

I wheezed out a voiceless laugh, caught off guard.

She chuckled again, but a second later, her humor faded, and she released a heavy exhale. "I know I've already told you this a thousand times in so many embarrassingly inappropriate ways, but you have a beautiful body."

This was more like it.

Wary of the knife at my side, I reached over and took her free hand, placing it on my stomach. Skin-to-skin contact at last. Sweet god, yes.

Her fingers were warm as they rested on me, and I was starting to wonder if she'd lost her nerve because of how long she kept them there when suddenly they shifted, bumping down over my abs.

"That video you sent me was such a tease," she said. "All your videos are. Is that what you're like in real life?"

I nodded. Yes. Teasing women was second nature. I'd already given her a glimpse of that in our DMs and texts, but my need to wind women up extended to the bedroom. Aly was my perfect victim in that regard. I already knew she was feisty. It was all too easy to picture her red-faced and panting as she begged me to make her come.

Her fingers dropped to the waist of my jeans and ran along the edge. I flexed. Hard. Not to show off but to keep from giggling like a lunatic. I was ticklish, and it was incredibly inconvenient at times like this. Mercifully, she stopped just above my top button, and I relaxed a little as the threat of ruining the moment passed.

She flicked the button open with practiced fingers. "Can I see it?"

Oh, fuck. This was happening. I hadn't hallucinated.

I nodded and shifted my hips forward to give her better access.

Her low moan filled the car as she slid her hand down and palmed my dick through my pants. "I knew you'd be big," she whispered.

I gripped the steering wheel so tight my knuckles turned white. Goddamn fucking snowstorm. My focus had to stay on the road, regardless of how much I wanted to look down and watch what Aly did to me.

The cold bite of steel slid up my side, and I went completely still. Jesus. How had I forgotten about the knife?

"You're so hard that I need two hands to get your zipper open. Will you behave if I set the knife down?"

Uh . . . would I? I wasn't sure. We were moving out of the city proper and closer to the suburbs where Aly lived. It would be all too easy to find an empty parking lot and tackle her into the backseat.

She turned the knife over and ran the blade up my side, so close she probably shaved off some peach fuzz.

"I won't do it if you don't promise to be a good boy," she crooned.

Praise kink: unlocked.

I nodded several times in quick succession, and she chuckled and set the knife, tip down, into one of the cup holders between us. Then those nimble nurse fingers were on me, one set tugging my jeans away from my straining cock while the other carefully eased my zipper open. She pulled the sides of my pants wide and went still. A glance showed her staring at the bulge in my boxers with a hungry look on her face.

Do not come in your shorts, do not come in your shorts, I started chanting in my head.

I kept my eyes trained on the road and slowed the car. Movement in my periphery was all the warning I had before Aly tugged the band of my boxers open and pulled out my dick. Silence reigned absolute between us. We must have both been holding our breath. Then Aly let out a ragged exhale and wrapped her fingers around my shaft, and I nearly came on contact.

"Don't misconstrue this," she said, picking the knife back up.

Terror slammed into me. A woman had one hand on my dick and the other on a knife. This could get so bad, so fast. My cock should be shriveling up in fear, but I only got harder at the thought, the danger pushing my arousal to an almost uncomfortable level.

Aly noticed, squeezing my shaft and running her thumb over the head of it to smear a drop of precum over my skin. "I see the knife kink goes both ways."

I guess it fucking did.

"I'm still mad," she said. "This isn't for you."

Okay, but it felt a *little* like it was for me. Her hand was stroking up *my* dick, after all.

"This is something I've dreamed about for months, and I'm not going to deny myself a chance to touch you just because we're in a fight."

Awww. Our first official fight.

I was absolutely going to mark this in my calendar so a year from now, we could celebrate the day she acknowledged there was something between us. Was I getting ahead of myself? Probably, but I couldn't help it. Aly was going to be mine. The end. I'd just have to find some way to make her think it happened organically, and she wasn't falling for my dastardly plan to brainwash her into loving me by spoiling her rotten and playing into every desire she'd ever had.

The blunted edge of the knife slid up my side in idle threat as Aly worked her way back down my cock. Her touch was gentle because both her hand and my dick were so dry that there wasn't enough lubrication between us for her to really go after it. She paused when she got to the bottom, squeezed my base, and then reached into the band of my boxers and tugged on my balls.

I let out a shaky breath and gripped the steering wheel so hard the leather creaked.

"I can't tell you how many times I've fantasized about doing this," she said as she started to lean forward. She paused halfway to my dick, and I nearly groaned. "Are you STD free?"

I nodded. I'd gotten tested a few weeks ago and hadn't been with anyone since.

"You wouldn't lie to me about something like that, would you?" she asked, starting to rotate the knife against my side, the sharp edge heading toward my skin.

I shook my head, horrified at the thought of someone doing that to a partner.

"Good, because I can't hold out any longer," she said.

And then she clamped her lips around the head of my dick and swirled her tongue over it.

My vision tunneled. Oh, fuck, I was going to come like a fire hydrant if she kept this up.

It was somehow even better than I'd imagined, and I'd done an unhealthy amount of daydreaming the past several days. Was it because I was off the drugs that had dulled my emotions and sensations for so long? Or because it was Aly, and having feelings about the person I hooked up with elevated my pleasure?

Maybe it was both of those things combined, paired with the fact that I had my mask on, and this was the first time I was living out a fantasy I'd had for years.

That realization fled from my mind when she squeezed the base of my shaft again and lowered her head, taking more of me into the wet heat of her mouth. The urge to thrust my hips upward was strong, but she said this was for her, so I held myself still with monumental effort and let her play with me.

She moved lower, lower, widening her jaw as she took me all the way to the back of her throat. I groaned as her tongue swirled over me again, coating my shaft in saliva as she pulled up. Would it ruin my scary masked stalker image if I came too early? Didn't badasses hold out for a long time?

Her hand wrapped around my now-lubricated shaft and started to pump, rotating on the way down just like I liked.

I prayed to the gods of longevity and then started naming baseball teams in my head.

She drew back up to my head and lapped at my slit with a moan. "God, you taste good."

Nope. I wasn't going to make it. I would blow like a two-pump chump, and my badass reputation would be ruined entirely.

I tried to drum up some regret about that, but Aly tunneled her cheeks as she bobbed back down, and the suction had me seeing stars.

I took a wrong turn down a dark street and slowed the car to an absolute crawl.

"Make a U-turn at the next stoplight," the British woman told me.

Aly froze.

Uh-oh.

Her lips popped free—*no, no, no*—and she sat up, knife fully rotated now, blade hovering over my skin.

"Did you just deviate from the directions?" she asked.

I whimpered in response.

I fucking *whimpered*.

In my defense, my dick was cold and lonely and pulsing with need, and the mouth that had so recently brought it pleasure was now several feet away. Who could blame me?

"Bad boys don't get rewarded," she said.

No. Goddamnit. I did not need a brat kink on top of my newly awakened praise kink. The two were supposed to cancel each other out, not act as amplifiers.

Or maybe I just had an Aly kink, and everything she said triggered this kind of response in me. Maybe being together meant that all her desires were about to become mine, too.

Please, god. Don't let her have a fisting kink, I thought. Being used like a puppet was not something I wanted to experience.

I put my blinker on and turned the car around at the light. She sat watching me in the dark, knife running up and down my side until we got back on the road my map wanted us on. Another torturous moment passed that made me worry Aly was going to leave me like this before she pulled the knife away and leaned forward again. This time, she started on my stomach, planting hot, drugging kisses on my abs before she parted her lips and nipped at my skin hard enough to pinch.

Was a biting kink a thing? It must be because I was rock-hard for it.

The snow picked up outside, and the car lights made it look like I'd just launched us into hyperdrive, even though we were barely moving, flakes flashing past us like stars as we raced through space. It made me feel like we were in our own little world as Aly's lips wrapped around the head of my dick again.

"If we weren't in this car," she whispered against me, breath heating my skin while her hand worked my shaft, "I would deep throat you until I choked. But this angle is wrong, so I'll have to do this instead."

She laved at the head of my dick, tonguing my frenulum and then my slit before she did that delicious swirling motion again, all while her hand pumped my shaft.

Aly was done playing around. The way she lapped and sucked and stroked spoke of a single-minded determination to get me off.

I switched from baseball teams to hockey teams. I wasn't a huge fan of the latter, and it took brain power to recall some of the names of—*holy fuck, what did she just do*?

I took my foot off the gas and glanced down. The back of Aly's head hid her mouth and hand from sight, depriving me of getting to watch her do whatever the fuck this was to me.

No. Hockey. Remember the hockey. Team things. You were trying to—

Pressure built at the base of my spine. My balls started to tighten.

Aly sucked me deep and did that *thing* again.

I was going to come.

Hard.

I tapped her shoulder, trying to get her attention. She swatted me away like she didn't need the distraction right now.

Fuck. Oh, fuck. Her *mouth*.

I tapped her again, more insistent this time.

A *pop* sounded as she pulled herself off my dick. "If you keep interrupting me, I'll never find out what you taste like when you come."

Lust roared through me as she bobbed back down and sucked me deep. I knew she said this was just for her, but I could no longer stop myself from moving, just a little, thrusting up into her luscious wetness. She moaned like she welcomed it, so I thrust harder.

A sharp stab of pain shot through my right hand.

What the fuck?

I glanced down, and my eyes flashed wide.

Aly had just accidentally stabbed me.

I jerked my hand away from the knife to see how bad it was, but Aly did that thing with her mouth again, and between the resulting spike of pleasure and the searing pain, I fell over the edge, spine bowing forward, losing all control as I came inside her welcoming, perfect mouth. She choked a little, trying to swallow it all down, and it only made me come harder, dragging my release out.

Aly gripped my cock when I was done and cleaned every last drop off it with her tongue. I elevated my hand and pulled it close. Blood was starting to trickle down my arm, and I didn't want to get any of it in her hair or on her car seat.

She gave the head of my dick one last, sweet kiss and then tucked it back into my boxers, rising with a satisfied smirk that quickly turned to horror when she saw my hand.

"What the fuck did you do?" she said, grabbing it to assess the damage. "Oh, Jesus, I think you need stitches."

Was there a nice way to tell her that I, in fact, had done nothing, and it was *her* who had done the maiming?

9

ALY

I'D STABBED HIM. Jesus take me now, I had stabbed a man while giving him head. There was no coming back from this. My days ended here. Any second now, I would spontaneously combust from the humiliation.

The Faceless Man seemed to be handling it pretty well, all things considered. If our roles were reversed, I doubted I'd be so forgiving about getting stabbed. Or was it just his commitment to silence that hid his true anger? Was he being stoic about it now, but after this, I'd never see him again?

And why did that thought make me feel like the floor had dropped out from beneath me?

"One last time," I warned, the words only slightly muffled by my surgical mask.

The hand lying before me didn't so much as flinch as he readied himself for the final stitch. I'd tried to get him to turn around and go back to the hospital and have a doctor do this with a localized painkiller, but he shook his head, and the stiff set of his shoulders told me he would have been stubborn about it if I'd pressed harder. I wasn't about to. My coworkers were in the middle of dealing with a tragedy; they didn't need me taking up a bed with my . . . whatever he was.

So here we were, sitting at my tiny dining table turned makeshift ER, my emergency kit spread out around us. He was lucky I had everything required for cleaning and stitching his wound, but I was still uncomfortable about this. I was an RN. Suturing was considered a minor surgical operation, and our state, like many others, didn't allow RNs to perform the procedure. You needed to be an advanced practicing nurse to do it. If anyone found out I'd broken the law, I could get in a lot of trouble, maybe even lose my job and get fined.

I told him all that as we pulled into my driveway, on the off-chance his wound got infected and he had to see a doctor, asking him to please not tell anyone it was me. He'd mimed zipping his gaping mouth shut like he planned to take the secret to his grave. Oddly enough, my instinct was to believe him.

Just one more stitch, Aly. You can do it, I told myself. It had been a long time since I'd done this, and I was out of practice. My exhaustion wasn't helping. Nor was the fact that I couldn't stop following the line of tattoos up his hand to his thick, veiny forearms.

I licked my lips and nearly moaned. I could still taste him on them.

This man had watched me at work, decided he needed to play white knight, and then broke into my car to give me a ride home. And what had I done? Oh, you know, waited all of five minutes before face-diving onto his dick.

"Are you ready?" I asked, glancing up at him.

He nodded, seemingly far less affected by this situation than I was, and stroked his free hand down Fred's back.

I spared my traitorous cat a glance. Fred had jumped into the Faceless Man's lap the second he sat down at the table, and now he lay there curled up and purring like my stalker was his new favorite human in the world.

My life had gotten really weird lately.

I dropped my gaze and refocused on the hand before me. The Faceless Man needed five stitches. *Five*. I must have sliced more than stabbed, lost in my own little lust-filled world as I worshipped what was arguably the most aesthetically pleasing dick I had ever seen. Because of course it was. His entire body was a masterpiece; why not his cock, too? Big, thick, straining, with silky smooth skin unmarred by veins or discoloration. I'd taken one look at it, and saliva started pooling in my mouth.

Yup, I had it bad for his body. But just that. This could only ever be fantasy fulfillment. I shouldn't have been so turned on by the maniacal way he'd frightened off those gross men in the truck. And I definitely shouldn't be smiling to myself as I poked a needle through his skin one final time, thinking of his flirtatious DMs and texts.

What was it about smartass men that was so attractive? Was it because they never seemed to take life or themselves too seriously? Or was it because I saw so much pain and death that I needed someone who could make me laugh with a well-placed one-liner after a terrible shift like the one I'd just finished?

Though it killed me to admit it, the Faceless Man's brand of smart-assery seemed like the harmless kind that spoke more of witty banter and self-deprecation than cracking jokes at the expense of others. I wanted more of it in my life, still couldn't believe he'd gotten me to laugh with that "sounds kinky" line when I was so pissed off at him.

He sucked in a breath as I tugged the final stitch closed, the only noise he'd made this whole time, despite the pain he must be in.

"I'm sorry," I said. "I just have to tie this side off."

I took deep, even breaths as I finished closing him up, trying not to let the panic drown me. Of course, I'd stabbed right through a tattoo. The scar would be super visible because of it. And he'd have a scar, all right. These stitches were rough work, thanks to my lack of experience.

"You can probably get a plastic surgeon to fix it for you," I said as I straightened. My back protested from being bent over for too long after all the time I'd been awake and on my feet. I needed aspirin and about fifteen hours of sleep.

The Faceless Man shook his head and pulled his hand from Fred to start typing one-handed. It took him a while to get it all out, and I used that time to clean his wound and the mess we'd made. I must have hit a vein when I stabbed him because he'd bled a fair bit. At least I now had his DNA.

I slipped a wad of gauze into a plastic baggie and slid it off the table while he was distracted. It would be going in my freezer with a note attached that said if anything happened to me, the blood belonged to my killer. I hoped it wouldn't come to that, but a girl had to be careful.

He turned his phone my way, and I read, *No plastic surgeon. I'll wear your mark like the badge of pride it is.* To drive his point home, he made a fist, placed it over his heart, and bowed to me like someone from a Tolkien movie.

"You are ridiculous," I said, turning away so he wouldn't see my amusement.

I took my mask off, gathered the trash, and went to throw it away. "Do you want something to eat?" I asked, opening the freezer. The door hid me from view while I chucked the plastic bag into the far corner. "I have frozen pizza, or . . ." I opened the refrigerator. Moths flew out of it. Okay, so moths didn't actually fly out, but they might as well have. My fridge was barren except for wine, a small bottle of half-and-half for my coffee, and a to-go container from my favorite local deli.

I shut the door and turned back to him. "Or frozen pizza."

He shook his head, carefully set a protesting Fred onto the floor, and stood. From his videos, I knew he was tall, but seeing him in the flesh, taking up far too much space in my dining room, was something else. He was several inches over six feet, with broad shoulders and the tree trunk thighs of a football player. His black Henley clung to him in a way that almost made me jealous. Lucky cotton.

I wanted to say something, crack a joke, or find some way to fill this pregnant silence, but words escaped me. He was here. In my house. Within touching distance.

My body was keyed up, hyper-aware of his every move as he grabbed his phone off the table. I didn't know if it was like this for all women, but giving head turned me on. The act was so intimate, so vulnerable for both parties, and I just plain enjoyed getting someone else off. Feeling a dick go rigid between my lips and start to pulse as a man lost himself to pleasure? I loved it, which meant that I was horny as hell right now.

At this point, all it would take was a single brush of his fingers against my clit, and I would come, but I doubted he was thinking about sex after I'd *stabbed him*.

I felt a brush against my shin and looked down to see Fred butting his head against my leg. "Oh, now you remember me? The human who rescued you and has done nothing but spoil you rotten since the day you turned up like a half-drowned rat? I see how it is."

Fred sat back on his haunches and meowed up at me, unapologetic.

The sound of footsteps had me lifting my head. The Faceless Man padded toward me, holding his phone out.

You should shower and get some sleep, the text read. *Thanks for stitching me up. It was the least you could do after brutally mutilating me, but I appreciate it anyway.*

I clapped a hand over my eyes and groaned. I was never going to see him again. "I know I've said it about a hundred times, but I am so sorry."

I heard the sound of typing, and then his long fingers wrapped around my wrist, tugging my hand away as he showed me his phone again.

Aly, that was so good that I will happily let you maim me whenever you're feeling frisky.

My cheeks heated. I didn't blush easily, but this man seemed to be my kryptonite. "Uh, you're welcome then?"

His broad shoulders shook like he was laughing. At me, I was sure, but I couldn't blame him. The reality of a kinky hookup was proving a little different than the fantasy I'd harbored for so long. First off, I'd been the one with the knife. Secondly, it included snacks.

Whenever I daydreamed, it was always of some brooding alpha male pushing me around, aggressive and borderline ruthless as he used my body. I still wanted that for myself at some point, wanted it with this man in particular, but I doubted I'd get it after what I'd done to him, regardless of how nice he was being about it.

The hand around my wrist tightened, all the warning I had before he tugged me close. My chest bumped against him, nipples tightening in my bra. My breasts felt fuller somehow, aching like they longed to feel his big hands cupping them, and my underwear was absolutely soaked. Every few seconds, my inner muscles clenched as if to remind me that they didn't have a dick to squeeze, and they were *not* happy about that fact. I'd watched too many thirst traps of this man, and now my past behavior was coming back to bite me in the ass.

Do not rub yourself against him like a cat in heat, I told myself. *You've already done enough to freak him out for one night.*

He released my wrist and lifted his hand to grip my chin, tilting my head back until I stared into the black voids of the mask's eye sockets. I looked from one to the other, wishing I could see beyond them to his actual eyes. What did they look like? What color were they? Were they staring down at me with the same lust that filled mine?

His thumb brushed over my lips, and even though I couldn't see his eyes, I swore I felt them drop to my mouth. Was he thinking about earlier, too? The feel of me sucking him down before everything went sideways?

Unable to help myself, I reached between us and brushed a hand over his jeans. Oh, fuck, he was hard. I flattened my palm on his erection and stroked upward, hungry for him all over again.

"Let me make it up to you," I said before fastening my lips around his thumb and swirling my tongue over it suggestively.

He shifted his hips forward in the most subtle of thrusts and let out a low grunt. A thrill of victory shot through me, only to be dashed a heartbeat later when he pulled his thumb free, stepped back, and shook his head, just once. He pointed at me, then toward my bedroom. Then he clapped his hands together, tilted them sideways, and rested his head against them, miming sleep.

I nearly kicked at the floor like a petulant child. *But I don't wanna go to bed! I want to stay up late and get railed!*

He must have seen the mutiny in my expression because he crossed his arms over his broad chest and widened his stance in a way that brooked no argument. Okay, that was kind of hot. But also, maybe he had a point. The fact that I felt like throwing a full-blown temper tantrum, tears and all, probably meant that I had whizzed right by overtired and was now deep into delulu territory.

"Fine," I said, and he relaxed a little. "How are you getting home?"

He uncrossed his arms and typed out a response. *I parked down the street.*

"Of course you did," I said, glancing skyward in exasperation. "And I can feel you smiling about that right now, you weirdo, so stop it."

His shoulders were shaking with silent laughter when I glanced back down. He made deranged look more adorable than concerning, which was why he was so dangerous. Because if he was deranged and mean or a bully, my instincts would have put me off him, made me want to run screaming in the opposite direction. His humor and needling only drew me closer and lowered my guard.

I really hoped he wasn't planning to murder me because I'd feel real dumb when it happened.

He started typing again, one-handed, and I scrunched my nose while I waited, feeling sorry again. There had been many times I'd felt like stabbing men in my life. It was just my luck that the one time I actually did was accidental.

He showed me his phone. *I'm going to leave now. Even though I don't want to.*

"Then stay," I blurted. Oh, god. Clingy much, Aly? If the stabbing didn't scare him off, surely my lack of chill would.

He shook his head, pointed at me, and mimed sleeping again. Then he closed the distance between us and leaned down to bump his masked forehead against mine. The plastic was cool and lifeless, almost jarring after all the time I'd spent anthropomorphizing it. I caught the slightest whiff of what might have been the soap he used, piney and crisp and clean-smelling, before he pulled away.

Even though he said he was leaving, he stood there, staring at me for a long moment before letting out a low, frustrated sound and striding away. I took it as a good sign that he'd lingered. He must have genuinely been into me if he had a hard time saying goodbye even after I'd stabbed him.

It made me feel better about my borderline obsession with him. People always said you shouldn't meet your idols, but after months of following his account, the reality of him left me even more intrigued than his online persona. In my fantasies, he was one-dimensional, an archetype I'd created for my pleasure alone. The man walking toward my front door, being chased by my equally unchill cat, was even better because of the enigma he presented.

Who was he? Why wouldn't he speak to me? And how long did he plan on toying with me like this before he got bored and moved on like all the other men in my life had?

He paused with his hand on the doorknob and turned back to me. We looked at each other for another drawn-out moment. There was so much I wanted to say to him that I didn't know where to begin. Did he feel the same pull between us? This borderline-unhealthy fixation? He'd been watching me at work, so the assumption was yes, but I wanted to know, without a shadow of a doubt, that the same need that had overtaken me was bearing down on him, too.

He nodded one last time, leaned down to scratch Fred behind the ears, and left. I stared after him for far too long before a headbutt to my shin and a demanding yowl broke me out of my thoughts.

I scooped Fred up and buried my face in him. "I should have named you Benedict, you little turncoat."

He purred and started making biscuits in my hair.

■ ■ ■

Twelve hours later, I woke to a noise. It sounded like a door closing, but I'd probably just been dreaming.

I rolled over and was about to go back to sleep when the past forty-eight hours crashed into me. The mass shooting. The Faceless Man breaking into my car. Me, getting into the passenger seat in a move that would have had horror movie aficionados screaming at their televisions. And yet, here I was, still alive. I was either one lucky bitch, or my instinct that I wasn't in danger was correct.

I was pretty sure it was the latter. After all, I knew danger. Intimately. I faced it daily. In the past week alone, I'd had to block a slap from one patient, dodge a grope from another, and bite my tongue while being cussed out by countless more. My instincts were so honed that I couldn't remember the last time someone caught me off guard. I always saw it coming, knew which patients I needed to be careful around. People only laid hands on me these days when I was distracted or had my back turned.

Most of my coworkers had the same sixth sense, with Brinley being the one exception because she was so new, but she was already learning, and if she stuck it out, she'd be as battle-hardened as the rest of us within a month or two.

All that to say, I was 98 percent sure that the Faceless Man didn't intend to harm me. The other 2 percent should probably be concerning, and it was, but unfortunately, it also lent an exciting edge to our interactions. It was that tiny little sliver that drove my desire higher, similar to how the risk of getting caught made fucking in public so much fun.

Last night, he'd asked me if I wanted him to take the mask off and ruin the fantasy, and I'd had to clench my jaw and turn away to keep from yelling, "NO!" Because what if he did, and the excitement disappeared? I needed the mask on to feel alive. Needed the knife in his hand to make me remember how precious my life was and that I was lucky to be living it.

The only thing that might up the ante was finding out who he was on the sly and keeping it to myself. The thought of turning the tables and breaking into his house to place my own set of cameras so I could taunt him back was almost as thrilling as getting fucked by an anonymous stranger.

And yes, I realized precisely how fucked up that was.

I sighed and rolled onto my back, wondering how I'd gotten to that point. Was I simply overworked, or was it genetic, and darkness had lingered inside me for years, waiting for the chance to come out and play?

No, I told myself. Most of my family had been law-abiding citizens. There was only one exception, and I decided not to count him.

It must have been trauma-induced, which meant I really needed to put in for a two-week vacation. For more reasons than one. I'd just woken up from a long day of deep sleep, but I was still exhausted, and if it wasn't for the fact that I needed to be back at work in a few hours, I could have easily dozed off for the rest of the night.

I'll put in for leave as soon as things settle down at the hospital, I told myself.

So . . . never? came an answering thought, unbidden.

I shook my head. Why did I always do this? Put off taking care of my mental health and prioritize the welfare of everyone else above my own? I knew what my therapist would say: that I was still internalizing Mom's death and blaming myself for it. After all the years of work I'd put in trying to recover from her loss, guilt still rode me. I couldn't save Mom, but with every life I saved at work, I felt like at least I could save someone else's loved one.

I sat up in bed and put my head in my hands. "The hospital will not collapse if you decide to take a few weeks of PTO," I told myself. "Between Tanya and Seth and all the other nurses, they'll be fine."

Maybe if I kept repeating those words to myself, I would believe them. It wasn't that I didn't have faith in my coworkers. Tanya and Seth, the senior day shift nurse, were the most competent nurses in the hospital. I would trust them implicitly with my life. It was the thought of not being there when I was needed that gave me pause. The chance that my absence might spell someone's demise. What if some critical symptom or sign went unseen because I wasn't there?

"Okay, stop," I said. Now I sounded full of myself. Like I was some super nurse, and without my presence, all the hospital's patients would die. That wasn't true, and it also wasn't what drove my thoughts. What I felt was closer to FOMO—the fear of missing out—than self-aggrandization.

Before I could talk myself out of it again, I grabbed my phone off the nightstand and emailed my supervisor, asking for the time off.

I let out a deep breath afterward and tried to come to terms with the thought of two weeks of freedom. It felt like so much time. Too much time, honestly. How would I fill all those hours? Going to the gym, certainly. Catching up on all the TV shows I had saved to my playlist sounded good, too. Maybe I could finally learn how to knit.

A soft meow interrupted my spiraling as Fred padded into the room. He leaped onto the foot of my bed and strode right up to me, arching his back when I reached out to pet him. I still couldn't believe how much he liked the Faceless Man. The fact that he'd sat in his lap last night was wild. Then again, he'd always been my little empath, snuggling close whenever I was sad or had had a bad shift at the hospital. Maybe he'd sensed the Faceless Man's pain and wanted to comfort him.

Yeah, let's go with that instead of Fred choosing a masked stranger over his mother.

"You ready for breakfast?" I asked.

Fred chirruped in response and jumped from the bed, leading the way to the kitchen. I followed him, tugging on my heavy robe and slippers before leaving my room.

My house was bathed in the golden light of the setting sun, rays glinting off the holiday decorations I really should have taken down by now. Or was that just societal pressure telling me what to do? There was no official mandate saying when holiday décor season ended, and the neighbors across the street still had their tree in their front window. I'd been low-key waiting for them to remove it before I packed my stuff away, and every time I got home and saw the merry glow coming from their house, I smiled, knowing that festive cheer had lived to see another day.

A thought occurred to me as I set about brewing a pot of coffee and preparing Fred's breakfast. What if my neighbors were doing the same thing I was? Were we stuck in an unintentional standoff, each waiting for the other to make the first move? Would January turn into February, and we'd become the ridicule of the rest of the neighborhood? Paula and George were from the Deep South, and if country music had taught me anything, it was that some Southerners took pride in leaving their lights up all year round.

I grimaced. Christmas in summer. Yeah, no. The decorations needed to come down.

I'd do it on my next day off.

I fixed Fred his plate of wet food and set it on the floor for him to devour. While the coffee brewed, I got out my favorite mug, which was soup-cup-sized and had the words "I've seen more dicks than a porn director" written on it. It was a birthday gift from Tanya last year, and the entire breakroom full of nurses had cackled when I opened it. Because we saw a *lot* of genitals.

I shuddered.

So many genitals.

The smell of coffee filled the kitchen as I headed toward the refrigerator. I opened the door and went to grab my creamer but froze. There were two takeout containers in there. Hadn't there been one last night?

I snagged the creamer and shut the door. Then I opened it again. Yup, the second container was still there.

I pinched myself, and it hurt. Okay, so this wasn't a lucid dream. Sometime while I'd slept, someone had broken into my house and put their leftovers in my fridge.

Gee, I wonder who could have done such a dastardly thing?

Worried I was going to find a body part waiting for me inside, I removed the new container and peeked beneath the lid. No severed hand, thank fuck. Instead, I looked in on a stack of pancakes covered in fresh strawberries and homemade whipped cream. The same breakfast I ordered every Sunday from the bakery down the street.

I lifted the container and checked underneath, and there, right in the center, was the logo for the bakery.

Carefully, I placed the pancakes back inside the fridge and shut the door a final time, wondering how to feel about this latest invasion. On the one hand, the Faceless Man noticed I had no food in my house and fixed it for me. On the other hand, I'd slept straight through him doing it.

That realization was terrifying. I knew I was a heavy sleeper, but holy shit. Anyone could have broken in over the past several years with much worse intentions, and I wouldn't have known I was in danger until it was too late.

I was suddenly way more grateful for my new security system than I had been.

Speaking of which.

I turned and went to grab my phone from my room, opening the security app as I strode back into the kitchen. There were several notifications, but they were all from cars driving past or neighbors walking by on the sidewalk. I frowned when I realized the time stamps showed a gap of several hours, stopping around noon and starting up again just twenty minutes ago—around the time I woke to the sound of a door shutting.

Goddamn it, he'd hacked my cameras.

I stomped toward the front of the house, planning to see if they were back on by waving my hand in front of the one outside, but when I opened the door, I froze for the second time in less than five minutes, blinking into the blinding white of my snow-covered neighborhood. The storm had dumped at least a foot on us, and my immediate reaction was to groan because that meant I'd have to shovel myself out before I left for work, which would take up the time I usually went to the gym.

The thing was, someone had already shoveled me out. My front steps and walk were clear, my car had been brushed off, and my driveway was spotless.

My next-door neighbors, a Black couple in their late sixties, were out in all their snow gear, almost done with their own storm cleanup. The husband, Clarence, saw me and waved. His wife, Wendy, noticed and waved, too, leaning her shovel against the side of their garage before ambling my way.

I stepped out onto my front porch and shut the door behind me. The wind nipped at my skin, and I tugged my robe tighter as I walked down the stairs to meet Wendy. She and Clarence had introduced themselves when I was moving in, welcoming me to the neighborhood with a homemade lasagna casserole. They had several grandchildren my age, and they'd taken one look at me that day, a young homeowner, exhausted and in way over my head with all the work this place needed, and decided to all but adopt me, helping with renovations, making sure I had at least one home-cooked meal a week, and checking on Fred when I had marathon shifts at the hospital like the one that ended earlier this morning.

Wendy tucked a loose curl into the hood of her jacket as she reached me, a sparkle in her dark eyes. She was tall, like me, and still in great shape, thanks to all the walks she and Clarence took together, paired with their bi-weekly golf games during the warmer months. Theirs was the nicest house on the block, a gorgeous two-story Craftsman they'd owned for forty years. They'd mulled over downsizing recently, but neither could bring themselves to sell the house they'd raised their four girls in, and I selfishly hoped they never would.

"Lucky girl," Wendy said. "That handsome man of yours shoveled you out."

My pulse skyrocketed. "What did he—" I cut myself off. How strange would it seem if I asked Wendy what he looked like? "Did he say anything?"

She grinned. "Not much. Just that you two had a little tiff, and he was trying to get back into your good graces." She regarded my pristine sidewalk and driveway before turning back to me with a look of gentle chastisement. "You didn't tell us you were seeing anyone."

"It's still new," I said by way of apology. No, they weren't my actual relatives, but Wendy had the grandma guilt down to a fine science, and I'd lost count of how many times I'd spilled my guts to her and Clarence whenever they invited me over for dinner.

"I don't mean to be pushy," she said, "but if you ask me, I say hold on to that one. Handsome as the Devil and willing to do manual labor to keep you happy?" She waved in the direction of her husband. "These men don't come around that often, and if you don't scoop him up, someone else will. I stole Clarence right out from beneath the nose of a woman who didn't appreciate him like she should have."

I gaped at her. Prim and proper Wendy had taken another woman's man? "Uh, ma'am? You were going to tell me this story when?"

Her smile widened, eyes crinkling at the corners. "It's not nearly as exciting as it sounds."

"I think I'll be the judge of that," I said.

She chuckled and shook her head at me.

We chatted for a few more minutes before the cold sent me back inside, and I left Wendy with the promise that we'd have dinner soon. It was their turn to host, and she said Clarence had all the ingredients to make chana saag—my absolute favorite thing they'd ever served me.

I whipped my phone out of my robe pocket the second I got inside.

Have you ever heard of the word boundaries? I texted the Faceless Man.

Doesn't sound familiar, he wrote back. *Can you use it in a sentence?*

Goddamn it, this wasn't funny. Not at all. My cheeks hurt because they were cold, not because of how wide I was grinning.

Did you do any other nefarious things besides shovel and stock my fridge that I should know about? I asked. *Watched me while I slept? Placed more hidden cameras?*

He sent a thinking emoji. *Nothing comes to mind. But you do snore real cute.*

My eyes flashed wide. *I do NOT snore.*

Like a chipmunk with a cold. Wheeze, wheeze, siiiiigh.

Keep making fun of me, and I might stab you again. And do not say "kinky"!

Kink—uh, I mean . . .

You're lucky I didn't find some sneaky way to get my neighbors to describe you and make it easier for me to track you down.

And risk having them look at you sideways after I told them I was your beau? I knew you wouldn't do it. Or make it easier on yourself. Don't lie. You're having as much fun as I am, Aly.

I shook my head. He was incorrigible. And I was having fun, but I wasn't ready to admit that to him yet. His ego seemed big enough without me inflating it.

Thank you, by the way, I said. *For breakfast and shoveling. You shouldn't have. I mean that literally, but I'm grateful anyway.*

I expected a sarcastic response, but he wrote back, *I like taking care of you.*

Shit. No, hormones. We're not going to be set all aflutter when the strange man stalking us does something nice.

How are your stitches? I asked, unsure of how to respond to his loaded comment. I'd been actively avoiding the memory of stabbing and then stitching him up, but I could only suppress the healthcare worker inside me for so long. I'd done everything I could to prevent infection, but the reality was my house wasn't a sterile environment, and the risk of something going wrong was real.

Red and itchy, he replied. *And are black lines leading up my arm from the wound normal?*

Oh, fuck.

No! You need to go to the ER. Now, I am not— I typed out before his next text came through, and I paused to read it.

Just kidding. It's fine. You totally freaked out, didn't you?

I braced my hands on the kitchen counter and leaned forward, wheezing in a breath as I fought to get my heart rate under control.

I was absolutely going to find him and figure out some way to get even. Maybe I'd break into his house and move all his furniture slightly out of place. Not enough to be super obvious, but just enough that his brain got stuck on it, knowing something was off, and he went crazy trying to figure it out. Or maybe I'd film a thirst trap in *his* bedroom and see how *he* liked it.

Ugh. Scratch that. He'd probably like it a little too much, and I was aiming for punishment, not reward.

My phone pinged again.

Aly? You still there? Or are you off somewhere plotting my demise?

How did he know me so well already?

Oh, right. The stalking.

You will never see me coming, I told him, hitting send before I noticed the double entendre in the words.

Welp. There go my plans for you tonight, he wrote back.

I nearly choked.

How the hell was I supposed to get through the rest of the night with the thought of him getting me off taking up so much space in my brain?

Another text came through, but it was from Tyler.

Hey, Aly. I know you probably work tonight, but do you have time to swing by here first and talk to Josh? He said he's free.

The smile that spread over my face felt maniacal. Let the first step toward finding the Faceless Man commence.

If I leave soon, yes, I responded. *Does half an hour from now work for him?*

It took a few minutes for Tyler to answer. *He said yes. I won't be here. Is that okay? Josh is cool.*

I'm sure I'll be fine, I told him.

K. Good luck. Here's his number so you can text him when you get here.

He sent it through, and I saved it to my phone before thanking him.

I switched back to my text thread with the Faceless Man.

Do you feel like sharing those plans? I asked.

In answer, he sent back a zipped-lip emoji followed by a knife and then a grinning devil face.

Cool, cool.

It was either his turn for knife play or he was planning to stitch my lips shut so I wouldn't be able to tell the Devil who stabbed me to death when I got to hell.

10

JOSH

"You're sure you'll be okay with Aly on your own?" Tyler asked from the kitchen. "I can stay if you need me to."

How bad had I gotten that my roommate considered bailing on a date to babysit me while I had company over?

I paused in the middle of setting up my laptop on our living room coffee table and turned to him. "I'll be fine as long as you're sure she's not into true crime."

Tyler scoffed, crossing his arms as he leaned back against the counter. "She's not," he said. "She sees too much of it at work and doesn't understand people's obsession with it. And come on, man. You really think I'd bring a murderino home?"

I frowned. He screened his dates for me? "I didn't realize you were so selective."

Tyler shrugged. "Why do you think you never met Eric last year? He was a *My Favorite Murder* fanboy, and they'd just covered your dad."

This was why Tyler was my best friend, despite all his douchey tendencies. He did the right thing when it mattered without me asking him to.

"So I've been avoiding all your hookups for no reason?" I said.

He flashed an unapologetic smile. "Yup."

"And you didn't feel like telling me about this until now because?"

"Because I didn't want the competition if anyone got a good look at you. The last thing we need is another—"

I pointed at him. "Do not say another Cara McKinley situation."

Tyler's college girlfriend had been a real piece of work, doing her damnedest to come between us, but not in the way he thought. Cara had "abuser" written all over her. I'd seen the signs early and tried to warn Tyler, but he wouldn't listen.

Her behavior was straight out of my father's playbook. She tried to separate Tyler from me and everyone else in his life. I lost count of the times I watched her blatantly lie to manipulate my roommate, always making herself out to be the victim, and she constantly rewrote events and gaslighted Tyler when he tried to correct her. I talked to him several times while they were dating, pointing her behavior out, but he refused to see it, too blinded by the way she love-bombed him.

So, I decided to take matters into my own hands. I'd found Cara rifling through Tyler's things one day while he was gone and cornered her, staring unblinking into her eyes and smiling with all my teeth while I told her who my dad was and that if she didn't leave my roommate alone, I would make my father's crimes look like child's play.

She'd run from the dorm. She also told everyone what I'd done and reported me to campus security, letting my secret out of the bag, which eventually led to Tyler and I bailing on that school.

I had no regrets, even though Tyler was still convinced I'd driven Cara away because she hit on me or something.

I shook my head at my roommate. "It sounds like you might be the one who doesn't want me left alone with Aly."

He pushed off the counter. "Are you kidding? If I thought something might happen between you two, I'd line the front hall with rose petals, fill this place with candles, and blast some Marvin Gaye. You need to get laid, man. You've been spending way too much time alone in your room, and at the rate you're going, you're either going to get carpal tunnel or early-onset arthritis in your wrist."

I went stock-still. He didn't have a problem with me seeing Aly? Excitement coursed through my veins. That was one less hurdle I had to jump, one less obstacle to overcome on the road to making her mine.

The second half of Tyler's statement hit me on delay because of my distraction, and I rolled my eyes at him. "I'm not sitting in my bedroom whacking it 24/7."

Wait, why was I arguing? It was better he thought I'd turned into a serial masturbator than learn the truth about how I'd been spending my days lately.

"I've just been working a lot," I lied.

He eyed me. "If you say so."

"Don't you have a date?" I asked. He needed to leave. Now. Aly was probably already on her way here.

Tyler checked his watch. "Shit. Sarah's gonna kill me if I'm late again."

The tightness in my chest eased as he raced into his room. If I had any hope of keeping Aly from figuring out who I was, Tyler couldn't be here.

I drummed my fingers against the coffee table as I listened to him getting ready.

Come on, come on. Your hair looks fine. Stop fixing it in the mirror.

The fact that I knew what he was doing without needing to see him probably meant we'd been living together too long.

A few minutes later, he returned, wearing a stylish black peacoat with the collar turned up, and stopped in the middle of our living space. A crease appeared between his brows as he looked me over. "You sure you'll be okay?"

"Get the fuck out," I said, the words a little harsher than I intended. I was running out of time.

He sent me a flat look. "Fine, but call me if shit goes sideways."

I waved him off, and he stalked out of the loft, looking pissy. I'd have to find some way to apologize later.

The second the door closed behind him, I leaped from the couch and turned off the heat before racing around to open every window in the apartment. I'd kept my injured hand hidden from Tyler, but that wouldn't work with Aly because I needed both of them to type. I bet I was already on her list of suspects—I was an obvious add because she'd met me and I was good with computers—so I'd have to be crafty if I wanted to ease her suspicions. To that end, I'd spent the past hour gleefully developing a plan.

Who knew stalking and games of deception were so much goddamn fun?

Uh, your dad? my brain helpfully supplied.

I stopped dead in my tracks and cringed. I needed to find some way to muzzle my subconscious. It kept popping up at the most inopportune moments to point out flaws in my logic or draw comparisons between me and the monster who'd contributed half my DNA.

So what if I shared a few traits with the man? As long as they weren't the bad ones, did it matter? After all, I'd also inherited my mom's propensity to overthink things, and that had been giving me more grief lately than any of the shit I got from Dad.

I shook my head and returned to the thermostat, watching the temperature drop into the low sixties. As soon as it hit fifty-five, I closed the windows again. There. That should do the trick. Cold enough to require layers but not so bad that Aly would start shivering.

Our thermostat was in the entryway where she might see it and notice I'd turned it off, so I hefted a canvas print of my mom, stepdad, and me from my visit with them this summer that Mom had sent me and hung it over the thermostat to hide it from sight. Not my best work, but it would have to do for now.

The loft was a large rectangle, and the door to my room was right off the entry hall. From there, the space opened up, with the kitchen to the left and the living room to the right, banked by massive windows dating back to when this building was an industrial factory. Tyler's room was on the opposite side as mine, and you'd think that would mean I didn't hear what went on inside it because we were so separated. Unfortunately, the big open space between us acted like some sort of sexual echo chamber, the exposed brickwork and overhead ducts carrying every moan and grunt straight to my room.

Three nights ago, I looked up from my computer screen and said, "Wait for it. Waaait for it. Now," right before Tyler let out an almighty groan, and the apartment went silent.

I shuddered at the memory, wishing I could unlearn the warning sounds my roommate made before he came.

We'd definitely been living together too long.

I dropped my focus to the floor and searched for anything I missed while cleaning earlier. Tyler liked to leave his socks lying around, but he'd been doing it less and less. He complained the other day that he was running out of them and the dryer must be eating them somehow. It wasn't. I was throwing them away to try to break his bad habit.

Mean? Maybe. But according to the whiteboard hanging by my desk, it had been five days since the last sock was left on the living room floor—a new record!—so I wasn't about to stop.

I paced into my room and grabbed a sweatshirt and fingerless gloves. I'd already intended to wear the latter to hide the tattoos on my hands, but with my stitches, they were doubly necessary now.

Two phones lay side by side on my bed. I made sure the burner I texted Aly from was switched to silent and left it behind as I grabbed my real one and strode out of the room. Just in case Aly felt snoopy when she arrived, I locked my door behind me.

I was as prepared as I could possibly be, so why was I freaking out? I was excited, yeah, and looking forward to playing more games with Aly, but I was also nervous. Was it because a girl I liked was coming over to see me for the first time, and I wanted everything to go perfectly?

No.

Yes?

I mulled that over. Yes, it was. Because, apparently, I was turning back into a teenage boy over Aly, and the fact that I got hard anytime I thought of her further confirmed that fact.

I'd pulled on a T-shirt that was a size too big earlier because it fell low enough to hide the obvious outline of my erection pressing against my jeans. I'd been turned on most of the day because every time I paused for more than half a second, my thoughts went back to last night and the memory of Aly bobbing up and down in my lap as she worshipped my dick.

Goddamn, the woman gave good head, and that was after telling me it was a bad angle for it. What would she be capable of if I laid myself before her and let her do her worst?

Probably spoil me for all other women. Not that I'd complain.

My phone chimed in my hand.

Deep breath. This was it.

I glanced down, and sure enough, the text was from Aly. She'd just pulled in and was on her way up.

I tugged on my gloves and sweatshirt and went to wait for her by the door. My fingers drummed against my thigh impatiently, and I couldn't stop tapping my foot. I'd gone for a run earlier to work out some of my nervous energy, but even though I'd pushed myself to the point of exhaustion, it hadn't been enough. I was keyed up, hyperaware, and hard as a fucking rock.

Aly was about to be within touching distance, and I couldn't lay a finger on her. This was going to be torture. The only thing that would get me through it was the knowledge that I'd more than make up for it later. Despite what I'd texted her earlier, I still planned on making her come. After a little light punishment for the stabbing, of course. I just hoped I'd done enough to earn her trust last night and that she didn't run straight for a gun when she found me sitting in her room covered in blood while holding a knife.

A knock sounded from the door. I took a deep breath, bracing myself, and opened it.

Aly stood in the hall, dressed in a fresh set of scrubs and the same jacket from last night. Her dark hair was pulled back into a long braid, and she had the barest hint of makeup on.

She was looking straight ahead when I pulled the door open, so her eyes landed on my chest. I held myself perfectly still as they widened a little and slowly climbed up, glancing over the breadth of my shoulders, lingering on my jaw, before finally rising to meet mine. Her pupils dilated the barest fraction, and a hint of color stole into her cheeks.

Was Aly turned on right now? Did she find me attractive?

I felt both elated and slightly betrayed. Well, this was a weird feeling. I was jealous of myself. Why? It wasn't like the masked version of me had any claim on her. She was a red-blooded woman with eyes in her head. She was allowed to be attracted to whomever she wanted. I should look at this as a good thing. When she eventually figured out who I was, it would be a bonus if she had the hots for me.

I smiled, reveling in the flush darkening her face. Oh, yeah, she was attracted to me.

"Aly, right?" I asked, extending my right hand toward her, which just so happened to be my injured one. I needed to work my way off her suspect list, and this was a great way to start.

She dropped her gaze to it and frowned, noting the gloves. "Yeah, thanks again for helping me."

Her eyes narrowed as she slipped her hand into mine, and I braced myself before we shook. If I knew anything about her, and I knew a lot thanks to how much I'd watched her, she was about to take the bait.

Right on cue, her fingers tightened around mine on the first pump upward, and by the time we came back down again, she was squeezing me much harder than necessary.

My hand burned like a sonofabitch, pain racing up my arm. A whimper built in the back of my throat, but there was no way I was letting it out because she would either realize she'd hurt me or recognize the pitiful sound from earlier.

I grinned through the pain. "Quite the grip you got there. Trying to intimidate me into keeping my mouth shut about all this?"

Her eyes flashed wide with the realization that if I wasn't her masked stalker, she was choking off the blood flow of an innocent man. She let me go and took a harried step back. "Sorry, no, I just . . ."

I raised a brow, waiting for her to finish the sentence.

She opened her mouth. Closed it again. Was Aly flustered? Oh, this was too good. My dark, devious heart sang at the sight of her searching for a way to excuse her behavior. I was going to torment the fuck out of this woman, and it was going to be so much fun.

"Just . . . sorry," she finished lamely, looking away.

I briefly took pity on her and stepped aside, holding the door wide. "Come on in."

"Thank you," she said, skirting past me.

"Sorry if it's chilly. The heat kicked off a while ago and won't come back on. I called the building's super, and he said he's on it."

Her gaze dropped to my gloves. "Oh, so that's why you're wearing those."

"Yup. If you get cold, we have more pairs lying around."

She smiled, still looking embarrassed about her imitation of a boa constrictor. "I'll let you know. Thanks."

I closed the door behind her and strode toward the kitchen. "Coffee?"

"Sure," she said.

"Just half-and-half, right?"

She was quiet, likely wondering how I knew how she took her caffeinated beverage of choice. From watching her, duh, but I'd known it for even longer, and that little nugget of truth would probably throw her off just as much.

I turned and grinned at her, wide enough to make my dimples pop. Her gaze dropped to them and lost focus for a second, and I was grateful my oversized shirt and sweatshirt hid the way my dick responded. I knew what I looked like, knew the effect I had on people. Up until now, I'd always resented how handsome I was because it reminded me of how easy it must have been for Dad to lure his victims.

For the first time in a long time, I was grateful for my looks because the girl of my dreams seemed rattled by them, caught off guard because she hadn't gotten a good look at me the first time we met and didn't know what to do about the fact that Tyler's roommate looked like he could get cast in the next Superman movie.

"I remember how you liked it from when you stayed over," I said, adding a wink to see if I could get her to blush again.

Sure enough, the pink fading from her cheeks came rushing back. "How I liked it?" she asked, having picked up on the innuendo in my words. Her eyes flashed wide as they glanced toward Tyler's room, and

I saw the wheels turning in her mind, wondering how much I might have heard that night.

"Yeah, your coffee," I said, tone innocent, expression anything but as I looked her over.

She sucked in a deep breath and turned away. "Yup!" she squeaked. "Half-and-half is fine, thank you. I'll just go over here and sit down."

Her ex-hookup's roommate was flirting with her, and she did *not* know what to do about it. Inside, I was cackling. Maybe I could keep her so off balance that she forgot why she was here.

But I should have known better than that.

By the time the coffee finished brewing and I ambled over to her carrying our cups, she'd gotten control of herself, back to the no-nonsense, competent woman I watched almost every night. It must have only been her surprise that threw her off at first.

"Thank you again," she said as I passed her coffee to her. "I know this is a strange request, asking you to hunt someone down for me, and I appreciate your help. Are you sure I can't pay you?"

"I'm sure," I said. "The challenge of it will be payment enough."

It was my turn to get flustered as I stared into her wide brown eyes. Up close, there were lighter hints of amber and topaz hiding amongst the deeper tones. Her eyebrows were thick, a shade or two darker than her hair, arching in the middle like one of the beauties out of a Renaissance painting.

Whatever you do, do not look at her mouth, I told myself.

I used the excuse of sipping my coffee to tear my gaze away before I gave in to that temptation. Looking at Aly's mouth was dangerous because it would remind me of what that mouth had so recently done to me, and my dick was already hard enough as it was.

I set my coffee on a coaster and opened my laptop. The screen came to life, displaying the emblem of the company I worked for. I'd scrubbed this machine down earlier, removing any trace of Aly from it just in case I had to get up and pee, and she got curious and started clicking around.

"Why do you need to find this person?" I asked. "Tyler was kind of vague."

"That's my fault. I didn't want to go into details with him," she said.

I glanced over to see her watching my screen intently. I waited a beat, but she didn't elaborate. *Really, Aly? You won't even tell the guy helping you find what you're after?* Fine. If she refused to be upfront about it, I'd have to wheedle it out of her some other way.

"Okay then," I said. "Do you at least have a starting point? A name or an address?"

She took a deep breath and pulled out her phone. "Please don't judge me for what I am about to show you."

I watched her unlock the screen, noting her passcode—because of course I did—and waited as she pulled up her social media app, found my profile, and then showed it to me.

I looked from it to her and back again. "You want me to find this guy for you?"

She nodded.

"You're not some rabid fangirl trying to find out where he lives, right? Because stalking is a crime, Aly." My tone was dead-ass serious, and it took every ounce of willpower to keep the rabid glee from my expression.

Her cheeks heated again, but it looked like it was from temper instead of lust. "*I* know it's a crime. It's someone else who has the boundary issues," she muttered.

Don't laugh, don't laugh, don't laugh.

"Oh?" I said.

"It's a long and insane-sounding story, and I don't want to get into it with a near-stranger."

Ouch.

She lifted her gaze to mine and had the good manners to appear apologetic. "No offense."

"None taken," I told her. "I'm just a little worried this ends with me getting charged as an unwitting accomplice in someone's murder."

She snorted. "It's my murder you should be more concerned about."

Was she serious? She still thought I might hurt her? Fuck, I hadn't done enough to reassure her after all. Maybe I needed to change tonight's plan around and give her the power again. She seemed to like having it last night.

"Are you joking?" I asked because that's what a non-involved, concerned person would do. "You think this guy is going to kill you?"

She blew out a breath. "No. I mean, I hope not." She dropped her head into her hands. "Fuck, I'm making this sound so much worse than it is." She lifted back up and looked at me imploringly, and I decided I would give her anything she asked for at that moment. My help. My undying loyalty. The password to my investment account and all the money inside it.

"If I thought I was truly in danger, I would have gone to the cops," she said. "This guy has just been messing with me a little, in a mostly harmless way, and I'd like to get back at him."

I continued to play the role of a concerned bystander. "I don't know. This seems like something the authorities should handle."

She shook her head. "No. I want to do this my way. Will you help me or not?" She placed her hand over mine, my right one, I noted, and squeezed again. "I totally understand if you're too freaked out, though."

Ow, ow, ow.

I kept my face stoic as I answered her. "I'll help. But please go to the police if things escalate or you feel unsafe."

She grinned up at me, squeezed once more, even harder this time, clearly watching me for any sign of pain, and then let go. "I will. Thank you."

She seemed almost disappointed that I didn't flinch as I nodded and turned back to my laptop. Did she want it to be me?

Did she think I'd make it so easy for her?

I made a show of pulling up my social media profile on a browser and locked it to the left side of my screen. Next, I opened a coding program, locked it to the right, copied and pasted my username into a line of code, and hit enter. Numbers and letters started flying over the right side of the screen while the program got to work.

It looked impressive as hell, like something out of a spy movie, but in reality, it did fuck-all. I wasn't really going to sit there and track myself down, nor had I replaced my fall guy with someone closer. If Aly was serious about looking for payback, that might mean breaking into someone's house, and I would never send her to a stranger's address if that were the case.

I'd have to find some way to run down the clock, tell her that her hacker was very good—I mean, he was, not to blow my skirt up or anything—and he'd done too much work covering his tracks for me to find him without risking getting caught and hacked myself.

"That's it?" Aly asked. "You just put it in there, and the program does it all for you?"

"I wish it were that easy, but no," I said. "This is just to figure out what IP address he used to create his account."

From there, I went into detail about how much work it would realistically take to track someone down. Her face fell as I talked. Good. Hopefully, she was second-guessing her harebrained idea.

"So you're not going to have an answer for me by the time I have to leave," she checked her watch, "in twenty minutes?"

"Nope. Sorry," I said. "What's it like being a trauma nurse?" I tacked on. Because I couldn't help myself. This was the first time I'd spoken to Aly, and despite how often I watched her, I was still ravenous for information. There was only so much knowledge you could gain through a camera. I had memorized her expressions and learned how to read her moods, but I didn't know what made her tick, didn't know how she truly felt about all the things I'd seen her go through.

"Oh," she said, looking slightly taken aback by the sudden topic shift. "It's . . . I don't exactly know how to describe it. Good isn't the right word. Rewarding might be better."

I glanced down at her lips, unable to help myself. Less than a day ago, they had parted around my cock. Less than a day ago, I had come inside that sweet mouth.

I jerked my gaze up and refocused on her words before I did something stupid.

"It's incredibly challenging at times," she said. "The lows are really low, but the highs are equally high. Nothing compares to the thrill of saving someone's life."

I nodded. "I bet. What made you want to get into it?"

She met my eyes before shifting to watch the letters flashing over my screen. "My mom, but I don't want to talk about it. Sorry."

"It's fine," I said. Shit, I'd touched a nerve. I needed to get us back on safer ground. "More coffee?" She drank at least a pot a night, and her cup looked like it needed to be topped off.

She held it out to me. "Yes, please."

I went to the kitchen and poured us more. Aly was typing on her phone when I turned back around, and I watched as she hit a final button and then looked toward my phone, which sat next to my laptop, as if waiting for something. Did she just text me? The masked me?

If so, she would get a vague, slightly teasing response in three, two, one . . .

Her phone chimed, and she looked disappointed for half a second until she read the text and grinned, shaking her head like she was amused and didn't want to be. I knew the expression well. She'd worn it almost constantly last night.

She fired off another text as I returned to the living room with our cups, grinning even wider when the next reply came through.

The auto-response program I'd loaded onto my burner was pretty sophisticated. It could carry on an entire smartass/flirtatious conversation with her in my absence, though I hoped she didn't keep this up for long. The program was good, but it wasn't perfect, and she looked like she had finally stopped suspecting me. Josh me. After all, I couldn't be her masked admirer if he was texting her back, could I?

"Thank you," she said, setting her phone down to take her coffee. She looked more relaxed than a moment ago, like her back was no longer up now that she didn't suspect me.

Mwah ha ha ha ha.

My evil plan was working. Step one: get Aly to drop her guard. Step two: fuck her on this couch.

Oh, wait, no. I'd skipped a few steps somewhere.

But, god, the temptation was strong. Relaxed Aly was almost as hot as feisty Aly, and I had to stop myself from staring at her instead of pretending I was watching my fake hacking program work its magic.

Unfortunately, she didn't seem to suffer such compunction, and I could feel her gaze like a physical touch as she watched me watch the screen. I'd been worried earlier that my need for her might be tied to our shared kink, and without a mask between us, the excitement would dull. I should have known better. I wanted her just as much now as last night, and from the way she stared at me so intently, I was beginning to think it went both ways.

Keep it up, baby, I thought, *and see if I don't out myself right now just so I can give in to this driving need to yank your scrub pants down and—*

"What's it like being a computer programmer?" she asked.

I cleared my throat and shifted my hips, trying to ease my erection sideways so it wasn't digging straight into my fly. Was she making small talk, or did she really want to know?

I took a sip of coffee and sat back, risking a glance at her. She looked genuinely interested.

"It's a little like how you described nursing. Challenging but rewarding, if in different ways."

"What made you want to get into it?"

I reluctantly pulled my gaze from her—I'd been staring at her mouth again and almost missed the question. The second it registered, my stomach plummeted. I was already playing enough games with her, and I didn't want to start piling lies on top of them, so I settled for a half-truth instead.

"My dad wasn't a good man. He tried to find us when Mom and I left him. Learning how to hide us from him online was the reason I first started coding."

"Oh, wow," she said. "I'm so sorry."

I shook my head. "Don't be. It's in the past. We're free from him now." The whole world was, thanks to his state-sanctioned execution. "Lighter topic," I said. "If you were locked in a room full of spiders, would you rather have the lights on or off?"

Aly leaned toward me until I had no choice but to look at her again. "That's lighter?" she asked, brows lifted in concern.

Her eyes were so pretty this close. "Than my dad? Yeah."

She sat back. "Lights on, I guess. So I could see the spiders coming. You?"

I nodded. "Same."

"Would you rather be trapped alone in outer space or at the bottom of the ocean?" she asked.

"Those are both terrible. Outer space."

"Same. But why?"

I grinned. "I'm banking on the chance of an alien rescue."

She smiled back, her gaze dipping toward my dimples again and going slightly unfocused.

My heart started beating so hard that it rattled my rib cage. When was the last time I'd done this? Sat and talked with a woman? I couldn't remember ever being so at ease around one, at least not as an adult. Part of me was always wound up, waiting for them to find out who I was and for that knowledge to ruin everything. Maybe I should have felt that with Aly, but Tyler wasn't a liar, and if he said she avoided true crime like the plague, he meant it.

"Would you rather change sexes every time you sneeze or not know the difference between a baby and a muffin?" I asked.

She laughed, throwing her head back and almost spilling her drink. "That second part is twisted. I'll take changing sexes. Sounds fun."

I nodded. "Same."

A mischievous look crept into her expression, and her gaze dropped to my lap.

I glanced down, but the hem of my sweatshirt still hid what was happening beneath it.

She lifted her eyes to mine, her gaze searing. "Would you rather ejaculate one tadpole-sized sperm every time you come or a hundred regular-sized ones that can all talk?"

I sucked in a breath full of coffee and immediately started choking. Aly patted me on the back while I leaned forward, hacking as my lungs tried to expel the liquid invasion.

"Sorry," she said. "Should have waited until you swallowed. I've caught a lot of people off guard with that one."

"That is a truly impossible question," I wheezed.

She quit patting me and rubbed her hand over my back instead, and I decided to stay right where I was until she felt like stopping. "I know. Because on the one hand, ow. On the other, you could never get rid of them." She raised her voice to a much higher register, sounding like a munchkin. "Nooo. Don't flush us, Josh. We're aliiive."

■ ■ ■

Aly had left my house almost eight hours ago, and I was desperate to see her in person again. I'd declared her the winner of our impromptu game of Would You Rather after she made me nearly choke to death again with a question about crying tiny rocks or sweating pickle juice.

My computer screen showed me that she was busy at work, still dealing with the fallout of the mass shooting. Another one of the victims had succumbed to their wounds during the day, and the news organizations and local politicians were both working overtime to either bring attention to or away from the event, depending on their affiliations.

Mom had called me in a blind panic earlier. She didn't watch the news these days, not that anyone could blame her for that, given her past, but someone had told her about the tragedy, and she hadn't heard from me, so her mind went straight to the worst-case scenario.

The half-sob she let out when I picked up the phone stabbed into my heart, and I resolved to call her and Rob, my stepdad, more often.

We caught up after she calmed down, and when she asked if I was seeing anyone, a hopeful tone in her voice, I caved and told her a little about Aly. Not much—Mom would probably have me committed as a precaution if she knew the truth about my behavior—but that I was seeing someone and it was still new and that she was a trauma nurse who was helping the victims of the shooting.

"She sounds like a good woman," Mom said. "And you must really like her. I can't remember the last time you told me about someone."

Yes, she could, but neither of us liked to think about how that relationship ended. My high school girlfriend had gone missing for five days the summer after graduation. I was arrested on day two and sat in a jail cell until she showed back up at her parents' house. She'd taken an impromptu road trip with her best friend and didn't bother telling anyone.

The cops let me out with an apology, but Mom still wrote a furious op-ed in the paper afterward, packed us up, and moved us. Again.

Here was hoping my relationship with Aly ended on a nicer note. Or better yet, didn't end at all.

I refocused my attention on my computer screen. Aly stood by the nurses' station, laughing with her coworkers. It was good to see that they could still laugh even under such duress. Hell, it was probably the coping mechanism they clung to the hardest.

I'd made the mistake of tapping into the ambulance bay cameras when they'd started wheeling victims in the other night, and it was the final nail in the coffin confirming that Dad and I were different in one critical way: real-life blood and death freaked me out. I'd taken one look at the most critically injured victim and started gagging. And what had Aly done? Climbed right on top of the gurney and replaced the exhausted EMT who'd been pumping their chest to keep their heart going.

She was a goddamn rockstar, and I hoped her patients told her that at least once an hour.

I blinked as I watched her wave goodbye to someone and turn to walk up the hall. The blink must have lasted a full minute because she was gone from the camera when I finally opened my eyes again. Fuck, I was tired. I meant to take a longer nap after she'd left the apartment earlier, but I'd woken up after a few short hours, the need to see her dragging me back to my computer desk.

I'd make another pot of coffee in a minute. That would keep me going. At least until Aly got off work. Then, the excitement and adrenaline would take over, and I'd be wide awake again.

I leaned back in my chair and let my mind wander to everything I had planned for Aly later. My eyes fluttered shut, the better to imagine her laid out beneath me, arms overhead, tits bouncing.

God, what a beautiful sight.

A blaring alarm snapped me out of it. Shit, was something happening at the hospital again?

I jerked forward in my seat, horrified that my room was several shades brighter than when I closed my eyes. Because the sun was rising.

I must have fallen asleep.

The alarm was coming from my phone. Aly's front door camera was noting a lot of activity. I yanked my phone closer and saw her getting out of her car. In her driveway.

She was home already, and I wasn't there waiting for her.

God-*fucking*-damn it!

I shoved away from my computer, grabbed my backpack full of supplies, snagged my car keys, and ran out the door.

11

ALY

JOSH WAS THE FACELESS MAN. I didn't know how I knew it, but I did.

The second he opened his apartment door, that certainty hit me like a punch to the gut. He'd already been near the top of my suspect list—I'd met him, he was good with computers, and he had the right body type—but seeing him in the flesh confirmed it.

How he'd managed to keep a straight face while I squeezed the shit out of his hand was beyond me, but not a hint of pain showed in his expression. I felt terrible about it now. It must have hurt like a bastard. Hopefully, his stitches were fine. I'd texted him cleaning and bandaging instructions, so if it bled afterward, he should have been okay fixing it alone.

Aside from the suspicious-as-fuck gloves, something in his manner reminded me of the Faceless Man. He'd been so concerned and sincere when telling me that stalking was illegal. On the surface. But there had been a gleam in his eyes while he spoke that made me feel like he was secretly having the time of his life making me squirm with discomfort.

Other things pointed to his innocence that I chose to ignore. The fact that he smelled different. Instead of the clean scent of soap, his cologne was dark and heady: cedarwood paired with smoky magnolia. His movements were more relaxed, too. The Faceless Man stalked.

Josh prowled. Most damning of all, when I texted my masked stalker, expecting Josh's phone to light up on the coffee table, I'd gotten a response instead.

I'm a little worried about your plans for me, I'd said.

Short-term plans or long-term plans? Both should be cause for concern, in different ways.

I'd smiled and shaken my head. *Short-term.*

He'd texted back a GIF of a cartoon villain laughing maniacally while lightning flashed in the background, and I'd lifted my head just in time for Josh to hand me my coffee. Josh, who'd been in the kitchen sans phone, so he had to be innocent, right?

Wrong. I was falling for none of it. My lizard brain had watched the Faceless Man along with the more evolved part, and it saw Josh and *knew*, picking up on subtle tells I couldn't put my finger on.

And if Josh was as intelligent as Tyler claimed, he could have anticipated me texting him and gotten one of his hacker buddies to answer for him or figured out how to auto-reply to me in a believable way.

I'd been half-tempted to take a sneaky picture of him to show Wendy, but I hesitated for two reasons. The first was the off chance that I was wrong. How would I explain showing her a picture of the person I thought was my "beau" only for her to look at me sideways and tell me it wasn't the guy she'd met? The second was it felt too easy. Almost like cheating. My stupid pride was pushing me to figure this out on my own. I wanted to beat the Faceless Man at his own game, which was why I'd stopped at the gun store after leaving Josh's place and picked up a tracking device. The next time I got the chance, I was slipping it into one of the Faceless Man's pockets and seeing where it went.

I hoped it led back to Josh and Tyler's apartment because I just plain wanted Josh to be the Faceless Man. It'd make me feel less guilty about how my body responded to him. He'd opened that door, and the second I caught sight of him, lust exploded through me. Because, holy shit, Josh was hot. Like, the kind of hot you didn't see walking around in the wild with the rest of us plebeians. His face was more suited to a movie screen or magazine page.

And when he smiled and those dimples appeared? It triggered ovulation. You couldn't convince me otherwise. Not after the way I stood there staring at him while my ovaries donned their warpaint and started metaphorically chucking eggs at the man.

I had no idea how I kept it together that whole visit when all I wanted to do was tackle him onto the couch and rip his shirt up to get a look at his tattoos. And then keep tearing clothes off until I had him laid out naked beneath me.

Fuck, I needed to get laid. It had been so long that my fingers and vibrator weren't cutting it anymore. I'd gotten myself off in the shower after the Faceless Man left this morning, but it did almost nothing to take the edge off. I needed a dick inside me, needed another person's hands on my body. I was touch-starved, skin hungry. It was what happened when people went too long without physical contact. Sure, I put my hands on others every day, but rarely did anyone touch me back, and certainly not in the way I'd been craving.

Was "craving" a strong enough word for what I felt at this point? It didn't seem like it. "Need" was better, but still not quite there. What I wanted was closer to possession. I wanted someone to own me, body and soul. The Faceless Man had the potential. So did Josh. The way he'd leaned back against the kitchen counter and winked at me, dark eyes smoldering, spoke of a man who knew what he wanted, and what he wanted would get him excommunicated from most religions. There was something devious yet playful in his eyes, like he'd make your descent into hell the most fun you ever had.

My mind was made up. Until proven otherwise, the Faceless Man and Josh would be one and the same. I couldn't fathom another explanation for why the pull Josh had on my body was so instantaneous and strong. And it hadn't just been my body that was drawn to him, but my mind, too. It had been so easy between us. We'd clicked in a way I hadn't with anyone in a long time. I never wanted that game of Would You Rather to end, and when I made him choke and got to rub his back? Heaven.

Something about the feel of heavy muscle really did it for me, and not just because it looked nice, but because of how much effort and intensity it took to create. It spoke of someone with drive and focus, someone willing to put in hard work even on the days they didn't want to. That dedication had the potential to transfer well into a relationship because relationships could be the hardest work of all.

If Josh were the Faceless Man, that meant I might get kinky sex, witty banter, easy conversation, and even a new gym buddy all in one. Uh, yes, please?

Speaking of the kinky sex. Work had been especially rough again tonight, and if ever I needed to go home and find a naked, masked man waiting for me in my bedroom, it was now. I thought about it the whole way there, which took longer than normal thanks to the black ice covering the roadways and the need to drive at a snail's pace to keep from sliding on it.

What would I realistically do if I opened my bedroom door and found the Faceless Man waiting on the other side, shirtless and covered in fake blood like he'd stepped out of one of his videos? Probably say, "Smash," and then pounce. These masked thirst trappers had no idea how feral they made people. Sure, our comments might give them some indication, but they probably thought we were all talk. We weren't. By the time I was finished with the Faceless Man tonight, *he* would be the one walking funny.

Anticipation sang in my veins as I pulled into my driveway. I glanced around the street but saw no strange cars nearby. He must have done the smart thing and parked a few blocks over again.

Fred did his usual scream-greeting as I opened the door, and I dropped my stuff just inside the threshold, scooped him up, and started walking.

"Where is he?" I asked.

Fred purred at me, eyes slanting in bliss like he hadn't gotten attention in a while. Hmm. That didn't seem right. If the Faceless Man were in my house, wouldn't Fred have been all over him, ignoring me like yesterday?

I smushed my cat and then set him back down, heading toward my bedroom, where I'd most likely find—

No one. There was no one in there.

Frowning, I went to the closet and pulled it open, half worried the Faceless Man would jump out at me like a life-sized Jack in the Box. Nope. Not there either. I checked under my bed and then in my bathroom, going so far as to pull back the shower curtain. Nada.

A search of the rest of my house revealed that it was just as empty.

I fought back a wave of disappointment. It wasn't like we'd set a time and date for our next encounter.

Was this his way of getting back at me for stabbing him? Making me think he'd be here with those ominous texts and then not showing up?

I ran a hand through my hair, digging my nails into my scalp. Argh! Why were relationships so confusing?

Not that this was a relationship.

No. Absolutely not. I shouldn't get attached. Not when I didn't have confirmation of the Faceless Man's true identity or what his end game was. For all I knew, my daydreams about more time spent together lounging on couches in between marathon bouts of sex were a pipe dream. He might be planning to show up once every few weeks when I least expected him, adding a thrill of fear and surprise to our encounters.

That sounded like fun but also torture—not the fear part, but the waiting in between. I'd barely had a taste of him, and already I craved more. I'd make an entire meal out of him next time I got the chance, savoring every lick and suck, making it so good for him that his cum tattooed the back of my throat.

I shook my head. Those thoughts weren't helping me. Nor would the pity party I felt like throwing myself. What would happen would happen, and worrying about it now wouldn't change anything. It was just that the Faceless Man had done so much to convince me I could trust him that I thought he felt it, too, this gnawing hunger for more.

I sighed, double-checked that my doors were locked, and went to take a shower. I half expected to find him waiting for me when I got out, but he wasn't, and alongside my disappointment, I was starting to feel bratty. There was one way to make him regret not being here, and that was revenge.

I shut Fred out of my room and yanked open the top drawer of my bureau. Nestled between my two favorite vibrators was the hidden camera the Faceless Man put in my room.

It was time to plug this bad boy back in.

There was a chance he wasn't even awake, but I hoped he was up and had some notification attached to the camera that would tell him when it was on because I was about to pay him back for all the times he'd needled me or made me laugh when I should have been furious. Not that I was complaining about either of those things. Secretly, I loved it.

Oh, hell, fine. I openly loved it. I wanted more of it, and quid pro quo felt like a great way to get it.

I plugged the camera into the socket with the best view of my bed and then dropped my towel, leaving me butt ass naked. The light in my room was dim, the only illumination coming from my cracked shower door, but it was still enough to see by and no doubt be seen on a computer or phone screen. I unwound the towel from my hair and let my damp strands fall loose to my elbows, chilling my skin and making my nipples pebble.

My phone chimed.

What are you doing? read his text.

Elation zinged through me. He was up, and he'd noticed the camera was live.

Keep watching and find out, I wrote back, adding a winking face followed by a grinning devil.

A typing bubble immediately popped up, but I switched my phone to silent and tossed it aside. I was done talking.

I'd never done anything like this before, and before my nerves got the better of me, I pulled my largest vibrator out of my top drawer and climbed onto the bed, taking my sweet time and making a show out of the way I crawled toward my pillows. I leaned back against them, spread my legs wide toward the camera, and pulled the lube out of my nightstand. The vibrator wasn't something to scoff at, and even though I was already turned on, I knew I'd need a little help taking it all.

I dropped a dollop of lube on the tip of it and used my hand to work it over the silicone. It was molded from a famous porn actor's dick, but I still thought the Faceless Man's was prettier. I briefly considered telling him that, but I didn't know if the camera had a microphone, and I was trying to torment him, not inflate his ego.

My chest rose and fell as my breathing picked up. Knowing he was watching me was a bigger turn-on than I'd anticipated, and now I needed to add voyeurism to my kink list because this was something I wanted to do again. Or watch someone else do.

Oh, fuck. The Faceless Man and I, hidden in the back of a dark, crowded room while someone onstage pleasured themselves? I didn't think I could get through five minutes without hiking my skirt to my waist and planting myself on his lap, still facing the stage so we could both watch while he fucked me from behind.

I ran my free hand over my breasts, cupping and kneading them, fingers bouncing over my tightened nipples in a way that sent sparks racing straight to my core. My other hand gripped the base of the vibrator as I braced the tip of it at my entrance and turned it on. The main source of the vibration was located at the bottom of the device, where a second, smaller nub stuck out that would lie flush against my clit when it was all the way in, but the vibration was so strong that just the head of it felt good against my aching center.

I'd barely even started, and this was already better than every other time I'd masturbated recently. Yup. This confirmed it. I wasn't vanilla, and vanilla wouldn't cut it for me from now on. Maybe the world of grays I'd been living in had less to do with my darkening mentality and more to do with the lack of spice in my life.

I pushed the head of the vibrator in, feeling myself expand around it, stretch to accommodate its girth. How much more would I have to stretch to take the Faceless Man? What would it feel like to be seated on his cock, so full that I could barely breathe around it? And then to feel him retract, leaving me aching and desperate before he came roaring back in with a hard, brutal thrust?

My legs trembled at the thought. I pinched and tugged at my nipples before easing the vibrator in another inch, relishing in the delicious, heady lust coursing through my body. I felt languid and giddy, the oxytocin lowering my inhibitions and making me want to be braver. Bolder. If I was going to put on a show, I was going for it. To hell with my lingering self-consciousness and worry that I wasn't doing this right.

Teasing myself was fun, and teasing him was even better, but right now, I was horny and frustrated, and I wanted it hard and fast and rough, all thoughts driven from my head as I abandoned myself to pleasure.

I grabbed a pillow from behind me and sat up, rising onto my knees so I could shove it between them, brace the vibrator on it, and let go, dropping straight down and spearing myself on the huge silicone cock.

Stars exploded across my vision as a throb of deep, dull pain told me I probably should have spent more time on foreplay.

Fuck foreplay, I thought. I welcomed the ache. Especially because it was already fading, and what was left behind was the feeling of being stuffed full in a way I'd been craving since I first fastened my lips over the head of the Faceless Man's thick cock.

I leaned forward, bracing my free hand on the bed and holding the vibrator in place with the other so I could ride it. The first thrust was pure delight, so good I paused on the downstroke and rotated my hips, letting the vibration thrum against my clit. I did it again, and my breath hitched. At this rate, I wouldn't last long.

The light in my bathroom went out, plunging my room into a darkness so complete that the whole block must have lost power.

I froze.

An unholy *BANG* echoed through the house.

I clicked the vibrator off.

What the fuck was that?

Was it the Faceless Man? Was he here? Or had someone else just kicked in my front door?

I shivered in the dark, the lingering water droplets cooling on my skin, lust shriveling up as fear took hold of me. If there was an actual unwanted intruder in my house, this was the most vulnerable position I could be in—naked and soaked in lube.

I needed a gun, and I needed it now.

I was just lifting off the vibrator when I heard Fred let out his welcoming yowl. He didn't do that for anyone but me and the Faceless Man.

There was another yowl, and then a deep, guttural voice broke the silence, too deep to be natural, so low it must have been modulated. "No, Fred. Mommy and Daddy need to have alone time right now."

I almost laughed, my relief was so strong. Mommy and Daddy. It had to be him. No one else was so presumptuous.

My door opened and closed quickly. I could see almost nothing, just a large shape looming in the darkness, growing bigger and bigger as it strode toward me. My bathroom light kicked back on, and suddenly I was face-to-mask with my stalker.

I reared away on instinct, caught off guard, but he grabbed me by the throat and pulled me back to him, those gaping black eyes staring straight into my soul, his grip firm. Inescapable.

"Don't stop on my account," he said, and my inner walls clenched around the vibrator. Of all the voice modulator settings he could have chosen, of course, it was the one that sounded like it was about to growl absolute filth into my ear.

His grip on my neck tightened, and he tugged. It was either rise or be choked. I hesitated for half a second, feeling the sweet thrill of fear course through me at the possibility of having my air cut off. He sucked in a harsh breath and pulled harder, and up I went, sliding almost all the way off the vibrator.

"Are we doing this?" he asked.

He didn't have to explain himself. Doing this meant finally playing out our shared fantasy.

"Yes," I said, my pulse thundering against his fingers.

He held me in place and reached between my thighs, clicking the sex toy back on. "No safe words," he rumbled. "You want me to stop, just say so. No matter when. No matter what I'm doing to this greedy little pussy." He flicked my clit, and I cried out. "Do you understand?"

I nodded in his hold.

His fingers dug into my skin. "I need you to say it, baby."

"No safe words," I agreed, my voice thready from a mixture of worry and lust. He was so much bigger than me, so much stronger despite all the time I'd put in at the gym. This man could do serious harm to me. Sure, there was a chance I could fight him off, but all it would take was one solid punch to put me on the ground.

I'd never been in such a vulnerable position in my life.

And I'd never felt so fucking alive before, either.

He used his grip on my neck to push me back down, all the way to the base of the vibrator, and hold me in place. "Swivel those sweet hips."

I whimpered and did as he said. Holy fucking shit, that felt good.

"Again," he said, and I complied, staring up at him with wonder.

Gone was his playfulness; gone was his sly teasing. The man who stood above me now was everything he promised in his videos: demanding, despotic, and absolutely ruthless.

He reached down again, slipped his fingers between my clit and the nub stimulating it, and clamped down on that sweet bundle of nerves. My spine arched as pleasure punched through me.

"Were you trying to punish me?" he asked.

I couldn't answer. Couldn't do anything but sit there and pant. The vibration was rolling through me from clit to core, but with the blood flow to my pleasure center nearly cut off, it was impossible to come. Instead, I spiraled higher and higher, sweat starting to dot my forehead. My skin felt electrified, like I stood too close to a live wire.

He squeezed my clit harder. "Answer me, baby."

"Yes," I rasped. "I was mad you weren't here."

His fingers eased off me slightly, and my legs started shaking as blood returned to my clit, and it started to grow engorged between his fingers, the returning pleasure multiplied because of its recent absence. I was about to come so fucking hard.

"You should have known I was on my way to you and waited," he said.

I barely caught the words, too busy thrusting my hips down as my inner muscles tightened around the vibrator. Close. I was so close. I just needed him to loosen his hold a little more on both my clit and my neck, and I would—

His fingers clamped down again, catching me off guard. "It's me who should be punishing you," he said. "You fucking stabbed me, Aly."

My gaze had been unfocused as I started to lose myself, but his words had it sharpening again. I grinned as I stared into his black eyes, my voice coming out as a wheeze because of the pressure on my windpipe. "Yeah, but you liked it."

He growled, and the modulator turned it animalistic, making it sound like a goddamn werewolf had just stalked into my room.

His fingers disappeared from my sex, and the flood of returning blood had my head spinning and spine bowing as I got closer to the edge, but then he pushed my hand off the vibrator's handle and pulled it out of me. I had just enough time to whimper at its loss before he shoved me backward. I bounced on the bed, and then he was on me, swinging a leg over my waist as he pulled his shirt off. He yanked me up by my arms, shoved the shirt under my head and neck, and then tugged his zipper down, freeing his cock.

I reached for it hungrily, but he pushed my hands aside and grabbed the lube I'd left discarded on my comforter. A splash of it landed in the middle of my chest, all the warning I had before he grabbed my hands and put them on my breasts.

"Press them together," he ordered. "Your first present is that necklace you've been begging me to get you."

I shoved my breasts in tight and smirked up at him. "I see you've been reading my comments."

He huffed out what might have been a strangled laugh—the modulator made it hard to tell—and thrust straight into my cleavage.

I craned my head up and managed to lick his frenulum before he grabbed my hair and pulled me away, holding me against the bed.

"What was it you said yesterday?" he asked. "*This isn't for you*?"

"It feels a *little* like it's for me," I shot back.

Another strangled laugh was quickly cut off by a groan as he thrust into me again, starting a steady rhythm. The bed squeaked beneath us. Our heavy breathing echoed through the room, and the smell of sex filled my nose.

If he was trying to punish me, he was failing. I was all for the feel of his hot, smooth, lube-slicked cock shoving between my breasts as he used me to find his release. And really, letting him paint a pearl necklace over my throat was the least I could do after stabbing him. Maybe I could find more ways to piss him off and see just how many of my comments he'd read.

"Your tits are perfect," he said, letting go of my hair to brace both hands on the bed and piston his hips back and forth, picking up speed.

Your whole body is perfect, I wanted to say, but I was too mesmerized by the sight of him looming over me, abs contracting, biceps straining as he held himself aloft. I pushed my breasts together even tighter, imagining it was my pussy he was slamming into. His monstrous cock would probably hit my cervix with every thrust—lucky me.

I lifted my gaze from his straining pecks to see him staring straight down at me, watching as he fucked my tits. His breathing hitched, and his cock swelled with a fresh infusion of blood. I felt his balls lift off my skin as they started to tighten up, and the sight of what he was doing to me, the *feel* of it, was so hot I had to squeeze my legs together to ease my unsatisfied need.

"I want to feel you come," I said, unable to keep my mouth shut any longer. "I want to feel you brand my throat where your hand just was, marking me."

"As mine," he growled.

It wasn't a question, but I answered him anyway. "Yes. Yours."

"Fuck, Aly."

With one last thrust, he was coming, hot seed splashing over my skin, dick pulsing between my tits, body trembling above me as he sucked in one breath after another, his hips changing rhythm as he lost himself to pleasure.

He shuddered and went still when he was done, bowing over me, and even though I hadn't done anything but hold my tits together for him, I felt a triumphant little thrill that he'd come so hard he needed a minute to regroup.

"My turn?" I asked, unable to keep the excitement out of my voice.

His answering laugh was evil, and at first, I thought it was because of the modulator, but soon, I learned better.

■ ■ ■

"Fuck you," I spat.

"Only good girls get fucked, Aly, and from the way you've been cursing my name for the past five minutes, I think we've established that you aren't one."

More vitriol spewed from my mouth as he braced his forearm across my shoulders and held me in place while he slowly started thrusting into me again. With my godforsaken vibrator instead of his cock.

It felt like he'd been doing this for an hour, though it had probably been closer to ten minutes. Over and over again, he fed the vibrator into me, holding it steady against my clit until stars danced across my vision, only to pull it out again, denying me the orgasm that needed to happen at this point, or I swore I would die from frustration.

"Please," I begged.

"You can always tell me to stop," he said.

No, I couldn't. Because then he would win. He'd had almost all the power in our dynamic from the start, and I couldn't bring myself to give him any more by tapping out. My stubborn streak was too big for that, and it would probably be the death of me.

He eased the vibrator out again just as I was getting close, and a sob slipped through my lips before I could stop it. The bastard had the audacity to chuckle. Fuck him. And fuck me, too. Past me, specifically, who'd read about edging and thought it sounded fun.

It wasn't fun. It was torture.

I thrashed beneath him as he pulled the vibrator out, leaving my pussy clenching on empty air. How did he think this was hot? I was a red, sweaty mess right now, hair plastered to my forehead, tears streaking from the corners of my eyes, but I knew he was into it because he was rock hard again, his pants still unbuttoned, showing off his picture-perfect cock. That he wouldn't give me. Or even let me touch. Every time I reached for it, he slapped my hands away and went back to tormenting me. The man must have been a goddamn sadist to be having so much fun.

I shook my head from side to side. "I need to, I need to," I repeated.

"Shhh," he said, brushing the hair from my face. "I know, baby. You're doing so good."

Another sob shook my body. I'd never look at arousal the same after this. He was shifting my entire worldview.

"Brace yourself," he said, all the warning I had before he rammed the sex toy home.

My back arched off the bed, and his hand landed on my throat again, just beneath my jaw, keeping my head tilted away from him as something warm and wet enveloped one of my nipples.

Had he taken his mask off?

His tongue laved at my nipple just as the vibrating little nub hit my clit, and if he didn't stop soon, there was nothing that would prevent me from coming this time. I could feel it building like a tidal wave just offshore, gaining momentum as it raced into the shallows, ready to slam through me with the same destructive force as a late-season cyclone.

He rotated the vibrator, simulating the act of thrusting, rubbing the nub over and around my clit. Spots danced at the edge of my vision, crowded close because of how tight he held my throat.

Shit, he was cutting off my airway.

His mouth latched onto my nipple, and he sucked, *hard*, fingers popping off my neck. I dragged in a single breath before he tightened his grip again. Oh, no. How was the pleasure still building? I couldn't do this. It was too much. My entire body felt like one raw, pulsing nerve, and if he pushed me any higher, I'd have brain damage; I just knew it.

His mouth left my breast, and I cried out in desperation.

"Let go, Aly," he rumbled. "I'll catch you when you fall."

He refastened his mouth over my other nipple and sucked, bore down on my clit with the vibrator, and loosened his hold on my neck enough that breath flooded back into my lungs. And then I was shaking, sobbing, legs slamming together and clamping down on his wrist as he tore the most soul-shattering orgasm I'd ever had from my ruined body.

It felt like my brain short-circuited. It felt like I died. It felt like I spoke to the Devil, and the Devil told me he was proud of what we'd just done.

And then I'm pretty sure I passed out for a few minutes because, by the time I came back to myself, the Faceless Man was cleaning my neck off with a warm towel and telling me what a good girl I was after all.

12

JOSH

I MIGHT HAVE PUSHED ALY TOO FAR. She'd probably been exhausted and emotionally drained after another punishing shift at work, and what had I done? Edged her right to the point of breaking.

I couldn't help myself. The second my phone pinged on the way over and I saw Aly getting herself off without me, something snapped. And then I walked into her room and found her perched on her vibrator, the terror in her eyes quickly turning into desire, and all my nerves disappeared.

A calmness had taken hold of me, shredding my lingering worry that I would turn out like my father. The feelings I had toward Aly had nothing to do with violence or pain, and memories of the man who fathered me didn't belong in that room with us, tarnishing what we were about to experience. I'd shoved them from my mind once and for all as I approached the bed, trusting myself to wrap my hand around Aly's delicate throat without worrying that I would go too far or squeeze too hard.

God, Aly was perfect, absolutely perfect. Not only while she got me off but afterward, when she thrashed within my grip, calling me every name in the book and cursing my very existence.

I hoped she wasn't too angry because what we just did was satisfying on a bone-deep, primal level. We'd played out our shared fantasy of a masked hookup—sans knife because, in my haste to get here, I'd left it behind like an amateur. Or maybe that was my subconscious trying to save me in case Aly got her hands on it again. Two stabbings in two days would have been a bit excessive.

A soft meow interrupted my thoughts, and I glanced down to see Fred sitting by my feet, staring up at me while patiently waiting for another piece of bacon like the little gentleman he was. He might have scared the shit out of me the first time we met, but now that I no longer worried I might get the sudden urge to skin him, he was growing on me.

I especially enjoyed the way he all but ignored his mother every time I was around. Mostly because it probably pissed her off, but also because it was nice to be chosen for once. I couldn't remember the last time someone laid claim to me.

I dutifully broke some bacon off and held it out for Fred, and he rose onto his hind legs and carefully took it before scurrying away to eat it underneath a dining room chair like a lion dragging its kill into a cave.

I fought back a gag and turned up the stove vent to suck away the smell of searing meat before flipping the bacon over in the pan and then stirring Aly's eggs so they didn't get lumpy.

As the nausea died down, a feeling of contentment washed over me. I was satiated, damn near lethargic, and all I wanted to do was curl up with Aly beneath her covers and sleep for about a week straight. Unfortunately, I'd never worn my mask this long, and certainly not while doing something as strenuous as titty fucking and then tormenting the woman I was obsessed with. I'd underestimated how sweaty and itchy the inside of it could become, and if I didn't get it off my head soon, I was going to break into hives.

Movement caught my attention, and I glanced at where my phone was propped on the windowsill. It displayed the camera feed from Aly's room—even now, I couldn't stop watching her. She'd just exited the bathroom, finishing her second shower of the morning, a towel wrapped around that luscious body.

She'd been so out of it after coming that I'd had to help her into said shower, supporting her weight with one arm while turning the water on with the other. I'd petted and praised her while we waited for it to heat up, hating that I had to abandon her there and couldn't climb in with her because of my mask. I was hoping to make up for that desertion with breakfast.

She refastened the towel around herself, and the urge to storm in there and rip it off was strong, but I knew firsthand the break your body needed after an edging like the one I'd just given her, so I shoved my need down and was just about to go back to cooking when I noticed the sly look on her face.

What are you up to, baby? I wondered as she paced over to her purse and pulled out a small brown box.

She tiptoed toward her door and gently shut it before turning the lock into place. Had she already forgotten about the camera? Or did she think I wasn't watching her through it because I was only on the other side of the door? If it was the latter, she'd clearly underestimated my obsession.

I absently stirred her eggs as I watched her open the box and turn it upside down, something silver—she was too far from the camera for me to make out what it was—dropping into her hand. She pressed the object like she was turning it on, then walked right over to the backpack I'd left propped on her armchair and shoved it deep inside the front pocket.

The self-satisfied grin on her face when she turned back toward the camera and went to unlock the door was downright diabolical. That little vixen. I was willing to bet good money Aly just put a tracking device in my bag.

Oh, this was going to be so much fun. I knew she'd be a worthy adversary in the game we played, and I was proud that she'd risen to the challenge so quickly. But what to do about her little spy device? I could put it in a plastic baggie and drop it into a river. Tie it to a subway rat and let her think her stalker lived underground like the mole people rumored to dwell below the city. Or I could—

Oh, fuck, there went her towel. Aly was naked. Aly was no less than thirty feet away from me. Naked.

My chest heaved as I sucked in a breath. All the blood in my body went rushing straight to my dick, and I was instantly hard again. And also kind of lightheaded. Goddamn, I needed a bigger screen than my phone to fully appreciate the sight of her in all her glory. Sure, I'd seen her like this less than half an hour ago and much more up close and personal, but her room had been darker, and seeing her swathed in shadows couldn't compare to the way the rising sun limned her form in golden light. She looked like a goddess straight from the pantheon of our ancestors, curvaceous and strong, like she'd be equally at home in an Olympic stadium or lounging on an Ionian beach.

The bacon popped, startling me, and I looked down to see it sliding past perfection and into the realm of fricasseed. I scooped it onto a paper towel-lined plate. Aly's eggs were ready, too, and I'd had about enough of this separation, so I scraped them onto another plate beside the orange slices and toast I'd already prepared, grabbed a fork, and headed into her room with everything.

She was pulling on a pair of blue and white striped pajamas when I pushed the door open, and seeing the breasts I'd so recently branded with my cock disappear behind her top was akin to watching my favorite bar burn to the ground. She should be naked. Always. I'd have to find some way to spirit her away to a cabin in the woods and then hide all her clothes. I'd make sure there was the odd blanket she could wrap herself in, and I'd stoke the woodstove until it was sweltering inside so she wasn't cold. That way, she might not be too mad at me to participate in all the fun things we could do throughout a long, naked weekend.

Yes. It sounded like a most excellent plan.

"Is that for me?" Aly asked.

I shook my head. "Absolutely not. I brought it in here to eat in front of you while mocking your hunger."

Her eyes narrowed. "After what you just did to me, I'm inclined to take you at your word."

I reached her in three strides and tugged her to me, holding the plate out to keep from spilling anything. I could tell she wasn't really mad by how she melted into the embrace, both arms snaking around my middle, her cheek pressed between my pecks as she nuzzled in close.

"You were perfect," I said, wrapping my arm around her shoulders and squeezing tight.

She shuddered. "I was a gross, sweaty mess. I half expected you to be gone when I got out of the shower."

I tried to drop a kiss on top of her head and nearly cursed when the voice modulator I'd glued to the inside of the mouthpiece clicked against my teeth. I needed to figure out a better setup, or this would get old real fast.

"You were beautiful," I told her. "And in the end, wasn't it worth it?"

She stepped backward out of my embrace, a brow arching. "I honestly don't know yet. I'm still trying to decide whether to beg you to never do that to me again or do it right the hell now." Her gaze slid down, landing on my crotch.

Aaand there went my cock again, right on cue. "Let me know when you figure it out," I said, ignoring the lust roaring through me, demanding I push her onto the bed, bury my dick into her hot, tight pussy, and fuck her until she forgot everyone else she'd ever been with. I wanted my name and my name only on her tongue, wanted to drink down every future cry of pleasure this woman ever made.

Fuck, I had it bad. And from the unfocused way Aly was still staring at my obvious arousal, I wasn't the only one on the brink of making another move.

I shoved her food between us. "Breakfast?"

It took her a beat to process the word and pull her gaze up to the plate. "Oh. Yeah. Thank you."

She took it from me and sat cross-legged on her rumpled bed. The bed I'd so recently pinned her to. The bed I needed to stop staring at if I had any hope of leaving this house and letting her get the sleep she so desperately needed.

I turned on my heel and went to get her bacon and chamomile tea.

Only two pieces of bacon were on the plate when I returned to the kitchen. Hadn't I made three? What the hell? Where did the missing one go? I started looking around, wondering if it slid off the plate or if I forgot to take it out of the pan. I was positive I'd made three.

The sound of crunching drew my gaze to the dining room, where Fred was holed up beneath the table with a squirrelly look in his eyes while he choked down the missing piece of bacon as fast as he could.

"You sneaky little beast," I said, ducking down to pluck it away from him. I might not know much about animals, but that amount of grease in such a small body could only end in digestive gymnastics, and I didn't think his mommy would be too happy with Daddy if she woke up to her house covered in explosive cat diarrhea.

I chucked the wayward bacon in the trash and grabbed the rest of Aly's breakfast.

"What did Fred do?" she asked when I re-entered her bedroom.

"Our angel baby did absolutely nothing wrong, and I resent the insinuation that he ever could," I said, setting the small plate of bacon beside her and handing her the tea.

She shook her head at me, but I knew she was fighting a smile from how tightly her lips pressed together.

I let out a relieved breath, glad to return to safer, more antagonistic ground. Not that I didn't want to fuck Aly—standing up, sitting down, sideways, backward, against a wall—but something was holding me back besides her need for sleep and recovery. It felt almost wrong to have sex with her before she knew the whole truth about me. Not just who I was but where I came from.

I hadn't told any romantic partners after my high school girlfriend about my dad. Hell, all my hookups and situationships ended when it felt like we were getting too close to that information. That was because I'd gone into them thinking they were short-term, but that wasn't the case with Aly. This wasn't just a kinky hookup anymore. Sometime in the past week or so, I'd begun to develop feelings for her, and though it had been a while since I'd had a real relationship, I knew that starting one on a foundation of lies was a great way to set yourself up for failure.

That didn't mean I was ready to stop toying with her yet. Our game had just gotten started, and as much as I wanted to stay here and watch her fall asleep, I was excited to make the next move and see how she reacted.

"Hey," I said, tilting her chin up to see her eyes.

Her expression softened, turning into something my traitorous mind tried to tell me was longing. "Yeah?"

"I'm gonna go so you can eat and then sleep in peace."

Her face fell, and I probably shouldn't have felt so triumphant at seeing her open disappointment, but I couldn't help it. Aly didn't want me to leave. Good. It might not have been a declaration of her undying love, but it felt like the first step toward getting there.

I leaned down and bumped my masked forehead against hers. "I meant what I said earlier. You were perfect. The hottest thing I've seen in my fucking life, and the next time I get the chance, I'm going to find some way to make you come even harder."

Her eyes flashed wide. "Is that safe?"

I chuckled. "Only one way to find out. You in?"

She let out a shaky breath and grinned up at me. "Fuck it. Yeah, I'm in."

"Good. I'll see you later, baby."

I turned to leave, but she surprised me by grabbing my hand. "Wait a second. I want to make sure it's healing okay."

"I was joking about the infection," I said.

She shot me A Look. "I know that, but I would never forgive myself if I didn't check and something went wrong."

I flinched as she tugged up the bandage and then poked and prodded the area around my wound, testing the skin and then leaning in close to inspect the stitches. "It looks okay. Have you been following the instructions I gave you?"

"Yes, ma'am," I said.

She released my hand and shook her head at me. "Then I guess you're free to go."

I snagged my backpack from her chair but paused before her on the way out to tuck a stray piece of hair behind her ear, unable to stop myself. It was impossible to have her so close and not touch her. "Take care of our son while I'm gone," I said, forcing myself away. "And don't give him any more bacon. He's had enough."

Her laughter followed me out of the room. "You are so presumptuous!"

I paused and leaned back through the doorway to have an excuse to look at her one last time, perched on her bed in her prim pajamas, balancing the food I made her in her lap, dark hair tumbling around her, sunlight streaming through the cracks in her blinds.

"Presumptuous?" I said. "Nah. I noticed how you look at me and decided not to fight your inevitable claiming."

She chucked a pillow at my head.

I laughed and ducked out of the way, pausing to say goodbye to Fred before turning off her front door camera and leaving.

I tugged my mask off as soon as I stepped outside, sucking in my first unencumbered breath in over an hour. God, it felt good to be out of that thing. I was going to scrub my face raw when I got home because, otherwise, I'd probably end up breaking out.

I pulled the hood of my jacket up to hide from Aly's view if she decided to peek out her window, then turned my back to her house and strode down the front walk, pausing to wave at her next-door neighbor, Wendy, who was out getting her mail.

Ten minutes later, I was in my car, heading back into the city. My phone was propped on the dash, showing Aly sitting in the middle of her bed beside her half-eaten breakfast while she stared intently at her open laptop, tracking me. I grinned and palmed the quarter-sized device she'd hidden in my bag. It was good that I'd been watching her, or I would have stumbled into her trap.

See, this was why you had to keep your eye on women. They were always up to no good, invading your privacy, pushing right past the boundaries you set for them, with no care for things like societal norms or laws. What next? She broke into my house?

I chuckled at my own bad joke as I turned right and drove east for several blocks before turning left. I went north for two blocks, watching my map so I knew when to make a U-turn and drive back to the street I'd turned off. I got onto it again and headed east for two more blocks, writing out the letter L before making another carefully timed left, heading north again for two blocks, and then making more lefts until I spelled out the letter O.

"What the fuck is he doing?" Aly asked, leaning close to her screen.

I was grinning so hard it hurt now. This tracker brand came with a trace on it so you could watch everywhere it went, which meant that any second now, she would realize what I was up to.

Fred jumped onto the bed beside her as I made another left, but she intercepted him before he could reach her forgotten piece of bacon.

"Does he think I'm trailing him or something?" she asked. "Is he trying to lose me?"

I made yet another left, drove for two blocks, then made a U-turn and went back down the same street I'd just come up.

"No," Aly said.

My shoulders shook as I tried to hold back my laughter.

She grabbed the edge of her laptop and shook it, startling Fred. "Don't you dare take another left."

I took another left and gunned it, cracking my window to drop her tracker onto the road, leaving her staring at what I'd spelled out for her.

"LOL?" she yelled. "LOL, you motherfucker?"

God bless the city planners who'd decided to lay these streets out in the grid pattern that made what I'd just done possible. This was, perhaps, the proudest moment of my life. If I died tomorrow, it would be with the knowledge of this one perfect prank.

Aly's head whipped up, her gaze locking onto the camera. "Damn it. He watched me while making breakfast?" She slid off the bed and stalked toward the device. "Why? I was only a room away from him. Wait. Are you watching me right now? You must be." She crouched down to look into the camera, which, in a happy coincidence, gave me a great view straight down her shirt.

Hello, boobs. I've missed you.

"I bet you're real proud of yourself right now, Josh," Aly said.

I jerked my gaze back up to hers. Uh-oh.

"You think I don't know who you are, but I do," she said, looking furious. "None of your bullshit threw me off. In fact, it did nothing but confirm my suspicions. I tried to do this the nice way, beat you at your own game, but fuck it. You're not playing fair, so neither will I. Guess what? I plucked a few pieces of hair off your sweatshirt while rubbing your back yesterday, and if you think I'm not going to DNA test them against the bloody bandages I stashed in my freezer, you're dead-ass wrong." She winked. "Later, Boo."

The screen went black as she ripped the camera from the socket.

Well, that just happened.

Unfortunately for Aly, I'd grabbed that sweatshirt from Tyler's dirty laundry basket just in case she was as devious as I was and did something like this.

She was going to be so mad when the DNA didn't match.

I spent the rest of the drive home laughing maniacally, picturing the range of emotions that would play over her face when she realized she was either wrong or, even worse, had been outsmarted again.

13

ALY

"WHAT DO YOU MEAN IT'S going to take a week?" I said.

I was three stories up from the ER in the hospital's clinical forensic lab, calling in a favor.

Veronica, a whip-smart Latina lab tech with flaming pink hair, held up the two baggies I'd brought her. "You gave me three pieces of hair that may or may not have viable roots and some bloody rags. This isn't like a fully automated paternity test that I can bang out in an hour, Aly. I have to follow a whole process of purification, quantitation, amplification, and capillary electrophoresis if you want the results to be accurate, and I'll be squeezing you in between my other work." She set the baggies on her counter and shot me a deadpan look. "You might have noticed; I have a *lot* of other work."

I grimaced, knowing exactly how many thousands of hours our lab was overbooked. Vern and her coworkers had an entire backlog of evidence to process, including rape kits. I suddenly felt like an asshole for jumping the line, but I honestly didn't realize how much work it would be for her. I thought she could pop my samples into a machine, and, *beep-boop*, I'd get my results.

I reached for the baggies. No way in hell could I put my desire to one-up Josh above identifying someone's rapist. "I changed my mind. Forget I asked."

Vern slapped my hand away. Her pinup-girl makeup was flawless tonight, and one perfectly arched brow climbed even higher as she eyed me. "Too late. I'm intrigued now. You want to tell me what this is all about?"

"Let's just say it involves a boy I like," I said.

Both brows went up. "You think he's running around behind your back? I heard Greg down in the janitorial department has mob ties. Maybe he can disappear him for you."

I forced a laugh, trying to act natural. Greg was a lanky Irish-Italian guy with black hair and freckles. He had a baby face but was also a relentless flirt, and he'd lured Vern in at the holiday party. He was also, most definitely, in the mob.

Vern and I got along in a way that made me feel like we could be besties if we had any free time for things like friends. I'd only seen her a handful of times over the past month, but I knew she had it bad for Greg because she'd found a way to bring him up at least once in each conversation. Which meant I needed to figure out a way to ruin her crush. Immediately. Vern was a good person; she didn't need to be associating with lowlifes.

"Greg?" I said. "Mallory told me he cheated on his last three girlfriends."

Vern grimaced. "Seriously?"

"Yes. And bragged about it."

"Ew. Never mind then," she said, dragging the bag of bandages toward her.

"Vern, no. I can't ask you to do this for me." I tried to slide my hand under hers to get my samples, but she scooped them up and held them behind her back.

She gave me a stern look. "I said it's too late. I'm invested now. And wipe that guilty look off your face. I'll run the tests during my breaks, so you won't feel like you're line jumping."

I scrunched my nose up. "But then I'll be taking away your breaks."

"Aly," she said, gripping my arm with her free hand. "It's okay to be selfish once in a while. You know that, right?"

"Yes?" I said, fighting the urge to squirm beneath her gaze.

She shook my arm. "Once more with conviction."

"Yes," I repeated. It still sounded more like a question than a statement.

Vern released me and huffed out a breath. "You trauma nurses and your bleeding hearts." She turned away to hit a button on a machine, and I was contemplating snagging the baggies and running when she spun back around and caught me with my hand outstretched. The unimpressed look she gave me spoke volumes. "That's it. Get out."

I sheepishly made my way toward the door. "Thank you."

"Yeah, yeah. I'll let you know when I have the results," she said, waving me away.

I left the lab feeling oddly deflated and more than a little guilty. Yes, I wanted the results, but I didn't like that I was taking time from Vern. I knew how sacred breaks were when you were overworked, and the forensic lab was as short-staffed as the nurses.

My phone pinged in my pocket as I made my way back downstairs. I knew without looking that it would be Josh, and I was hesitant to check the text in public in case he'd said something especially incendiary. The man had a way of needling me that led to expletives spewing from my mouth, and I didn't want to offend anyone who might overhear me.

I whipped my phone out of my pocket the second I stepped inside the breakroom. Yup. It was Josh.

On a scale of 1–10, how mad are you about the tracker? he asked. *One being you need a day or two to cool off, and ten being we need to start drafting a joint custody agreement for Fred.*

And just like that, I was grinning. I had no idea how he kept doing this to me: pissing me off one second and making me want to burst out laughing the next. I'd never met anyone quite like him, and his personality was addicting because of it. It didn't take much imagination to picture life with him, going home after a horrible shift and having him find some way to turn my tears into laughter.

I'm at a 3, I wrote back. *As in, I think I need a few days to regroup and form my next plan of attack.*

Lie. What I really needed was time to talk myself out of the feelings I was starting to develop for this man. A kinky hookup? Fine. That was allowed. We all had one-night stands with strangers. But to want more from the man who had a) broken into my house, b) broken into my car, and c) was actively stalking me had to be the height of stupidity.

Only I didn't feel like an idiot. I felt . . . right. He'd had countless opportunities to harm me, and he hadn't. All he'd done so far was make my life better. Food, shoveling, rides home when I was too tired to drive, security updates, the best orgasm of my life. Sure, he drove me up a wall half the time and couldn't cook for shit—the bacon was still raw in the middle, and I stopped eating the eggs after picking the third piece of shell out of my mouth—but no man was perfect.

I feared that I was getting too attached too quickly. It had only been a few days since he'd broken in the first time, but I'd spent almost every free moment since either obsessing over him or in his presence. If my disappointment at getting home yesterday and not finding him there was anything to go by, this man had the potential to hurt my feelings. I blamed all the time I'd spent obsessing over his videos. It made it feel like he'd been a part of my life for much longer than he actually had, like we'd been in a strange, one-sided sexual relationship since before Halloween.

Now I understood the female leads from all the sports romances I'd read. No wonder they were saying "I love you" by the halfway mark—their feelings for their famous counterparts had started months, sometimes years before they had their meet-cutes.

I snorted, remembering my own not-so-meet-cute, unable to keep from imagining someone years from now asking how Josh and I met. Somehow, I didn't think "He broke into my car at three o'clock in the morning and waited there for me with a gun and a knife" would be the answer they anticipated, even if I added the part about the seat heater and the snacks.

My phone pinged, and I looked down to see another text.

I'm sorry if I went too far, he said. *Both with the "LOL" and earlier.*

Great. Now he was worried he'd crossed a line and either offended me or pushed me into doing something sexually that I hadn't been ready for. This was what I got for being evasive.

I took a deep breath and started typing, pulling on my metaphorical big-girl panties. *You don't have to apologize, and you didn't go too far. I'm just trying to protect myself.*

I would never hurt you, Aly, he wrote back.

I sighed. Why did he have to be so sweet? My stupid, fragile, love-starved heart wasn't great at self-preservation to begin with, and this man was shredding what few defenses I'd erected around it.

Maybe not intentionally, I said. *But I've been watching you a lot longer than you've been watching me, and I'm worried*—Fuck. How did I say this without giving too much away?—*that this is only kink fulfillment to you.*

It's not, he said. *Watch my video later. Take some time if you need it. But Aly?*

Yeah?

I'm only willing to allow you a few days. After that, I'm coming for you, baby, whether you're ready or not. And until then, I'll be watching.

Well, that wasn't ominous or anything. And definitely not the hottest thing I'd ever read in my life. My panties were soaked not because of how achingly turned on I was but because I'd developed sudden onset incontinence, and that was the story I was sticking to.

Not knowing how to respond to Josh's sendoff, I set my phone in my locker and backed away like I'd just stowed a bomb in there. Of course, that's when Tanya walked in.

"You doing okay, Aly?" She stood halfway inside, arm outstretched as she held the door open, glancing warily between me and my locker. "You didn't leave Indian food in there again, did you?"

"No, I didn't," I said. "And that was one time!"

She stepped inside, letting the door close behind her. "Yeah, but that one time was enough to clear the whole floor. Four days, Aly. Four days of rotting curry in the middle of summer, the week the A/C was acting up. We sent Seth in here dressed in full PPE to dispose of it." She shuddered. "He still has nightmares."

I shook my head at her, oddly grateful for the familiar ribbing and the distraction it provided. "I'll pay for his next therapy session."

She strode toward the coffee maker. "Our therapy is free."

"Yeah, well, I'll buy him some wine," I said, joining her.

Technically, our shift didn't start for another half an hour, but Tanya and I always came in early to get the lay of the land. We chatted for a few minutes, catching up on life—mostly hers, as she actually had one with a husband and kids—before heading to the nurses' station to get the gossip from the day and learn which patients we'd be inheriting.

Josh's parting words kept repeating themselves in the back of my mind, and it wasn't until someone poked me in the ribs and asked if I was listening that I realized I'd been zoning out. Yup, I had it bad. Hopefully, I'd figure out some way to guard my heart in the next few days.

Several hours later, my hope went up in flames as I watched his latest video. It was darker than his others, not just in lighting but tone, with lyricless, haunting music playing in the background. He was shirtless in it, and the video opened with him grabbing the phone like he'd just wrapped his hand around someone's throat—my throat—before a pan transition revealed him rising over the screen, one hand braced somewhere overhead, his dark jeans unbuttoned as he reached into them like he was getting ready to pull out his dick—and fuck it straight into my tits again. The camera panned once more, showing him lying on his side, one hand propping his head up, the other disappearing offscreen, forearm flexing deliciously as he pumped his arm like he was fucking that vibrator into me again.

This was the most overtly sexual video he'd ever posted, and watching him recreate what we'd done this morning made me fucking desperate for round two. What a devious bastard. *Sure, take your time, Aly, but I'm going to torture you with my absence until you come to your senses.* It made me want to be bratty again, hold out until his patience snapped and he hunted me down.

Oh, fuck, that sounded like a good plan. Yes, I was definitely going to do that. And . . . wait. His video had another caption.

I nearly dropped the phone when I read it, my laughter so instantaneous that I choked on air. It said: *Mommy and Daddy time*. How? *How* was he able to be so fucking hot and funny at the same time? It didn't compute. Surely, one should cancel the other out, and I should either be turned on or amused and not both simultaneously.

My eyes skipped down to the comment section. It did not disappoint.

OMG is he married???

This just proves that all the good ones are taken.

I knew I'd been calling him Daddy for a reason.

@aly.aly.oxen.free GIRL, YOU WON.

Okay, but how are you going to tell your wife that this video just got me pregnant?

Are you accepting applications for a third?

If my future husband ain't like this, I don't want him.

I didn't think I wanted kids until I just pictured this man holding a baby.

I all but threw my phone into my locker. No. Nope. I did not need the image that the last comment invoked filling up my head.

Oh, god. Too late. Six-four, muscle-bound, heavily tattooed, shirtless Josh cradling a baby in his arms. I could feel my ovaries back at it again, opening the floodgates and screaming, "GO, GO, GO," as they released every single egg in my body. If I had sex with this man in the near future, we'd have to double up on birth control.

My pager went off, and I was glad for the excuse to get out of there before the next kink I developed was a breeding one.

■ ■ ■

The next several days seemed to both fly by and drag, making me feel like I was in a time warp. Going back to my usual routine was weird, even though I hadn't been out of it for that long. I half expected Josh not to honor my request for space, but the time stamps on my security cameras didn't show any gaps indicating he'd hacked them and broken in again, and other than the pining video he posted halfway through my shift Thursday night, complete with a sad '80s hairband soundtrack, he hadn't tried to contact me.

The comments on the video were priceless, with many wondering if Mommy and Daddy were fighting again. I'd gotten almost ten thousand follow requests since Josh had "claimed" me, which spoke volumes about the kind of pull he had online. No wonder he had such a big ego. All that power had gone to his head.

"Hey," I said as I joined Tanya, Brinley, and a few other coworkers at the nurses' station. Usually, I spent my downtime in the breakroom chugging coffee, but I didn't trust myself near my phone right now.

A chorus of greetings welcomed me into the fold. We were midway through a late-night lull, but we'd pick up soon once the bars let out and all the football fans hit the streets. Our city's team had made it to the final round of playoffs, and after games ended, we got an influx of shitfaced men who'd hurt themselves trying to flip cars or climb light poles.

The nurses' station faced our fast-track area, where we had six narrow, open bay rooms, almost like stalls. It's where we put patients with minor injuries and illnesses like sprains, fractures, lacerations, and sore throats. Three were occupied, but only two of the patients were being seen. The third bay contained an average-looking white man with light brown hair. He had one of those faces that were ambiguous, like he could have been anywhere from his early twenties to late thirties, and he'd blend in well in a crowd. Still, he looked vaguely familiar, but I couldn't place him. His shoulders were broad like he worked out, so maybe he went to my gym?

"What's up with that guy?" I asked. It looked like he'd gotten into a fight, with one eye quickly swelling shut and a split lip. He held gauze to his forehead, no doubt putting pressure on a cut there. Someone should be helping him with that.

Tanya leaned in close, her voice low. "That's the rapist from the other night."

It felt like she'd dumped ice water over my head. I jerked my gaze from the guy, not wanting to make eye contact if he turned our way. "Why isn't he in jail?" I asked. "Didn't he get caught in the act?"

It was Deb, a white woman in her mid-fifties and the most senior nurse on shift tonight, who answered. "He didn't even get arrested. Some hotshot lawyer showed up before we could swab him, and he walked out of here scot-free an hour later." She shook her head in disgust, her shoulder-length gray hair swaying with the motion.

I gripped the edge of the nurses' desk to steady myself. "How. The fuck?" I couldn't get any other words out. Felt like I was choking on the anger that threatened to bubble up.

Brinley let out a sound like an angry cat, and I felt better knowing I wasn't the only one on the brink of going nuclear. "His family is loaded. The lawyer threatened to sue the shit out of the hospital and the cops for trying to coerce a DNA test out of him."

"But he got caught in the act," Erica, another junior nurse, said. "Why do they need DNA to arrest him?"

"Maybe because there was no video evidence?" someone said.

"Yeah, but the cops brought him in here," another answered. "And the victim and a separate witness both identified him."

We got into a heated whisper-debate about what happened that night, each of us sharing the knowledge we'd gleaned from the cops, hospital admin, and our own late-night Google searches and crime show binges. But none of us had law degrees, so it was all speculation, and in the end, we only had more questions than the answers we'd been after.

"Okay, but why is he here?" I asked once we'd calmed down.

Erica clicked the computer mouse and leaned in to read the screen. "One of the victim's brothers tracked him down in a bar after seeing a Snapchat."

I shook my head. "No. I mean, why is he still here? The faster we treat him, the faster we can send him back out so the brother can finish him off."

"No one wants to help him," Tanya said.

I glanced around the station. All women. Usually, we had several male coworkers on each shift as patients sometimes had preferences for whom they wanted to treat them.

"It's only Amit on shift right now," Brinley said, catching my confusion. "Zach called in sick, and Kevin won't be in for another hour."

Amit was a squat, barrel-chested Indian-American man in his early thirties who could deadlift twice his body weight. He was great with our "problem patients" because they usually took one look at his straining muscles and thought better of their bad behavior.

Tanya leaned over the station desk to grab a clipboard off it. "We're waiting for him to get done in room three, and then we're sending him over."

I shook my head. That would be a while. The patient in three was barely stable.

"I'll do it," I said.

Brinley sucked in a breath.

Tanya grabbed my arm. "Aly, no."

I pulled out of her grip and turned to face my coworkers. "I'll be fine. You guys can see me, and yesterday, I learned how to punch in someone's windpipe in my martial arts class." I grinned, wrapping myself in false bravado. "Maybe I'll get a chance to test it out."

Tanya didn't look convinced. "I'm coming with you."

I held up a hand, halting her when she made to take a step toward me. Tanya never treated sexual predators. Ever. There was a reason for her reticence that she'd only hinted at before, but it was enough for me to get the gist, and I'd be damned if that man got a chance to retraumatize her by saying or doing something terrible in her presence.

"I got this," I said.

A line formed between Tanya's brows as she frowned at me, and her dark eyes looked troubled. "You'll step away if he gets inappropriate and let Amit handle him."

I nodded. It wasn't a question from my friend but an order from a superior.

She eyed me for a long moment before blowing out a breath. "Fine. But we're watching."

"Good," I said, turning on my heel, glad I had backup ready to intervene.

The phone started ringing as I walked away, and I heard Erica answer it. "Wait, come back! There's a man on the line for you!"

"Tell him I'm fine," I called over my shoulder.

Josh must have hacked into the hospital again and saw what I was about to do. I almost smiled. He said he'd be watching me, but it was nice to have it confirmed. It was like having my very own guardian angel keeping tabs on my welfare, and it made me feel safe in a way that not even the hoard of coworkers at my back did.

I was sure I would have been okay, even without such close supervision. The man I was about to treat wasn't even the worst I'd ever seen. Something most "civilians" didn't realize was that when people in jail got hurt or sick, they went to the hospital just like everyone else. Last year, I'd treated a man with a stab wound who'd been convicted of brutally murdering two women. He'd been strapped to the bed, and there were two correctional officers in the room with me the whole time I'd seen him, but I still felt unsafe in his presence.

I would never forget the look in his eyes when he'd caught sight of me. It was inhuman, something I'd never seen before that was somehow completely dead and feverishly alive at the same time. He looked like he was starving, but not for food. It was the gnawing kind of starvation that hollowed you out until all that was left was the hunger.

The second I'd stepped out of his room, I'd turned toward the cop guarding the door and told him I didn't think that man had only killed two women. The cop looked me dead in the eye and said, "Neither do we."

I had nightmares for weeks afterward.

Nothing could get worse than that man, I thought. But as I approached the accused rapist and he turned to look at me, I wondered if I was about to be proven wrong.

Up close, he had the same eyes as the suspected serial killer, even though his were brown and the murderer's had been blue. They were dead and alive and wholly inhuman. I knew with certainty that I was looking into the eyes of a predator, the eyes of someone who didn't see me as a being with agency of my own but as a plaything put on this earth for their entertainment. It made me want to crawl out of my skin, but I pulled my professional façade on and brandished it like a shield. The faster I treated him and sent him on his way, the better.

I skipped the usual pleasantries and got straight to business, giving the bed he reclined on a wide berth as I went to the pulse oximeter, keeping myself half turned toward him so if he tried to make a move, I'd see it coming.

"Hello, I'm treating you tonight," I said, with almost no inflection because fuck him.

"And your name would be?" he asked, his voice low and pleasant and all the more unnerving because of who it was coming out of.

"Nurse Hanover," I said. It was the generic name we gave patients when we didn't feel comfortable offering them our real ones, and it would even go on his discharge paperwork when he was released, so he couldn't track me down afterward. We'd had a few incidents after patients found their nurses outside of work, one of which ended very badly, and now the hospital did its best to try to protect us.

"Do you have a first name?" he asked, a teasing note in his voice.

"Nope," I shot back. "Just Hanover. Like Madonna or Cher."

He chuckled, and the sound made me want to puke. Because it was infectious. If I'd heard it in a bar, I would have turned to see who was laughing, and it made me think of how charming some people with personality disorders could be.

I lifted the pulse reader from the machine and asked him to hold out his finger, careful not to touch him when I clamped it on. I let it work its magic, stepping away to pull his chart up on the nearby computer. Amit's name was on it, so he must have been the one to settle this creep in before getting called away to help the patient in room three.

The rapist's name was Bradley Bluhm, and if he was of any relation to the Bluhms that one of the tallest skyscrapers in the city was named after, he didn't just come from money; his family was worth billions. No wonder they found some way to bribe, coerce, or pay for him to avoid arrest. Laws didn't apply to the uber-rich, only to those without the money or means to subvert them.

Brad's chart told me he'd probably need stitches on his forehead and an X-ray of his ribs, but I still had to ask him what happened and get him to describe his injuries. I really didn't want to, so I clicked around on the computer for a while longer as the heart monitor pinged out a slow, steady rhythm. The bastard was staring straight at me. Hadn't stopped since I'd approached. I could see him turned my way out of the corner of my eye and feel his gaze tracing over me like it was corporeal.

Your coworkers are watching you, I told myself. *Josh is watching you. If he was so unhinged when a couple of strange men catcalled you, just imagine what he'll do if this guy lays hands on you.*

The thought almost made me smile. It wasn't that I needed a big, strong man to protect me or fight my battles—I'd kick-flipped a dude fifty pounds heavier than I was halfway across a judo mat yesterday afternoon—but it was nice to know that Josh was more than willing to. Part of me almost hoped that Brad tried something so I could learn how far Josh would go, and how far I'd be ready to go with him, because if he went after Brad, there was no way I wouldn't be along for the ride.

I stepped away from the computer and wheeled over the sphygmomanometer. "Can you hold out your arm? I need to take your blood pressure."

Brad leaned forward, trying to meet my gaze, but I avoided it. I had a habit of wearing my emotions for everyone to see, and I didn't want this piece of shit to learn just how much I both feared and reviled him. The fear wasn't because of what he might do to me; it was more from knowing that people like him lived and walked amongst everyone else—ones who were so broken inside that no amount of therapy or medication would ever make them "safe" for the rest of us. People like Bundy and Kemper and that one handsome guy from the recent Netflix documentary my coworkers kept talking about. What was his stupid nickname? The Ken Doll Killer?

"You seem uncomfortable," Brad said, voice low and cajoling as I wrapped the pressure cuff around his bicep. I noted the healing scratches on his arm and wondered if the cops had been able to photograph them. "Is this about the unfortunate mix-up from the other night?"

I kept my mouth shut, tightening the cuff more than necessary before stepping away and turning the machine on. Mix-up. The fucking *nerve* of this piece of shit.

"I know how it must look," Brad said, his tone almost bashful. "But if I'd really done what they said, wouldn't I be in jail right now?"

I didn't respond, refusing to be goaded by him. Instead, I clenched my jaw and half turned away to watch the machines. His pulse was steady at 61 beats per minute, and his blood pressure read a healthy 115/70. The fact that even his readings showed a man at ease made me want to scream. He wasn't nervous or elevated while discussing raping someone, which told me that he was either incapable of emotions like empathy or the woman from the other night wasn't his first victim. Part of me worried both were true.

I girded myself as I pulled his cuff off, trying to keep my breath steady while my heart beat nearly double the rate of his, and my blood pressure went through the roof.

"I'll need to look at your head before you're wheeled down to radiology for your ribs," I said.

"Oh, of course. I'd make that joke about how the other guy was worse, but that would be a lie," he said with a self-deprecating laugh.

The hair on the back of my neck stood on end. Despite my repulsion, I could see how someone might be charmed by him. But my lizard brain wasn't buying it. It was screaming at me to get away from Brad as fast as I could.

I took my time pushing the machines back into the corner, trying to gather my unraveling resolve to treat him.

"Did my chart tell you what happened?" he asked, not pausing long enough for me to get an answer out. "That man stalked me through social media so he could attack me from behind in a bar. Good thing there were so many witnesses, and the cops were close enough to make a quick arrest."

I said absolutely nothing again, but inside I was seething. How fucked was our justice system that a devastated family member sat in jail while a rapist walked free?

I couldn't take much more of this, but maybe if I stayed quiet long enough, Brad would get the hint and shut up. I sure as shit wasn't about to argue with a potential psychopath or play into whatever false narrative he was creating for himself.

Unfortunately, this monster was a chatty one.

Brad leaned toward me, attempting to catch my eye. "I tried to tell him it was a misunderstanding, and his sister had been more than willing, but he wouldn't listen."

My ears rang as my temper started to get away from me. From the amount of ketamine we'd found in her system, Brad's victim wasn't anywhere near being able to consent, if she was even conscious at the time.

Just do your job and get out, I told myself, pulling on a fresh pair of nitrile gloves.

"But I come from the kind of family that sees attacks like this all the time," Brad said. "You'd be amazed at the things people do looking for a payout."

Don't, I told myself. *Do not rise to the bait.* A response was clearly what he was after.

I kept my eyes trained on a small riser of shelves as I strode past the foot of Brad's bed, careful not to let him out of my periphery. My pulse was pounding in my ears, and I had so much adrenaline sluicing through my veins that I was starting to tremble. I could do this. I just had to clean his head and call an orderly to take him downstairs for his X-rays. After that, it would be a doctor's responsibility to stitch him up.

I glanced at the nurses' station to see Erica and Tanya standing behind it, watching me with stony expressions. Could they hear Brad all the way over there? Or was it just that they could see him talking that had them on guard? Either way, I was grateful for their vigilance. The sight of them buoyed me some, reminded me that I wasn't alone with this piece of shit.

"I should have expected something like that from her," Brad said while I pulled open the top drawer. "She wasn't exactly a high-quality woman, if you know what I mean. You think she would have been grateful for the attention of someone with my pedigree, but instead, she turned around and accused me of attacking her."

My fingers shook as I lifted the things I'd need from the drawer. Gauze. Cleaning supplies. Butterfly stitches to hold his wound closed until the doctor could see him. I focused on every single item to keep myself from turning around and punching Brad in the face. I'd never wanted to hurt someone like this before, and the violence screaming to get out of me was terrifying.

Movement caught the corner of my eye. I dodged sideways and whipped around to face Brad, who'd just tried to grab me.

A smile split his face, the charm slipping away as something cold and serpentine took its place. Damn it. I'd finally given him the reaction he wanted.

"So jumpy," he said. "You must be afraid." From the way his dick was starting to tent up his pants, he was thrilled about the possibility.

Unfortunately for him, my fear had been subverted by rage. I was so mad that I felt oddly calm as I cocked my head sideways and dropped my eyes straight to his lap.

"Afraid?" I said. "Of some shrimp-dicked spoiled brat?" I lifted my gaze back to his, knowing he would see my fury, my anticipation. "Go ahead. Try to grab me again." I stepped close to him for the first time all night, catching the smell of stale alcohol wafting off his breath. God,

I hoped he'd do it. If he touched me first, I could say I was defending myself. "I'd love to see how a coward like you holds up against a fully conscious woman."

He blinked at me, and I had just enough time to catch the triumph in his eyes before he scrunched his face in mock fear and started wailing. "Help! Help! This nurse just threatened me!"

I took a hasty step away, cursing myself for letting him manipulate me.

Several people came running in at Brad's continued outbursts, including Ben, one of our security guards.

"You okay, Aly?" he asked, and I almost swore at him for using my name.

"I'm fine," I said.

"Why are you asking her?" Brad whined, all evidence of the monster I'd just met gone, replaced by the spitting image of the spoiled brat I'd accused him of being. "I'm the one she threatened."

"We're not doing this again, Mr. Bluhm," Ben said, approaching Brad's bed.

Again? Had Brad pulled something like this the other night? Is that how he'd gotten out of here? Fuck. Had I just given his lawyers another excuse to target the hospital?

"I want my lawyer!" he yelled, right on cue. "And I want that one to treat me instead." He pointed straight at Erica, who'd rushed in with Tanya to help.

Thin, petite Erica, who I noted had the same build and dark hair as the woman Brad had assaulted. Oh, hell fuck no. Was this his plan all along? Replace me with his ideal victim so he could torment her instead, or worse, try to find out who she was so he could attack her next?

"Nope," I said, turning Erica around and marching her away while everyone else dealt with the shrieking rapist.

Tanya found us around the bend in the hall a few minutes later. "What did he say to you?"

I leaned against the wall and tilted my head back, trying to get myself under control. "Some bullshit about how his victim should have been thanking him for deigning to lay with such a low-quality woman."

"But . . . that's—what?" Erica sputtered.

"He's fucking crazy," I told her. "And I'm not being ableist. I mean that clinically. I might not be a therapist, but there is no way that man doesn't have ASPD." I shifted my gaze to Tanya. "He was just like that guy from last year."

Her eyes widened. "The murderer?"

I nodded.

She looked away from me as a plump white woman in her early thirties joined us. Uh-oh. Someone had called HR.

"Hey, Aly," Hannah said as she reached us. "You want to come to my office and tell me what happened?"

I sighed and pushed off the wall. Technically, I hadn't broken any major rules, though I'd probably get a slap on the wrist for the shrimp-dick comment and the taunting. "Sure, lead the way."

An hour later, Brad had been discharged, and I was back on the ER floor, ready for my next patient. Hannah had given me an unofficial warning and very kindly told me to watch my mouth while also insinuating that had she been in my shoes, she would have stabbed Brad with the nearest sharp object.

Hannah was good people.

I felt like I'd faced the worst of the night and came out mostly unscathed on the other side. That was until I got called to the ambulance bay to help with a car accident victim. These were always rough for me because of my past, but tonight proved to be my undoing.

The victim was a woman in her mid-fifties with dark hair and olive skin. Like my mom. And just like my mom, she'd been impaled by something on impact, only instead of the pipe that had plunged straight into Mom's chest, this woman had an unidentifiable, thin piece of metal sticking out from her right shoulder. She would survive where Mom hadn't, and though I told myself that it wasn't her, all I could see was Mom looking at me from the passenger seat, blood pouring from her mouth as she tried to speak.

"I can't," I said, backing away from the gurney while one of my coworkers rushed in to take my place. "I can't."

I was sixteen again, sitting uselessly beside my mother as she died, my hands covered in her blood while I tried to staunch the flow, the broken car horn drowning out my cries for somebody, anybody, to help us.

14

JOSH

SOMETHING WAS WRONG WITH ALY. Something was *really* wrong with her.

I paced in front of my computer desk, unable to sit still any longer. She was grabbing her things out of her locker, and to anyone who didn't know her well, she probably seemed fine. But I knew her. At least I knew her expressions, and right now, her face was wooden. It was like someone had sucked all the life out of her, leaving her shell behind to go through the motions.

Was it something that rapist said to her? The stupid cameras in the ER didn't have microphones, and I couldn't hear the conversation, but I knew from Aly's face that it must have been ugly, especially at the end when he'd almost grabbed her.

I didn't know what I would have done if he'd succeeded in touching her. It was bad enough knowing Aly was in the presence of such a bastard. I'd pulled up his file as she headed his way, and what I'd seen had sent me scrambling for the phone. She'd asked for space, but surely that didn't extend to warning her of impending danger?

My jaw still hurt from how hard I'd ground my teeth together after she told the nurse on the line to tell me she was fine.

I could tell the second she caught sight of the rapist that Aly wasn't "fine." She'd been scared. And not the kind of scared I liked—the brief kind that was quickly replaced by lust—but a bone-deep fear that drained the color from her face. I understood why when I zoomed in on Bradley Bluhm. He had the same eyes as my father, and Aly, used to working in such a dangerous environment, was probably better than most at recognizing monsters and realized she was in the presence of one.

For a moment, it made me feel marginally better that she'd never looked at me that way, but then the gut-punch realization hit that she was within touching distance of someone like that, and I'd been on my feet with my keys in my hand before I could think better of it. I was halfway to my car when I got ahold of myself. Driving down there and barging into an ER wearing a horror movie–inspired mask wasn't the move. I'd get arrested or probably shot. And as much as I wanted to go to her, going as myself pulled me up short. I wasn't ready for our game to end yet.

Fuck. That wasn't entirely true. No, what stopped me was the potential fallout when I told Aly everything about myself. There was a real chance she'd bail, and I'd just gotten my hands on her. I wasn't ready to give her up so soon.

I returned to my room and planted my butt in front of my computer, reminding myself that Aly was a badass. I'd watched her kick the shit out of a dude almost twice her size yesterday. She was a good fighter: fast, bold, borderline reckless. And from the smile on her face, she liked fighting. I was certain she could defend herself against someone like Brad, especially because men like him were fucking cowards. At their cores, they feared women as much as they hated them. There were countless stories about people like Bundy and the Night Stalker and even my dad running away when their intended victims fought back and started to get the upper hand.

Aly had various objects around her that could double as weapons and plenty of people who could rush in to help. She would be okay.

I thought that right until Brad opened his mouth, and Aly's jaw jumped like she'd bitten back a retort. What had he said? I leaned forward, lasered in on Brad's face, trying to read his lips, wanting to knock the smarmy grin off his mouth. His gaze was as glued to Aly as mine was to him, trailing over her from head to toe in a covetous way that brought out my inner caveman.

"Punch him in the face," I told an unhearing Aly.

"Bash his head against that glass panel."

"Oh, no, you're right. It'd be much better to strangle him with the cord of that machine you're reaching for."

Unfortunately, she did none of those things. And she didn't look directly at Brad either, not after that first glimpse. He must have truly unnerved her.

She crossed the foot of his bed, and I got a good view of her face. Nope. She wasn't unnerved; she was fucking livid. What was that piece of shit saying to her?

"Look out!" I yelled as he reached for her. If that motherfucker hurt her, it would be one of the last things he ever did.

She easily dodged him, but instead of stepping away, she got close, wearing an expression I'd never seen before. It was almost serene, but her eyes burned like she was trying to set Brad on fire with her gaze. She looked slightly deranged, so of course, my dick chose that moment to enter the conversation. I didn't even try to stop my body's reaction to Scary Aly because, goddamn, watching her go full bad bitch on Brad was fucking hot. If she actually hit him, I might come.

Unfortunately, she didn't get a chance. Proving my point about cowards, Brad screwed up his face and started screaming, probably for help, the manipulative little shit.

I opened a new window in my browser and started pulling up everything I could find on the guy, and now, five hours later, I'd come to a conclusion: Bradley Bluhm needed to die. The sooner, the better.

I'd figure out the logistics of that when I had more free time. Right now, Aly needed me.

Despite what went down between her and Brad, I didn't think he was the one to put her in her current mood. She'd been pissed, but from what I'd seen, recovered pretty well. Even the dressing down she got in that HR woman's office hadn't looked too bad.

I'd turned away when they started laughing and got lost in my research. Had something else happened to Aly while I'd been distracted? I'd checked in on her here and there throughout the rest of her shift, and she'd seemed okay, if a little muted. Was her shutting down now a delayed response to the ugly interaction with Brad, or was my gut right, and I'd missed something?

Not knowing was driving me bugfuck.

I scooped my phone from the desk and texted Aly, unable to help myself. *Please don't drive home like this. I know you said you needed space, but let me come and get you. Or at least take an Uber.*

Onscreen, she checked her phone, staring at it woodenly. I didn't like this.

I'm taking an Uber, she wrote back, with none of her usual vitriol about me watching her. Maybe she'd finally accepted my continuous oversight, but I didn't think that would keep her from ribbing me under normal circumstances.

One of her coworkers, a trim Black woman I'd seen Aly chat with so often that they must have been good friends, put an arm around Aly's shoulders and spoke to her. I wished I could hear what she said. Her expression was full of understanding and empathy. Had Aly lost a patient while I'd been learning about Brad's past crimes? I knew that hit her especially hard.

Their conversation was brief, ending in a long hug. Aly turned from her coworker afterward and headed toward the door. I used the cameras to follow her the whole way out of the hospital, and by the time her Uber started to pull away from a side door, I'd made up my mind. I was done with space. I'd given Aly the days she asked for, stopping myself every time I picked up the phone to text her.

I'd hoped our reunion would be sexual in nature, but she clearly shouldn't be alone right now, and despite the fact that I was still hard, sex was the last thing on my mind. She needed comfort, companionship. Someone to listen to her or hold her while she cried.

I left my mask behind in favor of a balaclava. I had a feeling it would be a long morning, and I didn't want to be stuck inside a plastic shell the entire time.

Tyler would be up soon, so I texted him about needing to get out of the apartment, grabbed my keys and backpack, and headed out.

For the first time since I'd started watching her, Aly left the hospital when she was supposed to, so the sun wasn't up yet, and I had the roads almost entirely to myself. Even so, she lived closer to the hospital than I did to her, and her front door camera showed her beating me there by several minutes.

I parked around the corner, out of sight, and doubled back on foot. It was freezing. The news had warned that we were in for a polar vortex, but this was the first one of the year, and I'd forgotten just how cold it could get. My breath hung in the air around me, and although I didn't need it yet, I pulled on my balaclava to keep the frost from my skin. Fuck this weather.

I didn't bother turning Aly's cameras off since my face was covered, and I didn't bother knocking either, using the key I'd made to let myself in the front door. Fred came running right up to me, his tail held high and mouth wide open as he sang me the song of his people.

I shrugged out of my jacket and scooped him off the floor before heading into the house. "We need to work on your social skills, buddy. Imagine if Mommy and Daddy acted like you and ran in here screaming every time we got home."

The sound of my voice brought me up short. My *unmodulated* voice. Shit. In my haste to leave the apartment, I'd forgotten the modulator was stitched into my mask. What a rookie move. I wasn't going back to get it—now that I was here, only Aly ordering me to leave would get me out—so I'd have to find some other way to talk to her because I was done with the texting thing, and I was pretty sure she was, too.

As I approached Aly's room, I heard her shower running. I had a few minutes.

"How's this?" I asked a purring Fred, dropping my voice as low as I comfortably could. "I am Batman."

Fred half-slitted his eyes and dug his claws into my jacket, kneading it, so I assumed he approved.

I nuzzled him through the face mask and set him back down as I made a beeline toward the kitchen. Some people lost their appetite when upset, so I didn't want to make Aly another elaborate breakfast only to have it go to waste. I especially didn't love the idea of frying more bacon. It brought up memories of when Dad got an ingenious idea for how to dispose of his latest victim during a now infamous Fourth of July neighborhood cookout. I've been vegan since, and even now, almost twenty years later, the smell of sizzling meat still made me want to puke.

What might Aly want instead of food? Wine, or maybe a nice soothing tea? I'd get both ready. That way, she would have her choice.

The shower cut off shortly after the tea finished steeping, and I scooped the mug and wine up and headed toward her bedroom. She was dressed in a thick white bathrobe, combing her hair with her back to me when I walked in.

"I didn't know what you wanted, so I brought—ARGH!"

She whipped around and threw the brush at my head, and I burned the shit out of my hand with scalding-hot tea as I ducked it.

"Fuck!" Aly and I both yelled before speaking over each other.

"You can't just sneak up on me like that!"

"I thought you heard me."

I set the wine and tea on her bureau and turned to go rinse my scalded skin in the kitchen.

Aly was hot on my heels. "What's up with your voice? What are you, the scary mask version of Batman?"

"Maskman?" I shot back. "I like it."

"I hope you like the sound of ringing, too, because I'm getting you a collar with a bell on it so you can't sneak up on me again."

Despite my pain, I grinned. "Kinky."

"Goddamn it," Aly muttered.

I clamped my lips shut to hold in my laughter.

"Here, let me look at it," she said when we reached the sink.

I turned the faucet on cold and spared a glance at my angry-looking skin before lifting my gaze to watch Aly's brows pull together as she took my hand in hers. She gave my latest injury a quick, professional once-over, shifted the faucet from cold to lukewarm, and guided my hand beneath the water.

"It's not too bad," she said. "And at least it wasn't the hand I stabbed."

I wanted to reach out and smooth the line between her brows, but seeing her slightly upset was better than no emotion at all. "Yeah, much better that I lose the use of both of them than just the one."

She shook her head and muttered something unintelligible that sounded slightly threatening, and I was glad she couldn't see how wide I was grinning. Women tended not to like it when people found their dark moods cute, and I was betting Aly was no exception. But I couldn't help it. She was adorable, especially because after watching her with Brad, I knew she was all bark and no bite with me.

"Nice touch with the blue contacts, by the way," she said, glancing up at me. "But I can see a line of brown around them."

Damn it. I knew I should have gotten a custom-fitted pair.

Her eyes didn't stay on me for long, just enough to shoot me a look of reproach for continuing with this duplicity before dropping back down. We fell quiet while she watched the water move over my hand, and I took the time to drink her in. Her wet hair left damp patches on her bathrobe, and her eyes were a little bloodshot like she'd cried in the shower. The skin beneath them was slightly bruised, a telltale sign of exhaustion, and watching the life start to drain from her expression again made me want to scoop her up and never let her go.

"You're here," she said, so low I almost missed the words.

I slipped my hand from hers and pulled her into a hug. "You needed me."

She rose to her tiptoes, wrapped her arms around my neck, and buried her face in my chest, taking such a deep breath that her sides pressed into my biceps. She started to tremble as she exhaled, and I gave into my need to hold her, dropping my hands to her thighs and hefting her up. Her long legs wrapped around my waist, arms tightening on my shoulders as she hid her face in my neck.

"What happened?" I asked. "It couldn't have just been Brad."

"It was my mom," she whispered against my skin.

I frowned. "I thought your mom passed away."

She stiffened.

Fuck. I probably should have kept that bit of knowledge to myself.

She pulled back enough to meet my eyes, not bothering to hide the tears that slowly leaked from hers. "You're so nice that sometimes I forget what a creep you are."

A sarcastic response was on the tip of my tongue, but I held it in check. "What do you mean, something happened with your mom?"

She sighed and started to pull away, but I hung on, unwilling to let her put any space between us. She must not have truly wanted to escape because she gave up when she realized my intent and snuggled back in. "I killed her."

It was my turn to go stiff as a board. What the hell was she talking about? "I thought she passed in a car accident."

"She did," Aly said. "I was driving. She was trying to teach me how to operate a manual transmission, and it was our first time out on a real road. Before that, we'd practiced in empty parking lots, and she thought I was ready for the next step. I almost stalled out at a red light and panicked when the car jerked forward, slamming my foot down, only I missed the brake and hit the gas, and we shot into the intersection."

Oh, fuck.

"A car clipped the rear end, spinning us around, and a work truck rammed us head-on," she said. "The truck driver managed to hit his brakes at the last second, but the impact was still hard enough that all our airbags deployed, and both of my ankles were broken when the front end crumpled. I hit my head hard enough that everything went fuzzy for a few minutes, and when it all came back into focus, I was in so much pain that it took me a moment to notice the pipe sticking out of my mom's chest. It came loose from the truck during impact and impaled her."

"I'm so fucking sorry," I said, squeezing Aly tight. The words felt useless. Why wasn't there a better way to verbalize empathy in moments like this? Some way to say that you were sorry that encompassed how your heart broke for someone and that you'd do anything you could to take their pain away.

Aly's sides shook as she lost the fight against her tears, her next words coming out between sobs. "I couldn't save her."

Everything clicked into place. Aly couldn't save her mother, so now she spent every waking hour of her life trying to save everyone else, to the detriment of her own mental and physical health. It made me even more protective of her. Someone so unselfish and caring should be safeguarded at all costs, even from themselves, if necessary.

"There was a car accident tonight," she said. "The woman looked like Mom, and I just . . . lost it. I couldn't treat her."

I strode from the kitchen into the living room and sank onto the couch with Aly still in my arms. "No one could blame you for that."

She sniffled. "I blame me."

I brushed her hair over her shoulder and stroked my hand up and down her back. "You shouldn't. Retraumatizing yourself isn't the answer."

"It's been almost ten years. I shouldn't still be traumatized."

I pressed my fabric-covered lips to her temple. "There isn't a time limit on grief or trauma."

She pulled back enough to look at me, eyes red, cheeks blotchy, all the more beautiful for trusting me with her vulnerability. "You sound like my therapist."

My answering laugh was humorless. "Probably because I've been in therapy for so long that I know what one would say right now."

"And what's that?" she asked, studying my eyes.

"A therapist would tell you that you didn't kill your mother. What happened was an accident."

"Fair enough," Aly said with another sniffle. "But it's still my fault she's dead."

"Counterpoint: it's that truck driver's fault for not swerving around you. Or that first driver's for clipping you. Or even your mom's for taking you onto the road before you were ready."

"Hey," she said, eyes flashing with reproach as she started to slide off my lap.

I tightened my arms around her and tugged her back to my chest. "I'm serious, Aly. Everyone involved was just as complicit as you. It's not fair to put all the blame on yourself. Would you tell another sixteen-year-old in your shoes that it was their fault their parent died?"

She shuddered. "God. Never."

"So why are you doing it to yourself?" She had nothing to say to that, so I pushed my advantage. "I didn't know your mom, but I bet she wouldn't want you punishing yourself for her death. She'd want you to live your life free from guilt. She'd want you to be healthy and happy, and by neglecting yourself and pulling these nonstop shifts, you're actively headed in the opposite direction."

"It's so hard, though," she said, digging her fingers into my shirt. "The hospital is so short-staffed."

I hefted her by the thighs and hauled her closer, wanting to banish what little space remained between us, wishing I could crawl right inside of her and fix the thoughts in her head.

"I know," I told her. "But you'll be no help to anyone if you run yourself into the ground. Exhausted people are sloppy people. They make mistakes that get them caught." Goddamn thoughts of my father slipping into every conversation. "I mean in trouble. You'd never forgive yourself if you treated someone after pushing past your limit and slipped up in a way that made them worse instead of better."

Her warm breath heated my neck as she blew out a heavy exhale. "You're right. I know you are, but it's almost a compulsion at this point." She sounded better than a moment ago, more like herself, and it made me want to needle her a little.

"Well, we have the next two weeks off to fix that," I said.

She reared back, and I should have gotten a medal for keeping my gaze on her face instead of dropping it to where her robe had slipped open, revealing a line of olive skin all the way to her navel. Even lower, in my periphery, I realized her robe had parted below the tie as well, and Aly was nude beneath it.

Fuck.

"How did you know my vacation got bumped up?" she asked. "And what do you mean when you say 'we' have two weeks off?"

I ignored her first question. She already knew the answer. "I took a vacation, too. I thought we could spend some quality time together as a family. You, me. Our maladjusted son who just scooted his butt across the carpet behind you."

She spun around, robe gaping even wider. "Fred, ew! Do you have worms again?"

He lifted his head from where he'd been fast asleep in his little felt house by the TV and gave her a look like, *Me? What the fuck did I do*?

She turned back around, features shifting into a long-suffering expression. "You just can't help yourself, can you?"

"Not when it's so easy to get a rise out of you."

The hint of a grin tilted up the corners of her mouth, and something unwound inside me to see it. She had every right to be upset, and I was sure this wasn't the last of our "you push yourself too hard" conversation, but it was still nice to know that I could get her to smile, even at the worst of times. That had to mean something, didn't it? That this was bigger than a hookup, more than casual dating. This had real long-term potential, and I hadn't been deluding myself when I formed my plan to make her fall in love with me.

I shifted my legs up, jostling her forward so she fell against me, hiding all that beautiful skin before I gave in to the urge to touch it.

She rested her cheek on my shoulder. "That was you on the ER line earlier, right?"

"It was."

"What were you going to say?"

"I was going to warn you about Brad. I pulled up his hospital records and had a bad feeling about him."

"You were right to," she said.

I stroked a hand down her back. "Oh, you have no idea."

She tilted her head up enough to meet my eyes. "What do you mean?"

"His family has been covering up for him or paying off his victims since he was a teenager," I told her.

"So, I was right. He's a monster."

It wasn't a question, but I answered her anyway. "He is."

Her gaze fell, darkening as she stared at the wall. "I wanted to kill him."

I went completely still beneath her. "What did he say to you?"

"A bunch of bullshit about how his victim had wanted it and was only lying to get money out of him," she said. "But it was more than that. Everything about him made my hackles rise. After he tried to grab me, I taunted him, hoping he'd try again or throw a punch so I'd have an excuse to unload on him." Her voice dropped. "I'm glad he didn't because I don't think I would have stopped. I felt out of my mind. I know that doesn't sound good, but I don't know how else to describe it. I felt completely unhinged, like I would have done anything in that moment."

I hugged her close, careful not to squeeze too hard because there was so much adrenaline pumping through my veins that I felt like I was in that ER bay with her, more than ready to go to jail for killing a man.

"I know I sound like a broken record, but I'm sorry," I said. "And if it makes you feel better, I felt the same way, and I didn't even hear what that bastard said to you. The look on his face was enough to push me to the brink. It took all my willpower to keep from barging in there. If I'd known he was taunting you—" I turned my head away so she wouldn't see the battle playing out in my mind.

No, I didn't want to be like my father, and no, I didn't think I was in danger of turning out like him anymore, but sometimes, I still worried there was a risk of being overtaken by urges that led to me falling down a dark rabbit hole and becoming a monster-adjacent person.

Like Dexter or Joe. Someone who did terrible things but found a way to justify them to themselves.

Aly lifted off my chest enough to frame my chin with her hand and turn me back toward her. "I wish you'd barged in." Her eyes roamed over me, taking in my black fitted tee and the way my dick strained against my jeans, even as we discussed violence. I was worried she'd be repulsed by my arousal, but instead, her lips curled in a wicked grin. "Watching you beat the shit out of him would have been the hottest thing I've ever seen."

"There's still time to make that happen," I told her, only half joking.

She sat up in my lap, and I nearly groaned at the way her robe gaped open. As I watched, she reached down and tugged the end of the fuzzy sash barely holding the garment on. She glanced down and kept pulling, torturously slow, biting her lower lip in a way that had my dick straining against my fly.

"Aly," I said, a hint of warning in my tone. This wasn't what I came here for. She'd had a terrible night. We should discuss it more and dig deeper into her compulsion to put everyone else above herself.

Her eyes rose to mine, and without breaking my gaze, she tugged the sash free, letting the robe fall open. My mouth watered at the sight of her perfectly rounded tits, the globes just big enough to fill my palms, her nipples a dusky pink several shades darker than her skin, already peaked with desire. She lifted my hands and placed them on her breasts, and it was only with monumental effort that I stopped myself from rolling my thumbs over her nipples.

"We should talk more about what happened tonight," I said.

She blew out a breath. "I don't want to talk anymore. I've been thinking about it for hours, and I just want to turn my brain off for a while." She leaned forward, rubbing her tits into my hands. "I want to be bad," she said. "I want you to make me forget about Brad and all the awful shit I've seen. I want you to use my body like your plaything."

Unable to hold out any longer, I dragged my thumbs across her nipples.

She shivered and ground her hips down, rolling her bare sex over me. "I want to be dark."

I jerked my eyes up from her tits and found her watching me with an intensity that had my balls tightening. "How dark?"

"Darker than the other night. I know you held yourself back." She reached a hand between us and palmed my dick through my pants. "Don't."

I groaned. "Aly, fuck. Do you know what you're asking for?"

Christ, did I even know? I'd come here wanting to comfort her, but she'd just set that plan on fire with her declaration. There was so much terrible shit in my head that I couldn't figure out where the line should be, how far I should drag her into the darkness with me.

"I know I want you," she said. "And I know I trust you enough to put myself at your mercy."

I panted as she squeezed me through my jeans, remembering how good her mouth felt wrapped around my cock, the way her tits bounced as I fucked into them. So far, most of what happened between us had been about me and my desires. Here she was, brave enough to trust me with her pleasure, brave enough to tell me what she wanted. The least I could do was deliver.

Calm descended like a second skin. Gone was my desire to tease her. Gone was the man she thought was cute and funny and safe, who hid from the world for fear of recognition. What was left behind was the part of me that stripped off clothes and covered himself in blood so I could horrify and titillate millions of strangers on the internet. This side was all ego. I wanted Aly on her knees for me, humbled and worshipping. I wanted to watch her crawl to me, naked, before kissing my boots and licking the flat of my knife.

She dragged in a breath as the change came over me, watching my eyes as the humanity bled from them and my need for her took hold. Her pupils widened with a mixture of anticipation, lust, and a small hint of fear. Good. She should be afraid. I felt like destroying something.

I wrapped my hands around her thighs and stood. "No safe words."

She clung to me, sounding breathless when she responded. "No safe words."

I strode into her room and threw her on the bed. She let out a strangled yelp of surprise as she bounced across the mattress. I left her to grab my bag and ensure Fred was still minding his business in his felt house and hadn't snuck into her room while we'd been distracted. What I was about to do to his mother, no child should see.

I yanked the knife out as I strode back into the room, throwing my bag to the side and pulling the blade free as I kicked the door shut. We were dropped almost entirely into darkness, but Aly must have sensed the danger in the room with her because she scrambled away as I stalked toward her, fear edging out lust.

I raised the blade high.

She threw herself to the far side of the bed. "What are you—"

I stabbed the knife down.

Straight into the corner of her mattress.

She clapped her hands over her mouth to muffle her horrified scream.

I crooked a finger at her, beckoning her forward.

"Come here, Aly," I said, wrapping my other hand around the knife handle so there would be no mistaking my intent. "I want to watch you ride it."

15

ALY

My heart beat against my ribs like it was trying to break free from my chest. Holy shit, for a second there, I thought Josh was going to kill me. I needed to remember that this man took me at my word. Online, I'd begged him to break in, and he had. Now I asked for dark, and he was delivering. I should have known it would come at a cost.

I dropped my eyes to the knife handle sticking out of my bed. My beautiful bed that I'd paid so much money for.

"Your new one gets here tomorrow," Josh said, his voice deliciously low in his continued effort to disguise it.

I jerked my gaze up to his.

He tilted his head, indicating my mattress. "This one is too small for me, so I got you the same frame, headboard, box spring, and mattress in a California king."

My breath came out in a rush. He called my cat his son. He bought me a bed for both of us as if he planned on spending a lot of time in it together. When I needed him, he came to me, held me while I cried, helped me work through my issues, and listened without judgment when I confessed to wanting to kill someone.

I couldn't remember the last time anyone had been there for me like he was. Definitely none of the men I'd slept with or dated lately. They'd all bailed when I got busy at work. What had Josh done? Watched me on shift instead, unwilling to let me out of his sight even when I asked for space.

Twice now, he'd assured me this wasn't just a kinky hookup for him, but he must have known that words only went so far because he was doing a hell of a job showing me, too. It was time I started believing him instead of waiting for the other shoe to drop. Yes, he might end up breaking my heart, but if I didn't give this a chance, I'd be breaking my own heart instead, and possibly his along with it.

I sat up and slipped my arms free from the bathrobe, letting it fall to the covers behind me. His eyes roamed over my body with feverish intensity, like he didn't know where to look, so he tried to drink all of me in at once. I would never get sick of being looked at this way: like I was someone to be cherished and lusted after at the same time. It made me feel safe with him, even though he still managed to scare me sometimes.

And yet, the slight fear of never knowing what he would do next only had me wanting him more. It made me want to be brave for him, but I still had a few concerns about his request. The knife handle was long and wide, with a rounded head and a slight undulation more suited to a kitchen knife than a hunting blade. I didn't think it would hurt me, but that still left the risk of infection or slicing myself open.

He reached behind him and dragged his backpack closer. Keeping his eyes on me, he pulled what looked like a disinfecting packet out of it. "If you think I would ever let something happen to that perfect pussy," he said, gaze dropping to the apex of my thighs, "you're not paying attention." He tore the packet open and tugged out a wipe, rubbing the knife handle down. "Get over here, Aly. I'm losing my patience, and you're not ready for that to happen yet."

My inner muscles clenched with anticipation. Oh, fuck, why was the thought of him going off the rails so hot?

I slid from the bed and rounded the side toward him, stopping so close that I had to tilt my head back to meet his eyes. I hoped he saw the same thing I did when I looked at him—desire paired with genuine affection. Yes, I coveted his big, gorgeous body, but his personality turned me on just as much.

"I want to kiss you," I said, the words tumbling from my mouth as the thought entered my head.

"Then turn around," he rumbled.

I frowned, an argument on the tip of my tongue—because how could we kiss like that?—but something in his gaze told me this wasn't the time to play fuck around and find out, so I turned and was left to wonder what he planned when I heard rustling from behind me.

He stepped close, his chest brushing my back, and then dropped what felt like a satin sleep mask over my eyes. My world went black as he tied it in place. Okay, this was fine. I could deal with being blindfolded if it meant I got to kiss hi—

I yelped as he jerked my hands behind my back. A little warning would have been nice, but then again, nice wasn't what I had asked for, was it? I felt the bite of steel on my right wrist, and, yup, he was handcuffing me. Still fine. No need to panic over the thought that I had never been more vulnerable in my entire life.

Please, God or Buddha or whoever the fuck might be listening, do not let me be wrong about this man, I prayed.

"You're breathing hard, Aly," he said, a hint of amusement in his tone as he used the handcuffs to tug me into him. His arousal dug into my lower back, and I had to stop myself from rubbing up against it like I was in heat. "Are you scared?"

"Yeah, but I like it," I confessed, and speaking those words felt freeing in a way I hadn't anticipated.

I'd expected to feel guilty for it, dirty, but when Josh let out a tortured groan and wrapped his large hand around my throat, all I felt was horny. Images of what he could do to me while I was trussed up like this flashed through my mind. He could tie me to a bed rail and edge me until I passed out. Or bend me over and fuck me doggy style, using the handcuffs to yank me backward into every brutal thrust.

Yes, please.

He tightened his hold on my neck briefly before letting go and trailing his fingers lower. I held my breath, anticipation coursing through me as his fingertips bumped over my clavicle. With my vision obscured, my other senses came to life. My skin became hypersensitive to his touch. The soft exhales stirring my hair sounded like whispered sighs. We were pressed so close that I felt his heart beating against my back, just as fast as mine, the only sign that he was as affected by this as I was.

As one hand slid down, the other started trailing up, and they met in the middle, cupping my breasts just like they had on the couch. The difference was that there was no hesitation this time, Josh's thumbs stroking over my nipples, back and forth, off tempo so that each peak was stimulated before I even processed the pleasure radiating from the other. It went straight to my core, making my knees weak and my pulse trip. I wanted him to feel good, too, so I shifted my hands higher and tried to reach for his erection.

He made a tutting sound and tilted his hips back, denying me. "This is about you," he said, gently pinching my nipples one after the other. "You're going to sit. I'm going to play."

I squirmed within his hold. If he kept this up, I'd be sitting sooner than he intended. On the floor at his feet. My legs weren't going to last much longer against this sweet torture.

One hand left my breast and slid lower, and he was so much taller than me that he had to lean down to reach between my legs, bringing his lips to my ear. I held my breath, waiting for that first delicious stroke, but it didn't come. Instead, he traced a teasing line down my upper thigh and then sideways, stopping just shy of where I needed him.

"I want to kiss you, too," he said, his lips ghosting over the shell of my ear.

I shivered and turned my head toward him. This wasn't a great angle for making out, but I was so desperate that I was willing to risk a permanent crick in my neck if that's what it took.

He let out a low laugh. "Not on your mouth."

My head spun as he turned me around. I heard a thud like he'd dropped to his knees before me, and, oh, god, if it weren't for the handcuffs, I would have ripped the mask off to see such a thing. I was left panting as I awaited his next move, and I had a feeling that he was well aware of what he was doing to me and reveled in making me wait for it. It figured that even now, he was trolling me.

Somehow, I managed to keep my mouth shut instead of cursing him or demanding he touch me, and my anticipation only spiraled higher with every passing second. What was he doing? Where was he looking? How much longer did he plan on dragging this out?

I jerked back in surprise when his hand touched my ankle, nearly stumbling because the stupid handcuffs left me off balance. He grabbed my hips, steadying me as his low chuckle echoed through the room.

"You're a jumpy little thing this morning," he said, and I could hear the smile in his voice—the bastard.

"You try being trussed up like this," I shot back.

His fingers dug into my hips, hauling me closer. "If you're the one doing the trussing, gladly."

My brief annoyance evaporated. Josh blindfolded and handcuffed. Immediate yes. The possibilities were endless, but the thought that popped into my head and stuck was revenge for the edging he'd given me. I had no idea how to pay him back—I'd never edged anyone before—but I'd always been a good student, and I would spend my time until I got the chance studying up on all the ways to bring a man to the brink of climax and keep him from actually coming.

"I'll take it from your evil smile that you like the idea," he said.

I opened my mouth to respond, but he chose that moment to lift my right foot off the ground, and all my focus was suddenly on not tipping over sideways. The hand still on my hip clung harder, helping to keep me upright as he guided my leg over his shoulder. I had to press my heel into his back to find my balance, and it only pulled him closer.

I was just getting used to the position when his warm breath rushed over my sex, and the resulting shiver made my ankle wobble. If not for his other hand returning to steady me, I might have gone over. It hit me then, that if I felt his breath, he'd probably pulled the balaclava off.

"You're soaked, baby," he said, his words warm against my skin. "You should see the way you glisten." I felt the soft brush of a kiss against my upper thigh and nearly moaned. "I thought I'd need to work you up to take the knife, but you got there on your own."

"You got me here," I said. "I've spent so much time watching your videos that the second I see you, my body is just . . . ready."

He leaned his forehead against my lower stomach and let out a tortured sound. "Fuck, Aly. You can't tell me things like that."

"Why not?" I asked.

"Because every time I see you, I'm gonna know you're wet for me," he rumbled.

"It might be this blindfold, but I don't see the problem here."

He huffed a laugh and shook his head, the feel of his hair against my skin confirming the mask was gone. "We have the next two weeks off together. Now that I know that, all I want to do is keep you locked in this house, naked."

"Smash. Next question."

He shook beneath my leg as he chuckled, and I tottered again. He felt it and tightened his grip, pulling his forehead from my stomach and dropping a kiss on my raised thigh. "How do you do that?" he asked. "Make me laugh even as I fight the urge to take you to the ground and fuck you?"

Oh, good. So it went both ways. "It must be a talent we share. Also, you don't have to fight the urge."

"I do," he said. "We'll get there eventually, but I have plans for you before then, and I'm nothing if not patient."

"A talent we do not share."

"I see that," he said, breath hot against my core again.

I felt him take a deep breath, all the warning I had before he let out another low groan and leaned in, fastening his lips around my clit. He swirled his tongue across it and then sucked. I shuddered, and he gripped my hips harder and slid his tongue lower, lapping at my entrance. From the slick sound it made, I was even wetter than I realized, damn near dripping for the man.

"You taste incredible," he said, slipping his tongue as deep as it would go.

My body tried to clamp down on it involuntarily, seeking resistance, needing something bigger and harder filling it up. He angled it and stroked back out in a way that had my toes curling before he circled my clit again. Then his lips clamped down, and he sucked, and I dug my fingernails into my palms, probably leaving half-moons in my skin from how hard I was squeezing my fists. This was amazing, but I needed more. Shallow stimulation wasn't going to do it for me right now. He either needed to keep those lips where they were or let me sit on that knife.

I blinked. Yup. I just had that thought.

As if he could sense my need, Josh sucked harder, and I lost the ability to think at all. My head fell back, cuffs digging into my wrists as I strained against them. I wanted to reach out and thread my fingers into his hair, hold him in place against me while I rode his face. Maybe if I used some self-defense moves, I could take *him* to the ground instead. Unfortunately, with my hands shackled, there were only so many I could perform right now, and none of them ended with me straddling his face.

A pop sounded as he released me and went back to stroking his tongue over and around my clit. One of his hands shifted from my hip, sliding across my thigh before snaking between my legs. He teased my entrance with his fingertips, coating himself in slickness while his tongue laved at my sensitive bundle of nerves. I was so desperate to feel something, anything inside me, that I nearly sobbed as he pushed two big fingers in.

God, that felt good, and if he kept this up, it would be more than enough to get me off.

He crooked his fingers inside me in a "come here" motion like he'd used earlier, hitting a spot that left me gasping.

"My leg will give out if you do that again," I warned.

He pulled his mouth off me just enough to whisper. "Then you should take a seat."

Oh, lord. This was happening. I was about to ride a knife handle while blindfolded and handcuffed. I should have been petrified, but all I felt was anticipation of what was to come.

Fingers still inside me, Josh let go of my hip and guided my leg off his shoulder. I felt steadier back on two feet. Right until he crooked his fingers again, and my knees wobbled. He took advantage of my unbalance by putting his shoulder into my pelvis. Caught off guard, I tipped forward. His fingers slid out of me, and he wrapped his arm around the back of my thighs and stood with me sprawled over him like a sack of potatoes.

It shouldn't be sexy. It really shouldn't. But the fact that he hefted my weight like it was nothing made me go all mushy inside. I was a bigger woman, tall, broad, muscular. Part of me had always been jealous of those videos of petite women getting picked up by their partners, and inside, I was squealing that it was finally my turn.

He took a few steps and dropped back to one knee to set me on my feet.

"The corner of the bed is right behind you," he said. "I'm going to guide you down. The knife handle has a thick guard on it, and the blade is stuck deep enough that it shouldn't move, but I'm still going to keep a hand under you, both as a barrier and to hold it in place."

"But your hands are hurt," I said.

"I like the pain."

Oof. That declaration was as hot as it was fucked up.

"Okay," I managed, barely above a breathless whisper.

"I meant what I said earlier," he told me, stroking his fingers through my folds once more. I gasped as he clamped them around my clit, having flashbacks to the edging. "This pussy belongs to me now, Aly, and I protect what's mine."

And they said the perfect man doesn't exist.

"Yours," I agreed.

He made a masculine sound of approval and released his hold on my clit so he could place both hands on my hips and push me gently backward. I took a cautious step and then another, stopping when the back of my knees hit the bed.

"Sit. Slowly," he said.

I did as he bade, grateful for all the leg workouts that gave me the control to manage this. It was just like a tempo squat, where—

Oh, Jesus. That's cold!

The rounded tip of the knife handle pressed against my folds just shy of my entrance, and I shifted forward enough that I was properly lined up. Here went nothing. Taking a deep breath, I lowered myself onto it. It was different from the vibrators I was used to. For a start, it was colder. So cold that my inner muscles clenched around it in protest, and I had to pause for a second before my body heated it enough that I relaxed and could keep going, only to repeat the process. It was also stiffer, unforgiving inside of me as I sank all the way to the mattress. As promised, Josh's warm hand was there waiting for me, the handle sticking up between his fingers, his palm pressed to my clit when I settled.

I let out a shaky breath, adjusting to the feel of an honest-to-god knife handle buried hilt-deep in my pussy.

Josh released an equally loaded exhale, and I knew he must have felt some kind of way because he forgot to modulate his tone. "You're a fucking goddess, Aly."

I recognized his normal voice instantly. I fucking *knew* it was him.

Sitting there, I felt like the goddess he likened me to. Not only because he was so undone by the sight of me perched on his knife handle that he forgot himself but because I'd never done anything so brave and reckless before. It made me feel powerful and untouchable, like after this, nothing could ever get to me again. Next time a patient tried to give me a hard time, I'd remind myself what kind of woman I was. The kind who didn't run screaming from her masked stalker but fucked his knife handle instead.

I rolled my hips forward, rubbing my clit into Josh's palm and testing the feel of the handle as I moved. Part of me was worried that it would be uncomfortable, but it felt fine. This wasn't much different from the first dildo I'd had—simple and metallic. The only exception was it didn't vibrate.

"You good, baby?" Josh asked, voice gone low again as he swiveled his thumb around and pressed it just above the hood of my clit, applying pressure exactly where I needed it.

A soft moan slipped through my lips. "Better than good."

I heard him shift forward and felt his arm slide around my waist before he grabbed the chain linking my handcuffs and tugged it down, pinning my wrists to the mattress behind me and forcing my spine straight.

"Then what the fuck are you sitting still for?" he purred into my ear. "I told you to ride it."

Hot damn. Dom Josh could *get it*. I braced my feet on the floor and thrust into his hand again, the metal warming inside of me as it pressed deliciously against the place his fingers had so recently stroked.

"Again," he said, and I obeyed the command.

I heard a thud like he'd dropped to both knees between my spread legs, and then his mouth was on me, sucking at the skin of my neck before he bit and nipped his way lower. One hand still kept the handcuffs pinned to the bed while the thumb of his other started moving in slow circles at the top of my clit as I thrust into him. His lips found my breast, tongue flicking over my nipple, and I cried out. The walls of my pussy squeezed against the knife handle, an orgasm already building inside me.

I was so wet that his hand was coated, and I felt his long middle finger glide through my slickness before sliding toward my ass. Was he going to do what I thought he was? Did I want him to? I mean, I didn't *not* want him to, but it had been a while since I'd done any anal play, and I didn't know how it would feel right now.

"You can do it, baby," he said, rubbing my arousal over that tight rear entrance, prepping the area. "The sooner we start breaking you in, the sooner you can take me here."

He waited a beat for me to tell him no, and when I didn't, he pressed the tip of his finger just inside. I stilled, trying to force myself to relax when my body tightened on instinct. It felt invasive, but not necessarily in a bad way, just different, a slight burn as I stretched around him.

Intense. That was the only word to describe it. So overwhelming that I went motionless for a moment and just *felt* what he was doing to me. His thumb still worked my clit, and when he laved his tongue over my nipple, the combined stimulation was enough to make me melt into him, his middle finger sliding deeper.

Carefully, I shifted my hips in the subtlest of thrusts, and oh, wow. Okay, that wasn't terrible. It was kind of hot, actually, still intense and slightly disconcerting, but if anything, the taboo of what we were doing just made me want it more, and I ground myself onto him and the knife a little harder.

"Good girl," he said, and yup, I had a praise kink all right because hearing those two little words had me immediately tipping closer to the brink. "Look how well you're already doing."

A thready moan slipped through my lips as I started to ride him again. I was experiencing so many sensations at once—anal penetration, clit stimulation, and nipple play, not to mention the knife handle filling me up—that soon they started blending into one overwhelming feeling of fullness and pleasure. I was going to come. Soon, and hard.

He curled his finger forward inside me, and I could feel him pressing my inner wall against the knife. "Fuck, I want to be inside you," he ground out before pinching my nipple between his teeth, just shy of painful.

"Yes," I panted. I wanted that, too, so bad it made me want to cry.

This was amazing, and I'd never had a more eye-opening, freeing experience in my life, but the thought of him buried balls deep in me made me mindless with desire. I was ravenous for him, wanted to stroke and kiss and lick every inch of his flawless body, wanted him to claim every inch of mine in return. I craved the closeness that came from wrapping myself up in someone and feeling their chest move against mine and their arms squeeze me close while they rocked into me.

"I want that so bad," I said, thrusting down harder, faster, the pressure building inside me.

"Soon, baby," he promised. "But first, I want to watch you come on my knife. Can you be a good girl and give me that?"

"I can," I told him, thighs bunching, ass tightening around him as I rose and fell.

He put his mouth on me again, worshipping one nipple and then the next, keeping his finger crooked and his thumb right where I needed it. It was all so much. Better than anything I'd felt before.

If this man broke my heart, I was screwed, because I had a feeling he was forever altering my sexual cravings.

"I would never hurt you, Aly," he said.

Oh, fuck, I must have spoken that last thought aloud, and now it was too late to take it back and too late to slow things down because I was coming, my hips bucking at a frenetic pace, moans falling from my lips, stars dancing across my closed eyes as the pleasure rocked through me so hard that my ears began to ring.

To my horror, tears started leaking from my eyes. I couldn't help it, though. It was so good, such a perfect release after the awful shit I'd been through tonight, hell, the past several years, that all the emotions I'd held in check came pouring out as the dam gave way.

"Aly, fuck. Are you okay?" Josh said as I curled forward into him. "Hang on, baby."

He slipped his finger carefully out of me and grabbed my thighs, lifting me off the knife. I burrowed into him like a lost child.

"I have you," he said, standing, one arm banded around my back, the other beneath my ass.

It took him a minute to get the handcuff keys from his bag because he refused to let me go, holding me to him while he crouched down and riffled around until he pulled them out. As soon as I was free, I wrapped my arms around his neck and clung to him, sobbing. Jesus Christ, what was wrong with me?

"You should have told me to stop," he said, sitting with his back to my bed, me straddling him.

"Oh, g-god, no," I choked out. "You were perfect. *That* was perfect. Everything else from tonight just hit me."

He let out a heavy breath and squeezed me tight. "Just tonight? Or have you been holding on to other things?"

How did he already know me so well? I couldn't even blame it on the stalking. You could only learn so much by watching someone through a soundless video camera or reading their files online. No, this man had an almost intrinsic understanding of me, like he was more adept at seeing through bullshit than most and could reach right down to the core of a person.

"It's okay to let it out," he said, rubbing my back.

"I can't. This is such awkward timing."

"It's perfect timing," he countered. "One release triggered another. Let go. I told you, I've got you, baby."

Goddamn it. He was going to be my undoing, wasn't he? Just hearing that made me feel like I finally had permission to stop hiding, stop bottling everything up and letting myself go numb instead. Tonight was terrible. Last night was almost as bad. This whole fucking month had been a nonstop shitshow, except for the man holding me, who was the only bright light in it.

And what had I tried to do? Push him away. Why did I think I didn't get to have good things? Was it because so much had been taken from me at too young an age, Dad passing from a heart attack only months after Mom died in the crash? Was that when I'd stopped letting people in and started pushing them away, only proving to myself that everyone would eventually leave me?

I needed to stop. Josh was right when he said Mom wouldn't want this for me. Knowing her, she was somewhere in the afterlife cursing me out for how hard I worked and how much my social life had suffered as a consequence. I could almost hear her now: "Just because I'm dead doesn't mean I don't expect grandbabies from you!"

The thought stemmed the flow of tears. Everyone I knew who had lost someone talked about their deceased relatives like they'd been saints. My mother had been a hellion: fiery, unapologetically outspoken, and the bravest woman I'd ever met. I once watched her face down an attempted mugger by reaching into her purse and yelling, "I see your knife and raise you a gun, motherfucker!" He'd taken off running, and she'd chuckled as I'd looked on in horror. There was no gun in her purse.

"Thank you," I told Josh. "I think I needed to hear it was okay to be upset."

"You're welcome," he said, stroking a hand up my back. "For a second there, I thought I ruined everything."

I sat up and yanked off the eye mask. His balaclava was back in place, and I hated that I stared into the icy blue of his contacts instead of the warm brown eyes I knew he hid behind them. "You couldn't if you tried," I told him.

He glanced away from me, brows pinching together like he didn't believe me.

I turned his face back to mine. "What we just did *changed me*."

He huffed out a laugh. "You and me both. I've never seen a more beautiful sight than you speared on that handle. Look." He jerked his head down, and I followed his gaze straight to the wet spot on his crotch.

I frowned. "Did you . . . ?"

"Come in my pants when your ass clenched around my finger, and you came so hard that you squirted on me? Abso-fucking-lutely. That's how fucked up you've got me, baby. You don't even need to touch me to get me off."

I lifted my gaze back to his. "If it's like this now, what's going to happen when I finally get you inside me?"

He groaned, head falling back against the mattress. "The poles will probably re-align, and we'll be responsible for an extinction-level event."

I couldn't form a response. Now that my tears were drying on my cheeks, I realized two things: I was still naked, and I had the man of my dreams sprawled out beneath me. The sight of him was arresting after I'd been deprived of his beauty for so long. My gaze drank in the way his muscles strained against his T-shirt before falling to the gorgeous kaleidoscope of color crawling down his arms. His body was a work of art.

He'd just rocked my world, and I'd just sobbed on his chest, but I was still hungry for him. I wanted him again. Now. All of him this time, to hell with waiting.

"Don't look at me like that," Josh said.

"You can't even see me right now."

He craned his head up. "Yeah, but I could feel you undressing me with your eyes."

I ran a finger down the center of his shirt. "Can you blame me? You've seen me naked twice now, and I have yet to see you once."

His eyes crinkled up at the corners. "If I get my way, you'll see so much of me over the next two weeks that you'll be sick of me by the end."

I shook my head, letting my gaze wander over him again. "I highly doubt that."

He pointed a finger at me. "Uh-uh. None of that. We need to get cleaned up, and then it's food and bed. You had a bad night, and you're exhausted. Your eyes are as sleepy as they are seductive right now."

My heart somersaulted. "Are you staying?"

He started to rise, hauling me up with him. "Do you want me to stay?"

"I . . ." The words stuck in my throat for a second. I'd shown so much vulnerability tonight that pulling more out of me was hard. I felt raw and overexposed, but then I wondered if maybe he needed to hear me say it because, so far, all he'd done was show up uninvited. "Yeah. I want you to stay."

He let out what sounded like a relieved breath, and I felt like I'd made the right choice.

"Then I'm staying," he said, scooping me up and carrying me to the bathroom, where he cleaned us both off. Afterward, I dressed in comfy pajamas and tried not to laugh as he tugged on the sweatpants I'd lent him. They were too big for me, meant to be worn loose, but they looked more like capris on him. The man could have doubled as a middle linebacker.

A yowl sounded from my bedroom door, followed by the sound of Fred scratching at it. Honestly, I was shocked that he'd lasted so long; Fred usually whined at my door within five minutes of me closing it.

Josh turned toward it and yelled, Batman-style, "Have you no respect for our alone time?"

Yowl.

"I'm not having this argument with you, young man!" Josh called back.

Yowl.

"Excuse you, sir. You better not talk to your mother like that when I'm not around."

I shook my head as he strode to the door and yanked it open. Fred was right on the other side, tail swishing as he gave one final, almighty yowl.

"That's it," Josh said, scooping him up and carrying him out of sight. "Ow. Jesus, be gentle, Fred. You're clawing through my shirt again. Yes, I know you're glad to see me." His voice grew quieter the farther away he walked. "Yes, I missed you, too, but screaming at people isn't the way to show that you care, and don't you dare point out my stalking. We're talking about your eccentricities right now, not Daddy's."

It felt like my heart grew three sizes listening to him. He needed to stop being so damn cute, or it was going to be a problem.

"Babe?" he called. "You want eggs and bacon again?"

Oh, shit, no.

I scrambled out of the room after him, trying to think of a kind way to ask him to please never cook for me again.

16

JOSH

THE BLARING OF AN ALARM jarred me out of sleep. I shot up in bed, and for a second, I couldn't see anything. Fear punched through me. Had the contacts rolled into the back of my eyes while I slept and severed my optic nerves? Was that even possible?

Aly groaned somewhere nearby. "What is that sound?"

"I don't know. I've gone blind," I said, voice laced with panic. Fuck, that was the second time I'd forgotten to disguise it.

"What?" she yelped, and the mattress shifted with her movement.

"Help me," I whimpered, Batman-style, and yes, it was just as pathetic as it sounds.

"Oh my god," she said with a shaky laugh. "You're not blind. Your dumb baklava slid sideways."

I flopped backward, so relieved that I was shaking. Aly's frowning face appeared, rising over me as I tugged the mask into place. It was so dark in the room that we must have slept through the entire day, and now it was night again. I couldn't remember the last time I'd gotten so much uninterrupted sleep, but after we filled up on the breakfast she insisted on making, we'd curled around each other in her too-small bed, and I was out the second my head hit the pillow.

"It's called a balaclava," I told her.

"And what did I say?" she asked.

"Baklava. One is a mask. The other a delicious dessert."

"Whatever." She reached over me, and I had to fight the urge to wrap my arms around her and tug her onto my chest. "You must have forgotten to turn your alarm off."

I went still, the sound finally registering. My phone had many alarms, but this one, which was loud and particularly blaring, was tied to Aly's security system—specifically, her back door camera. I'd tweaked the settings so it would only go off if someone was within a foot of the sensor and stayed there for several seconds, which would rule out animals passing beneath it.

Suddenly, I was wide awake, anxiety and adrenaline warring for dominance as I snagged my phone from the nightstand before Aly could reach it. I silenced the alarm and unlocked the screen. The sight that greeted me sent ice sluicing through my veins. The camera was dark. And not the dark of night, but the kind of dark that only came from being covered.

I swore.

"What's wrong?" Aly said.

"Someone's at your back door."

She smirked. "No, that was last night."

"I'm serious," I said. "I think someone's trying to break into your house."

"What?" she whisper-squeaked.

I jumped out of bed, clad only in my boxers. Where the fuck was Fred? My eyes snagged on his black and white form, curled on the nearby armchair. I grabbed him and handed him to his mother.

"Protect the baby," I told her.

"What do you mean?" she said, clutching Fred close. "What are you doing?"

"I'm going out there."

"No way," she said. "We need to call the cops."

I froze halfway into the too-small sweats she'd lent me. "No cops. I can't explain it right now, but . . . no cops. Where's the nearest loaded gun?"

"Bottom drawer of the dresser," she said. "And we are absolutely going to circle back to what you just said later."

"I figured as much."

With a final tug, I got the sweatpants up, then paced to the bureau. Aly's gun was right where she said, and I snatched it out of the drawer and chambered a round. By the time I turned back to the room, she was out of bed, pulling on her pajama bottoms.

"You're staying in here," I said.

"Nope," she fired back, heading toward me.

I angled the gun toward the floor and grabbed her shoulder with my other hand, halting her mid-step as I bent down to look her in the eyes. The thought of her leaving this bedroom was even more panic-inducing than someone breaking into her house, and no, the irony of the situation wasn't lost on me.

"You are a fucking badass," I told her. "And I don't doubt you could handle this alone if you had to. But I beg you, for my sanity, please stay here." I shook her to drive the point home, my ears strained as I wondered how much time we had until whoever was outside tried to kick down the door. "Please, Aly."

"I don't like this," she said, frowning at me in open worry.

"I know, baby, but if you're out there with me, I'll be too distracted, and all my focus needs to be on whoever might be outside."

She bit her bottom lip, brows pinched together. Fuck it. If I were about to die, it wouldn't be before I felt her sweet lips on mine. I'd denied her last night, wanting to delay the moment we finally kissed until she was begging for it, but now it was me who was desperate.

I jerked my mask up to expose my mouth and crashed my lips into hers. She met me hungrily, greedily, her hands gripping my shoulders as she hauled me closer. My head spun, blood rushing straight to my dick when she parted her lips, welcoming me in, and our tongues brushed.

Maybe I was already dead because kissing Aly felt a lot like heaven. Her body molded so perfectly to mine that it was like we were a matched set, made for each other. Our mouths worked in tandem like we had already done this a hundred times and knew exactly how the other liked it. It was the best kiss of my goddamn life, and it made me even more determined to make sure I got a thousand more from her, just like it. No, a million.

I broke away, both of us gasping, my world tilting on its axis as my true north realigned, pointing straight toward the woman in my arms.

I pressed a final kiss to her lips. "Lock this door behind me and get that other gun out of your nightstand in case anything happens to me."

She blinked, eyes as wide as saucers. "It might just be a raccoon."

I forced myself away from her. "Last I checked, raccoons don't know how to cover cameras." She sucked in a breath as I strode toward the open doorway. I paused to take what might be my last look at her, memorizing the sight of her standing there in her rumpled pajamas, hair falling loose around her, lips swollen from my kiss. "Get the gun, Aly."

"I'm not even going to ask how you know where all my weapons are." She paused halfway to her nightstand and turned to point at me. "And don't you dare get hurt."

"I'll try not to," I said. "But just so we're clear, I'm the only masked man you asked to break into your house, right? I wouldn't want to go kick the shit out of some innocent guy over a misunderstanding."

She looked past me, expression contemplative. "Masked men? No. There was that shirtless jump roper and a firefighter or two, though."

My spine stiffened. "Woman, you better be joking, or we are about to have our second fight."

She threw a pillow at me. "I'm kidding. Get out of here, psycho, before I change my mind and go with you."

I turned and shut the door on her whispered "Please be careful."

For you, always, I thought.

The Christmas tree Aly still hadn't taken down lit my path through the living room. I briefly debated unplugging it but discarded the idea; the person outside might notice the light cut off and know someone was awake and waiting for them. My best chance to avoid injury was catching them off guard.

I moved closer to the far wall, out of sight from the back door, and slowly made my way toward the kitchen where it was located. The sound of the knob rattling was the death knell of any hope that this was an animal. Someone was outside Aly's house in the dead of night, picking her lock.

The rage that burned through me was so intense I started shaking. I was going to fucking murder them. No. Wait. That could end with me in jail, and then I'd only get to see Aly during visiting hours.

Not if you don't get caught, a helpful little voice offered.

I shook my head. Now wasn't the time to have an internal debate with my intrusive thoughts. There was nothing to say this wasn't just a simple home invasion. Crime rates were average in this part of the city—not as high as some parts but not as safe as others. Aly's car wasn't in the driveway because she'd taken an Uber home. The person on the other side of the door probably thought the house was empty. It was only my catastrophizing brand of generalized anxiety that made me immediately assume it was something more nefarious.

I focused on the door, plastering myself to the wall as I neared it. Once the potential burglar got the knob unlocked, they'd realize there was still a deadbolt, and I didn't want them to break Aly's door and rouse the whole neighborhood with the noise. Slowly, silently, I reached out and painstakingly slid the bolt free.

Now I just had to decide what to do when they tried to enter. Stand here with a gun pointed right in their face, or hide somewhere nearby and jump out at them from—

The door flew open.

I reacted instinctually, all thoughts gone from my head, my body moving on its own thanks to the years I'd spent practicing martial arts. My fist pistoned out as a man wearing a balaclava like mine stepped into view. I threw my full weight behind the punch, picturing my knuckles moving through his head like my first karate teacher taught me all those years ago.

My fist crunched into his face as I cold-cocked him, and he collapsed in the open doorway like a puppet whose strings had been cut.

To ensure he was out, I hauled him up by the shirt front and shook him. His head bounced around in a boneless way that was hard to fake. I lowered him carefully to the floor and shut the door behind him, relocking the deadbolt in case he had a partner waiting nearby. Between the balaclava and the large backpack he wore, this was looking more and more like a home invasion.

The sound of an indrawn breath drew me up short.

No. She. Didn't.

I clenched my jaw and turned to see Aly standing not five feet away with her gun pointed at the intruder. Of course, she hadn't listened and stayed put in her room.

I narrowed my eyes at her, but she was lasered in on the unconscious man and didn't see the censure in my gaze. "We are 100 percent about to have our second fight."

Her face was pale in the darkness, her expression drawn with what looked like genuine fear. Instead of some snarky response, she motioned at the man with her gun. "Take his mask off."

"Aly," I said, wariness snaking up my spine.

"Do it," she bit out.

I reached down and yanked the man's balaclava free.

God. Fucking. Damnit.

It was Bradley Bluhm.

His face was still swollen from his previous beating, and his nose was now ruined, too, blood gushing down his mouth and chin, but there was no mistaking the rapist—and most likely murderer if the cops were correct in their suspicions—that Aly had a run-in with last night.

The implications of him being here were horrifying. Aly had pissed him off, called him a coward, and he'd tracked her down to do what? Get revenge? Make her his next victim? If not for the alarm I'd set, we might have woken to the sound of him kicking in the back door. He could have caught us off guard and done something to Aly before I realized what was happening.

The sound of her chambering a round snapped me out of it. I wheeled toward her, my arms outspread in front of Brad's prone form. "You can't shoot him."

She immediately pointed the gun toward the floor but still motioned at me with it. "Move."

"No. Aly, listen to me," I said in my normal voice. Talking like Batman was giving me a sore throat, and I'd already slipped up enough that it felt foolish to keep the charade going. "If you shoot him, you'll wake the whole neighborhood, and then someone will call the cops."

She flicked the safety into position and set the gun on the nearby table. "Fine. We'll beat him to death. Quietly. I know people who can dispose of the body." The look on her face as she strode forward told me she was dead serious.

I held my hands up to stall her. "Think for a second. He has a backpack."

She stopped at Brad's feet, fingers curling into fists, her face a thundercloud. "So, what?"

"So, he might have a phone in there," I said. "And if he does and then goes missing, it will get traced straight to your house. Grab me a pair of those latex gloves so I can check."

Her expression turned mutinous, but after a tense moment, she stomped away from me toward a kitchen drawer and produced the requested gloves.

I tugged them on and riffled through Brad's backpack, my rage returning tenfold as I realized I was looking at a kill kit: zip ties, rope, a bottle of chloroform, trash bags, a serrated knife, bleach, rags—everything you would need to murder someone and then clean a crime scene. It made me certain that Brad had killed before. You didn't get this bold unless you'd gotten away with it a few times.

I knew that better than most. When I was six, I found one of Dad's victims in our basement freezer. He said it was a mannequin and he was going to play a prank on Mom with it, and if I told her, he would beat me, so I kept my mouth shut and only realized when he got caught what I'd really seen.

I moved on to the smaller pockets, but there wasn't a phone in them either, so I set the bag down and flipped Brad over, checking his jeans and jacket. Nada. He wasn't as sloppy as I thought, which was as relieving as it was concerning. On the one hand, I might get the chance to enact my plan to end him; on the other, there was still a risk that his phone was somewhere nearby, most likely left in a parked car.

"No phone?" Aly said.

I sat back on my heels. "No phone."

She stepped forward and hammer-stomped Brad's crotch so hard that his legs lifted off the ground. He wheezed and curled in on himself like he was starting to come out of it. I might have been planning the man's death, but I still wanted to puke, thinking of how much that must have hurt. Before I could stop her, Aly stomped on his ribs next. A crack ricocheted through the room, and then a low, tortured moan as the pain pulled Brad back to reality.

"No, you don't," she said, leaning down and punching him in the temple so hard it snapped his head around. He went boneless again, and Aly straightened, shaking her arm out. "Fuck, that hurt."

I took her hand, inspecting her knuckles in the dim light. "Are you okay?"

"No," she said, tears springing to her eyes. "Did I see rope and a knife in his bag?"

I pulled her into a hug, both of us trembling with unspent adrenaline and more than a little fear. "Yeah."

"He came here to rape and kill me," she said.

"Most likely."

I tugged her closer, petrified on her behalf, on behalf of all women, because men like Brad were something they had to worry about constantly.

God, I was a fucking asshole. Brad and I might not have had the same intentions, but we'd both broken into Aly's house, and I hated the idea that I'd caused her similar distress. What had I thought to myself less than two weeks ago? That I would never regret what I'd done? I wanted to go back in time and kick the shit out of my past self for it now. This kind of violation was unforgivable, and I couldn't believe Aly had given me a chance instead of shooting me in the face like I deserved. If I had to spend the rest of our time together making it up to her, I would, happily.

"Brad needs to die," she said, her voice muffled from how tight I held her to me.

"He does," I agreed. "But I can't be the one to do it, and I don't want that for you either."

"So what do we do?" she asked.

"First, we need to hogtie him and figure out whether or not he has a phone or a vehicle stashed nearby," I said. "If he doesn't, we'll drop him off at his last victim's house. Her extended family lives outside the city on a big farm, and between her ex-army father and her ex-marine husband, I'm sure they'll do the rest of the work for us."

"What if they call the cops instead?" she asked.

"So far, Brad hasn't seen either of us, so he can't identify us if he survives. And it's not like he could tell the cops the last thing he remembered before getting knocked out because 'I was breaking into a woman's house with a bag full of weapons' wouldn't do him any favors. Afterward, we'll find another way to get him."

She pushed back from me enough to meet my eyes. "You've thought this through."

I didn't bother lying. "Yes." Here it was, the moment she realized how disturbed I was.

Instead of looking horrified, she nodded. "Good. I would have made a rash decision and probably ended up in jail."

"Hey," I told her, lifting her chin as I gathered my courage.

"Yeah?"

"I'm sorry I did this to you."

She frowned. "You didn't do this to me."

"I literally did," I said. "Or are you forgetting that Brad's not the only man in this kitchen who broke into your house?"

She released a shaky breath and tugged her chin out of my grip. "I haven't forgotten. Trust me, that first time, I was just as ready to shoot you as I was Brad. But," she looked away, worrying her lower lip between her teeth, "after that, I never felt like you wanted to hurt me.

I can't explain it, and I know it sounds stupid and illogical and dangerous, and, god, it is, but something in my gut told me to trust you."

I leaned down and bumped my forehead against hers. "It was the snacks, wasn't it?"

She huffed out a laugh. "What can I say? I'm a sucker for homemade trail mix."

I pulled her into another hug, wanting to hold her right there for the rest of her life, shielding her from this terrible world with my body if that's what it took to keep her safe from it. Unfortunately, the unconscious man at our feet would only stay that way for so long, and the sooner we got him out of there, the better.

I unwound my arms from Aly and dropped down beside Brad's backpack. "I think tying him up with his own rope has a kind of poetic justice, don't you?"

"I do."

Now probably wasn't the time for those two little words to make my stomach somersault, but hearing Aly say them warmed my heart in a way that made me want to hear them from her again, preferably while standing in front of an altar of some kind, or on a tropical beach, just the two of us—whichever she preferred.

She grabbed a pair of gloves and squatted beside me as I unzipped the bag.

"Son of a bitch," she said when she got an up-close look at its contents. Her fingers shook as she reached in, flicked aside the knife, and pulled out the rope. "He's done this before, hasn't he?"

"Based on the police files I read, yes," I told her.

"How has he gotten away with so much?"

"Money, and he's not an idiot," I said. "Most of the evidence tying him to his recent crimes is circumstantial. His only conviction happened when he was still a teen, and it got expunged from his record. He must have gotten complacent the other night."

Together, we tied him up, with me hauling his arms and legs tight as I talked Aly through the motions. It would have gone faster if I had done it, but this was the kind of skill everyone should learn, and after such a close call, I was desperate to teach her everything I knew about self-defense and survivalism.

"Do I want to know how you know how to do this?" she asked halfway through.

"Probably not," I told her. "No, not like that. That part of the rope goes under instead of over."

She corrected her mistake. "Does it have something to do with why you didn't want me to call the cops?"

"Surprisingly, no," I said, and she shook her head.

Once Brad was trussed up, I made Aly double-check her knots, tugging as hard as she could to prove he couldn't get free. We put his balaclava back in place and, inspired by my earlier freakout, dragged it over his eyes like a blindfold. Then we gagged him, and I went to grab my laptop from my bag.

An hour later, we had all the answers I could find in such a short amount of time. Brad's phone was still at his house in a wealthy suburb north of the city. He'd disabled the GPS location services on his vehicle, so it might have been parked nearby, but if we couldn't find it, the cops would have a hard time, too. Even if it got found, it'd be difficult to prove how it had gotten where it was or where Brad had gone after ditching it, so I felt confident that Aly would be in the clear.

"You should stay here," I told her as I closed my laptop and met her gaze over the dining room table.

She shook her head, her expression turning mulish. "Absolutely not. This is a two-person job, and I'm not letting you shoulder the burden of it on your own. We're doing this together, or not at all."

I let out a heavy breath, knowing when I was beaten. Lowering my voice, I pulled her from her chair onto my lap and wrapped my arms around her waist. "We are talking about kidnapping and complicity in a potential murder."

She gazed toward the sound of Brad struggling against his restraints just out of sight in the kitchen. "I'm well aware, but that son of a bitch broke in here planning to do unforgivable things to me, and I'm not a very forgiving person as it is. I'm not exaggerating when I say I could kill him myself and not lose any sleep over it."

She turned to look at me then, and the absence of her usual light drew me up short. No, she wasn't exaggerating. Right now, I was staring into the eyes of a dangerous woman. And to think I'd been worried about being too fucked up for her. What had she said the first time I watched her through her computer? That Fred only liked me because cats were sociopaths, and he recognized one of his own? I should have picked up on the subtext then: Fred liked two people, Aly and me, making us two peas in a pod.

She blinked, and life returned to her expression, her lips tugging up as she shook her head at me. "I can feel you getting hard right now."

I met her gaze, uncaring, embracing the fucked up for the first time in my life because at least I wasn't alone anymore. "And I bet if I reached into your panties, you'd be soaked."

She rolled her eyes and pulled free from my embrace, standing. "I never should have told you what you do to me."

"Yeah, sure, let's chalk it up to that."

She glared at me.

I booped her nose and was just about to pull her back into my lap when Brad tried to scream through his gag.

Twenty minutes later, we'd changed into real clothes—thank fuck I'd washed and dried my jeans before we fell asleep—I'd dosed Brad with his own chloroform, slapped duct tape over his gag, and shoved him into Aly's snowboard bag.

While she made us coffee for the road, I left to get my car, keeping the lights off as I backed into her driveway to avoid unwanted attention. It was two a.m. on a Saturday, which meant the risk of someone still being up was greater than on a weeknight. Aly's front lights were off, and thankfully, her Christmas ones were on a timer, so they'd gone dark hours ago.

This section of her block didn't have a streetlight, but I still wasn't taking any chances. I had another mini-blackout waiting to go, and I triggered it right before opening my car door. As the neighborhood plunged into darkness, I popped the trunk and sprinted toward Aly's front porch. She threw the door open when I reached it, and together, we hauled the Bag o' Brad up and shuffle-carried him outside, dropping him into the trunk with little ceremony and quietly shutting him in. That done, Aly doubled back for the coffee while I climbed into the driver's seat.

The neighborhood lights flashed back to life right after I eased out of the driveway, and Aly and I shared a relieved look over the fact that we'd pulled our escape off.

"Here's your coffee," she said, passing over a travel mug. "Black with a little sugar, right?"

I raised my brows at her as I took it. "Yeah."

She flashed me a pleased grin and turned forward in her seat. "I pay attention, too."

The woman was down for kinky sex, knew how I liked my coffee, and was more than willing to aid in the murder of a rapist. What had I done to get so lucky?

I returned my focus to the road as I pulled out of her sleepy neighborhood onto the busier throughway. There were still cars out and about, but the farther we got from the city, the fewer we passed, and in less than an hour, we were the only vehicle on pitch-dark country roads that wound through snow-covered cornfields.

Aly and I barely talked during the drive, both of us stuck in our heads over what we were doing and how much worse this night could have gone if Brad had succeeded in breaking in. What little we did speak revolved around me catching her up on everything I'd learned while she was still on shift last night.

The police and hospital had done an excellent job trying to protect the name of Brad's latest victim, but I'd managed to find Macy Harold, a twenty-seven-year-old schoolteacher who'd been in Chicago the night of the attack to celebrate a college friend's bachelorette party. From what I'd pieced together, they'd run into Brad and his friends during their bar crawl, and at some point during the night, he'd honed in on

Macy, buying her and her friends rounds of drinks even after they tried to decline them politely. One of the last things Macy remembered was finally accepting a shot because she didn't want to seem rude, and less than an hour later, someone heard Brad assaulting her in a bathroom stall and kicked the door open.

Macy and her husband lived in a small cottage adjacent to her parents' house on a hundred-acre farm. The brother who had already gone after Brad lived in a similar place nearby. I hoped that even if Macy's dad and husband failed to hurt Brad, her brother would step in and get the job done.

I relayed all this still using my regular voice, wondering if she recognized it. My time for hiding from her was drawing to an end, and I had a feeling that if we managed to pull this stunt off, one of the first discussions we'd have when we got back to her house would revolve around confirming my identity and digging into why I'd avoided admitting who I was for so long.

I was dreading that conversation. Aly had already forgiven me for so much, put up with so much. How could I possibly ask her to continue trusting me after she found out who my dad was and started questioning why the son of a notorious serial killer would cover himself in blood and film knife-wielding thirst traps? She'd probably assume I idolized him when nothing could be further from the truth.

I cut the car lights and turned down a dirt road that bisected two corn fields, driving until I reached a narrow band of trees that sprung up around a small brook. The satellite images I'd poured over online showed a narrow footpath leading through them to the main house. I'd hacked into Macy's parents' Wi-Fi and couldn't find any evidence of security cameras, but even so, Aly would stay in the car while I dragged Brad onto their back porch, ready to gun it out of there if shit went sideways and I came sprinting back.

"Are you ready?" I asked, putting the car in park and turning toward Aly.

Her expression was troubled. "Yes?"

"Would it make you feel better if I told you that I'm so scared I feel like I might puke?"

She released a shaky breath. "Oh, good. I've been fighting the urge to hurl this entire drive."

"We'll have to hold it in," I told her. "Wouldn't want to leave behind gross little piles of DNA for someone to find."

She huffed a laugh. "Let's do it then."

I popped the trunk, and we got out of the car.

Aly unzipped her snowboard bag but stopped after exposing Brad's face, her eyes wide. Had she finally hit her limit? Did it just now occur to her how fucked up this all was, and she was having second thoughts?

We'd come too far to turn back now, so I reached forward and was about to finish unzipping the bag when she grabbed my arm.

"Don't," she said.

I turned toward her, frowning. "I can do it without you if you want to wait in the car."

She shook her head and released my arm. "We're going to have to go with my backup plan."

"Backup plan?" I said, starting to get confused. She hadn't mentioned a backup plan.

She nodded and leaned forward, placing her gloved fingers on Brad's neck. It looked like she was checking his pulse.

Wait. Why the fuck was she checking his pulse?

She turned toward me, sympathy written across her face. "You put the duct tape over both his mouth and nose. He's dead."

I snapped my focus to Brad, and, oh, fuck, she was right. His eyes were wide and unblinking, and his skin already had a pale sheen that seemed unnaturally bloodless in the moonlight.

My guts heaved.

I ripped the balaclava off and ran to the nearby bushes, dropping to my hands and knees as my stomach tried to expel everything I'd ever eaten. So much for not leaving piles of DNA behind.

Aly squatted next to me, rubbing my back and making soothing noises as I retched. "This is probably a bad time to gloat over the fact that I was right about your identity, isn't it?"

Reader, I puke-laughed.

And, no. I do not recommend it.

I'd just killed a man, and my unhinged partner in crime was cracking jokes. "Fuck me," I muttered.

"Kind of a weird time to offer," Aly said without missing a beat. "Can I take a raincheck until after we've disposed of the body and you get a chance to brush your teeth?"

17

ALY

IF SOMEONE HAD TOLD ME two weeks ago that I would end up driving a car with a body in the trunk, I would have . . . I don't know. Laughed? Told them they had lost it? And yet, here I was, driving back toward the city with a queasy killer and the corpse he'd created.

I glanced at Josh, slumped sideways in his seat with his forehead resting against the window. "You doing okay?"

He craned his head sideways, slowly, like he couldn't believe I was even asking him that because he was obviously not okay. "I'm great. Definitely not in the middle of an existential crisis. You?"

"Disappointed."

He sat up a little, frowning. "What?"

I shrugged and refocused on the road. It was pitch-black outside, and with the night I was having, it would have been just my luck that a deer would jump in front of us. "Brad's death was too anticlimactic."

"Anticlimactic," Josh repeated.

"Yeah. I mean, a piece of shit like him? His demise should have been more violent and, ideally, included getting lit on fire at the end."

That surprised a snort out of him. "Bonfire o' Brad."

"Barbecue o' Bluhm," I said, grinning.

Josh groaned. "We're going straight to hell."

"Good. Maybe we can get another shot at him down there." I glanced over my shoulder toward the trunk. "I'm lowkey considering pulling over so I can stab him a few times and make myself feel better."

"Haha," Josh said humorlessly.

I gave him a blank look.

His eyes flashed wide. "Jesus Christ, Aly."

I winked to let him know I was kidding—kind of—and faced the road again.

He shifted beside me, sitting fully upright in his seat. "I can't believe I just murdered someone."

I held up a finger. "Technically, I think what you did classifies as involuntary manslaughter."

"Oh, good. That makes me feel much better."

"It should," I said.

"Why's that?"

I shot him a wink. "Less jail time."

"How are you so calm about all this?" he asked.

"Because death is nothing new to me," I said. "I see it on a weekly basis. Mostly, it's good people who pass way before their time due to illness or injury. So much of the loss I witness is senseless and tragic, leaving far too many heartbroken family members in its wake. It's nice to see someone like Brad get what they deserve for once. I doubt even his parents will mourn him."

Josh was quiet in response, and I glanced over to see him staring out at the passing snowscape as he processed my words.

God, the man was beautiful. His profile in the dashboard light was a thing to behold. It made me wonder why he'd ever want to cover his face with a mask.

I'd seen shitty people in his comments say things about how men like him were all butterfaces, and that's why they wore masks, but that wasn't true of Josh, and I'd watched enough face-reveal videos from other creators to know those commenters were wrong. So what drove the masktokers to it? Was it the anonymity? The opportunity to don an alter ego like a second skin and become someone else entirely?

That felt oddly fitting for Josh. He was like a soft dom—sweet in the streets and mean in the sheets. But, like, mean in the *best* way. Bossy and demanding and relentless, and oh, no, I was getting turned on within five feet of a fresh corpse.

I jerked my gaze back to the road. That cemented it. I'd officially become so numb that not even the body of a dead rapist affected me like it should.

I snuck one last glance at the passenger seat. Or maybe Josh was so handsome that the laws of morality broke in his presence.

"The worst part about it is that I don't even feel bad," he said.

"What do you mean?"

"I'm freaked out that I killed someone, but beneath that, I don't have any guilt over it. I'm more fucked up over not being fucked up if that makes sense."

"It does," I said as we approached a four-way stop. My map helpfully told me to turn right, so I threw my blinker on and followed the directions as I mulled over a more detailed response. "I think most people would feel the same way in your shoes. Death in and of itself is terrifying. The first time I watched someone pass, I stepped into the hall afterward and puked all over the floor. I've watched other new nurses pass out. Your response is pretty normal. As for not feeling bad, why would you?"

He turned toward me. "Because I took a human life."

I shook my head. "That's societal pressure. You've been taught that killing is wrong and only monsters do it, but that's not right. People kill for all sorts of reasons. Sometimes, it's in the heat of the moment, and they spend the rest of their lives regretting what they've done. Other times, it's out of desperation, like a woman killing her abuser because she knows that if she doesn't, she'll end up dead instead. And then there are accidents like what happened tonight. I'm honestly relieved we did it ourselves. Part of me was panicking over the thought of those people calling the cops instead of taking care of Brad on their own."

I reached out and gripped Josh's knee. "Just keep reminding yourself that it was an accident, and making one mistake doesn't mean you're a bad person. Especially when the result is removing a rapist and potential murderer from this earth. Between his family money and his obvious escalation, he would have gone on to target someone else if we didn't stop him. Who knows how many lives we might have saved by taking his?"

Josh shifted, his leg flexing beneath my palm. "You keep saying we, but I was the one who did it."

"Yeah, but I'm just as complicit," I said. "Maybe I didn't put the duct tape over Brad's mouth, but I went into this planning for him to end up dead, one way or another."

Josh slipped his hand beneath mine and threaded our fingers together. "Thank you for saying all that. It helps."

"You're welcome. And I hope you know I'm not blowing smoke up your ass. I truly believe we made the world better by removing Brad from it. I know vigilante justice is problematic as fuck, but sometimes I think it's necessary, especially when the system put in place to deal with men like Brad fails because it's susceptible to loopholes."

"Don't forget bribery," Josh said. "Brad gave off plenty of warning signs that went ignored, including peeping through windows, animal cruelty, and sexual harassment. All as a teenager. I read a quote from a judge who let him off without so much as probation after he got drunk his senior year of high school and drove his car into the house of a classmate who'd turned him down. It was, 'He's a bright young man with his whole future ahead of him. It'd be terrible to ruin it over something like this.' The judge was a golf buddy of Brad's father."

I pulled my hand from Josh's before I broke one of his fingers from squeezing too hard. "That right there is why I won't ever feel bad about this."

Josh let out a low, angry sound. "It barely scratches the surface of what Brad got away with."

I glared at the road ahead of me. "I keep getting stuck on how it went on for so long. That one judge? I get. Not that I understand, just that there are corrupt shitheads in every profession. But years and years of Brad getting away with his crimes? *That* no one will ever be able to explain to me in a way I'll understand, even if they give me a detailed bullet list of every misstep along the way."

"Maybe it all led up to tonight," Josh said. "Maybe I was meant to kill him."

I frowned. "Like fate?"

"Yeah," he said. "Maybe I was always meant to be a killer, and it would have happened one way or another."

What the fuck? How could Josh possibly think something like that? Him? Destined to be a killer? I couldn't accept it. He was too good, too kind, and yes, he'd broken into my house and stalked me, but I'd asked him to commit the B&E, and I'd never told him to stop watching me. I had a feeling that if I had, he would have listened and never bothered me again. His actions might be similar to Brad's when examined through a wide lens, but when you zoomed in, the two men couldn't be more different, and I refused to let Josh compare himself to such a garbage human being.

"No," I said. "I reject the idea that this was your fate. It's too fucked up when you take into account the pain and suffering of Brad's victims. There's no way they were put on this earth to fall prey to him."

Josh ran a hand over his face and released a heavy sigh. "I sound full of myself when you put it like that."

"Not full of yourself, just conflicted and confused after a traumatic event."

A glance at him revealed the worry on his face, brows drawn together, full lips flattened into a hard line.

I needed to drive my point home, and what better way than using his logic against him? "You asked me if I would ever blame another teenager for killing their parent, so let me turn that around on you. If it was me who'd accidentally killed Brad, would you be wondering if I was always meant to be a killer?"

"Never," Josh said. "But it's not the same."

"It is, though," I argued.

"It's not. This is something I've worried about since I was a child."

My blood ran cold. Who had thoughts like that as a kid? "What do you mean?"

"Uh-uh," he said. "We're not doing this now. If there was ever a worst time to have the Josh's Tragic Backstory conversation, it's right after I killed someone."

"No fair. I spilled my guts to you about mine."

He let out an exasperated sound. "Aly, my backstory is the stuff of people's nightmares."

I glanced over at him, starting to worry. "Have you ever killed before?"

He shook his head. "No."

"Have you ever hurt anyone?"

"Not outside a martial arts studio, and even then, only accidentally, and never seriously."

"Are you a criminal?"

"I'm a hacker, so technically, yes. I've broken countless laws, but the worst thing I've ever done was break into your house and stalk you."

I lifted a brow at him and then sent a pointed look over my shoulder toward the trunk. "Really? That's the worst thing?"

He shot me a grin. "I said what I said. Weren't you just telling me we did the world a favor by killing Brad?"

I smiled. Yeah, I had, and it was nice to see some of Josh's sass returning. "Then that's all I need to know. I trust my gut that you're not a bad person. Anything you have to tell me can wait until you're ready. No rush."

He leaned over the center console and pressed a kiss to my cheek. "You are the best girlfriend a guy could ask for."

My eyebrows flew up so fast it felt like they were trying to jump off my forehead. "Uh, what was that?"

"Too soon?" he said. "I mean, I know we haven't had the official conversation yet, but we share a child, and I feel like disposing of a body is a boyfriend-girlfriend activity and not something you do with a casual hookup."

I schooled my face. "Are you saying that the couple who commits homicide together, stays together?"

He snorted. "Too wordy. I prefer the couple who slays together, stays together."

I choked out a laugh. Yup. Straight to hell. The both of us.

"Where are we going, by the way?" he asked. "I feel like you were about to tell me right before the last time I had you pull over so I could dry heave some more."

My humor evaporated. I'd been working up the courage for this conversation for the past half hour and still hadn't figured out a good way to explain my plan B. "How much did you look into my family?"

"I stopped with your parents," Josh said. "Digging any deeper felt too intrusive."

I looked over at him. "Really? That's where you drew the line?"

One big shoulder lifted in a shrug. "What? It had to be somewhere. Would you prefer that I'd dug deeper?"

"I honestly would have because it would save me from having to tell you some uncomfortable things about my family."

I turned back toward the road. We were entering the suburbs, and I couldn't keep looking at him whenever I felt like it—which was approximately every 1.2 seconds. He was too good-looking, and it was a goddamn distraction.

His hand landed on my thigh, and I must have been beyond redemption because even such a comforting, innocuous touch made me want to squirm in my seat. If he'd just inch it a little higher . . .

"Aly, nothing you could say about your family would ever drive me away."

"Okay then. My uncle Nico is in the mob."

Josh turned toward his door. "Pull over. We're breaking up." He jiggled the handle like he was trying to open it. "Let me out."

I slapped at him. "Stop that. I'm serious."

He swiveled back to me. "I thought you didn't have any other family. There's no mention of them anywhere on your social media profiles or other digital records."

Was it weird that confessions like that didn't even phase me anymore?

"That's because I've been ignoring their existence," I said. "Nico is my mom's younger brother. He fell in with a bad crowd when he was a teenager, and the family pretty much disowned him. My grandparents fled here from Sicily because of the mob, and to have a son join their ranks was anathema after everything they'd been through. The last time I saw Uncle Nico was at my mom's funeral. I thought that was the final time I'd ever hear from him, but he reached out a few months ago and coerced me into getting my youngest cousin, Greg, a janitorial job at the hospital."

"Random," Josh said.

I shook my head. "I wish. Let's just say that there's a coroner's assistant whose last name ends in a vowel, and I'm pretty sure the real reason Greg got hired has something to do with how certain bodies get handled. I've only seen Greg a handful of times at work, and we've come to an unspoken understanding about pretending we don't know each other, which, I mean, isn't hard because we only met at Mom's funeral. And no, I don't want to get to know him now. He's following in his dad's footsteps like all my other cousins, and my job is too important for me to risk losing it over whatever shady mob shit he's involved in."

"So why are we involving them now?" Josh asked.

I sighed. "Because before my dad died, he told me that if I ever got into serious trouble, I should go to my uncle. Nico might be a soulless bastard, but family still matters to him, and apparently, he never stopped trying to reconcile with my mom and grandparents before they passed."

"When you put it like that, I almost feel bad for the guy," Josh said.

"You really shouldn't. He's not a good person. Maybe not as bad as Brad, but close. Unfortunately, I think he's a necessary evil right now. From what Dad told me, Nico's not high up in the organization, but because of what he does for them, he's our best bet at getting out of our current situation without getting caught."

"What does he do?" Josh asked.

I grimaced. "He's a cleaner."

"Money laundering?"

I shook my head. "More like sanitizing crime scenes."

"Oh."

"Yeah."

"And you're sure this is how you want to handle our current trunk situation?" he asked.

I glanced over at him. "I guess that depends. How do you feel about slicing off Brad's fingerprints, ripping all the teeth from his mouth, hacking him into pieces, setting those pieces on fire, and then dumping them all into a river or lake?"

Josh blanched. "Like I might be sick again."

I nodded. "Same. Death, I'm okay with; dismemberment, I'm not so sure. And because we're amateurs, the risk of getting caught somewhere along the way is too high for me to stomach. I'd much rather let the professionals handle it."

"Consider me team mob then," Josh said.

"It's going to come at a cost," I warned him.

He gripped my shoulder, and the urge to turn and nuzzle my cheek into his hand was too strong to resist.

He stroked his thumb up my neck. "Do you know what the cost will be? Are we talking money or, like, favors?"

"Probably favors. Just because I'm family doesn't mean I'm exempt from blackmail and coercion. I'll probably have to convince the hospital to hire another mobster or something." I sent him an apologetic look. "I can only imagine what they'll ask someone with your hacking skills to do."

He squeezed my shoulder. "If it means staying out of jail and the media, I'll do whatever they want."

I frowned as I took a left turn. He was concerned about the media? The thought of winding up on the news hadn't even occurred to me. I was still too worried about getting caught driving with a dead guy in the car to think much past that, but maybe I should have. Brad did come from a lot of money, after all. Rich white boys were always considered newsworthy by the media. It made me even more convinced that going to Nico was the right choice, despite whatever fallout might come from it.

"You never gave me an answer," Josh said, snapping me out of my dark thoughts.

"About what?"

"Whether or not you're my girlfriend."

My pulse ratcheted up, and there went my stomach, going aflutter. "Are you asking me to be your girlfriend?" I said, sneaking a glance over at him.

He flashed a wolfish smile at me, and honestly? I forgot about the body in the trunk. Hell, it felt like the sight of those dimples was altering my brain chemistry so that all my future thoughts would revolve around this man.

My body's response to his was bad enough, but I was doomed now that I had a face to go along with it. Doomed, I tell you. Whatever self-preservation remained went out the window. This was what I wanted—*he* was what I wanted—to hell with the consequences. And yes, it was all happening faster than was probably normal, but with him, I didn't need months to make up my mind. These past few weeks had been enough for me to decide what my answer would be.

He made me feel alive. He'd dragged me out of the gray world I'd been living in and taught me how to see colors again. In a sea of men who barely put in any effort, this man stood out for going above and beyond. He was the definition of "If he wanted to, he would." Because he'd done for me what no one else ever had: he not only met but exceeded my needs, both physically and emotionally. He kept me on my toes, never knowing what he would do next. And he did it all while making me blush and laugh, often at the same time.

Of course I wanted to be his girlfriend. Hell, if I had it my way, every free moment I wasn't working would be spent in his company from now on. I hoped he understood what he was getting himself into because while his obsession had started relatively recently, mine had been going on for months, and once I got my claws in him, I didn't plan to let go.

He shifted forward, crowding into my space in a way that made my breath hitch and my nerves spark. "Aly? Do you want to be my girlfriend? The position comes with snacks and orgasms and maybe a little light stalking."

I grinned. "Yes."

He swooped in and kissed my cheek, and I couldn't remember the last time I'd been so happy. Even with a dead body not five feet from me. Even on my way to ask the last person I wanted to for help. Josh distracted me from all the awful bullshit and made me feel good instead. Maybe this relationship had started out on questionable footing, and maybe we still had a lot to learn about each other outside of our mutual stalking, but saying yes to being Josh's girlfriend felt like the easiest decision I'd made in a long time, and no matter what was to come, or what secrets Josh still held, I doubted anything would ever make me regret it.

18

JOSH

"I THOUGHT YOUR UNCLE WAS a low-level mobster," I said. To Aly. My girlfriend.

"That's what Dad told me." She peered through the windshield at the Italian-style villa we approached. "I guess dirty work pays well?"

I was gonna dirty work her as soon as I got her alone. The smile on my face was starting to hurt at this point, but all I could think about was how we could get this over with as fast as possible so I could drag her back to her place and consummate our relationship.

Maybe we could back the car up like a dump truck, tip Brad's body out on the driveway, and wish her uncle good luck as we raced away like the horny miscreants we were. And yes, I felt comfortable speaking for both of us. Aly had zero skill at hiding her emotions, and she'd been sending me hot-for-stalker looks since I took my mask off.

Reluctantly, I pulled my gaze from her and peered out at the towering front gate. It was closed, but there was a small console to buzz up to the gatehouse just beyond. Was anyone even awake at this hour?

I had my answer a minute later when Aly rolled down her window. She'd barely reached out to press the little red call button when the speaker crackled to life.

"Who are you, and what the fuck do you want?" a gruff male voice asked.

I knew it was the asscrack of dawn, but I still didn't appreciate him talking to my girlfriend that way.

There went my mouth, pulling up in a too-wide smile again.

My *girlfriend*.

Aly leaned out into the cold night air. "I'm Alyssa Cappellucci, Nico's niece."

The gate swung open on silent hinges.

Aly put the car in gear, and we shared a surprised look. That seemed far too easy. No verification of identity necessary? Were they expecting us, or was there a standing order to let her in if she ever showed up? Considering what Aly said about how important family was to Nico, the latter seemed likely.

A thought struck me then, and ah, fuck—mobsters were probably more into true crime than most. I'd been so busy planning fun, naked couple activities that I hadn't thought about how this might play out. What if someone fixated on my appearance and brought up my dad? I needed to be the one to tell Aly; I couldn't risk her finding out from someone else when I didn't have the time to sit her down and explain everything. She'd probably lose her shit if that happened, and I wouldn't blame her.

I reached into the front pocket of my bag and pulled out my trusted disguise: glasses and a fake mustache. In my defense, it was a very high-end fake mustache, and it looked incredibly real, even up close, but yes, I still looked like a reject from an '80s buddy cop movie in it.

"What the actual fuck are you doing?" Aly said as I flipped down the sun visor and used the mirror to guide me while I stuck the mustache into place.

"I'll explain later. I promise," I said, patting the sides down.

"Are you famous or something?"

"Or something," I said, turning toward her.

She glanced at me and shook her head. "You look . . ."

I waggled my brows. "Hot, right?"

She jerked her gaze back to the driveway as we passed the gatehouse and the shadowy figure watching us out of its windows. "You shouldn't. That thing is ridiculous."

Unable to help myself, I closed the distance between us and whispered, "And yet you still want to ride it." For good measure, I brushed it over the shell of her ear.

She jerked away, eyes fixed on our destination, pink coloring her cheeks in the dashboard light. "I think we've already established that I'll try anything once."

I straightened in my seat, trying to remind my dick that we were about to meet a notorious mobster, and doing it sporting a full erection was less than ideal. Unfortunately, all I could picture was me lying flat on my back with Aly straddling my face. I needed a distraction.

How about the dead body in the trunk?

Oh, right. I'd just killed a man. And while Aly had done a great job of weaponizing my logic and using it against me, part of me still wondered just how "accidental" Brad's death was.

I couldn't remember taping his mouth. Yes, I knew I'd slapped the duct tape in place, but I'd been distracted by something Aly said at the time, and was half-excited, half-terrorized by what we were about to do. Had I just been sloppy? Or had some subconscious part of me acted on impulse and placed the tape intentionally? The fact that I wasn't sure and probably never would be was going to haunt me for the rest of my life.

I slipped my glasses into place as we pulled into the wide, circular driveway. This part was cobbled with red brick. It must be a nightmare to maintain. Our springs were weird, and the freeze/defrost cycle caused havoc on the city's roads, making them heave and buckle. I could only imagine how that would impact the tightly packed brickwork.

As Aly slowed the car, one of the large bays of the five-car garage opened, revealing a man in a blue flannel bathrobe. Uncle Nico? He motioned us into the bay, stepping back so Aly had room to pull in. It put him on my side of the car as she parked, and I tried not to stare as we passed him. He didn't look like a soulless mobster. The man was maybe five and a half feet tall, thin, and unimposing. His hair was salt-and-pepper gray, his skin was a darker shade of olive than Aly's, and his nose was a tad too large for his face.

Aly put the car in park and turned to me. "You ready?"

I shrugged. "Not really, but what choice do we have?"

She shook her head. "None. Let's do this."

Together, we got out of the car.

Nico was still on my side, and I towered over him as I rose to my full height.

He stared up at me, brows lifted. "Nice stache, Porno Joe."

Great. Smart-assery ran in Aly's family.

A killer rebuttal was on the tip of my tongue, but I held it in check. Trading insults was not the way to ingratiate myself with this man, and thanks to the body in the trunk, he had a lot of power over me. It was best not to anger him right off the bat.

I held out my hand. "Close. It's Josh."

He snorted but slid his palm into mine, his grip surprisingly strong. "Too bad. Josh doesn't have the same ring. I'm Nico."

I nodded as we let each other go.

"You Italian?" he asked, eyeing me.

"A quarter. My mom is Italian and Algerian."

He looked me over again. "I thought you might have a little—"

"Don't say anything racist," Aly cut him off, rounding the car's hood.

Nico turned toward her with arms outspread and a wide grin that seemed genuine. "I would never."

Aly shot me a glance, clearly uncomfortable with Nico's familiarity and the conversation she'd interrupted, but she stepped into his embrace anyway, leaning down slightly to hug him. "Thanks for letting us in. I hate to do this, but we have a bit of a—"

"EH!" Nico barked. "Not out here." He pulled away from her and went to close the garage. Then he motioned us toward a side door.

We passed through it into a functional yet opulent mudroom, complete with marble flooring and what looked like a full doggie spa in the corner.

Nico pointed at our feet. "Shoes off," he said. "Moira will have my head if you track that in here."

I glanced down. Not only were my shoes muddy, but so were my jeans from when I'd puked in the bushes. The house was warm, so I shrugged off my winter coat when I finished kicking off my shoes and hung it next to Aly's on a hook by the door.

Nico led us from the mudroom to a very ornate, busily designed kitchen. "Coffee? Wine?"

"Coffee's fine," Aly said.

I squinted as I tried to take everything in. The overhead lights were bright enough to glint off all the marble and glass. It was like the Palace of Versailles had thrown up in there. Everything was done in cream and beige, and I couldn't understand why the mosaic backsplash was full of naked people. It looked like it was supposed to be some ancient Italian design, but some of the pieces were slightly off, so one person's arm sat much lower than the other, and another guy's dick was separated from his body by a full tile space. It looked like it was just floating there on its own.

Like a phantom cock in the middle of a party.

Oh, god. Don't laugh, I thought, pulling my eyes up. Unfortunately, my gaze landed on the mirrored chandelier, and the reflection of the fluorescent lights in it nearly blinded me. What was that phrase about money not buying taste?

Aly elbowed me. "You want coffee or something stronger?"

"Oh," I said, dropping my focus to her uncle. "Coffee, please." The thought of wine on an already sour stomach was a no-go, but I thought I could do with some caffeine since I'd barely touched the to-go cup Aly had made me.

Nico strode toward a fancy white and steel machine with far too many buttons. "So, what brings you here so early?"

"We killed someone," Aly said.

I turned toward her with wide eyes.

She gave me a *What?* expression.

"You didn't want to ease into that?"

She shrugged. "I must have missed school on the day they taught us the polite way to tell people about bodies in car trunks."

Nico whipped around. "You brought a goddamn body to my house?"

Aly swiveled toward him. "Yes? Dad said to come here if I was ever in trouble."

"Fuck!" Nico bit out. "I might have feds watching me. You can't just bring me corpses like I'm the morgue."

"Hey," I said, stepping in front of Aly. He might be her uncle, but hearing him speak to her in that tone was enough to have me second-guessing whether or not I cared about making a good impression. "She didn't know."

Nico threw his hands up. "Tell that to the feds!" He wheeled around, yelling as he left the room. "Greg! Stefan! Alec! Junior! Get your asses up! We got a problem!"

Aly sidled next to me, and I wrapped an arm around her shoulder, glancing down to see her looking chagrined.

"Whoops?" she said.

I squeezed her close. "What were we supposed to do? Call the guy and warn him and the feds who might have tapped his phone?"

Footsteps thundered overhead, Nico's shouts rousing everyone as he raised the alarm. Someone ran down a set of stairs nearby, and we turned toward the sound as a young man burst into the room, still pulling on a gray T-shirt. He was maybe Aly's height at five-eight with dark hair and a rail-thin frame. Despite his baby face and freckles, something about the hardness in his eyes made me think he was older than he looked.

"Keys!" he yelled, gesturing toward Aly.

"Hey, Greg. Nice to see you, too," she grumbled, digging around in her purse for them.

So this was Greg. I eyed her youngest cousin. Maybe he was exactly as old as he looked, and the hardness came from what he'd already done for his father. God knew I understood the way parents could prematurely age someone.

"Come on," he said. "We gotta go."

Aly extended her keys toward him. "What do you mean, we?"

Greg shook his head. "Keep 'em. You drove in. You gotta drive out." He turned toward me. "Where's your coat?"

"Mudroom," I said automatically.

He nodded and gestured toward his cousin. "Let's get out of here."

Aly took a hesitant step forward, pulling out of my embrace. "What about Josh?"

Greg's eyes flashed to mine. "I'm gonna pretend to be him so anyone watching won't get suspicious, and he's gonna stay here and fill Dad in."

"Uh-uh," Aly said. "He's not getting separated from me."

"He'll be fine," Greg told her. "You think Dad wants to get on your bad side by messing with your boy toy?" He glanced at me again, giving me a once-over. "Plus, it looks like he can handle himself. Now, move, Aly. We don't have much time."

She turned back to me, expression worried.

I stepped in and kissed her forehead before lifting my eyes to Greg. "I get that you're in a rush, but I have to know what your plan is."

He shifted from one foot to the other, talking so fast that he almost tripped over his words. "We're gonna get to a safe spot and have someone remove the body."

"What if the feds trail you?" I said.

"We'll lose them."

I held his gaze for a long moment. Jesus, he was just a kid, barely out of high school. "Don't let anything happen to your cousin."

"I won't," he said, stepping toward the door like he was trying to prompt Aly into action.

I looked down at her. "I'll be okay. You?"

Her brows pinched together as she frowned. "I hope so. I don't like this."

"Me neither, but they're the experts, and we have to trust that they know best."

Greg snapped his fingers. "We don't have time for a mushy goodbye, Aly. Come *on*."

Annoyance flashed across her face as she turned away from me. "I'm coming. Jesus, calm down."

I met Greg's eyes over Aly's head and gave him the barest shake of my own, my stomach churning with anger. Dad used to snap at my mom, and it was a huge pet peeve of mine. "Don't do that again."

I'm not sure what my face looked like, but it was enough to make the child of a hardened mobster take a step backward.

"Sorry," he said.

I tipped my head toward my girlfriend. "To her."

He looked at Aly. "Sorry. Now, can we please go before my da—"

Nico reentered the room from a side door. "What the fuck are you two still doing here? *Andate, idioti!*"

Greg, obviously more afraid of his father's wrath than mine, grabbed Aly's wrist and hauled her toward the mudroom. She broke his hold halfway there and threatened him with bodily harm if he touched her again.

She shot me one last look before she left. "Be safe."

The words were a warning. Be safe, or else. I forced a reassuring smile and nodded. "You too."

Greg said something sharp from the other side of the door, and Aly stepped out and shut it on the sound of their continued bickering. A rumbling noise told me the garage was opening again.

And then I was alone with Aly's mobster uncle.

I turned toward him, wary, but he was already stomping out of the room again, head craned toward the ceiling as he yelled at his other sons to get a move on. Soon, three more men tumbled into the room, ranging from their mid- to late twenties. They looked like Greg, only filled out more.

Nico returned to the coffee maker and started pushing buttons. "What happened?" he threw over his shoulder, and suddenly, I was the center of attention.

I hated being the center of attention. It made me want to fold in on myself, hide, but Aly was relying on me, so I had to keep my shit together for her.

"First, where are Greg and Aly going exactly?" I asked.

"Back into the city to an autobody shop we run," Nico said as the fancy coffee machine whirred to life. "Our guy there will clean your car while others take care of what's in the trunk."

"And you think Greg and Aly will be okay?"

He nodded with his back to me. "Greg knows what to do. He's one of our best drivers, and he'll get other people on the road with them to run interference if he and Aly pick up a tail."

I let out a heavy breath, more nervous for Aly than before because it finally hit me that my girlfriend was about to be back on the road, driving around the city with a dead body. Fuck, I should have argued more or found some other plan that didn't involve her taking such a risk, but it all happened so quickly.

"You still with us, Joe?" Nico asked.

I jerked my gaze up from the floor and found him staring at me, arms crossed over his chest.

"It's Josh," I said. "Tell me she'll be okay."

I thought my continued delaying would piss him off, but he only grinned. "You really like my niece, huh?"

I nodded, looking around to see all four men eyeing me in the same speculative manner. Why did this suddenly feel like a trap?

"And are you responsible for the body in the trunk?" Nico asked.

I nodded again, and the men around me tensed. It occurred to me then that the idea of Aly dating a killer might not be a welcome one to her male relatives.

"Then you need to tell me what happened," Nico said, and I had a feeling that if he didn't like my story, not even Greg's promise to Aly that I would be okay would keep me alive.

"A rapist and likely murderer named Brad Bluhm was in the hospital two nights ago," I said. "He and Aly had a verbal altercation, and she insulted him. Earlier tonight, he tried to break into her house."

The room filled with the rumblings of angry men, and I started to feel a little safer now that we had a mutual hatred of Brad in common.

Nico's dark eyes burned with anger. "Why was he there?"

"He had a kill kit on him," I said, not bothering to elaborate since they likely knew what it was. "We overpowered him, tied him up, and planned to leave him on the back porch of his latest victim's family, but he died en route. Aly said we should come here, so we did. Brad's cell phone is still at his house, and he turned his car's GPS tracker off, so I don't know where it is, but I'm guessing somewhere near Aly's house."

"How do you know that?" Nico asked.

Fuck. Walked right into that one. "I'm a hacker."

One of Aly's cousins shifted forward, drawing my gaze. "What model and make is Bluhm's car?"

I told him.

Nico snapped his fingers at the son who'd spoken, and I tried not to grind my teeth. It must be a family thing. "Call Jimmy," Nico said. "Get his guys over there, and don't leave until you find the car and haul it out."

His son nodded and peeled away, heading for the door.

Nico turned to another one. "Her house needs to be scrubbed down. Have Aly and Greg meet you there when they're done with Josh's car so she can get her cat and her things before you start."

That son headed for the door next, leaving just me, Nico, and Nico's oldest child—Junior?—standing around the island.

The family patriarch eyed me. "What else?"

"All Brad learned about Aly at the hospital was her first name, so he must have done some digging to find her," I told him. "I'm worried that his phone or a computer at his house might point the cops straight to Aly when he gets reported missing."

Nico turned toward Junior. "Go to Vinny's and tell him you need a whole crew at Bluhm's house."

"He comes from money," I warned them. "He'll probably have security cameras and alarms and—"

Nico held up a hand, silencing me. "All due respect, but this isn't our first rodeo."

"Are you going to steal the computer or hack it?"

Nico glanced at his oldest.

Junior met my eyes. His gaze was even harder than Greg's. "This needs to be a smash-and-grab because we don't have time to prepare. We're gonna steal it."

I shook my head. "That's too suspicious. Take me with you, and I'll hack it."

His brows lifted as he looked me over. "You sure?"

I blew out a breath. "Yes. I do this for a living, and I can get in and wipe Brad's drive in less than ten minutes without leaving a digital footprint."

Junior turned toward his father, brows raised in question.

Nico threw his hands up and whirled back to the coffee machine. "I'm gonna have to make this all over again in a to-go mug."

■ ■ ■

Forty minutes later, I was still alive, having passed whatever weird test that was with Nico in the kitchen, and now I sat in the back of a van, sipping a piping-hot macchiato out of an insulated mug. The sides of the vehicle bore the markings of the local power company. I couldn't figure out if it was stolen, a good copy, or, worst-case scenario, actually belonged to said power company because it was mob-controlled.

I made a mental note to stop messing with their grids whenever I wanted to break into my girlfriend's house. I was already going to owe the mafia a favor for this; there was no need to paint an even bigger target on my back.

"You like the coffee?" Junior asked.

He was seated across from me on a bench with two much larger men I hadn't been introduced to—probably for the better. There were two more on either side of me, and at first, I worried they were *my* cleanup crew until they started talking logistics about what we were about to do.

"The coffee is great," I said.

Junior nodded. "Make sure to tell my old man if you want to get on his good side. He's vain as hell about his barista skills." He frowned and turned toward the man on his right. "Baristo? Is that a gendered term?"

"No idea," the guy grumbled.

My phone chimed in my pocket, and I slouched backward on the bench to fish it out. The second I saw Aly's text, I blew out a relieved breath. "They made it to the garage safely."

"Took them long enough," Junior mumbled.

Where are you? Aly asked.

Doing secret agent shit, I told her.

What do you mean? Are you not at his house anymore?

Smart woman, being vague on the details.

Nope. Out and about, I told her.

What do you mean? Are you already doing something for him?

Maaaybe, I texted back.

WHAT DO YOU MEAN?

I sent her three laughing emojis.

Josh, I am serious right now. Do not do anything for him. This is how they get you.

She was probably right, but there was no way I was backing out now. Not when the alternative was the cops becoming suspicious when Brad's shit went missing along with him.

I took a deep breath and texted her back. *I'll be safe, I promise. But this needs to get done. Please trust me.*

I think you know how much I trust you, she said, and nope, I did not need the reminder of how willingly she'd worn my hand like a necklace while crammed in a van with seven other men.

It's everyone else I don't trust, she said. *If anything happens to you, I'm going scorched earth. Tell whichever of my asshole cousins you're with.*

I glanced up and found Junior watching me.

"Yeah?" he said.

"Aly wanted me to pass along a warning."

He raised his brows and canted his head, waiting.

"She said to make sure I get home safe," I said.

He snorted. "I'm sure it was that PG. You know, for someone not in the family business, she sure shares a lot of our traits."

The guy next to Junior elbowed him in the ribs. "Maybe it's genetic."

Junior turned slowly toward him. "What are you saying? That all Italians are meant to be in the mob?"

"Uh, no," the guy said, backtracking.

"Because that's racist, Phil."

I ducked my head and refocused on my phone. Nope. Not contributing to that argument.

I told him, I said. *You'll be pleased to know that he was shooketh.*

Impressive, she texted back. *Few people know the old English form of that word.*

I grinned. Now that Aly had stopped pretending to be annoyed by my needling, she'd started giving it back to me, and I liked it. A lot.

I slipped a key in your purse, I told her. *It's to my place. If you want to get yourself and The Chosen One settled there, I can meet you after I'm done.*

What about Tyler? she asked. *Won't that be awkward?*

I blinked. Right. Somehow, I'd forgotten about him. And the fact that he and Aly had been together. My brain had probably buried the information to protect me, but now it didn't feel necessary. They'd never been serious, and I knew neither of them still harbored feelings for the other, so there wasn't a need to feel threatened or insecure.

I texted my roommate. *Remember how I agreed to help Aly?*

It was barely five in the morning, but Tyler was an early riser, and even on the weekends, he had difficulty sleeping in. His response came through almost immediately.

Please tell me you two hit it off, he said.

I grinned. I'd lucked out in the best friend department.

A little bubble appeared, telling me he was typing. Another text came through a second later. *Because you've been creepier than normal lately, and I was starting to think I needed to call Maria and Rob for another intervention.*

And just like that, he ruined it.

No need to involve my parents, I told him. *I asked Aly to be my girlfriend.*

Grats! Tyler texted. *Wait, she said yes, right?*

Yeah. Do you mind if she comes over?

Not a problem, he said. *Are you not going to be with her?*

No, I told him. *I have to take care of something, and then I'll be back in an hour or two. Her house needs to get fumigated, so she'll have her cat with her.*

Great. That little shit hates me.

My grin returned. I'd never get over how special it made me feel that I was one of only two humans Fred tolerated. *How dare you impugn the good name of my son.*

Your son?

Yes. Sir Frederick Cappellucci-Hammond, the first of his name.

Tyler texted me an eye-roll emoji. *Thank fucking god there's a woman in your life to take some of your weirdness off my hands.*

Unlike Aly, Tyler didn't seem to appreciate my particular brand of humor.

Thanks for this, I said. *She'll be there in a little while. I gave her a key so she could let herself in.*

Daaamn. A key already? You went in hard. She know about your dad yet?

My grin slipped as a fresh wave of guilt washed over me. *Not yet. She knows my childhood was rough, but not the full extent of it. I plan on telling her when I get home.*

Let me know if you want me there to help explain it all, he said.

I think I'll be okay, but thank you.

I switched back to Aly's text thread. *He's cool with it.*

You sure? she asked. *This will sound horrible, but I didn't even think about how he might feel about us until now.*

Ha! I did the same thing. I blame you for it.

Me?! she wrote back. *How is this my fault?*

Oh, I think you know, I said. *And don't worry. He's just happy I'm happy.*

I'm happy you're happy, too, she wrote.

The van jerked forward like the driver had stomped on the gas. My phone flew out of my hand, and I had to grab onto the bench to avoid joining it on the floor.

Junior slammed into the guy beside him and glared toward the driver's seat. "What the fuck, Vinny?"

"The goddamn cops are at Bluhm's house!" he yelled back.

Junior swore. "Slow down. Speeding past it will look suspicious."

"I got warrants out on me," Vinny said, his voice laced with panic.

Junior shot from his seat, pulling a gun from the inside of his fake power company jacket. He kneeled out of sight behind Vinny and pressed the muzzle to the man's side. The sound of a safety clicking off echoed through the cabin.

"Slow. The fuck. Down," Junior said.

Vinny eased his foot off the gas, and a chorus of relieved exhales rose around me. Jesus Christ, that was tense.

Junior whipped around and pinned me with a glare. "How the fuck are they here already?"

Every set of eyes in the rear of the van swiveled to me like I had all the answers, but all I could do was shrug. "I have no idea."

Junior pulled the gun from Vinny's side and dropped back into the seat across from me. He leaned over, elbows on his knees, and pinned me with his stare. "Start from the beginning and tell me everything that happened again. You guys must have slipped up somewhere."

I reached for my phone on the floor. "Let me just tell Aly to be careful."

Junior kicked the phone out of reach and pointed his gun at me. "Aly will be fine. You need to worry about yourself right now. Start talking, pretty boy."

Oh, fuck.

19

ALY

I COULDN'T HAVE BEEN AWAKE for more than six hours, and I was already exhausted. I guess having my house broken into, aiding in the kidnapping and killing of a rapist, hauling his body halfway across the state, getting screamed at by a mobster, driving back into the city in full-blown terror that I was being followed, and then waiting for two hours in a cold autobody shop while my boyfriend's car was repeatedly deep cleaned by a middle-aged Black man named Lucius would do that to a woman.

And no, Lucius did not appreciate being asked if he'd learned any fun new spells recently.

I still wasn't convinced he wasn't some kind of wizard. The fact that he'd spent the past hour and a half trying to set me on fire with his eyes was suspicious as hell. Unless he'd heard that joke before, in which case . . . fair.

A yowl came from the back seat of Josh's car.

"I know, bud," I told Fred. "Just hold on a few more minutes. We're almost to Daddy's."

Great, now Josh had me saying it, too.

I checked my rearview for what felt like the hundredth time. I'd ordered Greg not to follow me when we parted ways at my house, but I didn't trust the little shit not to lie. Josh already owed my uncle a favor for this; the last thing I wanted was to lead Nico straight to Josh's apartment. Although, if Josh ghosted me for much longer, maybe I'd get mad enough to change my mind.

The light ahead turned red, and I slowed to a stop behind a line of cars, taking the opportunity to check my phone. Again. Still nothing from Josh or any of my male relatives, despite my increasingly threatening texts to the latter. If they hurt my boyfriend, so help me, god, I was going to spend the rest of my life making them regret it. It would be a nonstop campaign of terror. Roadkill left on their cars. Thumbtacks in their shoes. Random pizzas delivered to their house with notes saying they were sent from the feds.

They would never know peace again.

I prayed that I was actually getting ghosted and something horrible hadn't happened since Josh stopped texting me. The last thing I said to him was that I was happy he was happy. If he were any other man, I would have spiraled, thinking that I'd driven him away by being too romantic, too soon, but this was Josh we were talking about. He gleefully saw my "too soon" and raised me a "we now share a child."

Which meant something had probably gone wrong. Fuck.

Unfortunately, there wasn't much I could do about it. I had Fred with me, and if his increasingly pitiful yowls were anything to go by, he needed to get to a litter box, pronto. Even after I got him set up at Josh's, it wasn't like I could leave him there and go back to my uncle's house. Greg told me to lie low for a while, which meant staying away from my fed-attracting family.

Going to them had clearly been a mistake. Josh and I should have taken our chances, hacked Brad apart ourselves, and dealt with the aftermath in therapy later. Or at least I should have. After Josh's initial reaction to Brad's body, jumping straight to dismemberment probably would have been a step too far for him.

The light turned green.

"Just focus," I told myself, easing my foot off the brake.

Greg gave me a list of instructions I still had to follow, including scouring myself in the shower and scraping underneath my finger- and toenails. I'd changed at my house, handing my dirty clothes and shoes over to a guy named Guido, minus the bra and underwear because, ew, no. I wasn't about to give my unmentionables to some gross old mobster.

The phones Josh and I had been texting on were burners. He'd had a spare for me "just in case," and yes, I had side-eyed him for that statement. We'd left our real ones at my house, so if our phone records were ever looked into, it would show we'd been there throughout the night. I had them with me now, along with Josh's laptop and two bags filled with mine and Fred's things.

Another yowl echoed through the car, louder and longer than before.

"Cross your legs or something," I told Fred. "We're almost there."

A second later, I realized it wasn't him but a siren.

The leather covering the steering wheel creaked as I death-gripped it. A check in my rearview revealed a cop car screaming up the street behind me, lights flashing. My heart slammed into my ribs as I slowly eased the car toward the side of the road along with everyone else.

Please don't be after me, I prayed.

The cop slowed alongside the car, and I started to panic before I realized we were right before the intersection, and they were probably checking to see if anyone was coming from the other direction. I turned my face away as they eased past and then picked up speed again on the other side of the intersection.

"Holy shit," I wheezed, dropping my forehead onto the steering wheel. Nope. I wasn't cut out for a life of crime. Blood and gore, I could handle. Constantly worrying about being arrested? Hard pass.

Someone behind me honked, and I jerked upright. Now wasn't the time to have a breakdown.

I waved to the person and started driving again, careful to keep beneath the speed limit. Yes, the car was clean, and no, there wasn't any reason for the cops to be after me so soon, but telling myself that didn't magically erase my paranoia. I had a feeling it'd be weeks, if not months, before I could fully relax again. What would happen to Brad's body? Could Lucius be trusted? He'd seen my face. He could ID me to the cops if questioned.

Goddammit, I just had to go and piss him off with that joke. Maybe I could send him flowers or a new wrench set by way of apology and weasel my way back into his good graces.

Five minutes later, I pulled into Josh and Tyler's parking lot and rolled into the guest spot next to Tyler's SUV. Fred was nonstop meowing, so I eased the strap to his carry bag over my shoulder and grabbed his litter box before heading up. I had their entry code but paused to buzz in instead, giving Tyler a heads-up that I was there. It'd be super awkward to walk in on him when he wasn't expecting it, even though Josh said he was cool.

"Hey, Aly," his voice crackled through the speaker before he buzzed me up.

He met me at their door a few minutes later, holding it open. "Well, hello."

His dark blond hair was wet like he'd just gotten out of the shower, and it looked good slicked back from his face like that. He was shorter than Josh, maybe six feet, and just as muscular, though he appeared more so somehow, without any tattoos to mask his physique. There was no mistaking how handsome he was, but he didn't hold a candle to his roommate in either looks or personality, and I felt nothing for him as I strode past.

"Sorry," I called over my shoulder, heading toward Josh's room. "Cat bathroom emergency."

I saw nothing as I rushed inside the bedroom, too focused on getting the litter box set down and Fred out of his carrier. He bolted straight into the box once free, and I swear I heard an audible kitty sigh before he started peeing. Poor little guy.

I lifted my head and—oh, damn. I was here. On the set of all my favorite videos. There was the couch along the far wall. To my right was a massive bed, complete with hook holes for bondage play. Straight ahead was the wide bank of windows that Josh had stared out of while pretending to be sad.

I was instantly, painfully aroused. My lizard brain expected me to turn around and find the Faceless Man waiting just behind me, chest heaving and covered in blood, and, god, I hoped Josh got home soon. I'd never been so ready for kinky, athletic sex in my life.

Of course, that's when Tyler knocked on the still-open door. "You want coffee or anything?"

I grimaced, glad my back was to him so he wouldn't see my expression and misunderstand. "Coffee sounds great, thank you," I said, my voice two octaves higher than usual.

So awkwaaard.

I waited until I heard him walk away before turning around. Fred was pretty well-behaved, but I didn't know how Tyler would feel about him having free rein in the apartment, so I closed the door to Josh's room behind me to keep him sequestered.

"I'm just going to grab the rest of my stuff!" I called as I paced through the entryway.

"You have the code?" Tyler asked.

"Yup."

"Cool. Just leave the door unlocked then."

I raced out of there, glad to have the frigid winter air on my too-hot skin once I was back outside. Somehow, I hadn't paused to think about what staying at Josh's place would do to me. So far, it was a strange combination of emotions. I had fantasized about doing the darkest, most lascivious things with a man I was obsessed with in one bedroom, while in the other, I'd had real-life, boring sex with a man I had no feelings for.

Josh said Tyler was fine with everything, but now I wondered if I was. Was I adult enough for this situation? Or would the awkwardness of it prove to be too much? I wanted to be chill. Hell, I thought I could be, under normal circumstances, but after the night and morning I'd had, I'd just about reached full mental capacity, and making small talk with a guy I used to get naked with felt like a step too far right now. I'd have to avoid him until I could catch my breath.

I popped the car's trunk and was just reaching in for my things when my phone rang inside my jacket pocket. I whipped it out.

"Josh? Are you okay?"

"Uh . . . not Josh," a woman's voice said.

I pulled the phone from my ear. It was Veronica, my lab tech friend.

"Shit, sorry, Vern," I said, grabbing my bags and shutting the trunk. "I thought you were someone else."

"No worries," she said. "I just wanted to tell you I finished your bloodwork early."

"Vern," I whined, punching in the apartment door code. "I told you not to worry about it."

"I know," she said. "And you still shouldn't feel guilty. No line jumping occurred. I stayed an hour late the past two nights to finish it."

"Vern!" I yelled, my voice echoing up the stairwell. "That makes me feel just as guilty."

"You'll live," she told me. "Want to know the results?"

"Let me guess: they didn't match?"

"Ding, ding, ding!" she said. "We have a winner."

I rolled my eyes and let myself back into the apartment, making a mental note to ask Josh how he'd pulled that off. "I'm sorry I put you through all this for nothing. I feel like a dick."

Fred was waiting for me at Josh's door, and I almost tripped over him on my way inside. "Jesus, Fred. Watch out." I could hear Vern talking, but the phone was away from my ear while I juggled the bags and tried to keep my cat from sprinting past me to freedom. "One second, Vern."

Finally, I got everything inside and Fred corralled back where he belonged. I lifted the phone to my ear. "Sorry about that. What did you say?"

"I said I did some more digging."

Something about her tone had me sinking onto the edge of Josh's bed. It sounded like she was about to give me the kind of news you should hear sitting down. "Okay?"

"Like I told you the other day, you made me curious, so I decided to look past a simple match and see if I could find anything else."

"And?"

"Uh, I don't know a good way to tell you this," she said.

I gripped the phone, starting to get worried. Was there something wrong with Josh's blood? "Rip it off like a Band-Aid," I told Vern.

She took a deep breath. "I checked the sequencing from the bloody rags against the open DNA database we use, and, well, the contributor shares 50 percent of their DNA with the Ken Doll Killer."

I shook my head. "Wait. What are you saying right now?"

"That the man who bled on the rags is the son of a serial killer, Aly."

The phone slipped from my fingers. I could hear Vern calling my name, but a low buzzing filled my ears that drowned her out. The edges of my vision went fuzzy, and my head spun. I was going to pass out. I'd never fainted in my life, but I knew all the symptoms, and after all the shocks I'd suffered today, this last one had clearly pushed me over the edge.

My nursing kicked in, and I laid back on the bed while the room blurred around me. The man who had stalked me, broken into my house, and killed someone was the son of a serial killer.

Oh my god, he filmed himself covered in blood. Did he want to be his dad or something?

Was he already?

I pushed upright. I had to get out of there. True crime wasn't my thing, but I had a working understanding of personality disorders and knew some people with them were good at faking real emotion. Good enough that Bundy had worked alongside one of the best crime writers of our time, and she'd had no idea he was a monster. If Bundy could fool someone like her, what chance did I stand against someone like him?

For all I knew, this was nothing but a big game to Josh—I'd already learned firsthand how much he liked them—and this girlfriend/boyfriend/father-to-my-cat talk was just to butter me up and get me to trust him so I'd be all the more horrified when the real him came out to play.

My head swam as I tried to stand, sending me crashing back to the bed. Fred jumped beside me and made a chirruping noise like he was asking if I was okay.

"Aly!" someone yelled.

Right. Shit. I'd dropped my phone.

I scooped it up. "I'm here," I told Vern. "Sorry. That just threw me."

"Are you okay?" she asked. "Are you safe?"

I looked around, seeing the hooks in the bedframe with new eyes. Was I safe? Josh was still AWOL, so there was time to escape. I couldn't go to my house because he'd already proven how easily he could break into it. Greg told me to stay away from the family, but right now, I couldn't think of anywhere safer than inside the compound of a mobster. Nico probably had more weapons and security than even Josh could circumnavigate.

"Aly?" Vern said, sounding frantic.

"Yeah, sorry. I'm safe. I promise." Or at least I would be soon. "Look, I gotta go. Thank you for telling me."

"Are you sure you're okay?" she said.

"I am. Can you please keep what you found to yourself?" My head was a mess, but one thing was clear: Vern spreading gossip that there was someone related to an infamous serial killer living in the city would send panic through the hospital and bring more attention to me than I needed right now.

"I can," she said. "You can trust me with this because, technically, what I did counts as mishandling hospital assets, and I like my job too much to lose it."

Thank fuck for that.

We said goodbye and hung up, and I stayed on the edge of the bed for a few minutes while I tried to get my heart rate under control. This was the dark past Josh didn't want to tell me about, and now I understood why.

What had he said about the worst time to tell me being right after he killed someone?

I laughed, and it sounded slightly hysterical. Yeah, that timing would have been shitty, but hearing it from him then still would have been better than finding out like this.

Or maybe it was good that he wasn't present to manipulate my response.

I cringed. That thought didn't seem fair. Now that the initial shock of hearing the news was wearing off, I was starting to question my knee-jerk reaction. No, I didn't know Josh that well, but . . . it felt like I did. Not facts like what his favorite color was or who he'd taken to prom, but who he was as a person. He was funny, sweet, and more caring than anyone I'd ever dated, and it was hard to believe he was a good enough actor to fake all that.

I wasn't a true crime writer, but now that I thought about it, I'd probably been around more dangerous people than that woman had. She only interacted with them through highly controlled interviews, whereas I met them in the wild daily. If anything, my instincts were likely sharper than hers because she had correctional officers nearby to save her if anything went wrong, and I only had myself.

My family knew about him. So did my next-door neighbors. And Tyler knew about me. That was a lot of people for the cops to talk to if I suddenly went missing. Wouldn't someone planning to murder me do everything in their power to keep the witnesses to a minimum?

A knock sounded from the bedroom door.

"Aly?" Tyler called. "Coffee's done."

It hit me then. Tyler wasn't just Josh's roommate; he was his best friend. He'd once told me that he and Josh had been besties since they were kids. That meant he probably knew all about Josh's dad.

I pushed up from the bed on shaky legs, my earlier reticence about interacting with my ex disappearing. If anyone could answer my questions and give me more insight into whether or not Josh was who I hoped he was, it was Tyler.

"Woah, are you okay?" he asked as I emerged from the bedroom.

"No. I just had a bit of a shock."

"Here, sit down," he said, pulling one of the barstools from beneath the kitchen island.

I slumped into it, watching him pour me coffee, wondering how to breach this topic. I couldn't think of a casual way, so I decided to dive right in. "Do you know who Josh's dad is?"

Tyler stiffened, his back to me. "Why do you ask?"

"Do you know or not?"

He jerked his head in an abrupt nod.

"Well, I just found out about him and have some questions."

Tyler sent me a wary look over his shoulder. "I really don't think I'm the one who should answer them. Josh would probably be better."

I shook my head. "I want to hear it from you."

He frowned and turned to face me. "Why?"

Fuck, how to explain this? "Because some of my questions are harsh, and I don't want to hurt his feelings."

"Yes, because Josh is so delicate," he said, returning to the coffee.

I tamped down my rising annoyance. "It doesn't matter if someone is delicate or not. You should care about their feelings either way." Speaking of feelings, no wonder I'd never developed any for this guy. Without the lust for his body blinding me, he was more of a douche than I remembered.

He turned and set my coffee in front of me. "Whatever. Ask your questions."

"He's not like him, right?"

Tyler jerked like I'd slapped him. "Jesus, no. Why would you think that?"

I contemplated bringing up Josh's social media account but thought better. Knowing Josh, not even Tyler knew about it. And I definitely couldn't bring up Brad, but I needed clarity on something Josh said concerning his death.

"He made a comment about worrying he was fated to be a killer."

Tyler's expression darkened. "That fucking psychologist."

"What?" I said, confused.

"After Josh's dad got arrested, his mom took him to see this renowned psychologist to help heal Josh's trauma," Tyler said. "The doctor had just taken part in this study trying to prove that psychopathy was genetic. He was convinced he was right even though the data was slightly questionable. And there was Josh. A golden goose dropped right into his lap. Within a month, he had Josh and Maria convinced that Josh needed to be on antipsychotics for the rest of his life or he'd turn into his father."

I leaned back in my seat, horrified. "What kind of doctor does that?"

Tyler shook his head. "He isn't one anymore. Josh wasn't the only kid he manipulated in an attempt to validate his study, and his victims ended up taking part in a civil suit against him. He lost his license to practice, but the damage was done. Josh only recently got off most of his meds, and if he's still making comments like the one you mentioned, he must still be questioning that decision."

"So, he never should have been on them?"

"No," Tyler said. "He has some quirks, sure, but who doesn't? The important thing is that he has none of the more troubling signs that would point to antisocial personality disorder." He rested his elbows on the counter and met my eyes. "I knew his dad, and Josh is nothing like him. The fact that I'm still alive should be all the proof you need." He grinned. "I'm not sure if you've noticed, but I can be a bit much sometimes."

I took a sip of coffee. Yeah, I was starting to see that. "Why didn't Josh tell me about all this sooner?"

Tyler pushed upright and snagged his mug from the counter. "Probably because he knew you'd try to bolt."

"Hey," I said. "Does it look like I'm bolting?"

He snorted. "From how pale you were when you came out here, I think it's safe to say that you would have if I weren't home to talk you down from the ledge."

Okay, that was fair. But still. "Look, I had good reason to worry. Your roommate broke into my house and planted a camera there. And also hacked into my work to watch me."

Instead of being appropriately horrified, Tyler laughed. "Finally, someone to take some of the burden of his love off my shoulders." He reached over and grabbed my wrist, looking grateful. "Bless you."

I jerked out of his grip. "I'm serious, Tyler."

"So am I," he said. "Those are the quirks I was talking about. Josh spent his childhood trapped beneath the thumb of a serial killer. Once he and his mom got away, he spent every second of free time ensuring they never ended up back there. Even as an adult, he needs to know everything about the people he cares for, where they are, and who they're with. One time, I forgot to tell him I was staying out for the night, and he showed up at my hookup's house at three o'clock in the morning to lecture me about it."

I grinned. That sounded like something Josh would do.

"You have no idea what kind of nightmare he escaped from," Tyler said. "That he still lives. News agencies and media outlets are constantly trying to track him and Maria down for interviews. It's made him a paranoid recluse, and it's been even worse since that documentary came out this summer. He barely left the house before you two started seeing each other."

"Why?" I asked, confused.

"You really don't like true crime, do you?" Tyler said, fishing his phone from his pocket. "Josh looks exactly like his dad."

He pulled something up on his phone and slid it across the island toward me. I picked it up and, holy shit. He was right. Their hair might have been different, and Josh's skin was darker, but aside from that, the men were identical.

No, wait.

I leaned in, studying the serial killer's eyes. Those were different, too. They were that weird dead/alive combo, like the other killer I'd met, like Brad's, with none of the warmth and humor I regularly saw from Josh. I scrolled down from the photo and quickly scanned the attached article. Josh's dad was right up there with Bundy and Dahmer when it came to the horror of his crimes, and I could only imagine what life must have been like with him as a parent.

I handed the phone back to Tyler.

He slid it into his pocket and studied me over the top of his mug. "Josh has to know things, Aly. Feeling safe is important to him, and keeping the people he cares about safe is even more so. If you're going to be with him, you'll have to accept that he doesn't give a shit about normal boundaries. My car has a GPS tracker that he put there the day I drove it off the lot. I have location data turned on in my phone so he can constantly check up on my whereabouts. If you were a true crime fan, I never would have invited you back here because they're not allowed in the apartment."

"That . . . weirdly doesn't bother me," I admitted.

Tyler nodded. "Yeah, me neither. It's nice having someone always looking out for you. Like your own personal guardian angel."

"It sounds like you look out for him, too, though," I said. He frowned, and I motioned toward the apartment. "The not bringing people here who might recognize him thing, taking time to explain this to me, and being cool about us seeing each other."

He huffed a laugh. "If I'd known you two were a possibility, I would have immediately ended things between us and shoved you at him. No offense."

"None taken," I said, waving him off.

He leaned back against the counter. "I know it's a lot to take in, but Josh is the most trustworthy, loyal person I know. Does he have his quirks? Yes. Will you get annoyed at the way he turns everything into a joke? Sooner than you expect. But Josh is the kind of ride-or-die you could go to with a body, and he'd help you hide it."

I choked on my coffee. If only Tyler knew how true that statement was.

He spun and grabbed me a wad of napkins.

"Thanks," I managed in between bouts of hacking. "Swallowed it the wrong way."

"No problem," he said. "And look, if you don't think you can deal with Josh's baggage, you should back out now. He lets so few people in that if you drag it out, you'll only hurt him more."

I nodded. "I get that. I don't let people in either."

Tyler raised his brows and gave me A Look. "Yeah. I know."

I cringed. "Sorry."

He waved me off. "No hard feelings. We obviously wouldn't have worked out had we tried for anything serious."

I nodded. Yes, Tyler was a douche, but somehow, I was starting to think he was a likable one. As in, I could see myself becoming friends with him if Josh and I stayed together for a while.

"What else should I know?" I asked.

"He's vegan," Tyler said.

I frowned. "But he made me bacon and eggs the other day."

And now I knew why they'd been terrible. Because Josh probably had no idea how to cook them properly.

Tyler whistled. "He must have it bad. I've never been allowed to cook meat in here."

"Why not?"

"Uh, how do I put this lightly?" Tyler said, tapping his chin. "His dad stirred one of his victims into hamburger patties and fed her to our entire neighborhood at a block party."

I gagged. "What?!"

"Yeah. That kind of thing sticks with most six-year-olds."

I held up a hand. "Yup, I get it. No more details, please. Wait." I narrowed my gaze at him. "How can you still eat meat?"

"I ate a hot dog instead of a burger that day."

"Yeah, but you still smelled her being cooked" was a sentence I never thought would come out of my mouth.

Tyler shrugged. "Fair. But smelling and tasting are two different things."

"Ew. Enough," I said. Even for me, this conversation was too much, especially after I'd made that offhand comment about burning Brad's body parts. Poor Josh. He must have been retraumatized when I said it.

I felt like such an asshole for my momentary freakout after Vern's call. Thank fuck I'd always been a logical person and was able to come to my senses, even after all the shit I'd been through over the past twenty-four hours. Imagine if I'd stormed out of there without giving Josh a chance and let a misunderstanding potentially ruin our relationship. Unforgivable.

Josh and I were alike in so many ways, and the more I learned about his past, the more I was beginning to see that. Things were clicking into place about why Josh was the way he was and why he'd started his social media account. I just hoped he would listen to what I had to say about all this when he finally got home. I hated the idea that he still questioned himself, and if there was anything I could do to set his mind at ease once and for all, I would do it.

As if I'd summoned him, the front door opened, and Josh walked in. He was beautiful, even pale and exhausted, and wearing a stranger's clothes that were obviously too small for him. The stubble on his chin was growing out, lending him a rough edge that wasn't there when he was freshly shaven. I liked it. A lot.

All my earlier worries disappeared at seeing him unharmed, and I threw myself off the barstool to go to him. He scooped me up in his big arms and lifted me right off my feet, hugging me close.

"You're safe," we said at the same time.

"Glad you're back, man," Tyler said. "Oh, and Aly knows about your dad." Josh went stiff in my arms. "I'll kindly see myself out and let you two deal with this alone."

I pulled back enough to glare at Tyler as he strolled past us with a shit-eating grin. "Turn me toward him."

"Why?" Josh asked.

"So I can kick him," I said, lashing out and missing by more than two feet.

Tyler's chuckle echoed through the exterior hall before he shut the door behind himself.

Josh set me back on my feet, his expression guarded as he stared down at me. "He told you?"

I shook my head. "The lab tech I gave your samples to did more digging than she should have, and DNA matched you to your dad."

Josh swore. "I knew I should have broken in and stolen them."

"Don't worry, she promised to keep her mouth shut."

"And you trust her to?" he asked.

"Yes. She's my friend, and her job depends on it."

The words did nothing to stem his open worry. "Are you . . . ?" He ran a hand over his face. "Fuck, this isn't how I wanted things to go."

"It's okay," I said, gripping his biceps. "I'm not freaking out."

He eyed me.

"Anymore," I added. "Tyler cleared things up for me."

"Then I should really be worried," Josh said.

I shook my head. "He's a good friend."

He huffed out a breath. "I know. A douche, but a good friend."

"I understand why you do it," I said.

"Do what?"

"Wear a mask. Cover yourself in fake blood."

His brows rose. "Really? Because I'd love an explanation."

I took one of his hands and led him toward the kitchen. He looked just as tired as I was, and I thought he could use a cup of coffee, so I had him sit on my vacated barstool as I poured him one.

"You're doing the same thing I am," I said. "Trying to rewrite history."

"How so?"

"I try to save every patient as if it might somehow make up for not saving my mom." I turned and handed him his coffee. "And you dress up like a scary serial killer but do the opposite of what your dad did."

He blinked.

"Think about it," I said, scooping my mug from the island. "You broke into my house and stalked me, just like your father did to his victims, but you never meant to hurt me, only bring me pleasure. You do the same thing for millions of people on the internet three times a week. You distract them from this shitshow of a world and make them feel good instead of bad."

He leaned back, looking contemplative. "I never thought of it that way."

"You're the opposite of him, Josh," I said.

He shook his head, eyes sad as they met mine. "I like fear like he did."

My heart stuttered for a second. "My reaction to Brad breaking in turned you on?" Oh, god. I didn't know how I would handle that if it were true.

"Christ, no," he said. "Not that kind of fear."

"What, specifically, then?" I asked.

He broke our gaze, staring past me as if searching for the right words. "It's hard to explain, but those moments when I catch you off guard and watch your eyes flash wide with fear before bleeding into desire is what turns me on."

I grinned. "Play back what you just said because it sounds to me like you don't like fear so much as you like it when I stop being afraid and start being horny."

His eyes returned to mine, and I could see the wheels turning in his head. "I don't care about other people besides those in my inner circle."

I shrugged. "So? Most of them are garbage anyway."

"I have no regrets about stalking you."

"Me neither. You might have noticed that I never asked you to stop. No safe words, remember?"

He nodded, eyeing me. "I remember, baby."

I shivered. Why did that pet name turn me on so much? Or was it more about the ownership he sunk into the word every time he used it?

"Now," I said. "If you're done trying to scare me off, I'd like to know why you stopped texting me two hours ago."

The heat cleared from his eyes. "We didn't get into Brad's house. The cops were already there when we arrived."

I swore and nearly dropped my coffee. "What? How?"

"It wasn't anything you and I did," he said. "They were there to serve an arrest warrant related to Macy's assault."

I pinched the bridge of my nose. "That's some godawful timing."

"I know," he said. "Your cousin held me at gunpoint until we figured it out."

I dropped my hand and stared at him, lips curling in a snarl. "Which one?"

Josh leaned away from me, circling a finger between us. "You got a real creepy vibe going on right now, and I don't know if I should be worried or turned on." He glanced at his lap, hidden by the island overhang. "Never mind. My body figured it out."

"This isn't the time for joking," I told him. "This is the time to start planning our second murder."

"I thought you said it was involuntary manslaughter."

"Quit stalling and give me a name."

"Nope," he said. "Not until Scary Aly gives me my girlfriend back. Plus, it was all a misunderstanding. He apologized afterward and invited me to his weekly poker game. I think we're friends now."

"No making friends with my mobster cousins," I said. "Nothing good can come of that. Wait. Did they drop you off here? Do they know where you live now?"

He nodded, and I had to set my coffee on the counter to keep from crushing it in my grip. So much for trying to keep him safe from them. I guess it was a losing battle anyway. I was sure either Greg or Lucius made note of Josh's license plate, and it was only a matter of time until they used it to find him.

"What happened after you left Nico's?" Josh asked.

We spent the next ten minutes filling each other in on everything we'd missed after being separated. From the sound of it, my uncle had everything well in hand, and I could only imagine the favor I would owe him when all was said and done. I was especially worried about what he'd ask Josh to do, and I planned to be there when it happened so I could negotiate the terms down and threaten Nico with never seeing me again, his last remaining extended family, if he pushed for too much.

"Come here," Josh said when we finished talking.

I rounded the island, and he turned in his stool and pulled me between his legs, wrapping his arms around my waist.

"Thank you for being so understanding about everything with my dad," he said.

I shook my head. "Don't thank me. I went into a blind panic right after finding out."

He tipped my chin up and stroked his thumb over my lower lip, his gaze fixated on the motion. “I don’t blame you for that. The fact that you were able to work through it is what matters.”

“It wasn’t hard when I stopped to think for a second,” I said, snaking my arms around his neck. “I’ve met my fair share of bad people, Josh, and I can safely say you’re nothing like them.”

“No?” he said, still staring at my lips.

“No. And if I have to tie you up and edge you until you agree with me, I’ll do it. I’ve been studying up.”

He grinned, his dark eyes finally rising to mine. “Oh, I know you have. I’ve been watching.”

We smiled at each other for a moment, and I wanted to lean in and kiss him so bad it hurt.

“How are you?” I asked. “Really?”

He shifted forward and rested his forehead against mine, his eyes bottomless pools of black as his pupils edged out the brown of his irises. “Exhausted. You?”

“Same.”

“Wanna go shower together and then sleep for another twelve or thirteen hours?”

“I do,” I said, tightening my arms around his neck.

“God, I love hearing you say that,” he rumbled, and then I was airborne as he scooped me up and strode toward his room.

It was as he was opening the door that I remembered the tripping hazard waiting on the other side of it.

“Be careful!” I got out just as the door swung open, and Fred scream-ran between Josh’s legs, making him stumble.

Thank god for Josh’s athletic ability because he managed to take a few staggered steps forward, and we fell onto the bed instead of the concrete floor. Unfortunately, Josh was a big sonofabitch, and even though he threw a hand out to brace himself at the last minute, most of his weight landed on top of me, knocking the air from my lungs.

“Ow, fuck, my knee,” he said, rolling off me.

“My ribsss,” I wheezed.

He turned his head, a grin lifting his full lips as our gazes caught. “Now I see why people say having kids puts a cramp on your sex life.”

“Is that what just happened? Or did Fred just wingman us? I mean, we are on a bed.”

“He’s such a good boy,” Josh said, rolling back my way. “Extra treats for him tonight.”

And then he was on me, big body rising over mine, my very own unmasked fantasy come to life.

20

JOSH

I BRUSHED ALY'S HAIR BACK from her face. She knew. This gorgeous, kind, sexy woman had found out about my past, and instead of running away, she dug her heels in and taught me things about myself that shifted my perspective.

How the fuck had I gotten so lucky?

I'd spent my entire life convinced that I couldn't have someone like her. That I wasn't safe. That a ticking time bomb lived inside my mind, and once I reached some unseen point, it would go off, and *boom*, I'd become just like my father. Mom and Rob had tried to tell me that wasn't true. So did Tyler, in his own way. So had my therapist. It wasn't until Aly that I started to think they were telling the truth.

And no, it wasn't because meeting the right person at the right time had magically healed me. I'd been warming up to the idea for a while. Aly was simply the final hurdle. She'd let herself be vulnerable with me, and instead of taking advantage of that and harming her, all I wanted to do was cherish her instead.

It was time to accept it once and for all: I was nothing like my father, at least not where it mattered most.

A distant meow caught my attention. Right. Fred.

"Stay right here," I told Aly.

She scratched her nails down my back. "Or what?"

I shot her a dark look. "Or I'll decide it's time for your punishment."

She grinned. "For what?"

It was obvious she had no idea what I was talking about or how much she'd scared and worried me earlier, or she wouldn't have been giving me such a flirtatious look. I gripped her chin, not hard enough to hurt, but hard enough that she'd know I was serious. "For coming out of your bedroom after you told me you'd stay put."

Her smile faltered. "But I heard someone get punched and worried it was you."

I shook my head. "And if it had been, seeing you would have been such a distraction that I probably would have gotten hit again. You gave me your word, Aly. And then you broke it."

"I was scared you were hurt, and I did what I felt was right," she said, her stubborn streak emerging. "And I was careful. I snuck out with a loaded gun. If you'd been on the ground, I would have shot Brad. I'm not sorry for what I did."

"You will be by the time I'm done with you," I said, leaning in to bite her lower lip.

Her eyes were wide as I pulled away, her expression a mix of surprise, worry, and what looked like anticipation. I reached down and stroked a thumb over the spot where her nipple pebbled her thin sweater, just long enough for her to arch into the pleasure before I pinched her, drawing a shocked gasp from her lips.

"Josh," she said as I stood and turned away. "You can't be serious about punishing me."

I paused at the door and looked back at her. "I am. But not right now. We don't have time. I have no idea how long Tyler plans to give us, and I need to be inside you. Go start the shower while I gather our wayward child."

She nodded, my fierce, strong girlfriend turning compliant at the command in my tone. That switch had been thrown inside me again, and now that I no longer feared my needs turning dangerous, I didn't have to hold back. It made me impatient, borderline grouchy that I wasn't already balls-deep in Aly's tight, welcoming pussy.

She scrambled up as I turned and left, and I heard her rushing for my en suite bathroom, as ready for this as I was. It was becoming increasingly apparent that Aly had a switch similar to mine. Her job demanded that she always be in control. She was solely responsible for her house, car, yard work, Fred's care, and her own welfare. It was easy to see why she was so submissive with me in the bedroom—she needed someone else to take control. She craved feeling safe and protected just as much as she wanted it rough and dirty. We were the perfect pairing in that regard.

The sound of the shower turning on followed me out of the bedroom as I looked for Fred. He was nowhere to be seen at first glance in the living room, and thanks to the acoustics in there, the echo from his next yowl made it sound like he was behind the couch. I leaned over it, searching for him, but he wasn't there. Another yowl had me stalking into Tyler's room. He'd left the door open, and it would be just my luck that Fred would decide to piss on Tyler's dirty laundry pile, conveniently located right next to his empty hamper.

My roommate was going to drive his future partner insane one day with shit like that. Maybe I could tell them about my successful sock experiment, and they could use it to fix the rest of Tyler's bad habits.

Thankfully, Fred wasn't inside the bedroom, so I closed the door and turned to face the open living space. He had to be somewhere in it. There weren't any other rooms in the apartment for him to hide in.

"Come on, bud," I said, checking behind the curtains. "You just wingmanned me. I need you to not be a cockblock right now." My dick was straining against my zipper, almost painfully erect. I needed Aly like I needed air.

Another yowl had me lifting my gaze to the top of the kitchen cabinets. There Fred sat, looking pleased with himself as he stared down at me from on high.

"How the hell did you even get up there?" I asked, dragging one of the island barstools over so I could grab him.

By the time I got him back into my room and the door closed behind us, steam was billowing out of the en suite. I told Fred to behave and went to find his mother. Her clothes sat in a pile on the bathmat, which meant that all that separated me from a naked, soaking-wet Aly was the flimsy shower curtain between us.

I ripped my shirt over my head before jerking my belt loose. A few seconds later, my clothes landed in a pile next to my girlfriend's, and in two strides, I stood just outside the shower. I yanked the curtain open, savoring the sight of Aly's wide eyes, drinking in the sound of her gasp before her momentary fear and surprise quickly turned to lust.

She was right. It wasn't fear I liked; it was the moment it shifted into desire. The woman was as intelligent as she was beautiful, and the sight of her standing there, frozen beneath the stream of water, arrested me. She was so striking, her long, dark hair clinging to wet skin, her body an artwork of muscles and curves. Her dusky nipples had tightened into stiff buds, either from arousal or the cool air streaking past me into the stall, and I wanted to take my time worshipping them, laving them until she was so needy she was begging for it. But we didn't have time for any of that, and from the hungry look on her face, foreplay was the last thing on her mind.

I stepped into the shower, right beneath the stream of water, forcing Aly backward. Her eyes roved over me like she didn't know where to look first, and belatedly, I realized it was her first time seeing me naked. Even though my hands shook with the need to hold her, I let her take her time inspecting me, leaning my head back into the water so the warmth rushed over me, flexing just a little for her. The heat in her eyes made me understand why Tyler was always posing for people. I could quickly become addicted to the open need on her oh-so-expressive face.

She shook her head as her eyes met mine. "You're so beautiful. I know I've said it an embarrassing amount of times online, but I mean it."

I went still beneath the water. "You don't look at me and see my father?"

"No," she said, and I let out a relieved exhale as her gaze slid down to my cock. "I just see my boyfriend. And I need him right now."

Fuck. She was about to get more of him than she was probably ready for. I hadn't missed that brief moment of hesitation when she saw the monster straining between us. She'd had my dick in her mouth and sandwiched between those perfect tits, which meant she knew damn well how big it was, but now that it was time to take it into her body, it looked like it was hitting her for the first time just how much she'd have to stretch around me. Good thing she'd had plenty of prep with that huge vibrator of hers.

It still wouldn't be enough, and yes, I knew exactly how fucked up it was that the idea of her having trouble taking all of me turned me on even more.

"Turn around," I told her. "Put your hands on the wall."

She spun without argument, palms flattening over the tile, back arched, ass out like a present. I nearly groaned at the sight of her tight, rounded cheeks. One day, I would claim every single part of this woman, but I didn't have the patience for the prep work she'd need for anal. Hell, I didn't even have the patience to prep her pussy the way she deserved.

I stepped right into her, my dick framed by her ass as I placed a palm next to hers on the tile. My lips brushed the shell of her ear. "I need you too much to go easy on you right now."

A low whimper slipped through her lips. "I don't want you to go easy on me."

She spread her legs nice and wide for me, an anticipatory shiver wracking her body as she ground against me. The moan she let out was enough to push me toward the edge of my control. I shoved her lower back down, arching her like a bowstring, my palm leaving the cool tile to snake between her thighs. She was soaked, and I could tell from the slickness coating her sex that it had nothing to do with the shower. Aly wanted me just as much as I wanted her, and here was my proof.

I stroked my fingers up from her slit to her clit, rubbing a circle around it as I slid down just enough to get my dick beneath her. If I didn't do this right, she'd end up too sore to take me again when we had more time, and a little patience now would pay off later. As soon as her house was safe for us to return, I was locking us inside until I had my fill of her, which would likely be never. Thank god for modern technology and grocery delivery services. I might manage to keep her naked for the next two weeks if I played my cards right.

"Please," she whispered, grinding against my fingers.

I shifted my hips forward just enough to nudge at her entrance, just enough for her to feel how wide the head of my dick was. She sucked in a breath, tensing up at the threat of such a brutal invasion.

"Relax, baby," I told her, brushing her hair from her neck. "You can take it."

I rolled my fingers over her clit again, and she shuddered, shoving back against me on instinct. I thrust forward at the same time, just enough to sink my tip into her. She was soaking wet, but it was still a tight fit, tight enough that it felt like a soft, warm vise was wrapped around the head of my cock, and oh, fuck, did it feel good.

I slipped my hand from her clit to her hip, holding her in place, gripping her hard enough that I would probably leave marks, but my hold on her was the only thing keeping me sane, keeping me from losing the last of my sanity and pounding into her like a mindless beast.

My other hand rose to her neck, snaking around her delicate, vulnerable throat in the possessive way I knew she loved. I leaned over her and whispered, "Don't tense up again."

She sucked in a ragged breath and shook her head. "I won't."

"Good girl," I said, and without warning, I kicked her feet farther apart, sinking in another inch as she dropped onto me.

I groaned. She hissed. But instead of tensing, she braced her hands on the wall and breathed through it.

"You're so big," she said.

My balls tightened. "Too big?"

She shook her head, neck muscles flexing beneath my fingertips. "No. Give me more."

I slipped out just enough to coat myself in her slickness before shunting my hips forward, fighting for another glorious inch. Fuck, she was so tight. Tight enough that I knew she was having to work to keep from clenching up around me as her body tried to fight the invasion.

"More," she panted.

I gripped her neck. "So impatient."

"For you, always," she said.

"I need to go slow to keep from hurting you."

She writhed in my grip, her words strangled. "I don't care if it hurts. I need you, Josh. Now. Please."

"Fuck, Aly," I said, working another inch into her and then another, trying to be careful, trying to keep my desperation for her at bay even as my thrusts quickened. "I need this pussy."

She straightened her arms, head dropping as she pushed herself against me. "It's yours. Take it. Claim it. Don't hold back."

"You don't know what you're asking," I warned.

She made a low, angry sound. "Yes, I do. Fuck me, Josh. Fuck your girlfriend."

The last of my control splintered. I shifted my angle, pulling out until only the head of my dick was nestled inside her, and then shoved forward with a ruthless thrust, hitting something deep inside that made her yelp and stiffen.

I went still, breathing hard. I'd tried to fucking warn her it would be too much, but would the woman listen? No, she had to go and use the "girlfriend" word on me, knowing it would be my undoing, knowing that—

"Again," she demanded, the word half-pained, half-needy, her pussy clenching around me.

All thoughts of hurting her fled from my mind. She was a grown-ass woman who knew what she wanted, and if getting railed by her boyfriend in the shower was what she demanded, then I was going to give it to her, just as hard as her greedy little cunt needed it.

I let go of her neck and hip, lifting my hands to pinch and tease her nipples as I started a steady, relentless rhythm. She bucked against me, using the wall to push herself back and meet every savage thrust.

It was rough. It was wild. I was so deep inside her that I was starting to lose sight of where I ended, and she began. It felt like our bodies were one, like she was made to take me, and I was made to give her every thick inch I could, stretching her until no cock but mine would satisfy her from this moment onward.

She'd asked me to claim her, so I leaned forward and bit her shoulder hard enough to make her hiss, hard enough to feel her stiffen in my grip before she shuddered and threw her hips back with even more intensity than before. I held her in place with my teeth, my dick branding her pussy, my fingers tormenting her nipples. This woman was fucking mine, and if I had to mark every inch of her skin, I would.

I'd never felt more feral in my life, like I could fight every man who looked at her, put a fucking collar on her neck and lead her around on a leash just to prove that she belonged to me.

Aly didn't have to lay claim to me in return. She already owned me, body and soul. Every snap of her hips, every sweet, needy sound that echoed through the shower only served to tighten her hold on me.

She writhed, moaned, widened her legs, and circled her hips, and oh, fuck, the way her pussy clenched around me was going to milk me fucking dry.

"Tell me you're on the pill," I said.

"Yes," she moaned. "Don't pull out. I want to feel you unload inside me."

I leaned back just enough to stare down at what I was doing to her, watching my straining dick disappear into her tight little pussy, loving the way she made my skin glisten with the evidence of her arousal.

"You should see how good you take me," I told her, and she moaned and ground back into me. I pinched her nipples, fucking into her. "I can't wait to feel you come. You squeeze me so good, baby."

She cried out, thrusting back, her spine stiffening, fingers scrabbling on the tile as she started tipping over the edge. "More," she moaned. "Please, Josh."

I slipped a hand down her stomach, knowing what she needed, and gently pinched her clit between my fingers as I pistoned my hips forward, crashing into her. She came screaming, sobbing, begging, her pussy gripping my dick so hard I could barely move.

The second she started to come down from her orgasm, I pulled out of her and spun her around, grabbing her by the legs and hauling her upright so I could look her in the eye while I finished fucking her.

"Watch me," I said as I slid her down, spearing her with my cock.

She wrapped her arms around my neck and clung on as I straightened to my full height and shoved her against the wall.

Her eyes flashed wide. "This angle. How do you feel even bigger now?"

I grinned, knowing it was smug. "I held back on you."

She had just enough time to frown in confusion before I rammed fully home. I'd been waiting for this moment, waiting until she came and was loose and languid and fully aroused before I gave her the last inch of me. Her mouth popped open on a shocked inhale as I bottomed out, but I didn't give her time to adjust as I pounded into her, watching her surprise and borderline panic lose the battle against her lust.

She whimpered and rolled her hips experimentally, and she must have liked the result because the moan that tore free from her was deeper, rougher than the ones I'd heard so far.

"Do that again," I told her.

She did, and we both moaned.

"I'm going to come again," she said, head tilting back.

I squeezed her thighs. "Eyes on me, remember? I want to watch you this time."

She swore, nails digging into my shoulders, a line appearing between her brows as she frowned in concentration. "I don't know if I can. I've never looked into someone's eyes as I came before."

"You can do it, baby," I told her, shifting my hips so I hit a spot deep inside her that had her scratching at my back as she writhed. She'd better fucking do it soon because my balls were starting to tighten up, and I could feel pressure building low on my spine. "Give me another one, Aly. Be a good girl, and come on your boyfriend's dick."

The dirty talk sent her back arching, hips shifting at a frantic pace that I had no choice but to meet, and a heartbeat later, I got to watch from inches away as her eyes lost focus and her pussy tightened around me again.

"Josh," she moaned.

The sound of my name, spoken with such reverence, was enough to push me over the edge, our gazes holding as my dick grew even larger and stiffened, drawing out her orgasm as I unloaded deep inside her like she'd asked me to.

"Fuck, Aly," I groaned. "Fuck, you feel so good."

I thrust in one last time and went still, my heart thundering, legs turning to jelly even as she went boneless in my grip. It took me a moment to realize I'd buried my head in her shoulder and bitten her again like a fucking animal, but from the way she stroked her hands up and down my back and kissed the side of my cheek, she must not have minded very much.

"I need to pick up the morning-after pill," she muttered.

I unlatched my jaw and jerked back. "I thought you said you were on the pill?" Not that I minded if we had an "accident" even this early into things. I'd never regret bringing a miniature version of this woman into the world, and don't ask me why I knew our firstborn would be a wild-child little girl—I just did.

"I am," she said. "But my ovaries can't be trusted around you."

I buried my head back into her neck. Of course, she would make me laugh ten seconds after giving me the best orgasm of my goddamn life.

"Probably smart that we pick it up," I said. "I'm pretty sure my sperm can't be trusted around you either."

She started to giggle, a dopey, sex-drunk sound, before I eased out of her, and her laugh turned into a hiss.

I winced. I'd probably gone a little too hard there at the end. "You okay?"

She nodded. "I'm sore, but in a good way."

"You sure?" I asked.

"Yes," she said, rising on her tiptoes, a hand snaking around my neck to draw me down. "Thank you. I needed that."

And then her mouth was on mine, and she was kissing me like she was ready for round two. She tugged me closer, plastering her naked body against mine, and fuck if I wasn't getting hard again for her already. The feel of her wet tits against my chest was too good to resist, and I didn't bother stopping myself from reaching down and gripping her ass, hauling her closer.

The front door slammed shut, and Tyler called out a greeting.

Aly writhed against me, pulling back just enough to whisper, "I can be quiet if you can."

I shook my head. "I'm not risking it. Your noises aren't for anyone but me now."

Her lips parted. "That shouldn't be so hot."

"What? My possessiveness?"

She nodded.

I arched a brow at her. "So you'd be fine with another woman listening to me grunt and moan for you?"

She wrinkled her nose. "Guess not."

I bumped my forehead against hers. "That's what I thought. Now, come on, let's get cleaned up. I'm as hungry as I am tired after that."

She leaned back, eyes running over my body. "Huh. I thought you'd have more stamina than this."

I mock-growled at her. "Blame yourself. Your pussy just milked me bone dry, woman."

She slapped a hand over my mouth, wide-eyed. "Say that a little louder, will you?"

I bit her palm, and she yelped and pulled back. "I said I didn't want people to hear you, not that I wasn't fully okay with telling everyone I meet from this point forward just how well you take my cock."

She shifted her gaze from mine, cheeks flushing, and tried to slip past me into the shower stream. As she did, I caught her muttering, "It shouldn't be hot," over and over again, like she was trying to convince herself she wasn't into it.

I stepped aside and let her past me, daydreaming of all the fun I'd have getting her to admit things to herself.

She moved to stand directly beneath the cascading water, and unable to help myself, I stepped behind her and wrapped my arms around her waist, bending down just enough to trail a lazy line of kisses up her neck.

"Promise you're okay," I said.

She nodded. "Better than okay. I hope you're serious about this boyfriend-girlfriend thing because that was the best sex of my life, and if you try to break up with me right now, you're going to be the one with a stalker."

I chuckled. "Don't threaten me with a good time. I'd love to round a corner and find you waiting for me in the dark."

She shuddered in my arms. "Fuck. Same."

I perked up. "In the mask?"

She whimpered and nodded, and I clapped a hand over her mouth to shut her up. "In a house or the woods?"

She nodded again, and I took it as a yes to both.

I leaned down and nipped at her neck, reveling in the way she squirmed in response. "We are going to have so much fun together."

In response, she wiggled her ass into my semi-erect dick, and only the thought of my roommate overhearing us stopped me from bending her over for round two.

21

ALY

THE THING ABOUT GETTING FUCKED hard is that it leaves you both sore *and* horny. It was midday Sunday, just over a day after Josh dicked me brainless in the shower, and we were back in his car headed to my place. My cousin Alec assured me the house was sparklingly clean. His crew had even gone so far as to set up my new bed—that Josh and I forgot was arriving thanks to the Brad debacle.

That bed was all I could think of right now. Every time I shifted in the passenger seat, a little pang of soreness radiated between my legs, making me think of exactly how I'd gotten so sore. I couldn't stop picturing my hands braced on the shower wall. If I closed my eyes, I swore I could feel an echo of Josh pounding into me, hitting something deep inside that had driven my pleasure to new heights.

Then there was the second orgasm he'd given me, his dark, heated eyes staring straight into mine, the tile cold against my back as he thrust inside, filling me and stretching me so much that it felt like my body would never forget the feel of his thick cock. The man was ruining me for anyone else. He was the perfect blend of competent and domineering. And when he came, and I got to both feel and watch it happen? It brought a new closeness to our relationship that I hadn't anticipated.

Josh threw his blinker on and pulled into the turn lane that led to my neighborhood. He'd cranked the heat up for me and Fred, and it was toasty enough in the car that he'd shoved his sleeves up to his elbows. I'd learned over the past few nights what a furnace the man was, and I loved it. There was nothing like slipping beneath cool sheets and snuggling up to my own personal heater. Even though Josh ran hot, he was a cuddler—because of course he was—and the last two times we'd slept together, he'd draped his heavy limbs around me and pulled me tight against him.

Being in his arms felt like the safest place in the world. Normally, I didn't linger in bed. I had so little free time because of my job that I couldn't bear to waste it. I usually jumped right up after my alarm woke me and started my day.

Waking up next to Josh had cured me of that. We'd lingered beneath the sheets for over an hour, talking quietly with Fred snuggled between us as we listened to Tyler moving about the apartment, making himself coffee and turning on the TV. He'd kept it quiet, but we still heard the newscasters talking about market numbers on what Josh said was Tyler's favorite financial channel. It drove home how weird the acoustics were in their place and made me desperate to get out of there so I could have Josh all to myself.

I'd asked him again if he was serious about punishing me, and the clipped "Yes" he'd given me had both worried me and turned me on. What did he have planned? Were we talking about another vicious edging or a bit of light spanking? The possibilities had me squirming in my seat, which sent a pang of soreness through me, making me think of how I'd gotten so sore, and the torturous cycle started again.

Josh drummed his fingers over the steering wheel absentmindedly, and I almost whimpered at how it made his tattooed forearm flex. My eyes were drawn upward from it to his bicep straining against his shirt sleeve.

"Why is this light so long?" he said, almost to himself. Fred yowled in response, and Josh glanced in the rearview. "I know, bud. We're almost there." He shot me a grin before turning his focus back toward the light. "I told him to go before we left, but would he listen?"

I made a noncommittal sound, too distracted by his profile to talk. God, I would never get tired of looking at him. He had to know how gorgeous he was. I understood that he hid away for fear of someone saying he looked like his father, but I was betting that 99 percent of the stares he got in public had nothing to do with his dad and everything to do with the fact that Josh was so hot that if he pulled up next to someone and told them to get in his van, he wouldn't even need candy to lure them. They'd take one look at him and decide that the risk of being serial murdered was worth the potential reward of getting fucked instead.

Or maybe I was trying to rationalize how easily and quickly I was falling for him. My stomach fluttered every time he looked at me. I couldn't stop watching his mouth when he spoke, like I was trying to memorize the way his lips formed words. His body seemed to take up more space than it should, drawing me toward him like he had a gravitational field, and I was the moon he'd pulled into his orbit.

We'd been in the car for over fifteen minutes, and I hadn't taken my eyes off him even once. I felt like I physically couldn't do it. Nothing else was as fascinating as the man beside me. We'd just endured what should have been an incredibly traumatic experience, but all I could think about was Josh fucking me against the shower wall. Thank goodness we'd picked up the morning-after pill. Between my untrustworthy ovaries and the amount of cum I'd cleaned off my legs when we finished, doubling up on birth control felt necessary if we didn't want to bring a little Josh into the world.

No. Do not, I told myself. *You are not allowed to picture him tossing a baseball with a miniature version of himself.*

The thought should have freaked me out. We'd just become official. It was way too soon to start thinking about what our kids might look like, and I didn't even know if I wanted kids. But I wasn't joking when I told Josh that he'd be the one with the stalker if he tried to end things. My obsession with him was growing to worrying levels. Like,

I suddenly understood why he watched me at work because if I had his hacking skills, there was a hundred percent chance that I'd return the favor.

Fred yowled again as the light turned green.

Josh glanced in the rearview before stepping on the gas. "If you hold it until we get home, Daddy will buy you a new toy."

Shit. He needed to stop saying things like that. It was making me not only want kids, but want them soon.

I leaned toward him and stroked a finger down his bicep. "And what will Mommy get?"

The steering wheel creaked in Josh's grip. He shot me a pointed look, then glanced meaningfully at the backseat, lowering his voice. "Daddy will tell Mommy later when there aren't delicate ears within hearing distance."

I grinned and leaned closer. "I'm pretty sure it's our responsibility as parents to scar our children. Builds character."

He grunted and shifted in his seat. "Keep talking like that, and we're going to need to triple up on contraceptives."

I glanced down to see the outline of his erection shoved down the leg of his pants. That couldn't be comfortable. Maybe if I unzipped his jeans and gave him a little "adjustment," he'd feel better.

I started to reach for him, but he grabbed my wrist. "Aly," he said, voice low with warning. "We'll be at your house in less than a minute."

"I can't wait that long," I told him, breaking his hold.

He blocked me again. "Well, you need to because there's someone in your driveway."

I jerked my head up. Sure enough, an unfamiliar luxury SUV was parked in front of my house. I was still banned from contacting my uncle, so I hoped it was one of my cousins come to fill me in on everything that had happened in the last twenty-four hours and not an undercover cop.

Josh parked next to the large vehicle but kept the engine running.

"There's no one inside," I told him, peering up at the empty driver's seat. "Must be a cousin. Those bastards better not have copied my keys and handed them out to the whole family. I don't want to have to change my locks."

Josh frowned at the vehicle. "The real question is, has he just been waiting here for you to come home eventually, or did he know we were on our way back?"

I shrugged. "We can touch the hood when we get out to see if it's still hot, and then we'll have our answer. You ready?"

Josh shook his head and gestured toward his lap. "I'm going to need a minute here. For some reason, I don't think your mob relatives would appreciate my erection as much as you do."

I grinned. "You might be surprised."

Josh chuckled and reached out to tuck a stray piece of hair behind my ear.

I closed my eyes and leaned into his hand. "I've been wondering something. Maybe you can fill me in while we wait."

"I can try."

I opened my eyes. "How did this all happen?"

He frowned. "What do you mean?"

I gestured between us. "You and me. Did Tyler tell you he broke things off, and you decided to make your first creepy move?"

He grinned and pulled his hand away. "Tyler showed me the text you sent him."

I gaped at him. "No, he didn't."

Josh nodded.

"And he didn't recognize your tattoos in it?"

"No. You might have noticed, but my roommate is more than a little self-involved."

I leaned back, remembering how grateful Tyler had looked to have some of Josh's focus on me now, and it made me wonder. What if Tyler had known about Josh's masktok account all along, and when I sent him that text, he decided to play matchmaker?

"What is it?" Josh asked. "You've got the same squirrelly look on your face that Fred had when he stole that piece of bacon."

"I'm sure it's nothing," I said. Tyler was probably too full of himself for something so diabolical. "So what happened after he showed you the text?"

Now it was Josh's turn to look squirrelly. "I, uh, might have spent several hours looking for you in my comments and reading everything you'd ever written." He turned away from me, rubbing the back of his neck. "And then I decided to see if you were all talk or if you were really as into the mask thing as I am."

"Who would have thought that a few weeks later, you'd get yourself a girlfriend out of it," I said.

Josh turned back to me, his gaze steady on mine. "The first night I watched you at the hospital, I knew I wanted this to be more than the kinky hookup I'd planned."

My insides went all mushy at the confession. "And there I'd been, ready to shoot you. You must have been shitting yourself when you watched me clear the house after you broke in."

He sent me a wink. "Yeah, but they say you can tell a lot about a woman by the way she handles a gun, and I was more than—"

A loud yowl echoed through the car.

Josh and I shared a panicked look.

I unlatched my seatbelt. "Finish that sentence later. Peepants McGee sounds desperate."

I climbed out and grabbed Fred's carrier, careful not to jostle him too much as I dashed for my front door. There was a second litter box in my laundry room, and as soon as I got Fred's carrier unzipped, he beelined toward it.

I followed after him into the house, wary. It smelled like bleach and the fabricated scent of pine. My hardwood floors shone like they'd been freshly polished.

How much had my cousin's crew cleaned? Brad was mainly on the kitchen floor and then briefly carted through the living room, but he'd already been in my snowboard bag by then. From how my house sparkled, it looked like every surface had been wiped down. Out of an abundance of caution? If so, I wasn't about to complain. It would save me from having to clean for a while.

Josh stepped inside behind me, carrying our bags and the litter box. I turned to help him, wondering where my guest was.

Josh leaned toward me and dropped his voice. "The hood was still hot. I'll need to sweep our things and my car for a tracker later."

Son of a bitch. What was it with all these stalkers lately? Was it me? Was I giving off some weird, come-at-me pheromone? Or was Mercury in retrograde again?

We left our things by the front door and went to find my latest home invader. Sure enough, my cousin Junior sat at my kitchen table, sipping coffee from a paper to-go cup. He was the spitting image of his father, short and trim with bold facial features that were more striking than handsome.

His gaze shifted from me to Josh, and he arched a dark brow. "I see you shaved and lost the glasses."

Behind me, Josh swore.

I stepped between the men, putting Josh at my back. "What are you doing here?"

I liked it when Josh invaded my space and pushed my boundaries, but it turned out he was the exception to the rule. Anyone else doing it made me grumpy, bordering on homicidal—family included.

Junior stood, spreading his arms. "Is that any way to greet your oldest cousin?"

I eyed him, making no move to accept his offered embrace. "That depends. Did you or did you not point a gun at my boyfriend yesterday?"

He dropped his arms and had the decency to look sheepish. "It was a misunderstanding."

"Your face is about to have a misunderstanding with my fist," I said, stalking forward.

Or at least I tried to. I made it one step before a yank on my jacket had me crashing backward into Josh's chest. He wrapped his arms around me like he was hugging me, but I could tell from the way his muscles tensed that this was less about affection and more about restraint.

"Let me go," I said.

"I could, but then what kind of example would I be setting for our son if I let you beat up a family member in front of him?"

I glanced past Junior and saw Fred padding out of the laundry room toward us. "That you shouldn't take shit from anyone, not even relatives."

Junior frowned, looking around the room. "Your son? I didn't know you—" He caught sight of Fred in his periphery and turned to stare at him. His confusion deepened as he looked back at us, jerking a thumb toward Fred. "You talking about the cat?"

"Yes," Josh said. The "duh" was silent but heavily implied.

Junior grimaced. "Cat people are so fucking weird."

Josh's arms stiffened.

I sighed. "What do you want, Junior?"

"We need your boyfriend."

"For what?"

"For the same thing as before," Junior said. "To hack Brad's computer."

Josh made a low noise of contemplation. "Isn't it a bit risky to return to the house so soon after the cops were there?"

Junior nodded. "Yeah, which is why we're not going. We got another team for stealthy shit. They'll sneak in tonight, and you can hack it remotely." He raised his brows at Josh. "Right?"

"It's not that simple," Josh said. "Is Brad's computer password locked? How secure is his network? What kind of software does he use?"

Junior shrugged. "How the fuck should I know?"

Josh's arms eased around me. "They're rhetorical questions, but depending on the answers, it could slow the work and require different tools to get the job done. It'll be faster if I'm there."

I stiffened. "I don't like that option."

My cousin looked troubled as he glanced past me to Josh. "Me neither."

Josh huffed out an unamused laugh. "Trust me when I say this isn't how I wanted my night to go." His arms tightened again, pulling me into him so he could press a kiss to the top of my head.

I closed my eyes and leaned back, wishing we were alone, wishing this bullshit was over so Josh and I could get on with our lives. And maybe I should have felt guilty about that or selfish—a man was dead, and all I cared about was what an inconvenience it was—but I couldn't bring myself to drum up anything more than a mild concern that this could blow up in our faces. What better way to ensure that didn't happen than having a world-class hacker cover our tracks?

I let out a deep breath and opened my eyes. "Josh is right. He needs to be there, and I'm going with him."

Junior shook his head. "No. Absolutely not. This isn't a job for a woman."

I reared back in Josh's arms.

Overhead, I heard my boyfriend suck in a sharp breath and then let it out with the kind of *ooh* noise better suited for a playground. He let go of me with one hand and held it out in front of me. "This is the part where you take your earrings out, right?" he said. "I can hold them for you while you beat his ass."

I craned sideways to look at him. "What about not resorting to violence in front of the baby?"

Josh's expression was stoic. "I changed my mind. Sometimes, examples must be made."

I turned back to my cousin just as Josh's other arm fell away from me.

Junior, to his credit, seemed to realize he'd fucked up. He held his hands out placatingly and stepped backward. "Hey, I didn't mean it like that. I meant my dad will fucking skin me if I let you in on this."

I took a step toward him. "I'm coming."

He shook his head. "Aly, you can't. I'm serious. The men on the team are rough. You shouldn't be around them."

Another *ooh* came from behind me, followed by a crunching sound. I glanced over my shoulder and found Josh staring at us with rapt attention. He'd pulled a single-serving popcorn bag out of the box of food he'd packed and was eating it with the kind of glee reserved for someone watching a *Real Housewives* reunion episode.

I shook my head at him, instantly deflating—which was probably his goal—and turned back to my cousin. "I work around rough people every day, Junior. I can handle myself. Find a way to make it happen because if Josh is going, I'm going."

Junior's face turned into a thundercloud, and for a second, he was the spitting image of his father after I'd told Nico about Brad's body. "Fine. But you're staying in the van."

I nodded. I could accept that, and from the look on Junior's face, I'd pushed him as far as he would go. "What else has been happening?"

My cousin's expression turned cagey. "What do you mean?"

"With the whole Brad situation. Did you find his car?"

"Yes," Junior said.

More crunching filled the room. Josh sounded like he was still enjoying the show, whereas I was starting to get annoyed again.

"And?" I said.

Junior shrugged. "And what?"

"Did you get rid of it?"

Junior rolled his eyes. "No, we left it where it was."

I pinched the bridge of my nose and ignored Josh's poor attempt to cover his laughter. "Junior, please fill us in on what's going on with the coverup of Brad's death."

The little shit grinned. "Well, since you asked nicely." He retook his seat and took a swig of his coffee before indicating the chairs opposite him. "Please, join me."

I tried not to grind my teeth as I sat. Beside me, Josh looked like he was having far too much fun. His eyes pinged back and forth between Junior and me like he was at a tennis match. I was beginning to think that Josh didn't just enjoy needling me himself but took great pleasure from others giving me a hard time, too. Why? Because he was antagonistic by nature, or did he just like it when I got all riled up?

And where was the line? I hadn't missed the moment Greg crossed it when he snapped at me in Nico's kitchen. Josh had gone from an easy-going, loveable golden retriever to a full-blown hellhound in the blink of an eye.

Seeing him upset like that only further confirmed how different he and his father were. Instead of having cold, dead eyes, Josh's had been a blazing inferno, the promise of retribution burning so bright that even my youngest, snarkiest cousin had realized the danger and rushed to apologize.

Junior set his coffee down and lifted his gaze to mine. "Brad's car was a few blocks away," he said. "We were able to get in while it was still dark without setting the alarm off. One of our guys drove it to a chop shop we own, where it'll get broken down into parts and sold in pieces."

I blinked, impressed. The cops would have a hell of a time trying to run that down.

Josh sat forward beside me. "Aren't you worried about door cameras from nearby houses?"

Junior shrugged. "Not really. Brad parked in an area between streetlights so he wouldn't be noticed, which meant our guys benefited from it, too. Given how far he went to cover his tracks coming here, I'm sure he had his mask on the second he got out of his car, so if any cameras did catch him walking by, it'd be nearly impossible to ID him. And at the end of the day, the cops would have to know Brad was in the area to subpoena people's door cam footage."

I nodded. "Which is why we need to get to Brad's computer."

Junior held up a finger. "Which is why your boyfriend needs to. You're not leaving the van."

I glared at him. "I know that, dipshit."

Junior sniffed. "Uncalled for."

Josh popped another piece of popcorn into his mouth, grinning as he chewed. "This is fun for me."

I rolled my eyes at him and fixed my gaze on my cousin. "What about Brad's body?"

Junior's expression shut down. "Nope. That's the one piece of information we don't get to have."

I frowned. "What do you mean?"

Junior shrugged. "Dad has two guys who deal with this stuff that he trusts with his life."

"You mean those goons who came and got Brad while the car was cleaned?" I asked, remembering the men who'd grabbed the body-filled bag out of Josh's trunk and disappeared without so much as a hello. They'd been middle-aged, trim, and dressed in nondescript clothes. Nothing about them stood out—to the point that I didn't think I could pick them out of a lineup, which was probably their aim. Get in, get out, be forgotten.

"Those are the ones," Junior said. "Only they know what happened to Brad, but I can tell you from experience that you don't need to worry. No one has ever found someone after those two disappeared them."

I shifted in my seat and shared a glance with Josh. His amusement had faded, and he didn't look pleased with this news either.

"Isn't it better we know what happened?" I asked.

Junior shook his head. "No. This way, if the worst does come to pass, you can't tell the cops where the body is. No body, no evidence of a murder. Pretty hard to convict on circumstantial evidence alone when you have mob lawyers representing you. They've gotten some of our people out of much worse charges."

"I still don't like it," I said.

Junior huffed out a laugh. "You'll get used to it."

I highly doubted that.

He twirled his coffee absentmindedly and glanced past me, his gaze turning troubled and distant like he wasn't seeing my house anymore but some buried memory. "And trust me when I say that sometimes you're better off not knowing things."

I grimaced. God only knew what he'd seen with a dad like his. As far as I knew, Nico wasn't as bad as Josh's, but it had to be close.

Nico's outward eccentricities and charm didn't fool me because I'd never forget the haunted looks my parents and grandparents shared when someone brought him up. Family didn't fear family for no reason, especially not someone like my mom, who'd feared almost nothing in life.

"Oh," Junior said. "I almost forgot. Dad wants you to come over for dinner."

I stiffened in my seat. "Um . . . no, thank you?"

Junior shook his head. "You don't have a choice, kid."

"I absolutely do," I told him. "And I'm not a kid."

His expression turned to pity. "You owe him a favor, remember? His payment for all this is dinner once a month with the family."

I turned to Josh, wide-eyed. "Am I being Gilmored right now?"

He nodded. "Yup. He's going full Emily on you."

Junior looked back and forth between us, confused. "The fuck are you talking about?"

I didn't bother explaining, and I didn't attempt another argument. If Lorelai could get through a few hours with her mother for Rory's sake, I could get through dinner with Nico and his spawn. My uncle was bad, but Emily Gilmore made him look like a peach in comparison.

"I'll go," I said.

Josh cleared his throat and sent me a pointed look.

I shook my head. "Oh, no. I'm not forcing you to join my misery."

He gripped my knee beneath the table and turned to Junior. "We'll be there."

I tried to tamp down my small, pleased smile and probably failed miserably.

Junior clapped his hands. "Good. If that's settled, we need to go."

I glanced at the clock. "It's barely one."

He nodded. "Yeah, but the sun sets in a few hours, and the plan is to pretend Brad's place is the last service call of the day. We need to be there by 5:30, and now that you two are coming, we have to change some stuff around."

I was a grown-ass woman. I would *not* pout about the fact that instead of having kinky sex with my boyfriend, we had to go help fix the mess we'd made.

Josh met my eyes, his sparking with amusement as he reached out and brushed my cheek with the back of his fingers. "Just remember that we'll have the next two weeks to ourselves once we finish this."

Junior made a gagging noise and rose from his seat. "You two are gross," he called over his shoulder as he stomped toward the front door.

I ignored my cousin, leaning into Josh instead. He pulled me from my seat onto his lap and wrapped his big arms around me. I buried my face in his neck, breathing deeply. He smelled like laundry detergent and cheddar popcorn, and for a moment, I allowed myself to be still in his embrace, to live in this brief, perfect moment of being held by my boyfriend.

My anxiety about tonight, my greater fear over what the coming days and months would bring, I pushed aside. No matter what happened, Josh and I would face it, and maybe it was being in his arms, but despite the severity of what we'd done and the very real risk of jail time if our crimes were ever discovered, I felt like together, he and I could get through anything.

22

JOSH

JUNIOR PULLED OPEN THE REAR of the power company van and motioned us in. I couldn't be sure, but it looked a lot like the one I'd been in before, and after the whole held-at-gunpoint situation, it made me wary of getting inside it again.

We were on a back street near an industrial complex on the city's outskirts, shielded from the setting sun by the surrounding buildings. It was that weird time called gloaming when daylight was dying, and even though the streetlights had kicked on, it wasn't dark enough for them to do much, leaving us in a murky world of gloom.

I squinted into the gaping maw of the van, barely able to make out the six-man crew we were joining. These were *not* the same guys from before. They looked more like something out of a military movie. Despite their differences in age, race, and stature, there was a sameness about them that spoke of a cohesive unit of people who'd trained and worked together for so long that they barely even needed to communicate anymore because they inherently *knew* what came next.

I gathered my resolve and climbed inside, ignoring the way the men made my hackles rise. There was room close to the door on one of the bench seats, so I folded myself down and nodded toward the others. "Thanks for letting us tag along."

All I got back was a single grunt and several blank looks.

"No, you're right," I said. "Better to stay mysterious."

Movement caught the corner of my eye, and I turned to watch Aly climb in.

I tucked her beside me on the bench so I could whisper, "Bet you twenty bucks I can get one of them to laugh before the end of the night."

She grinned up at me. "You're on."

Junior plopped down across from us, and the way his gaze shifted from me to Aly made me feel like he hadn't missed the way I'd placed her closest to the door, shielding her from the others with my body. A subtle jerk of his head told me he approved before he turned to the man next to him and said something I missed because the van's engine rumbled to life.

I took Aly's gloved hands in mine and blew into them. "You warm enough?"

Her eyes crinkled as her smile shifted from amused to something else. Something filled with affection and warmth. "I'm good."

"Well, I'm freezing," I said to have an excuse to wrap an arm around her and pull her closer.

She poked me in the ribs. "Liar."

I kissed her forehead, ignoring everyone else in favor of the distraction she provided. I couldn't remember the last time I'd been so nervous. Maybe the first night I broke into her house?

Junior said his dad had ordered someone to watch Brad's place after our first aborted break-in attempt, and according to that person, the cops hadn't come back yet. They were still waiting for their search warrant to get approved. The Bluhm family lawyers were fighting it, but Nico thought they would lose that battle sooner rather than later, which was why we were here now. Tomorrow could be too late.

Aly peeked past me to take in the other men in the van. Everyone inside was dressed in the power company's uniform. We even had official-looking badges hanging around our necks—including Junior and Aly, who were staying behind with the driver and "tech guy" while the rest of us went in. The badges were our only forms of ID, and Junior said they'd check out if anyone looked into them. It made me feel marginally better that so much thought had gone into this, but no amount of planning could lift the brick of unease out of my stomach.

I was about to break into the house of the man I'd killed, and part of me worried that this was a setup. We'd been told the mob handled Brad's body and his car and any DNA evidence left at Aly's place, but all we had to go on was their word. It didn't feel like a stretch to think that someone like Nico might have an ulterior motive or at least a backup plan if anything went sideways, and it definitely wasn't lost on me that I'd make the perfect scapegoat.

Unfortunately, there wasn't much I could do about my suspicions. If I didn't wipe all potential traces of Aly from Brad's computer, she'd be vulnerable, and I'd rather risk myself than her.

I steadied us both as the van rolled forward, tightening my hold on Aly to ensure she didn't slide into the door. She squeezed my thigh in silent thanks, and I knew I was freaking out because, for the first time, her touch didn't make me instantly hard.

She shifted forward beside me, her gaze trained on her cousin. "What happens if the cops are there again?"

Junior shook his head. "They won't be. We have people watching."

"What if they show up while we're there?" she pressed.

"We'll get everyone out before they reach Brad's," he said. "And again, we have people watching."

"What if they sneak past your people?"

Junior rolled his eyes. "Brad's house is in a gated community. There's one road in and out of there, and we have three cars on the street leading to it. If the cops come from either direction, we'll know in plenty of time to escape."

Aly narrowed her eyes. "Won't a utility van tearing out of Brad's driveway look suspicious to neighbors?"

A muscle jumped along Junior's jawline, and he answered her slowly, like he was trying to keep his temper. "We're not going to tear out of anywhere. We'll leave at a non-suspicious speed."

Aly's gaze swiveled toward the front of the van. "You sure about that after the way your last driver panicked?"

Junior shook his head. "Vinny isn't driving today. Now, will you quit it with the twenty questions? We've been over all this."

Aly flopped sideways into me. "Sorry, but I'm nervous, and the best way to ease my anxiety is to learn as much as possible."

Junior blew out a breath, his temper fading. "I get it, but there's not much for you and me to do but sit here and look pretty."

She frowned at him. "I'm not nervous for *us*."

I bumped my knee into hers. "That's sweet, but I'm sure our new friends will be fine despite their delicate appearances." A glance showed me that I didn't get so much as a lip-twitch with that comment. These guys were going to be harder to crack than I thought.

"I'm not talking about them either," Aly said, then grimaced. She leaned forward again to look past me. "No offense."

She got a head nod from one but nothing else. Oh, to have such self-control. Silence was descending on the van, and the urge to break the tension with another joke was almost too strong to resist.

Thankfully, Aly saved me from myself by wrapping her fingers through mine and looking up at me. "Are you going to be okay?"

My insides turned warm and fuzzy as I stared into her large brown eyes. She looked so concerned, her brows drawn together, lower lip pinched between her teeth. If it wasn't for our audience, I would have swooped in and kissed her worry away.

Instead, I raised my free hand and brushed her hair over her shoulder. "I'll be fine. And if shit goes sideways, don't try to wait for me." I leaned down and bumped my forehead into hers, dropping my voice so only she would hear it. "You might have noticed, but I'm very good at sneaking around. I'll be able to get myself out of there if I have to."

The corners of her eyes crinkled. "Then let's hope nothing happens because I don't know if I could leave you behind."

"Hey," Junior called out, "love birds. You need to mic up."

I reluctantly turned from Aly and accepted a contraption made of slim plastic from the guy beside me.

"Throat mic," he said, pulling his on.

I glanced down at the one in my hand and wondered if they'd miss it if I "accidentally" forgot to take it off later, and it ended up coming home with me. It looked military-grade, the collar so slim that I'd probably barely feel it once it was on. A nearly transparent, whisper-thin cable wound up from it to a small earbud speaker. I'd never seen anything like it before, and the urge to dissect it and figure out how it worked was strong.

"Here," Aly said, taking it from me. "I'll help you put it on."

I turned toward her in silent acquiescence, grounding myself in her presence, trying to tell my racing heartbeat that everything would be okay. The men in the van were professionals, and their strategy was solid. I just needed to get in, wipe Brad's computer, and get out. They would handle the rest, and if everything went according to plan, this whole operation would take less than half an hour.

"Lean down," Aly said.

I bowed, breathing deep as she lifted the collar over my head. This close, I could smell her shampoo, and it took me right back to the shower we'd shared. After the mind-blowing sex, I'd turned her around and washed her hair for her, lathering her strands and kneading her scalp while she went boneless within my grasp.

"Head up," she said, and I complied. Her nimble fingers tightened the collar around my neck. "How's that?"

I raised my voice to a squeak. "Little tight."

She grinned and loosened it. "How about now?"

"Perfect," I told her. *Just like you,* I wanted to add but stopped myself when I remembered our audience. This woman had a way of making me forget where I was, and I'd never been more grateful for it than now.

She tapped my chin. "Turn your head."

I did what she said and ended up facing Junior.

"You remember what to do?" he asked.

I nodded. "Let the A-Team lead the way, and don't touch anything but the computer."

Aly slipped my earbud into place, and I lifted my hand and adjusted it until it was comfortable.

"We're almost there," the guy at the far end of Junior's bench called out. He had a laptop open and balanced on his knees. He was the tech guy staying behind to monitor our progress and help with anything we might need, including cutting the power long enough for us to get inside Brad's place undetected so we could disarm the security system from inside.

Junior shifted across from us. "You sure you can pull this off?"

I grinned. "It'll be a cakewalk."

■ ■ ■

It was not, in fact, a cakewalk. We were only ten minutes into our little operation and had already encountered several problems. The first was that Brad's house had a beefy generator, and the moment Junior's guy cut the power, it rumbled to life. Of course, the security system was hooked up to it, and I watched with my jaw clenched while the "hacker" bumbled his way through disarming it remotely, repeatedly telling me to shut up and let him concentrate when I tried to point out there was a faster way.

The second problem occurred as we rounded the property. A raised fist from the front of our five-man line signaled a halt. I waited, breath steaming in the frigid night air, while the leader slunk to the edge of the house. He leaned down and picked something up that I couldn't see from my distance because Brad's closest neighbors didn't have generators, so it was darker than sin between the houses.

The man made a motion like he'd thrown something, and a heartbeat later, floodlights lit up Brad's backyard like a Roman candle. We flattened ourselves against the side of the house to keep to the shadows.

Someone swore, their voice loud in my ear because of the earbud.

"What is it?" Junior asked. "What happened?"

"We told you to keep the line clear," someone snapped at him, and the urge to *ooh* was so strong I had to bite my lip to shut myself up.

"The lights are tied to the generator," our lead man said. "We'll have to disable them remotely." He turned and motioned to the guy in front of me. "Get up here with the jammer."

The squat man scurried forward, pulling a device that looked like a radar gun from his Batman-style toolbelt. Watching him carefully aim it around the corner of the house before clicking a button that instantly killed the lights was one of the coolest things I had ever seen, and I wondered if the pocket-picking skills I'd developed during my brief, rebellious teenage stage were up to the task of lifting it off him.

Apparently, I turned into a kleptomaniac around advanced technology, but who could blame me? A magical jammer that killed lights with a single flick? There wasn't a tech geek alive who wouldn't have developed a sudden case of grabby hands in my place.

"Let's go," the lead man said.

I kept my hand braced on the wall as we started forward, wondering how he could see where he was going after those floodlights had ruined our night vision. The answer of "he can't" came a second later when he tripped over something buried in the snow and went diving head-first into the shrubbery.

The noises coming over the line from his struggle to free himself were so loud that I nearly pulled the speaker out of my ear.

"What's happening?" Junior demanded, ignoring the earlier call for quiet. "It sounds like you're fighting. Was someone inside waiting for you?"

I couldn't keep myself from answering. "Our fearless leader just faceplanted into a Rhododendron, but he's coming out of it now. He looks embarrassed." The man swiveled toward me, and even in the darkness, I could tell he was glaring. "Oops, now he looks pissed."

A snicker echoed over the line.

Victory!

"Aly, you owe me twenty bucks."

"Doesn't count," she said. "That was Junior."

"Keep the line clear," someone barked.

I covered my mic and tapped the guy nearest to me. "I'll pay you ten dollars to laugh at my next joke. I need to win a bet against my girlfriend."

"Hey!" Aly said. "I heard that. No cheating."

The lead guy pointed at me. "For the last time, keep the *fucking* line clear."

I saluted him and mimed zipping my lips.

We managed to make it into the house without more difficulty, but as soon as we closed the door behind us and stepped farther inside, the third problem slapped us in the face. The men ahead of me pulled up short and exchanged looks, and it made me feel marginally better that I wasn't the only one who recognized the gag-inducing scent of a decomposing body.

The leader pointed at the two guys behind him. "Find out what that smell is." He turned to the next two in line. "You go find the cell phone."

That left just him and me behind. Goody. I got the grumpiest one for a babysitter.

"Let's get to that computer and find out if you're all talk," he said, turning toward the grand staircase to our right.

I followed him up it, trying not to gawk at the displayed wealth. My salary wasn't anything to scoff at, but I'd never make the kind of money Brad came from. The staircase was lined with dark paneling, above which hung gold-framed paintings that probably cost more than my car. Overhead, a chandelier dripped with crystals that caught the moonlight shining through the high windows, sparkling silver in the darkness.

The plan was to traverse as much of the house as possible in the dark. Traditional flashlights could be seen through windows by neighbors, but we had fancy low-light red UV ones on us if absolutely necessary. Mine was strapped to my toolbelt, and I was itching to test it. And yes, it was another piece of spy gear that would probably go "missing" by the night's end. Aly had been so turned on by our talk of future mask play that I had a feeling I could put all these tools to good use with her.

"Everyone's in, right?" the man left behind with Aly and Junior asked.

The guy in front of me responded in the affirmative.

"Then I'm kicking the power back on if everyone is ready," came the reply.

We reached the top of the stairs and ducked low in case a nearby light sparked to life.

"Ready," the leader said.

The other two-man teams chorused him, and all the machinery in the house beeped when the power returned. A soft glow illuminated us as a distant light lit up the downstairs, but thankfully, none close to us had been left on.

The leader turned to shoot me a look. He was a white guy of medium stature with hair that had turned mostly gray. Like Brad, he had one of those faces that would be hard to pick out of a crowd, and I bet his ability to blend in had made him an excellent soldier once upon a time. Maybe that was why he had such a chip on his shoulder—his military days were over, and civilian life didn't suit him.

Our neck mics were powered by little battery packs attached to our toolbelts, and he reached down and killed his transmit switch. "We need to stay low."

I cut mine off, too, and nodded. "I can do that."

He eyed the way I was folded up like a pretzel, his gaze wary, obviously distrusting my abilities.

"I work legs twice a week," I told him. "I'll be fine."

He snorted and flicked his mic back on. With a "follow me" gesture, he turned and started down the hall, knees bent, spine bowed so he could slip beneath the window sills.

I sighed, knowing my height was working against me, and followed after him, dropping to all fours whenever I reached a window and scuttle-butting past them like a *Teen Wolf* wannabe.

We scanned every room we came across, which was a lot. During our briefing earlier, Junior told us this was an eight-bedroom house complete with two home offices, a library, a study, and multiple bathrooms.

There was even a wine-tasting room in the cellar, but when Aly asked if we could filch a couple of the good bottles since it wasn't like Brad would miss them, she got a look of censure from her older cousin and a staunch no.

We found what looked like Brad's office halfway down the hall. The guy with me closed the blinds and the door while I went to the computer. I was turning it on when the fourth problem struck.

"Uh, we got a situation down here," someone said, and for the first time, the stone-cold façade they all shared sounded like it was cracking.

"What is it?" their leader asked.

"There are two huge piles of cat litter on the basement floor, and the smell is coming from them."

"What the fuck?" Junior asked. "Does Brad have a tiger or something?"

"No," I said. "The litter is meant to cover the smell of rotting bodies and absorb the decomp liquids."

Only when the words were out did I realize I'd probably revealed too much about myself.

The leader craned his head toward me, frowning.

I shrugged, trying to act nonchalant. "I watch a lot of true crime documentaries."

He eyed me for a long moment before speaking. "Everyone out."

I frowned. "I just got the computer booted up."

He jerked his head toward the door. "Out. Once the cops find those bodies, their warrant is going to shift from a simple search order to a top-to-bottom investigation. Every surface will get dusted. We can't risk leaving anything behind.

"I just need five minutes," I told him.

He shook his head. "We're leaving. And if you're smart, you'll join us."

With that, he slipped out the door.

Well, shit.

"Josh?" Aly said. "Are you going with them?"

I glanced from the door to the computer screen, ready for me to enter a password. My hair was covered with a baseball hat that sported the power company's logo. The gloves I wore were leather, so there would be no prints or fibers from them to find. Our boots were from such a popular brand that there were probably thousands of people in the city who owned them, making them nearly impossible to trace.

The likelihood of getting caught was akin to being killed by a gopher: low, but never zero.

I took a deep breath. "I'm staying behind. I'll meet you at the rendezvous point when I can."

"I'm staying with you," Aly said.

There were so many shouted noes to that statement that I barely heard my own over them.

Aly's voice came through clear as day afterward. "Don't try to stop me."

Her cousin wasn't having it. "Dad will fucking kill me if I let you out of this van. Hey! Where do you think you're—get back here!"

The sound of a scuffle came over the line, followed by a loud groan and then silence.

I was almost afraid to ask, but I forced the words out. "What just happened?"

"Your girlfriend," Junior said in between wheezes, "just kicked me in the junk and ran off into the night."

"Oh, so she's *your cousin* when she's being good and *my girlfriend* when she's misbehaving? I see how it is."

"Will you quit dicking around?" Junior snapped. "I'm guessing you have incoming."

"We can intercept," the lead man chimed in.

"Absolutely not," I said, suddenly stone-cold serious. "If anyone so much as lays a finger on Aly, I'll make all your lives a living hell. Don't think I'm not capable of draining your bank accounts and putting illegal shit on your computers and phones."

Was I happy with Aly right now? Fuck, no. But that didn't mean I was okay with someone else restraining her.

"Do you understand?" I said, my voice so low with warning that I barely recognized it.

"Copy that," the lead guy said.

"Junior?" I pushed.

"Yeah, fine," he grumbled.

I let out a sigh of relief. "Was anyone able to locate Brad's phone?"

The response was an immediate negative.

Fuck. There was no way I could leave without trying to find it. At least most of the hacking software I brought with me was automated. I could hit run on all the applications and search the house while they churned away.

"Aly, baby," I said. "Can you wait for me in the shadows out back? I don't want you entering the house since less of you is covered."

Her sweet voice was a relief when it came over the line. "I can wait, but hurry up. It's cold as shit out here."

"I'll hurry," I told her.

"We're leaving," Junior said. "We'll keep the watch cars in place and wait for you at the pickup spot. We won't be able to hear you guys once we get out of range, so you're on your own. Only use the burner phones as a last resort."

"Got it, thanks," I said. "I'll work as fast as I can, Aly."

"I know you will," she said, the open trust in her voice spearing straight into my heart.

"I'm going to be quiet for a bit so I can get this done."

Her tone turned saccharine-sweet. "How will I ever survive the silence?"

A snort-laugh came over the line, telling me the others were still in range.

I stiffened. "Please tell me that was Junior."

"Nope," he said. "I think that means you owe her twenty bucks."

Aly let out a quiet whoop of victory.

I groaned and got to work.

The first thing I did was pull a thumb drive from my toolbelt and pop it into a USB port. I'd loaded my favorite generative password-cracking

AI on there, and it took less than ten seconds for it to log me into Brad's system. Next, I opened a file that would scrape Brad's entire web history, set the keywords to every variation of Aly's name I could think of, along with her home address, and hit "run." It didn't matter if Brad had used Firefox or a stealth browser that promised it was untraceable. My crawl tool would find them all and mine them for the data I sought.

That done, I opened another handy piece of software that a hacker friend had created. He called it the Brick Layer, and no, I had never gotten him to explain the significance of that name.

The program searched for hidden files and hard drives. Once it started chugging away, I pushed back from the chair and left the room, careful to keep as low as possible and out of sight while I traversed the hall, searching for Brad's phone. I was aware that this would be easier with two people, but if I couldn't find Brad's phone and some digital trace of Aly was on there, the cops finding any physical trace of her inside the house could be disastrous.

The end of the hall was dark enough that I decided to risk turning on my flashlight, remembering the instruction to keep it pointed down at all times. The red beam functioned as promised. I could hardly see much in it, so I doubted anyone would notice the glow out of the windows.

I peeked in doorways as I passed them, but the bedrooms that lay beyond looked like they were for guests. Finally, at the very end of the hallway, in the darkest part of the shadows—because, of course—I found Brad's room. There wasn't much to point it out at first, just the subtle hints that it was more lived in than the rest, but I went with my gut, and as soon as I stepped inside and saw a pair of shoes discarded near the bed, I knew I was in the right place.

Junior told us that Brad lived alone and rarely ever had company, and now I knew that probably had something to do with the dead bodies in the basement. The realization made me shudder. I was in a house with two corpses, and god only knew how many other people had died inside these walls.

A spine-chilling feeling slithered down my back. It felt like someone had reached out to touch me but changed their mind at the last second.

I whipped around. No one was there.

Yeah, this place was definitely haunted. What had Mom told me to do if I ever encountered a ghost?

"I mean you no harm," I whispered.

"Who are you talking to?" Aly asked, making me jump.

I clutched my chest, trying to relearn how to breathe. "Uh, no one, sorry. Just looking for Brad's phone."

"Want me to come help?" she asked.

"No. Please stay outside."

"Fine."

"Aly," I ground out.

"I said fine! Just hurry up. My toes are starting to tingle."

"Could be worse," I said, resuming my search of the room. "You could be the son of a serial killer currently stuck in a murderer's house with his last two victims somewhere a few floors below you and are trying not to spiral or let the memories of your childhood send you screaming from the place."

Aly was quiet for so long that I thought my earbud must have cut out.

"Aly?"

Her voice came through so low that I barely heard her. "I think someone just pulled into the driveway."

I clicked my flashlight off, fear and adrenaline flooding my veins. "Can you check?"

"Yes," she whispered. "I'm trying to get to the front of the house, but the snow is loud, and I don't want them to hear me crunching toward them."

"Hang on. I think this room might overlook part of the driveway."

I slunk toward the window and leaned forward just enough to see outside, and—*fuck!*—there was a car right below me.

"Stay where you are," I told Aly. "Someone's here."

"Get out!" she hiss-whispered.

"Way ahead of you," I said, racing back to the office. "I just have to wipe you from Brad's computer."

"No, Josh. You have to leave. What if they catch you?"

"They won't," I told her. "Did Junior text your burner about his people spotting cops?"

"No, but they could be in an unmarked car, or it could be one of Brad's friends or family members. Josh, get *out*."

"I will as soon as I'm done. I'll go out the window if I have to."

I really didn't want to go out the window, but as I skidded around Brad's desk and saw just *how* much of Aly I'd have to erase from his search history, I realized it might come down to that.

Hoping to buy myself some time, I shut and locked the office door before starting to wipe the browser Brad used to look for her. He had two hidden ones, and a quick glance revealed that there was more than enough on there to damn him in the eyes of the police, so I left them intact and wiped the other. He also had an encrypted hard drive, so I immediately unencrypted it and ran my search software on that, too. There was no trace of Aly on it, and I didn't bother looking further into what it contained; I was short on time and figured whatever was on there would probably scar me. I'd already been scarred enough for one lifetime, thank you very much.

"Josh?" Aly whispered. "What's going on?"

"Shh," I said, straining my ears. "I think I hear someone coming."

Her only response was a low, panicked noise. I was right there with her. Footsteps echoed in the hallway as I performed one last-ditch diagnostic test, looking for Aly anywhere I might have missed her.

Come on, come on, I begged as the footsteps drew nearer. The progress bar seemed to slow to a crawl as the doorknob jiggled. Whoever was out there must have beelined straight to this office once they got inside the house. Were they after the same thing we were—Brad's computer? If so, why? And what would they do with it if they got their hands on it?

"It's locked," a low male voice rumbled. "I'm kicking it down."

Shit, shit, shit.

The voice that answered him was feminine. "Don't. It will look too suspicious when the search warrant gets executed. I think he keeps a key in his nightstand."

The man made an angry sound. "If he fled the country, I'm disowning him this time, Vivian. I swear, I'll do it."

The vise around my heart slackened. Were Brad's parents on the other side of the door? I vaguely remembered his mom's name beginning with a V, and talk of disowning could only come from someone with the power to do it, like his father.

"While I'm at it," the man said, "I'm firing the housekeeper, too. It smells like the trash hasn't been taken out in weeks."

Was it weird that I took Brad's parents not recognizing the smell of rotting corpses as a good sign?

The sound of their retreat was such a relief that I nearly collapsed, but I fought through it and, trusting my instincts, plugged another thumb drive into Brad's computer and started making a copy of his machine, hard drives, search histories, and all. If his parents planned to hide the evidence of his crimes by destroying his computer, I'd find some way to get the backup files to the cops without getting caught.

The downside was that it would take several minutes. I grabbed a chair and braced it beneath the door handle like I'd seen Aly do all those nights before. For good measure, I found a nearby candelabra with a wide base and quietly wedged it against the bottom of the door like a jamb. At least all the antiques in Brad's English gentleman's office were good for something.

A peek at the computer screen told me I still needed to stall for time, so when I heard footsteps reapproach the door, I sidled over to it and grabbed the lock from my side, praying my finger strength was up to the job.

The sound of metal-meeting-metal filled my ears as the key slid into place on the other side. Pressure on the lock told me someone was trying to turn it, but I gritted my teeth and pinched it in place. The pressure increased, and sweat began to bead on my forehead as I tried to force all the strength in my body down into my fingers.

"Damn it, this is the wrong key," the man—Brad's father?—said.

"What do you mean?" Vivian asked.

"It's not working."

"Here, let me. You might have been forcing it too hard."

"Fine," the man barked. "You try while I go look for another."

He stomped away, and I held my ground while the woman tried to open the door politely and, when that failed, attempted to force it even harder than her partner-in-crime had.

"Josh, I can hear people talking," Aly said. "Please be okay. I need you to be okay."

I held her words close while the woman put in one final effort. My fingers started getting clammy inside my gloves from pinching so hard, and I didn't know how much longer I could last without them becoming slippery enough to lose my grip.

Finally, the pressure stopped, and the woman let out a low sigh from the other side of the door before removing the key and following after the man I assumed was her husband. I stood there, stunned for a few seconds, my pulse thundering in my ears. Holy shit, it had worked.

Snapping out of it, I retreated to the computer, where the progress bar on my program had finally reached a hundred percent. I tugged the thumb drives out and erased all traces that I'd hacked my way in. By the time footsteps reapproached the room, I'd killed the computer's power and was just swinging the office window open.

A rattle told me my time was up.

The moon had risen over the tree line, giving me enough light to make out a drop of ten feet to the pergola below. It was better than nothing. With a silent prayer to any entity who might be listening, I swung out of the window and lowered myself as far as I could, clinging to the window ledge with my fingertips. I took a deep breath and glanced down one last time, trying to aim for the nearest crossbeam as I let go.

The drop was only a few feet, thanks to my dangling act, and I hit the beam just how I intended, feeling a momentary burst of triumph before my boots went skidding off it because of the snow. It was a goddamn miracle that I didn't let out a shout of panic or a roar of pain as I fell like a human-sized checker in Connect Four. My shins slammed into the beam first, jerking my body forward so my ribs hit it next. That strike bounced me backward far enough that I banged my right shoulder into the opposite beam before finally slipping between them and dropping like a sack of potatoes to the patio beneath.

I sat there dazed for several seconds, trying to figure out which part of me hurt most. Thank fuck I hadn't hit my head and knocked myself out. Aly was strong, but she wasn't drag-an-unconscious-two-hundred-and-twenty-five-pound-man-a-mile-through-snow-covered-woods strong.

A tug on my arm had me glancing up to see her panic-stricken face.

"We have to go," she whispered.

Between her pulling and my piss-poor efforts to stand, we got me mostly upright. Aly immediately threw my arm over her shoulder and tried to drag me toward the woods bordering Brad's backyard, but I fought her.

"Call Junior," I wheezed. "Tell his guy to turn the alarm back on."

"We don't have time for this," she insisted.

I grabbed her chin with my free hand and looked at her imploringly. "Please trust me."

Her expression turned mulish, but she whipped her burner from her pocket and called. "Hi. No, we're not fine. Someone's here. We need you to turn the alarm on." Junior tried to get more information, but she shook her head. "I don't know. Just fucking do it."

A second later, she hung up. "It's done."

I grabbed a nearby deck chair and slammed it against the French doors leading to the patio.

"What are you doing?" Aly hiss-whispered.

I slammed the chair into them again, hard enough to break them open, hard enough to set the alarm off.

I tossed the chair aside and turned toward Aly. "We have to run."

She didn't need to hear anything more, slipping beneath my arm and taking off so fast that I struggled to keep upright as she hauled me toward the tree line.

"Hey!" a man's voice called out behind us. "Get back here!"

We made it into the woods, where we had to slow down because the shadows were deeper beneath the snow-covered boughs.

Aly glanced behind us. "You want to tell me what that stunt was about?"

"I think it was Brad's parents in the house," I said. "They bee-lined right toward his computer. I'd bet you anything they were going to cover up for him somehow."

"And?" she pressed.

"And in this state, when a home alarm goes off, all the cops have to do is say they believe a crime is being committed to legally enter the house without a search warrant."

Aly's eyes flashed wide as she caught on. "You just gave them the excuse to enter the premises they've been looking for."

I nodded. "Once they get inside and smell the bodies, it'll be all over for the Bluhms."

She turned toward me and hauled me down to kiss me hard on the lips. The grin that lit her face as she pulled away was bright enough that it felt like the sun had split the darkness. "You're a goddamn genius."

I leaned down and gave her a proper kiss, one with tongue and a decent amount of groping.

She looked breathless as I pulled away, and I dropped my hand and twined my fingers through hers. "I'm only a genius if we don't get caught."

The lust cleared from her face in a split second. "Oh, fuck. Right. The cops are probably already on their way, and we just left footprints in the snow for them to follow."

Together, we took off into the night like the criminals we'd become.

23

ALY

I NOW HAD THE ANSWER to the question, "How fun is it to run through the woods at night during winter?"

About as much fun as having Hannibal Lecter for a gynecologist.

My feet were soaked through because of the snow, I had so many scratches on my face from low-hanging branches that it was going to look like I'd picked a fight with a shredder, and even though it was sub-zero, I was sweating from exertion. I was both hot and freezing at the same time, and between my litany of physical discomforts and the fear and adrenaline pumping through my veins, I was so uncomfortable and wound up that I was ready to burst into tears. I wanted a hot shower, homemade chicken soup, and all the blankets in my house wrapped around me while I made a nest on my couch.

Josh looked even more miserable than I was. I couldn't stop glancing at him in the moonlight, worried he might suddenly collapse. I'd rounded the corner of the house just in time to watch him ping-pong through the pergola, and though he swore he hadn't hit his head, I was still wary. I knew from treating people that sometimes, in a fall like that, it all happened so fast you couldn't be sure of everything that got hit until the bruises showed up.

Thank fuck he'd made it out of the house before getting caught. I'd tried to play it cool while he was in there, but internally, I'd been freaking out. The thought of Josh trapped inside Brad's mansion while two of Brad's victims lay somewhere far below made me sick to my stomach.

I didn't know the full horror of what Josh had been through with his father, but between Tyler's revelations and Josh's cryptic comments, it was safe to say that having a serial killer for a parent was the stuff of nightmares. Knowing there were bodies nearby might have retraumatized Josh, and the surreptitious glances I kept sneaking at him were as much about his mental health as they were about his physical well-being.

How he'd had the wherewithal to think of setting off the alarm after everything he'd just been through was beyond me, and it made me look at him with a whole new level of admiration. Not only was my boyfriend funny and kind and hot, but he was also smart as hell. I'd never been so attracted to anyone in my life, and if not for the genuine fear of cops barreling through the woods after us, I would have dragged him to a stop, dropped to my knees in front of him, and showed him just how much I appreciated him.

He looked over at me, his face shaded because of his hat, hiding his expression from view. "The meeting point should be just beyond the next rise," he said, keeping his voice low.

I followed suit. "Do you think they're still waiting for us?"

Junior's voice crackled through our earbuds, making us both jump. "We . . . here . . . are you . . . at?"

Josh and I shared a look and picked up the pace as we started climbing the hill. The van must have been just inside radio range.

"Can you hear us?" I asked, voice barely above a whisper.

"Not . . . can you . . . me?"

I blew out a frustrated breath and kept climbing. The snow was deep, and though the surface had frozen, it was soft underneath, and Josh and I kept punching through it and nearly stumbling. My legs protested every step. I was starting to lose feeling in my toes, which was the first sign of frostbite. We needed to get to the van and get the fuck out of there.

"How about now?" Josh asked.

"Better," Junior said. "Can you hear me?"

If not for the fear of being overheard, I would have whooped in celebration. "Loud and clear."

"There's cops all over the place," Junior said. "You set off the fucking alarm?"

"We'll explain later," I said. "Where are you?"

"Parked near the meeting spot. We had to get the van out of there because of what you two idiots did, so I hopped in one of the lookout cars. When you reach the road, turn right and look for a black SUV down an unlit dirt drive."

I cringed. The plan had called for stealth and secrecy, but now any neighbors who'd seen the van at Brad's before his parents turned up would think it was suspicious and tell the cops. At least the van hadn't been there when Brad's folks arrived. Junior had inherited his father's talent for bullshitting, but I doubted that it worked on elitist snobs.

No, this situation wasn't ideal, but in my opinion, it was still better to have cops crawling all over the area than to give Brad's parents a chance to cover more of his crimes.

"Where are you two?" Junior asked.

I bit off a curse as my foot plunged through the snow again. "We're coming over the—"

Josh grabbed my arm and yanked me down. "Cop car."

A fresh wave of adrenaline punched through me as a searchlight swung over our heads, lighting up the forest like the Fourth of July. Josh and I dropped against the side of the hill, and I sent up a small prayer of thanks that we'd been just shy of the top and still able to hide. A few yards farther, and we would have been caught in the open.

The beam swept across the forest once before coming back for a second, slower pass. I flattened against the snow, rocks and fallen branches digging into me, my clothes soaking through. I didn't even breathe because I was so scared that I'd miss some warning sound that might tell us someone had gotten out of the car and was heading our way.

Josh gripped my hand, and I turned just enough to meet his eyes. Gone was the soulful brown I was used to. They were nearly black now, with a steely edge that spoke of determination. He hadn't taken my hand to reassure me; he'd grabbed it so he could haul me to my feet at the slightest provocation.

I was right there with him. We were *not* getting caught. If that meant fleeing back through the woods, so be it. I suddenly had enough adrenaline coursing through my veins that I felt like I could run a marathon.

The spotlight cut through the trees again, even slower this time, painting the night in blinding white. A crunching sound reached my ears, and my pulse skyrocketed. Josh squeezed my hand, his fingers practically trembling with the need to flee.

"Wait," I whispered, recognizing the sound for what it was: tires crunching over the salt-caked pavement as the car rolled past. We must have been closer to the road than I realized to hear that from where we were.

Josh released a shaky breath as the spotlight moved on, dropping our section of woods back into darkness.

"Fuck," Junior bit out. "Back up! Back up!"

He must have seen the beam and realized the cops were heading their way next.

Josh and I stayed where we were, frozen in place as we listened helplessly to the noises coming through our earbuds.

"Turn!" Junior yelled.

Whatever the response was, we couldn't hear it.

"I don't care about your fucking paint job," Junior said. "Back into the fucking trees if you have to."

A scraping sound came over the line loud enough to make me wince. Goodbye, paint job.

"Cut the engine!" Junior barked.

I lifted my head just enough to see the spotlight slicing through the forest a few hundred feet past us. The trees were denser there, more conifer than broadleaf. Hopefully, they were thick enough to hide a car. I squinted, scanning the understory for any sign of light bouncing off metal. Nothing.

I glanced down and met Josh's eyes.

"Can you see them?" he whispered.

I shook my head, but his expression remained wary. He knew what I did: just because I couldn't see the car from our angle didn't mean the cops couldn't see it from theirs.

His gaze moved past me, and I knew from the unfocused look in his eyes that he wasn't seeing the forest around us anymore. He was coming up with another escape plan if Junior and his driver got caught.

I strained my ears while Josh brainstormed, but all I could hear were my cousin's ragged breaths. The spotlight swept over his area much like it had ours, and I kept my gaze laser-focused on it, looking for some sign of a car or an interruption in the light that might signal someone was out of the police vehicle, searching through the trees.

"I can't see you from here," I told Junior. "And I don't see anyone in the woods either."

"Keep looking," he said, a low note in his voice that I hadn't heard before.

Up until this moment, Junior had been brash, cocky, and controlling, but now he sounded scared, and it reminded me that he wasn't that much older than I was. For the first time since meeting my estranged uncle and cousins, I felt a small pang of something like familial responsibility radiating from somewhere in my middle. I didn't want Junior to get caught. And not just because Josh and I would need to find another way out of there, but because I didn't like the idea of Junior sitting handcuffed in a jail cell.

I nearly swore. What a great time for this particular emotional response. Absolutely perfect. If those cops made a beeline for the parked car, I'd have to do something about it, and I really, *really* didn't want to. I'd had enough risk for one night. Hell, for an entire lifetime.

Thankfully, it didn't come to that. The spotlight continued rolling on, scanning farther and farther away until the forest almost entirely obscured it.

"Fuck," Junior said. "That was close."

"They're past you?" Josh asked, sitting up.

"Yeah," Junior answered. "You'll have to come to us through the woods. There could be more cops out on the street."

I got to my feet and started brushing myself off. "Crank the heat. Josh and I need to get warm to avoid frostbite."

Josh was slower to stand, moving in a halting way that made me wonder just how hurt he was. By the time he reached his full height, he towered over me, more of a large shadow than anything else, thanks to my ruined night vision. He took my hands and leaned close enough to meet my eyes. "Are you okay?"

"My toes are numb," I said.

"Shit. I shouldn't have made you wait outside."

"No, you were right about that," I told him. "Me going in was too risky. Now, come on. We need to hurry."

Together, we made our stumbling way through the underbrush. It was denser this close to the road than in the rest of the forest, and I kept tripping over things because of the numbness creeping up my legs. After the second time I almost fell, Josh scooped me up, bridal style.

He let out a pained grunt, and I squirmed, trying to get out of his hold.

"I'm too heavy," I protested. "And you're hurt."

He shook his head, jaw clenched in a stubborn line, his gaze trained down as he placed one foot in front of the other. "I'm fine. And it's not much farther. You're safer in my arms than on your feet right now."

I twined my fingers behind his neck and kissed him on the cheek. "I feel safer in your arms always."

"Gag," Junior said, ruining the moment.

Any lingering feelings of familial warmth I felt toward him vanished.

Despite Josh's reassurances that he was fine, getting to the SUV was still a slog. He moved carefully, either because of his injuries or his fear of tripping and toppling us back into the snow. We had to pause several times on our way through the woods, once because Junior thought he saw something and twice more because we thought we heard something. Those moments passed excruciatingly slowly while Josh and I held our breath and strained our ears.

I was so relieved when we finally reached the SUV that I nearly started sobbing, and I could tell from the shaky breath Josh released that he was equally grateful we'd made it.

The driver, an aging man named Jimmy who'd helped locate Brad's car in my neighborhood, had a few blankets in the rear of the vehicle that he used to cover his seats when he had his dogs with him. He explained this in a low, raspy voice as he opened the rear door for us, apologizing for the wet dog smell, but I was so grateful that I couldn't give a shit that they reeked, and I thanked him profusely for letting us use them.

Josh and I took our shoes and socks off and wrapped our feet in the blankets while Jimmy pulled out of the trees and back onto the road. There were heaters beneath the front seats, and I told Josh not to get too close to his at first because we needed to raise our skin temperature slowly. Next, we lost our sodden jackets and dried the rest of ourselves as best we could while filling my cousin in on everything that happened after his team bailed on the mission.

Junior wasn't happy about us setting off the alarm, not even after Josh explained why he'd done it. To Junior, it was better that Brad's family dispose of evidence than for any heat to be brought onto the power company or his dad.

Josh sent me a disgruntled look as my cousin reamed us out over our behavior, and I tilted my head toward him and dropped my voice as I said, "I told you they weren't good people."

By the time we made it onto the highway, my worry over the fate of our feet started to abate. Josh's toes hadn't gone fully numb, just tingly, so he was in the clear. Mine had been pale enough for concern, but now that an uncomfortable pins and needles feeling was creeping into them, I knew I'd gotten off lucky for how long they'd been cold and wet.

Junior's cell rang as we neared the exit for the warehouse district. He held up a finger to everyone in the car and brought the phone to his ear. "What?" A crease appeared between his brows as he listened to whatever the person on the other end of the line said. "And they're cooperating?" Several moments passed before he nodded and spoke again. "Got it."

He pulled the phone down and turned to look between Josh and me. "The cops found the bodies."

My breath whooshed out in a rush of relief. "Oh, thank god."

"Brad's mom fainted when they told her," Junior continued. "His dad gave the cops free rein of the house. Apparently, they didn't realize what a sadistic little shit their son truly was."

Josh nodded beside me. "I figured that when they didn't recognize the smell of the bodies. They thought the housekeeper had forgotten to take the trash out."

Junior's gaze sharpened on him. "And how did *you* recognize it?"

Josh opened his mouth, but I cut him off. "None of your business. And what do you mean, his parents didn't know? They were in that house going after Brad's computer."

Reluctantly, Junior pulled his eyes from my boyfriend and resettled them on me. "They claimed they were trying to find him. Their assumption is that he left the area after the arrest warrant was approved."

I leaned back in my seat. "That's good for us, right?"

Junior nodded. "We might not have found his phone, but one of our guys snagged his wallet. We're going to have someone about his height and build use his debit card up north near the border to make it look like he fled into Canada. That should keep the cops and his family busy for a while."

Josh and I shared a relieved look. This felt like a best-case scenario. Brad's crimes were about to come to light. His family didn't seem likely to impede an investigation into them. The cops were going to think that he'd fled the country, which meant they wouldn't have any reason to look for a body.

Holy shit. Were we actually going to get away with what we'd done? It felt like we might, but I didn't want to jinx myself by thinking about it too much.

Instead, I sidled closer to Josh while my cousin turned back around in his seat and continued his phone call. Josh wrapped an arm around my shoulders and resettled his blanket so we were both covered by it. He leaned down and nuzzled his nose into my hair just above my ear. I closed my eyes and was starting to relax when he spoke, low enough so only I would hear his words.

"That's twice now that you've broken a promise to me, Aly. I hope you can handle the consequences."

My eyes flashed wide. Shit. I'd told him I'd stay behind and failed to keep my word. Again. But in my defense, there were extenuating circumstances in both situations. He had to realize that, right?

I wanted to mention it, plead my case, but this wasn't the time. Josh was a rational guy—for the most part. Maybe I could convince him to see reason once I got him alone. Anyone in my place would have done the same. Most important, *he* would have, but I could already hear his counterpoint of "Yeah, but then I wouldn't have promised to stay put in the first place."

You think I would have learned after the first breach of trust, but *nooo*, I just had to do it a second time. Honestly, I couldn't even blame Josh for being angry about that. Trust was the foundation of any good relationship, and I'd drilled holes in ours right after it had been laid. Maybe I could find some way to make it better by apologizing. By telling him I wouldn't do it again.

But, god help me, a large part of me was too excited by the idea of him punishing me to say anything. Unlike me, he'd done nothing to break my trust so far, and I had a feeling that anything he doled out would be as pleasurable as it was torturous.

The next twenty minutes passed in a blur as I dreamt up all the sinful ways my boyfriend could correct my bad behavior. I had visions of whips and chains, hand necklaces and nipple clamps. Before Josh, my sex life had been the epitome of vanilla, but between social media, the salacious books I read, and the kink-specific porn I watched, it was easy to imagine all the delicious punishments in my future, and thinking about them was much better than thinking of the night we'd just had.

I must not have been the only one lost to their thoughts because the drive back to the warehouse passed in near silence. As soon as we pulled up to the rear of the building where we'd started the night, Josh told me to stay put and then slipped out of the SUV to preheat his car so I wouldn't get cold again. On the surface, the gesture was sweet as hell, but there was a wolfish gleam in his eyes when he looked at me that made me feel like I was being hunted.

"Hey," Junior said.

I turned from watching Josh's shadowy form stride through the night and looked at my cousin. Judging by Junior's expression, he'd been trying to get my attention for a while. "Yeah?"

"You remember what to do if the cops ever show up asking questions?"

"Tell them I don't know anything," I said.

"And if they keep asking?"

"Demand to speak to a lawyer."

Junior nodded. "Good. I'll have our guy call you tomorrow so you know who's representing you."

"Thank you for everything," I said. After all, if not for my family's help, Josh and I probably would have gotten caught. When I thought about it that way, having dinner with them once a month felt like a small price to pay.

Junior shrugged. "You're family. It's what we do."

Was it really so uncomplicated to him? "Still, thank you."

"You're welcome," he said, starting to look uncomfortable. He glanced out his window at Josh's idling car. "How'd he know what a dead body smells like?"

Josh's story wasn't mine to tell, but this was Junior's second time asking the question, and I had a feeling that if I didn't tell him something, he'd start digging into my boyfriend's past. I'd do whatever I could to avoid that, for both mine and Josh's sakes.

Lying wasn't my forte, but I gave it my best shot. "He found a deer rotting in the woods when he was a kid, and it traumatized him. Said he'd never forget the smell."

Junior grimaced. "I bet."

"How'd your men recognize it?" I asked, hoping to turn the tables.

He met my gaze head-on, looking more like his father than ever. "How do you think?"

It was my turn to grimace. No wonder my hackles had risen the second I laid eyes on them. At first, staying behind in the van seemed like the easiest thing in the world because it meant I'd be able to put so much space between me and the dead-eyed crew of ex-soldiers.

I'd been equally happy to stay behind with Josh after they'd aborted their mission, deciding I'd rather risk my boyfriend's wrath than be trapped in a van with them. Now, watching Josh get out of his car and stalk toward my door, I wondered why I'd made that decision. Junior would have been with me if I'd stayed put, and I didn't doubt that he would shoot anyone who made a move for me. Had I stayed behind because, subconsciously, part of me hoped to add to my punishment? Or was it just that I couldn't bear the thought of abandoning my boyfriend?

I shook my head to clear it. Maybe my subconscious played a small part, but more than anything, my reaction had been knee-jerk. Josh was staying behind, so I would, too. End of discussion. I would have never forgiven myself if I'd left him and something happened. And deep down, part of me wondered if leaving him had been the plan all along. After all, Josh was responsible for Brad's death. If not for the basement bodies, would the team have found another excuse to bail prematurely and leave him to fend for himself and hopefully get caught?

The thought made me shudder. If I hadn't gotten out of the van when I had, would my cousin have ordered us to drive to the pickup spot? Or would he have tried to overpower me and leave Josh behind?

Maybe I was being paranoid or mean-spirited by thinking such things about my relatives, but my gut was telling me that I was on to something, and so far, it hadn't led me astray. I might have softened some toward my mobster family members, but I would never trust them, especially not with my boyfriend's welfare, which would likely make our upcoming dinners about as fun as running through the woods at night during winter.

Josh opened my door, pulling me from my dark thoughts. His gaze bored into mine, the anemic glow of the distant floodlights painting his face half in light, half in shadow, reminding me of his mask. "Ready?"

I nodded and held my arms out. One look at Josh was enough for me to realize that no matter the consequences or reasons behind my actions, I wouldn't change my decision to stay with him. Our fates were twined together, for better or for worse.

He reached in and scooped me out of the backseat, blankets and all, and I wrapped my arms around his neck and held on tight. "Thanks, Junior," he called into the cabin.

"You owe us one," my cousin called back.

Josh nodded. "You know how to find me."

With that, he turned and strode toward his car, shuffling me when we reached it so he could open my door and settle me into the seat. He even went so far as to move it forward so my feet were closer to the heater. Ducking down, he tucked the blanket tight around me. "You good? Comfy?"

"I'd be a lot more comfortable if you told me what I'm in for," I said.

His flash of teeth looked feral in the moonlight. I didn't think it was a good thing that he didn't answer me, instead shutting my door and going around to his, but the way he limped made me wonder if he was in any condition to be doling out punishment.

The nurse in me took over as he dropped into the driver's seat. "Regardless of what you have planned for me, I want to look at your ribs when we get home. Don't think I missed the way you've been wheezing."

He sent me a saucy wink. "You just want an excuse to get me topless."

"Always," I shot back. "But seriously, did you hit your ribs?"

He put the car in drive and eased out of the parking spot. "You just steal my breath away, Aly."

I nearly groaned. That wasn't a no. "Josh, if you carried me with a cracked rib, I'm going to punish you right back."

A wicked grin split his face, and I knew from the mischievous gleam in his eyes what was coming next. "Kin—"

I clapped a hand over his mouth.

He swirled his tongue over my palm, all the warning I had before he bit down. Hard.

I yelped and pulled my hand back.

"Ky," he finished.

24

JOSH

To quote one of my favorite TV shows, "Everything hurt, and I was dying."

Okay, so maybe not literally, but it felt pretty close. My shins throbbed. A deep, pulsing ache radiated from my right shoulder to my elbow. Despite the way I'd sidestepped Aly's questions, I'd definitely hit my ribs.

I probably wasn't in any position to teach my girlfriend a lesson about breaking her word to me, but was I about to tell her that? Hell no. The way she kept jumping every time I moved too quickly, like she expected me to pounce any second, was far too satisfying.

I reached for her front door handle a little faster than was necessary, and she flinched so hard that she almost fell sideways into a planter. Oh, this was too good. So good that I was starting to think it was better to delay the punishment I had planned and focus on mental warfare.

"You doing okay, babe?" I asked, fighting the urge to grin. "You seem kind of jumpy."

She sent me a disgruntled look that had no business being so adorable. "I'm just impatient to get inside."

Right. As much fun as it was to torment her, we couldn't linger out here. Our clothes were still damp, and we needed to get out of them and check ourselves over for any injuries that might require treatment.

I slipped my key into the lock and opened the door for Aly, indicating she should go first. She passed me sideways, eyes narrowed and body tense like she was bracing for an attack. The urge to lunge was strong, but I held it in check. We'd been through hell tonight, and the last thing she needed was another rush of adrenaline when her flight-or-fight response kicked in.

A high-pitched yowl hit my ears as I closed the door behind us. Fred came skittering out of Aly's bedroom with his tail held high and mouth wide open as he announced how pissed he was that we'd left him alone. Maybe it was time to start thinking about getting him a little brother or sister, someone to keep him company while Aly and I were working or having Mommy-Daddy time.

Before meeting Aly, I'd never let myself think about what having my own family might be like—I'd been too afraid of passing on my genes to contemplate it—but it felt like I was already forming one with this woman. Now that I trusted myself around small things, I couldn't get the idea of a fluffy little kitten out of my head. It seemed like the next logical step, and I could already see it now: the four of us snuggled together on the couch, Aly sipping wine, and me rubbing her feet while we talked about our days, the cats curled between us.

Ahead of me, Aly leaned down and scooped Fred up. "We weren't even gone that long."

Fred headbutted her in the chin hard enough that I heard a low *thunk* from the impact.

I let them have their moment of reunion while I shucked off my jacket and unlaced my boots. By the time I reached them, Fred was purring loud enough to wake the dead, eyes closed in bliss while he made biscuits in Aly's shoulder.

I ruffled the fur between his ears, grinning when he rewarded me with a little chirrup of welcome. "He's probably just clingy after all the upheaval of the past few days."

Aly hugged him closer. "Poor baby."

"I'll go start the shower," I said, leaning in to kiss her temple. "We need to get cleaned up and warm."

She turned to me, pupils dilating, cheeks flushing, and I knew she was thinking about the last time we'd been in a shower together.

I nearly groaned. More than anything, I wanted to be inside her again. I'd spent half the night terrified we were about to get caught and I'd have to watch my girlfriend get put into handcuffs. I needed the reassurance that she was safe, that she was okay, and nothing could give me that like having her wrapped in my arms, moaning my name.

"Don't take too long," I said before striding away from her.

I put my phone on the bathroom counter before starting the shower. I'd turned the device's volume as high as it went because I was paranoid after Brad's break-in and wanted to hear if any of the freshly tuned alarms I'd set for the doors went off. I didn't love that Aly's family had the keys to her place. They seemed as bad with boundaries as I was, and I didn't trust their intentions. Maybe I could convince Aly to change the locks if she wasn't already set on doing it. From the wary looks she'd given Junior on the ride back to the warehouse, she trusted him even less than I did.

I left the door cracked as I pulled off my damp clothes and set them on the tile floor. A glance in the mirror stopped me in my tracks. Deep purple was starting to bloom along my right side. I knew enough about first aid to realize it wasn't a great sign, so I dragged in a deep breath to see how bad it was. My ribs pinched with discomfort, but the pain wasn't as intense as the time Dad kicked me in the side with his steel-toe boots, so I didn't think any were cracked.

I lifted my gaze and nearly flinched. I'd been so obsessed with Aly recently that I'd skipped my last haircut, and between how long it had gotten and the dark circles beneath my eyes from exhaustion, the resemblance to the monster who fathered me was uncanny.

Unable to look at myself any longer, I jerked my gaze away and got into the shower.

Fuck, what a night. I had no idea how I'd kept it cool inside Brad's place for as long as I had. If not for my need to wipe Aly from Brad's hard drive, I doubted I would have even made it to that computer.

The sickly sweet smell of decomposition had plunged me into one of my most haunting childhood memories, and I'd spent the whole time in Brad's house breathing through my mouth to avoid it. I swore I could still detect a hint of decay clinging to my skin, and, needing to be clean, I grabbed a nearby soap bar and started scrubbing it off.

I was still scrubbing when Aly slipped into the shower with me, and as much as I wanted her in my arms, I couldn't make myself stop.

"Josh?" she said, placing her hand over my wrist.

"I smell it on me," I blurted.

From the way her face crumpled, she knew without having to ask what I was talking about. She took the soap from me and stepped close, putting her nose into my chest. "You smell clean."

"You're sure?" I asked, hating how small my voice sounded.

She rose on her tiptoes and sniffed my neck. Next, she lifted each of my arms and gave them the same treatment. "Nothing but lemon verbena."

I tipped my head toward the yellow bar in her grip. "Is that what that is?"

She nodded and set it on the soap tray, taking my hands as she turned back to me. "I'm guessing you recognized the smell of bodies because of something to do with your father?"

I squeezed her fingers, grounding myself in her touch. "Yeah."

"Do you want to talk about it?"

I lifted my head, looking past her, and the words started pouring out of me before I could stop them. "It happened the summer I turned eleven. Dad took me with him into town for some reason. His car stank to high heaven, so bad that even riding with all the windows open, I was gagging when he finally parked. I asked him what it was, and he said he'd hit a raccoon the night before, and some of it must have stuck to the undercarriage and was rotting because of the heat wave. Back then, I did whatever I could to stay in his good graces, so I went to the trunk to find something to clean it off with. Before I could get it open, Dad pushed me away so hard that I fell onto the pavement."

I lifted my right arm, bending it to show Aly my elbow. "That's where this scar came from."

She leaned in and kissed it, her expression full of sympathy. "I'm so sorry that happened to you."

I nodded and let my arm fall back to my side. "At the time, I was used to his anger, but that day, he looked scared, helping me up when people stopped to watch, telling them it was an accident, and apologizing to me like he never had before. Instead of going into the store, he told me to get back in the car so he could drive me home and clean my scrapes. Instead, he dropped me in the driveway and then took off for two days. I'm not sure where he went after that, but when he came back, the car was so clean it looked new, and it didn't smell anymore."

Aly stepped in close and wrapped her arms around my waist, careful to avoid my ribs, her breasts flattening against my stomach.

Had she been naked this whole time?

Wait, of course she had. We were in the shower. Jesus, I hated the way memories of Dad still put me in such a chokehold, blinding me to my surroundings.

"You think one of his victims was inside the trunk?" Aly asked.

I hugged her close and rested my chin on her head. "Yeah. Dad was pretty active that summer. I just wish I knew the exact date it happened."

"Why's that?"

"Because there are still several missing women he's suspected of killing who have never been found. If the date lined up with one of their disappearances, it might give the family some sort of closure or help the cops find her. I even tried hypnosis once to draw the details out, but it didn't work. I feel like a fucking asshole for not being able to remember."

Aly pulled back, frowning. "You know it's not your fault, right? That you shouldn't feel any guilt over it? You were a child, and your mind probably suppressed as much as it could afterward to protect you."

I nodded and tugged her back in. "I know that, but it still doesn't make it any easier."

"I understand," she said. "It's the same thing with me and the car accident. Not the memory part, but the guilt part. As much as I know it's not my fault, I can't shake the feeling of responsibility."

"We've got some baggage between us, huh?"

Aly choked back a laugh. "Sorry. It's really not funny."

I took her by the shoulders and leaned back enough to look at her. "What?"

She scrunched her nose. "I just had a flashback to the other night and the literal baggage between us."

I grinned. "I get it. It's not ha-ha funny; it's fucked-up funny."

The humor faded from her eyes almost as quickly as it had appeared. "I was so afraid for you tonight."

Her words speared straight into my heart. "I was afraid for you, too."

She shook her head, water droplets sliding down her face. "No, I mean it, Josh. I could *not* leave you behind. Not just because I couldn't stand the thought of you trapped in that house alone with Brad's poor victims, but because I didn't trust Junior to keep his word about picking you up after."

Ah, so she had similar fears about me making a great fall guy or, at the very least, being conveniently expendable. That wasn't ominous at all.

Before now, I was chalking my suspicion up to paranoia, but knowing my girlfriend had come to the same conclusion made it feel like a much bigger threat. I'd have to be more careful around her family from now on. And I definitely needed to do whatever was necessary to stay on Nico's good side.

I smoothed Aly's hair back from her face, wrapping my fingers behind her neck so I could drag her closer. She came willingly, lips parting like she was subconsciously preparing for a kiss.

I dipped down and pressed my forehead against hers, feeling coldness steel up my spine as I remembered how afraid I'd been when she said she was staying behind. "You should have gone with them, even if it put me at risk."

Her eyes flashed with stubbornness, and she tried to pull away, but I tightened my grip and held her where she was. The breath she released was ragged, and I didn't miss the fact that even though she looked pissed, her nipples had tightened.

"That isn't how this works," she said. "You don't get to sacrifice yourself for me. This isn't the medieval times, and I'm not some damsel in distress."

"The whole point of you staying in the van was so there was no sign of you at the house, Aly."

"I know that," she said.

"What if a neighbor saw you? What if a piece of your hair fell out, and the cops find it?"

Fast as lighting, she tipped forward and turned, breaking my grip on her. "My hair was in a braid," she said, stepping as far back as the shower would allow. "And the closest I got to the house was when I helped you off the patio floor. The likelihood of them finding any sign of me is much lower than them finding some sign of you."

I shook my head, closing the distance between us. "My hair was covered, and I had gloves on."

"You might have left behind fabric strands."

I tilted her chin up to make it easier to meet her eyes. "Fiber analysis is about as reliable as blood splatter these days, and all our clothes were generic polyester for a reason. Any fibers left behind could have come from anything."

She huffed out a breath. "Fine. I'm sorry I broke my word to you, but I'm not sorry I stayed behind."

I spun her around, wrapping my arms over her shoulders so I could lean down and speak my next words directly into her ear. "I wasn't trying to sacrifice myself for you, and the last thing I think you are is a damsel in distress. I just want to keep you safe. And I'm sorry if I'm overbearing about it, but I care about you, Aly. I'm sure Tyler warned you that I tend to go overboard when it comes to the people I care about."

"He might have mentioned it."

Noticing that her skin was starting to pebble, I pulled her back beneath the water with me. "I guess we're at an impasse then. We'll both do anything to keep each other safe, even if that means pissing the other one off."

She gripped my forearms and dropped a kiss onto the nearest one. "I'd rather have you care too much than too little."

I squeezed her tight. "Same."

We stayed like that for a few moments, the water running over us and heating our night-chilled skin until I felt like the warmth had finally soaked all the way to my bones, chasing away the last of the cold.

Aly hadn't cleaned herself off yet, so I pulled my arms free and snagged the soap from its tray. I'd take any excuse to touch her, make her feel good, so I took my time rubbing it into her back, making it as much about loosening up her stiff muscles as it was about getting clean. The suds trailed down her skin, and I watched them slip all the way to her perfect ass.

My cock stirred to life as the sight of my naked girlfriend finally drove the lingering darkness away. We'd made it out. We were okay. We were safe. I didn't know how long it would last, so I planned to make the most of whatever time we had, whether that be weeks or years or the rest of our lives.

I stroked the soap back up, my free hand trailing after it, following a long line of muscle.

Aly let out a soft moan and tipped her head forward. "That feels amazing."

"Good," I said, my voice rougher than I intended.

She turned toward me, lips parted as her gaze started to dip from mine to my straining cock. It jerked to a stop halfway there, landing on my side. "Okay, I cannot ignore your ribs any longer."

The next five minutes consisted of us chronicling our injuries. After some painful poking and prodding, Aly finally agreed that my ribs probably weren't cracked, just bruised. My shoulder and shins were in the same shape, and Aly, in full nurse mode, said I'd have to ice everything once we got out of the shower, which made me want to delay that moment as long as possible. The thought of pressing anything cold to my skin after how cold I'd been earlier was abhorrent, but from the stubborn look on Aly's face, if I tried to argue with her again, I would lose.

Luckily, none of the scratches on our faces or necks from all the rogue tree branches were deep or long enough to require stitches. They were unsightly, though, and it made me glad for another excuse to stay locked up in Aly's house for the next two weeks while we healed.

She stepped back after looking over the last of my scrapes, worrying her lower lip between her teeth in the way that drove me crazy. "Do you feel like we got off too easy?"

"Too easy? No," I said, indicating my ribs. "But part of me is still waiting for the other shoe to drop."

She frowned and started soaping herself up. I did my best to maintain eye contact, but goddamn it, her tits were right there, dripping with suds, and I could already feel them filling my hands, warm and slick and sensitive to my every caress.

"Maybe it's because we didn't handle it ourselves," she said, unaware of my plummeting thoughts. "At least, that's it for me. I'm used to being in control all the time. The fact that I'm just supposed to trust an estranged uncle and cousins after they said they did their part isn't sitting well with me. I want to know where the body is, who they're going to sell Brad's car parts to, exactly how they plan to trick the cops into thinking he's fled to Canada."

"Maybe you can butter Nico up with wine at family dinner and ask him then."

She nodded. "It's not a terrible idea. I really want to know how Junior had all those details about the investigation already."

"Dirty cops," I said. It was the most logical answer.

Her expression turned contemplative. "That's what I was thinking, too."

Unable to help myself, I reached out and stroked my hand over her shoulder. "As much as I hate the idea of dirty cops, having someone on the inside could benefit us. If they continue leaking the investigation to Junior, we'll know if they find anything pointing to your family or us. Depending on how dirty they are, they might even hide evidence."

Aly grimaced. "I don't like benefiting from this kind of thing. It feels too close to what Brad was doing."

I squeezed her shoulder. "Would you rather go to jail?"

"No," she said. "I just don't like it, and yes, I realize that probably makes me a hypocrite."

I grinned. "Huge hypocrite."

She slapped my hand away.

I grabbed her wrist and pulled her close. "But a hot one."

Her response came out muffled because of the way I'd smooshed her face into my chest.

"I'm going to assume you just called me hot, too."

She reached behind me and pinched my butt hard enough to make me jerk forward, which pinned my dick between our slick skin. I expected her to pull away and say something snarky, but she writhed against me instead. My need for her returned in a rush, all other thoughts drowned out by the memory of how good it felt to shove my cock inside her tight, wet pussy.

"Aly," I said, stepping away from her. "I want you so bad right now, but if I don't eat something soon, I'm going to pass out."

Her face fell, but she caught it and shook her head. "No, you're right. And same."

I lifted a hand and cupped her cheek. "Also, I'm not too proud to admit that I'm in so much pain that I don't think I can worship you the way you deserve right now."

She nodded, her expression full of understanding. "I can wait until you feel better. I know it'll be worth it." She lifted a hand to show me her wrinkly fingertips. "And I'm starting to prune, so I'm good with getting out of here."

I turned away so she wouldn't see me smile. Should I have felt bad for lying to my girlfriend? Maybe. But I had a feeling that when I woke her up in a few hours, she'd be more than willing to forgive me for it afterward.

25

ALY

A SOUND WOKE ME in the middle of the night. I'd been having the nicest dream about . . . something. It was already fading as I cracked my eyes open, but I thought it involved cold beer and a warm, sandy beach. What I wouldn't give for a mid-winter Caribbean vacation. I had some money saved up. Maybe sometime during the next two weeks, Josh and I could slip away to—

My ceiling was awash with red. Why was my ceiling red?

Oh, fuck, was my house on fire?

I tried to jerk upright, but a yank on my arms had me floundering back onto the mattress. I craned my head up, panicking, and froze. There were black silk cuffs around my wrists, and the ropes binding them led straight to my headboard, where a complex series of knots that looked impossible to unravel secured them.

Fear punched through my lungs, stealing my breath away. Josh wasn't in the bed beside me. We'd been curled up together when I fell asleep, with Fred perched on top of us. They were both gone now, and I must have been half out of it with sleep because all I could think was that Brad wasn't actually dead, and he'd broken back into my house to finish what he'd started.

"Oh, good," a deep, modulated voice tolled out. "You're awake."

I snapped my gaze up.

There he sat facing the foot of the bed, shirtless and lit with the deep crimson light he often used in his videos: the Faceless Man. His mask looked more threatening than I remembered, the cheekbones sharper, the black eyes deeper. His massive frame dwarfed my small armchair, making it look like something made for a child. Why had I never realized how ominous his tattoos were? Dark, twisted forms crawled up his arms like gothic nightmares emerging from hell.

One hand grasped a wicked-looking knife I'd never seen before, curved and razor-sharp—something made for skinning prey. The way he held it so casually, half dangling from his fingers as he twirled it in an idle circle, made it seem even more dangerous. Only someone well versed with weapons handled them with such little regard, as if they knew the tool so intimately it had become an extension of their arm.

It's just Josh, I tried to tell myself, but the knowledge did little to calm my racing pulse.

Gone was my kind, funny boyfriend. In his place sat a man who radiated menace. With the mask on, it was like he'd become someone else. Or maybe that wasn't right. Maybe he was still the same Josh I'd grown to care about so deeply, and wearing the mask allowed him to bring out a darker side of his personality that he kept hidden during the day. One that craved my fear as much as my desire.

He lifted the knife and pointed it at me, head tilting sideways in an unnerving, almost alien way because it was such an un-Josh-like gesture. I checked him over again to reassure myself that it was, in fact, my boyfriend and not a different masked stranger who'd broken into my house. The bruised ribs confirmed his identity, but my heart raced on.

"Spread them," he said.

I glanced down to see the sheets pooled at my waist. I still wore the matching black satin tank and shorts I'd gone to bed in, and for that, I was grateful. It was bad enough that I'd slept through being tied up, but if I'd slept through being stripped, I would have had to book an appointment with a sleep clinic to see what the hell was wrong with me.

The Faceless Man's tone brooked no argument, so I propped myself up on my elbows and slowly parted my bent legs. He leaned forward just enough to drag the sheets off them, torturously slow, and my skin was already so hypersensitive that I felt every inch of cotton slide over me like wandering hands.

What was he about to do to me?

He stood in a fluid motion. The red light must have been set on the floor somewhere near the foot of my bed because he bisected the beam, his massive form outlined on my far wall like some kind of kinky Bat-Signal.

Turn it on, and he will come—pun intended.

The thought made me want to smile, but I had a feeling that it would only get me into trouble, and I was deep enough as it was. Now wasn't the time to taunt the man who'd tied me up. Maybe after this was over and I knew what his retribution entailed, I would start acting bratty, but until then, I was too chickenshit to pile any more punishable offenses onto my plate.

He twirled the knife again, and my gaze dropped to it. So far, we'd only briefly talked about our shared bedroom fantasies, but we hadn't gotten around to outlining just how far each of us was willing to take them, and the realization that he and I might have very different stopping points suddenly made me nervous.

No safe words, I reminded myself. If he pushed me too far, I could simply tell him to stop. After everything we'd been through, I trusted him enough to keep his word that he would.

He slid a knee onto the bed between my spread legs. The hand not holding the knife landed by my hip, and he leaned forward, braced over me. Fuck, he was big. His shoulders were so wide they blocked my view of the ceiling. Muscles rippled across his chest and down his torso as he balanced in place. Somehow, being around him so much recently had numbed me to our size difference, but looking up at him now drove home just how large he was.

A flash of metal had me dropping my gaze to the weapon he held. I was tied up, with a knife-wielding masked man looming over me. This was a fantasy I'd had for months, but the reality of it was much different. Yes, I was turned on. I wasn't wearing panties beneath my silk shorts, and I could already feel the fabric of them soaking through with my desire. But I was also more afraid than I thought I would be. All I had to go on was my instinct to trust Josh and his insistence that he didn't want to hurt me. That it was the moment my fear turned to lust he craved. If I was wrong, this could go so, so badly for me.

It only made me wetter for him.

The sharp edge of fear tipped my desire into the realm of darkness and heightened my other senses, making my skin so sensitive that every inch of me was turning into an erogenous zone. The Faceless Man lifted his knife and dragged the tip up the inside of my thigh, and I shivered beneath him, fighting back a moan.

He studied the blade's progress before lifting his soulless eyes to mine. "You're beautiful when you're scared."

God, that was fucked up.

I loved it.

Only the threat of the knife kept me still beneath him. If not for its presence, I would have been writhing. My pussy throbbed, and I needed something to ease the ache, friction against my clit, or better yet, his monstrous cock filling me up. I'd never forget the initial sting of stretching around it, trying to take something so large and hard into my body. I was still a little sore from our first tryst, and I knew it would make this second time so much better—more painful at first, but then pure bliss when he was buried to the hilt, and I relaxed into pleasure.

He sucked in a breath above me, no doubt seeing the desire writ across my face. I used to think it was bad to wear every emotion so openly, but the way he reacted to them made me never want to change.

The knife slipped another inch upward, sharp enough to sting but not hard enough to break the skin. I held my breath as it got closer and closer to the apex of my thighs, my gaze moving over his straining muscles, twisted tattoos, and back to the bottomless black of empty eye sockets again. This was the hottest, most terrifying moment of my life, and holding still through it was absolute torture, which was likely his intent. I should have known my punishment would be as mental as it was physical.

"Don't move," he said.

I froze, going so far as to hold my breath when the knife swiveled against me, blade up as he slipped it beneath the hem of my shorts. There was a tug around my upper thigh as the fabric went taut, and then a soft sigh filled the room as he pressed the blade up, slicing through the satin. It sounded disturbingly close to a scalpel opening skin, and it sent my fear ratcheting up another notch.

I glanced down to see the right side of the shorts fall away. He pivoted the knife to my other thigh and cut that side free next. Only a small square of fabric was left covering me, and as I watched, he used the knife tip to drag it down until I was revealed to him. Cool air brushed against the heated, wet skin of my folds, making me shiver.

With a flick, he spun the knife to hold its blade pointed down, his fist wrapped around the handle. Then he braced his fist beside me, shifting his weight to it as he lifted his free hand. That hand went straight between my thighs, cupping my pussy. The urge to grind against him was so strong that I let out a whimper as I fought it back. His hand was so warm, so close to where I needed it.

"You're soaked," he bit out, sounding as tortured by my arousal as I was.

I tried to lift my arms, wanting to touch him, but I was so out of it with need that I'd forgotten about the goddamn restraints and landed flat on my back. As soon as I hit the mattress, he plunged his fingers inside me. I was so shocked by the sudden intrusion that my spine arched off the bed, and a gasp tore from my mouth. He gave me no time to adjust, shoving his fingers as deep as they would go, the heel of his palm grinding into my clit as he used his hand to fuck me.

I writhed, half trying to get away, half trying to get closer. It was so much, so soon, but as sudden as his invasion was, it was already making something tighten deep inside me. No. There was no way I was close to coming already.

He added a third finger, wet, slippery sounds filling the room, almost loud enough to drown out my continued gasps. His movements were harsh, relentless, thrusting so hard that my tits bounced, and my heels scrabbled against the sheets as I looked for some way to brace myself. He was fucking me like he was mad at me, like this wasn't about getting me off, but spinning me as high as he could as fast as he could, and it made me nervous for what would come next.

The last edging nearly killed me, and he'd been in a playful mood then. I couldn't imagine how torturous it would be when he was hell-bent on teaching me a lesson.

I should have been scared, and maybe I was, but the thought of being dominated like that, utterly out of control, was more thrilling than anything else. It was enough to end my momentary resistance to him, my heels going slack as I quit tilting my hips away and instead started thrusting them down to meet his palm.

Apparently, it was what he'd been waiting for. The second I started writhing against him, he pulled his fingers free, leaving my pussy clenching around nothing. I couldn't stop the low hiss of frustration from slipping through my lips. I needed him. The sudden shock of loss was too much to endure. How dare he do this to me again, leaving me so desperate for him.

I couldn't wait for him to make it worse.

The fingers that had been inside me glistened in the red light. He sat back on his heels and tipped his mask up just enough to slide his hand beneath it. A sucking sound told me he was cleaning my arousal off with his tongue. My inner walls spasmed at the thought of it, and more than anything, I wanted to watch, but the sight was denied to me, driving my frustration to new heights. Those fingers would be put to better use out of his mouth and inside me. As shocking as it had been, I craved the feeling of them pounding into me again.

"Show me," I said, voice hoarse from lust.

I didn't think he'd do it at first, but then he tilted his mask up even higher, just enough to reveal his lips. His tongue slid out, licking in a sinful circle as he cleaned every last drop of me off his fingers. I almost came from the sight alone.

With a tug, his mask was back in place, and I had just enough time to register the bulge in his dark jeans before his hands wrapped around my ankles, and he pulled me flat against the bed. My arms strained overhead, the ropes snapping tight as I found the edge of the restraints. He let go with one hand, reaching for something out of sight at the foot of the mattress.

His hand came back into view holding what looked like a smaller-sized anal plug, the dark blue silicone narrow at the tip and then swelling in the middle before tapering off again and ending in a broad base. Then he was moving between my legs, pushing one of my knees up as he came, all the way to my chest. He stroked the blunted tip of the plug down my stomach and then lower, slicking it through my folds.

"You're so wet, I don't even need lube," he rumbled, the words deliciously rough because of the modulator. His black eye sockets were trained between my legs as he slowly pushed the toy into my pussy.

"Always wet for you," I panted, shifting my other leg to the side to grant him greater access. The plug was narrower than I wanted, but my inner walls, starved for friction, clasped down on it regardless.

He made a low sound of masculine approval, twirling the plug inside me so it was coated in my arousal. Then he slid it out, the tip tracing down to my ass. I was worried that he would be rough after the way he'd fingered me, but he took his time pushing the plug in, allowing me a moment to adjust when I hissed out a breath at the initial discomfort. I thought I was okay until I got to the wider middle, and everything clenched up, my body resistant to take it.

The Faceless Man reached down, the pad of his thumb landing on my clit. My head fell back as he massaged around it in a circle, pausing to gently flick it before circling again.

Oh, fuck, that felt good.

He did it again, pushing the plug deeper as my muscles loosened from the pleasure. Once the widest part of it was in, the rest was easier to take, and before I knew it, the toy was fully seated. He lifted his thumb away, and I was left both too full and too empty at the same time. My pussy was still contracting, longing to be filled, and I could feel the plug every time my inner muscles spasmed.

He lifted something else off the mattress and held it up for me to see. It was a small plastic square, almost like a remote of some ki—

A sharp *click* was all the warning I had before the plug in my ass started vibrating.

I let out a yelp, feet scrabbling against the covers again, caught off guard by the sudden sensation. Holy shit, I didn't even know there *were* anal vibrators.

Two big hands landed on my thighs, pinning them down, forcing me to lay there and *feel*, and oh, god, did I feel. I'd never been so aware of that part of my body before. Nor had I been aware of how close things were on the inside. Somehow, it felt like the vibration in my ass was happening in my pussy, too, and while I'd found anal play mildly pleasurable in the past, now I was actually enjoying it. More than enjoying it. If he kept this up and gave me literally any other stimulation, I would come so hard I'd probably squirt.

With another click, the vibration cut off, leaving me panting. The hands on my thighs lifted to my hips, and before I realized what was happening, the bedroom spun as he flipped me onto my stomach. A jerk on my waist had me face down, ass up on the mattress, the ropes so tight I couldn't do much but turn my hands in and cling to them for support. My heart rate, which was already at a steady gallop, skyrocketed.

What was he doing back there? What was coming next?

A hand landed between my shoulder blades, pressing me down harder. I turned my face so I wouldn't suffocate, trying to look behind me but seeing nothing but a long line of jean-clad thigh as the Faceless Man positioned himself behind me.

Please, fuck me, I wanted to beg, but I had a feeling that he was so antagonistic right now he might refuse just to spite me.

A click hit my ears, and I tried to brace myself, but—*oh, fuck*—I didn't think there was any way to prepare for the feeling of something vibrating in my ass. Between the sound of the toy and my ragged breathing, I barely heard the zip of jeans being undone. That meant something, I knew it did, but I was so distracted by what was happening inside my body that I didn't realize what I was in for until the hand pinning me down lifted free, and my hips were yanked backward, spearing me straight onto the Faceless Man's cock.

I cried out, my pussy clenching around him, stars dancing behind my closed eyelids as I tried to adjust to the mix of pleasure and discomfort. Yup, I was still sore, but anyone who's been fucked hard understands the delicious sting of being stuffed full again before you're ready for it. Maybe it wasn't true for everyone, but for me, it was a *good* kind of pain. What made it even better was that with the addition of the plug, this was the fullest I'd ever been in my life, and I could tell from where I stretched around him that the Faceless Man was barely halfway in.

"I need to be able to trust you," he growled.

And then he spanked me hard enough that my entire body clenched up, my ears echoing with the sound of the slap. With a grunt, he pulled all the way out of me, having to shove my hips forward because of how much my pussy had tightened around him.

I froze.

He'd actually *spanked* me.

I'd never been spanked in my life. And he hadn't held back either. He'd hit me hard enough that it still stung. I didn't think it would bruise, but there was no doubt my ass was now as red as the blush stealing up my cheeks, heating my face with an unexpected mixture of shame and embarrassment. And not because my boyfriend was following through on his threat to punish me. But because of how much I liked it.

Behind me, he'd gone completely still, like he was waiting for my reaction. Yes, he was being a domineering bastard right now, but deep down, I knew he was probably trying not to panic, worried that he'd gotten caught up in the moment and gone too far.

The vibrator clicked off, and the hand holding my hip softened. "Say something."

In answer, I pushed my ass into him. "I don't think I've learned my lesson yet."

The voice modulator turned his heavy exhale into something more like a growl.

I arched my spine. "Again."

The fingers on my hips tightened. A low rumble filled the room before he thrust back in, even deeper this time, and between his dick and the plug, I was so stuffed that my toes curled against the sheets. I felt his shift of movement right before his palm slapped my ass again, a little lighter than the first time but still hard enough to burn. Even though I was ready for it, I stiffened up, and he clicked the vibrator on right as he pulled out.

My eyes snapped wide, a deep pulse of lust blasting through me. The sensation of his cock dragging out of me while every muscle in my body clenched tight, paired with the vibration kicking back on, was unlike anything I'd ever felt before. The pleasure was unparalleled; if he kept this up for long, I would probably shred the sheets with my nails.

I felt feral, needy.

Desperate.

"Hold on to the ropes," he said, clicking the vibrator off.

I clung to them for all I was worth as he rammed into me again, spanked my other cheek, and then pulled almost all the way out, clicking on the vibrator as he went. Stars exploded across my vision. I turned my face into the sheets and cried out into them.

He started a rhythm: in, spank, out, vibrate. I lost myself to it, became someone else to it, no longer Aly, but some wild version of her, shoving my hips back, moaning and pleading and apologizing, unselfconscious and fully uninhibited for the first time in my life.

"Fuck," the Faceless Man growled. "I can feel it vibrating against me."

He stopped clicking the plug off after that, leaving it on as his hips snapped forward, burying himself balls deep with every brutal thrust.

The longer it continued, the more out of control we both became. I let go of the ropes to claw at the sheets. My masked man wrapped his fingers in my hair and wrenched my head up. Instead of spanking me with every thrust, his strikes became intermittent, and the unreliability of them made each one that much sweeter, that much more painful.

That much more pleasurable.

I felt raw and overexposed, all my layers of humanity stripped away to reveal the animal underneath. She wanted to be fucked, hard, every part of her so full to bursting that the whole world fell away, leaving nothing between her and the man behind her. The next time we did this, I was asking him to gag me. I wanted to scream for him when I came, and I hated that I couldn't do it because there were neighbors close enough to hear me and probably call the cops, thinking I was getting murdered. At least if something was shoved deep enough into my mouth to muffle the noise, I could give in to that desire.

His dick started to swell inside me, and I nearly sobbed with relief. I'd been holding my orgasm at bay as long as I could, waiting to tumble over the edge with him.

"Come for me, Aly," he said, tugging my hair hard enough to sting. "Let me feel that perfect pussy choke this cock."

His other hand left my hip, and a second later, I felt the cold bite of metal against my throat. He'd picked the knife back up.

The spike of fear that stabbed through me was enough to tip me over the edge. My pussy spasmed, inner muscles clenching, trying to draw him deeper. Bare millimeters away, the vibrator buzzed on, stealing the breath from my lungs and making tears streak from my eyes. I'd never felt like this before, and I'd do anything to feel it again. He had officially ruined me for all others.

The Faceless Man groaned behind me, his hips starting to lose the rhythm as his cock swelled and stretched, hitting a spot so deep it stole my breath away. And then I was coming, sobbing, praising him even as I cursed his very existence.

I would never forgive him for doing this to me.

I couldn't wait until the next time he did it.

"Aly, fuck!" he yelled.

The knife fell from his fingers, and his hands returned to my hips as his thrusts turned furious and desperate. Feeling him come inside me only prolonged my release, black creeping into the edges of my vision, a low buzz filling my ears. Was I about to pass out?

By the time I came out of my daze, my hands were free from the restraints, and I lay boneless on the covers, being petted and stroked and rewarded for how well I'd taken my punishment. His touches were as soft as they'd just been hard, and his words were full of approval as he told me how beautiful I'd been, that none of his fantasies could ever compare to what we'd just done.

I reached up and pulled his mask off, and the Faceless Man became Josh again, his hair mussed and his dark eyes full of wonder as he stared down at me.

"It was the back of the blade I held to your throat," he said. "You were never in danger."

"I know," I told him, because of course I wasn't.

"Aly, that was amazing."

I threaded my fingers through his. "Unfortunately, we're going to have to work through our issues with dialogue like rational adults because if that was meant to prevent me from breaking my word to you again, I gotta tell you, it backfired."

His chest heaved as he chuckled. "Are you sure? Because you sounded apologetic as fuck about halfway through it."

I grinned. "I was more sorry that I wasn't sorry."

He lifted his free hand and gave the side of my ass a gentle slap. "Bad girl."

"I think I'm falling for you," I blurted.

Maybe it was the hormones, or maybe it was how well he'd just brought my fantasies to life. Or maybe it was how he could make me laugh even in the most stressful situations. The way he'd moved himself right into my life like he'd always belonged there. The way he treated my, no, *our* cat like a human child. The unselfconscious goofiness of the man. The beauty. The intelligence. The way he looked at me like I was his whole world. And yes, even the obsessive way he tracked my every move. Even the way he watched me, stalked me, and hunted me down.

He grinned. "If all it took was a little light spanking to get you to say that, I would have bent you over my knee the first time we met."

He called *that* light spanking? God, I'd gotten off easy.

I made a mental note not to piss him off again. At least not until I felt ready to face more pain than that during sex.

I reached up and stroked my thumb over his lips. "I was too jumpy that night in the parking garage to let you anywhere near my ass."

His eyes darkened. "I'm not talking about then."

Oh. He meant the first time we saw each other in his apartment, all those months ago. Had his obsession started then?

As I watched, he parted his lips and sucked my thumb into his mouth, swirling his tongue around it before biting the tip. The grin that split his face as I pulled free was wicked. In a flash, he rolled me onto my back, settling his hips between mine so I could feel the way his cock was hardening again.

He leaned down and kissed me, and after not being able to touch him for so long, it felt like the sweetest reward to be able to wrap my arms and legs around him.

His dark eyes crinkled at the corners as he broke the kiss and pulled away enough to look at me. "I think I'm falling for you, too."

Warmth spread through my core, the heat of pleasure mixed with pure joy. Even though I was sore, I needed him again. Now.

I tightened my arms around his neck and pulled him onto me, plying him with drugging kisses until he gave me what I wanted, pushing inside carefully this time, his thrusts deep and gentle and just as mind-blowing as before.

It was a long time before we emerged from my bedroom, freshly showered and starving after our marathon calorie-burning session.

We pulled up short after opening the door. Fred sat right on the other side of it, looking rattled. His eyes were large and glassy as he stared past our legs toward the rumpled bed like he knew what had just gone on in there.

Josh leaned close. “I think we’ve officially scarred our son.”

I lifted a hand for a high-five. “Parental achievement unlocked.”

26

JOSH

"How do I look?" I asked Aly.

She paused before ringing the doorbell to give me a once-over. "Hot. Want to get out of here and go have naked fun time?"

I clapped a hand over her mouth. "Shush! What if there are cameras out here?"

Her response was only slightly muffled by my palm. "Then it'll teach my meddling family not to listen in on conversations that don't concern them."

Three weeks had passed since the night we'd broken into Brad's house. The next day, I'd swept my car for trackers, and Aly was still pissed that I'd found one. We'd gone straight to the hardware store afterward and changed her locks.

I removed my hand from her mouth and straightened my dinner jacket, feeling uncomfortable in such formal clothes. "I need to stay on your uncle's good side. Remember?"

She blew out a breath. "I do. Sorry. I'll try to keep it PG for your sake."

"Good girl," I said, unable to help myself.

Her mouth popped open, a flush creeping into her cheeks that had nothing to do with embarrassment and everything to do with arousal.

I tried not to let it go to either of my heads. We'd been having so much sex that we'd started implementing forced breaks to keep from chafing. I worried she might become desensitized to me, but the fact that I could still turn her on like a light switch with just two words made me feel better about what her red dress was doing to me. It wasn't even that clingy or revealing, but I'd never seen so much of her on display in public, and I was reacting like a kid at his first school dance.

"You look beautiful," I told her.

She smiled up at me. "So you've said. We should do this, just the two of us. Get all dressed up and go out for a nice dinner."

I rubbed the back of my neck, feeling overheated even though it was freezing out.

Aly saw my discomfort and rushed on. "I'll find a place with low lighting and a table in the back where no one but our server will see us. And if they start to look squirrelly, or you don't like it, we can leave."

"I don't know," I said, still hesitant.

She rolled her eyes. "Look, I didn't want to say anything because I didn't want it to inflate your already dangerously oversized ego, but you do realize that the people who stop to stare at you aren't doing it because they think they recognize you, right?"

I frowned. "Then why?"

"Because of how hot you are."

I blinked. Was she serious? Was that a thing? I knew I was more attractive than the average bear but hot enough to stop people in their tracks?

I refocused on my girlfriend, looking for some sign that she was joking or exaggerating, but her expression was stone-cold. Oh, man. If she was right, I was going to have so much fun with this.

Aly caught sight of my widening grin and huffed out a breath. "I knew I shouldn't have said anything. You're going to be insufferable now, aren't you?"

I turned my face from left to right. "Which do you think is my better side? I'll need to know when it comes time to send modeling agents my portfolio."

She slapped my arm and then rang the bell.

The front door opened so fast that Nico must have been standing right on the other side of it. Listening to our conversation?

Awkwaaard.

Nico threw his arms wide and stepped onto the front porch with us. "There's my girl."

Aly shot me a panicked look as her uncle hugged her. His overfamiliarity made her as uncomfortable as going out in public made me, and I knew she only endured it for my sake. I'd have to find a way to thank her for it later. Maybe it was time to finally give in and let her use the plug on *me* for once.

"Alright, fella," came a lilting feminine voice. I glanced toward the front door as a petite woman with pale skin and light brown hair appeared inside it. "There's no need to overdo it and scare the girl off." Her Irish accent was so thick that the word "there's" sounded more like "tears." It must have been the infamous Moira.

Nico released Aly and turned toward his wife. "Who can blame me for being excited to welcome our niece back into the fold?"

"Uh," Aly said. "That's not what this is."

Moira gestured us inside. "Either way, get in. It's cold as a nun's twat out here."

Aly and I exchanged glances and followed the pair into the house. From what Aly had told me about her aunt, I knew that Moira's family had ties to the IRA, and she and Nico had met when they were still in their teens, back when the Italian mob was trying to court the Provos. Their dads had done business together, and theirs had been a Romeo and Juliet–style courtship but with a better outcome.

Aly had only interacted with her aunt a few times and said that was all it took for her to grudgingly like the woman. Moira had a whip-sharp sense of humor and didn't take shit from anyone, her husband included. I'd just met her and could already see what Aly meant.

Moira held the door open as I passed, doing nothing to mask the appreciative way she eyed me, and I decided that maybe Aly had a point about my looks after all.

Moira's gaze shifted to her niece next, and she winked. "Well done, you."

Aly slipped her arm through mine, looking like the *Mona Lisa* with a smile full of secrets. "If you only knew."

Moira's brows lifted, her green eyes sparking with interest as they slowly rose to mine.

Nico chose that moment to clear his throat, and I was so grateful that I could have hugged him. Whatever the reason I drew so much attention, it still made me feel like I was about to break into hives.

Nico shut the door behind us and lifted an arm, indicating we precede him deeper into the house. "There's wine waiting for us, and Moira put out a nice spread."

She snorted. "Don't get your hopes up. It's just some fancy cheeses and crackers arranged on a board."

Her husband rolled his eyes. "I'm trying to compliment you."

"Then be more obvious about it," she shot back. "Next time, try saying something about what a nice arse I have."

Nico looked scandalized. "Not in front of the kids."

Aly dragged me past the pair, but we didn't get away fast enough to miss Moira's rebuttal.

"Calling that man a kid is like calling the David statue a lump of marble. Stop trying to infantilize him because he makes you feel weird in the tummy."

"Moira! Jesus Christ. He does *not*."

Aly wheezed beside me as we sped down a hallway, doing her best to hide her laughter and failing spectacularly. "Weird in the tummy. That woman is a legend."

I didn't find it quite as funny. "So much for me staying on his good side."

She squeezed my arm. "You'll be fine. I threatened to tell the cops everything if he ever turns on you."

I stopped mid-step, dragging her to a halt with me. "When did you do that?"

"A week ago. Remember when you went back to your place to grab more stuff?"

I nodded.

"I came here while you were gone and read him the riot act over the tracker and the mass copying of my keys and keeping us out of the loop with everything."

"How'd it go?" I asked.

She shrugged. "He said he'd fill us in tonight, but we'll see if he keeps his word."

"He will," someone called out. We spun to see Junior rounding the far end of the hall. He gestured behind him. "We're in here if you want to join us."

I was about to have dinner with the whole clan. Nico, Moira, their sons, and all their romantic partners. Great. Splendid. I couldn't wait to get this started.

Why were my hands so clammy all of a sudden?

Aly squeezed my arm. "We'll just be a second."

Junior nodded and disappeared back around the bend.

Aly dragged me into a nearby powder room with barely enough space for us. We were pressed so close that I had a clear line of sight straight into her cleavage. Weirdly, it helped calm my racing pulse. Just last night, I'd nestled my head there after she'd made me come so hard I saw God, and I'd spent several minutes with my ear pressed to her skin, listening to the steady rhythm of her heart. I could almost hear the low *ba-dump*, *ba-dump* now.

She took my hands, her eyes large and imploring. "You don't have to do this."

I would have leaned down and kissed her if not for the risk of smearing her crimson lipstick. "Thank you, but if you're here, I'm here. I'll just have to find some way to deal."

"You're sure?" she asked.

"I'm sure," I said.

She looked amazing tonight, her long hair falling around her in loose waves, her natural beauty accented with makeup, and that dress. God, that dress. I couldn't wait to see it pooled around her feet later. I'd caught a glimpse of the bra and panty set she wore beneath it, all black silk and lace. An image of me slicing them into ribbons filled my head, but the fantasy would probably never come to life. It turned out fancy lingerie was expensive, and Aly had been low-key pissed after I cut a different set off her.

Maybe I could get away with it if I bought her more afterward.

She shook her head at me. "You're thinking about sex, aren't you?"

I grinned. "Dirty, dirty sex."

"Yeah, you'll be fine."

With that, she shoved me out of the bathroom, and we joined the rest of her family in a formal sitting room. Everything about this house was formal, I was coming to realize. The ceiling was sky-high, with white-painted beams bisecting each other in a square pattern. A stone fireplace took up most of the far wall, and a roaring fire had been built in it that turned the room toasty. In the center, beneath a crystal chandelier, sat a trio of white couches facing a circular table filled with refreshments and appetizers.

I'd been expecting a crowd, but only three of Aly's cousins stood with their parents, Greg nowhere to be seen. I was the only significant other in attendance and didn't know how to feel about it. Were these dinners supposed to be for the family, and I was intruding? Or had the boys' partners been excluded because there'd be shop talk tonight?

"Red or white?" Nico asked, gesturing to a pair of wine carafes.

"White," Aly said.

I eyed the pristine couches before seconding her request.

Nico passed us each a glass.

Aly took a sip of hers and then trained her gaze on the family patriarch. "What's going on with the investigation?"

Her second oldest cousin, Alec, lifted his brows. "What happened to 'Hello. How are you?'"

Aly didn't acknowledge him, still zeroed in on Nico. "You told me you'd fill us in tonight."

He gave her a reproachful look. "We don't talk business until after dinner."

"That sounds like bullshit," Aly said.

Moira interjected. "It does, but it's also a tradition. Food and booze first. People are nicer when they're tipsy and full."

"Yeah," Alec said. "It's called hangry for a reason."

Aly frowned. "So, what do we do until then? Exchange frivolous pleasantries and pretend we're not all waiting for that conversation to happen?"

Moira clinked her glass against her niece's. "You catch on fast."

Aly sent me a frustrated glance.

I took a deep pull of wine to keep from having to say anything. Cowardly? Absolutely, but I knew better than to meddle in other people's family drama, and I wanted to stay in Nico's good graces as long as I could. I just hoped no one crossed a line with Aly because my Switzerland status only extended so far.

I also understood my girlfriend's frustration. Brad was all over the news. A child of mega-rich parents had turned out to be a serial rapist and possible serial killer—so far, only the two bodies in the basement had been found, and you needed three for the "serial" title. He was suspected of killing more, and there were plans to excavate the backyard and search the woods we'd fled through looking for further victims.

Nico had stayed true to his word, and a man who looked an awful lot like Brad had been caught on CCTV withdrawing cash from an ATM close to the Canadian border. The crossings up there were on high alert, and Brad's passport had been flagged. No additional sightings had been reported, but every night, the local news reminded people there was a killer on the loose, and the entire city was on edge, wondering if he'd really fled or if his family was hiding him somewhere nearby.

His parents were housebound because of the media attention, and their lawyers had been extra busy dodging questions and dragging their feet as they tried to slow the police investigation. It turned out the Bluhms' initial acquiescence mostly came from shock, and now they were doing everything they could to save face in the public eye and distance themselves from what their spawn had done.

There was so much scrutiny on the case that I hadn't hacked back into the police system despite how desperate Aly and I were to know what was happening. That left Nico as our only source of information.

He gestured at Aly with his glass. "How's work been?"

She eyed him. "Has your little mole not been filling you in on my daily life?"

Nico grinned. "Greg's been preoccupied with his own responsibilities."

"And what would those be?" Aly asked.

"Janitorial, of course," Nico answered, looking nonplussed.

Aly glanced around. "Where is he tonight?"

"Busy," all of her cousins said at once.

Well, that wasn't suspicious.

Aly homed in on it. "With what?"

Nico's grin slipped. "Anyone ever tell you you're not great at small talk?"

"Tell me about the investigation, and I'll try to improve," Aly shot back.

I hid my grin behind another sip of wine. She'd lured him right into that trap.

The rest of the pre-dinner conversation didn't improve much from there. Aly and Nico spent most of it trading barbs. Moira attempted to get them back to safer ground several times with well-placed jokes, but neither was having it; they were too caught up in their battle of wills. Junior tried throwing me a lifeline halfway through by bringing up the latest football game, but I'd never been into sports, so that side conversation fell flat quickly.

As uncomfortable as the situation was, I was proud of Aly. The people pleaser in me would have been nice just to put everyone at ease, but she stood firm. We weren't here because she actually wanted to spend time with her family; we'd been forced. And as funny as Moira was and as welcoming as her sons were being, these people were all criminals. They'd gotten rid of a body for us so seamlessly that it spoke of years of experience.

It made me wonder how many others they'd disposed of. How many families were out there, broken, searching for a loved one who would never come home? The mob didn't just "disappear" fellow mobsters and gangsters who pissed them off. They targeted shop owners who didn't want to pay for the mob's forced protection. They went after government officials and community organizers who tried to stand up to them. Or they got rid of innocent witnesses to their crimes.

And Nico was the guy who made sure no one ever found them.

The opulence surrounding us had been built on the bones of victims. My father was a monster, but at least he'd never profited from his crimes. He committed them because he was sick, because he'd grown up in a violently abusive household, and had suffered several frontal lobe injuries that altered his brain function. I wasn't excusing his actions, but there was a reason he was the way he was.

It made me wonder what Nico's excuse was. Aly's mom told her they had a strict but stable upbringing. Their parents didn't hit them. Nico had simply fallen in with a bad crowd. But I wondered if it was more than that. I'd been in therapy so long and researched antisocial personality disorders so much that it was second nature to question charming people like Nico. Was he just naturally magnetic, or did he have sociopathic traits?

"Babe?" Aly asked. "You good?"

I blinked and came back to myself. Everyone was heading into dinner, leaving us a moment to ourselves. "Yeah, sorry. I zoned out for a second there."

She scrunched her nose and dropped her voice. "Sorry about that. I know it must have been awkward."

I stepped close enough to rub my hand up her arm. "Don't apologize. You did good. I'm proud of you for holding your ground and not pretending that this is something it isn't."

She beamed at me. "Thank you."

The urge to tell her I loved her was almost too strong to resist, but this was neither the time nor the place. I'd almost blurted it out yesterday over breakfast and the day before that when I caught Aly singing off-key Mariah Carey in the shower, but as much as a large part of me thought she was right there with me, a smaller part second-guessed it, keeping the words in check. It wasn't that I didn't think I was worthy of love; I just couldn't believe I'd gotten so lucky that *she* was the one who loved me.

Dinner went a little better than cocktail hour. We were too busy stuffing our faces for much conversation, and Aly and Nico were seated far enough apart that they would have had to raise their voices to continue bickering. What brief discussion we had focused on safer topics like how good the food was, how shitty the weather had been, and Moira's plans to gut their master bathroom and have a custom spa built in its place.

I sat back in my chair afterward, unable to eat another bite, feeling warm and sleepy and sated. No wonder they waited until dinner was over for serious conversation. It would be hard to get worked up when all I could think about was how nice a quick post-meal nap would be.

Aly set her napkin beside her plate and turned to where Nico lorded over us from the head of the table. "Now?"

He sighed. "Yes, fine."

Moira placed a hand over his. "Coffee?"

His expression softened when he looked at her, and I started questioning myself about the sociopath thing when I saw the warm affection in his eyes. "Yes, please." He turned toward us. "Would you like any?"

Remembering what Junior said about Nico's barista-related vanity, I nodded. "I'll never say no to one of those macchiatos."

He grinned. "Moira's even better at making them than I am." His gaze slid to his wife. "And she's got a great ass."

Their sons let out a collective groan and started excusing themselves from the table, taking their plates with them to the kitchen.

Moira, however, looked thrilled. "He can be taught," she said, leaning in to kiss her husband's cheek.

Fifteen minutes later, Aly and I joined Nico and Junior in Nico's office with our coffees. It was the one space in the house I felt like I could relax. The walls were paneled in dark wood. Soft lighting filtered down from a black chandelier. Beneath our feet, a well-worn Persian rug covered most of the slate-gray tile floor. Nico's desk took up the center of the room, but the two leather chairs facing it looked as comfortable as the dark couch against the far wall, and I decided I'd be happy sitting wherever Aly chose. Leather meant that even if I accidentally slopped a little coffee over the side of my mug, it could easily get wiped up.

Aly decided on the couch, and I settled down beside her as Nico and Junior turned the chairs to face us.

Once he was seated, Nico took a sip of his espresso before lifting his gaze to Aly. "They didn't find any trace of you or our guys in the house."

Relief hit me so hard that I had to set my cup on my knee to keep from spilling it.

Aly reached out and gripped my shoulder, and I knew she must have been just as emotional as I was from how hard she squeezed me. "What about the van?"

Junior grinned. "The power company confirmed it was just a routine maintenance call, and the records they sent to the cops back that up."

"What about all the footprints everyone must have left behind?" Aly pressed.

"What footprints?" Junior said. "The guys swept the snow as they were leaving."

I forced my fingers to relax around my mug. "So that just left ours?"

Nico nodded. "Remember how we had you wear shoes a size too small?"

"Yes," I said. "I assumed it was so there wouldn't be a match to my real size." I'd pulled a similar deception the first night I broke into Aly's.

Nico nodded. "The size you wore was also Brad's."

You could have knocked me over with a feather.

My mind worked on overdrive as I thought back to all the other instructions I'd received that night, how they'd wanted me to hack into Brad's machine but make it look like it was him who'd logged on, and the order to unencrypt anything that the cops might struggle with, like his secret hard drive.

Aly released my shoulder and sat forward. "Are you saying the cops think it was Brad inside the study that night?"

Nico nodded. "And an accomplice. That's why the police bulletin says to be on the lookout for two men. Lucky for us, you have big feet for a woman."

Aly grimaced. "Thanks for the underhanded compliment?"

Nico waved her off. "I didn't mean it like that."

I frowned. "What about Brad's phone? Did the cops find it?"

"Ah, that," Nico said, pausing to drain the rest of his espresso. "Yes, they found it. Brad did some rudimentary searching for Aly on it shortly after being released from the hospital, but she wasn't the only one he looked for. Most of his digging revolved around another nurse named Erica Willet."

Aly let out a shaky breath.

I gripped her knee. "Was that your coworker who fit his profile?"

Her expression was troubled as she turned to me. "Yeah."

I rubbed a thumb over her stocking-covered skin, wanting to soothe her. If not for our audience, I would have dragged her right into my lap. The need to have her in my arms when she was upset was only getting stronger by the day—more proof of how hard I had fallen.

She turned back to Nico. "Are the cops going to question me?"

He shook his head. "Unlikely. With no other trace of you found, there's no reason. If anything, they might want to speak to you about your run-in with him to get a feel for what kind of headspace he was in that night, but I don't think it'll be for weeks yet, if it even happens. They're too busy chasing down other leads and looking into missing women reports. Something like twenty hookers have disappeared in the city over the past four years."

"Sex workers," Aly corrected.

I sat back in my seat, stunned. "And the cops weren't worried about it before now?"

Nico raised a brow at me. "You should know better than anyone how little cops care about hookers." He held up a hand. "Sorry. Sex workers."

I went completely still. Shit. He knew about my dad.

Aly reached down and threaded her fingers through mine. "I'm going to say this once. That is the last reference like that you make."

Nico's gaze sharpened on her. "So you know?"

Junior looked between them. "Know what?"

Nico hadn't told him? Thank fuck for that.

"Nothing," Aly said, glaring at her uncle. "Right?"

He held her gaze for a long moment. It felt like another battle of wills was happening between them, this one silent.

"I'm the only family you have left besides your kids," she reminded him.

He frowned but finally nodded. "Fine."

Aly blew out a breath. "What else is going on that we should know about?"

It turned out, a lot. A twenty-person task team had been formed to take over the investigation, including local police as well as FBI agents. Their first priority was finding Brad, but the second was finding his victims. Cops were canvassing the city streets, finally looking into all the missing persons cases they should have given a shit about to start with. Brad's childhood record had been unsealed, and a criminal psychologist was using it to help build a more complete profile of his crimes and potential escalations.

His past victims were being reinterviewed. Judges and lawyers were getting subpoenaed in relation to his previous settlement cases. One of the FBI analysts was pouring over his phone records as they hunted for burial locations and tried to match his GPS data to areas where women went missing.

It was a huge case, and because of that, it made Aly's name just one word in a vast ocean of information, easily overlooked.

The longer Nico talked, the more I started to believe we just might get away with what we'd done. Brad had left his phone behind when he went to Aly's. He'd disabled the GPS in his vehicle. Her house and my car had been scrubbed clean. Even if a neighbor had caught him on a door camera approaching Aly's house, there was absolutely no physical evidence that he'd ever come near us.

Junior swore no one would ever find Brad's body. Brad's car had been stripped to the frame, and its pieces were scattered throughout other vehicles across the city. Hell, the cops thought Brad was still alive. When Nico said he intended to keep it that way, with several planned sightings in Canada over the coming months, my shoulders started to relax for the first time since the night Brad broke into Aly's. Thank fuck, because I'd been working on developing a serious crick in my neck, and my stop-you-in-your-tracks good looks would have been totally ruined by frown lines.

Did I feel like we were completely in the clear? No. But I did feel like I could stop looking over my shoulder every five seconds, and for that, I would be forever grateful to Nico.

We spoke for nearly an hour, Aly peppering her uncle and cousin with question after question until Nico pinched the bridge of his nose and begged off, claiming she was giving him a migraine. He promised to call if anything else came up, and only then did Aly rise from her seat and say that she was ready to go. Nico invited us to stay for dessert, but she declined.

On the way out, she stopped in to use the powder room, and I gathered our coats and waited for her by the front door with her uncle.

It was only the second time I'd been alone with him, and, hoping to smooth over some of the earlier awkwardness, I extended my hand. "Thank you again for everything."

He ignored my offer to shake, going so far as to slip his hands into his pockets while he eyed me. "I did it for my niece. Not you."

"I understand, but I'm still grateful."

His expression flattened. "I don't trust you."

"Okay," I said, because what else was I going to?

He stepped close, and though he was about half my weight, it looked like he planned to keep on coming, expecting me to back up. His eyes had gone cold, and there was a cruel glint in them that made me feel like I was getting my first real glimpse of Nico, the mobster. "If you ever do anything to hurt my niece—"

I laughed.

In my defense, I'd held it in as long as I could. God, he was so predictable. I'd been ready to kiss his ass as long as he remained civil, but I'd had a feeling it wouldn't last, which was why I'd taken a page out of Aly's book and was ready with plan B.

"Look," I said. "I'm sure this routine works on most people, but you know who my father is. Nothing you can say will ever compare to what I lived through with him." I lifted my phone out of my pocket and waved it at him. "Also, I recorded that entire conversation in your study and already sent a backup to a private server I own, so now we're even. You have shit on me, and I have shit on you. Don't ever threaten me, and certainly don't try to call in your favor for covering up for me, or I'll dismantle your entire organization from the inside."

I lifted my phone and tapped the screen to drive my point home. All the lights in the house flickered. Nearby, the alarm by the front door started beeping. Nico rushed over to it and punched in the code before it could go off.

"Hun?" Moira called from deeper inside the house. "What was that?"

I answered for him. "Must have been a power surge!"

Then I turned my attention back to Nico and did something I hadn't done in years. I went to that cold, dark place in my head where I used to hide when Dad was at his worst. There was no pain inside it, no emotion. I didn't give a fuck about anyone or anything there, not even myself, and I knew it showed on my face because this was the same place I'd gone to all those years ago when I scared off Tyler's shitty ex.

"I don't care about you, one way or the other," I told Nico. "And your family seems nice, but I don't care about them either. You could all disappear tomorrow, and I wouldn't lose any sleep over it. And no, I'm not threatening you, just stating facts. Do you understand what I'm saying?"

"That you're a psycho, just like your father," Nico spat.

"Nah, I'm not that far gone. I'm able to care about *some* people. And I care about Aly. I'll do whatever I have to in order to protect her, go as far as I must. With my skills, I'd make a much better ally than I would an enemy. So, I'm going to offer to shake one more time, and we can try this conversation again." I extended a hand between us. "Thank you so much for everything."

Nico's face looked like a thundercloud, red creeping into his cheeks that spoke of a deep well of rage. I'd have to be very careful around him and his sons from this point on, but if my father had taught me anything, it was that bullies like Nico only responded to threats and violence, and I would never let someone like him push me around again.

I waited several seconds, still in that emotionally detached state, holding Nico's gaze as I let him decide if he wanted to be my enemy or my friend. Part of me hoped he made the wrong choice. I hadn't gotten the chance to really flex my hacking skills for years, and the thought of slowly leaking mob crimes to the FBI one at a time made me smile.

I think it was the smile that decided Nico. He shuddered and, with a grimace, finally slipped his hand into mine. "You're welcome."

"I truly appreciate all your hard work keeping your niece safe," I told him, which was true.

He frowned. "You're pretty fucked up, kid. Aren't you?"

An indrawn breath announced Aly's arrival. "What did you just say to my boyfriend?"

In a blink, I came back to myself, my smile becoming more genuine than creepy as I released Nico and turned to face his niece.

"He was teasing," I said. "I made a dumb joke. Right?" I asked him.

His gaze slid from me to Aly. "Right."

I clapped him on the shoulder. "Thank Moira again for dinner. It was delicious."

Aly frowned as she reached us, sensing something was off. "Are you ready?" she asked me.

"I am," I said before turning back to her uncle. "Can't wait to do this again next month."

Nico looked a little green at the idea, but he managed to say goodbye to Aly and see us out the door without giving anything away.

"What the hell did you say to him?" she asked as we made our way toward my car.

"I told him he had a nice arse."

Aly choked on nothing.

"What?" I said. "He does."

I unlocked the doors, and we climbed inside. She turned to me as I started the car, her eyes narrowed to slits. "You threatened him, didn't you?"

"Yes, but in my defense, he started it."

"What about trying to stay on his good side?" she asked.

"Turns out, he doesn't have one."

She punched my arm. "Are you out of your mind? Do you know what he could do to you?"

I turned to face her. "The better question is, do you know what I could do to him?"

That brought her up short. I could see the wheels spinning in her head as she reviewed everything she'd learned about my computer skills. "But the risk . . ."

I reached out and smoothed her hair back from her face, looking for an excuse to touch her. "I understand the risk, but I don't think it'll ever come to that. Nico is a smart guy. He knows a truce between us is preferable to setting his whole world on fire just to prove he has the bigger metaphorical dick."

She grimaced. "Gross. No relative dick talk."

"You understand what I'm saying, though. The threat was just a threat. He needed to realize that he can't bully me like everyone else. And he also needed to know that he can't push me out of your life just because I'm not Italian enough for his liking."

Her gaze shifted from my eyes to my mouth and back again. "Did you have to wait until I was out of the room to do it? I would have liked to see you go all alpha on him."

I cocked a brow at her. "Alpha, huh? Is that something out of your porno books?"

She rolled her eyes. "They're called spicy romances, and they've taught me as much about myself as your masktok account has."

"Yeah?" I asked. "Like what?"

"Like when we're at that Airbnb we booked in the mountains, I want you to chase me down and fuck me in the woods like an animal."

It was my turn to choke on nothing. Yup. Yes. I could definitely do that for her.

"Speaking of my masktok account," I said. "You want to hold the camera for me again tonight? People seem to like the new content since you've started helping."

She groaned and turned to buckle herself in. "As long as you don't publicly thank me again. I've gotten, like, a thousand new followers since Wednesday."

"You know people pay for that kind of social media growth, Aly," I said, unable to keep the teasing note out of my voice.

She turned back to me, deadpan. "Yeah, but do they also pay their new followers to threaten them? Because that's all I seem to get."

"They just want to make sure you're treating me right. They're still not sure about you after that one time you made me sad."

She rolled her eyes. "If they only knew the truth about what happened."

I grinned. "They'd probably think it was hot."

She sighed. "You're right. Who am I kidding? I'm living their fantasies. I will always be the enemy."

I gripped the back of her neck and pulled her toward me. The car had barely heated up, and our breath frosted between us.

"Hey," I said.

She looked into my eyes from an inch away. "Yeah?"

"I love you," I told her, unable to keep it in any longer.

"I know," she said.

"You do?"

She nodded, her hair tickling my forehead. "Yeah, you've been saying it in your sleep for the past week."

"Oh."

"Hey," she said.

"Yeah?"

"I love you, too. And no matter what happens, we'll get through it together. I don't have anything tying me here. If we have to, we can copy Pretend Brad and flee the country."

"Let's hope it doesn't come to that," I said. "But if it does, I'm down, too. I can do my work from anywhere or become a hacker for hire. We have options."

She grinned. "Okay, but can we agree on someplace warm? I'm over this cold."

"Wherever you want, baby," I said, leaning in to kiss her.

EPILOGUE

ALY

I CRASHED THROUGH THE UNDERGROWTH with all the grace of a water buffalo. Twigs snapped beneath my heels. Birds shrieked overhead, announcing my presence. I ignored it all and kept on sprinting.

Right now wasn't about stealth; it was about speed. I was being hunted, and if I had any hope of escaping my fate, I needed to put as much distance between myself and the man who chased me as possible.

The midsummer sun sat high in the cornflower blue sky, baking the forest with its heat. Sweat beaded along my forehead as I leaped over a fallen log and kept on running. The trees were laden with leaves, their lower branches reaching out to grab at my hair and clothes as if trying to slow me down, and the air was so humid that I could feel it pressing in on me like a weighted blanket.

I put on another burst of speed, defiance burning through my veins. Josh was *not* going to catch me. Why the hell had I made that bet with him? I must have been out of my mind at the time or suffering from sex-induced diminished capacity.

Was that even a thing?

Six months ago, I wouldn't have believed it possible, but since then, I could think of several times that I'd been dicked so good I'd briefly forgotten how to do basic things like walk unaided or solve simple math equations.

The wager was straightforward: if Josh caught me within the next twenty minutes, I lost.

I really didn't want to lose. Losing meant making my first-ever appearance in one of his thirst traps, and he would have full creative license over exactly how I took part. Knowing him, he'd use it as another chance to needle me, and I would either be embarrassed by it or become the internet's most hated woman for the second time in less than a year.

That would happen over my dead body.

Maybe literally, if I didn't start paying better attention to where I was going.

I skidded to a stop just before a drop-off. A glimpse over the edge revealed a long, steep descent into a boulder-filled ravine. My heart nearly fell out of my ass as I realized how close I'd come to having a Very Bad Day.

I glanced behind me. Shit. I must have gotten off the main path somehow and ended up on a game trail. Doubling back would cost me precious minutes I couldn't spare, so I forged onward, following what looked like another game trail that ran parallel to the ravine and farther up the hill. I had to slow down because of how close it skirted to the ledge. One wrong step could send me tumbling over, but I took heart in the knowledge that if I had to be careful, so would Josh.

As much as I didn't want to lose, part of me couldn't wait for him to catch up so the chase could start for real. He'd given me a five-minute head start. To be sporting, he'd claimed. He'd grown up in the boonies, after all, and some of his fondest memories were bonding with his stepfather during their camping trips. Rob was a country boy through and through, and Josh had learned a ton from him about tracking animals and how to survive if he ever got lost in the wilderness.

I didn't know anything about bushcraft, but I did have two advantages on my side: speed and endurance. I'd been a sprinter on my track team in high school, making it to the state championships my senior year. Unbeknownst to Josh, I'd spent the past three months skipping the gym two days a week to go to a local track instead. I alternated between sprint and distance training, pushing myself to the max because I had no desire to make this easy on him.

Yes, I longed to be hunted down and fucked in the forest, but I wanted the full experience more than anything. I wanted the chase. I wanted to make Josh *earn* the right to claim me. From the hungry gleam that entered his eyes whenever we discussed our plans leading up to today, he wanted that just as much as I did, and I couldn't wait for him to let his darker side out to play.

We didn't have many rules, but the ones we'd agreed on were iron-clad, and if either of us broke them, we forfeited. First and foremost, there was no cheating. We had GPS trackers on us in case we got lost, and promised not to check them unless an hour passed without Josh finding me. Dirty play was forbidden as well. We couldn't throw sand in each other's eyes or try to set booby traps—not that I would even know how to go about doing that.

The last rule was that only penetration counted as a catch. If Josh caught up to me, I could still win if I managed to keep his dick out of me until time ran out.

On paper, it toed the line of dubious consent, but I was more than into it, so maybe it was more like con-dub-con? Plus, Josh was adamant that all I had to do was tell him to stop, and he would. Just like always.

Part of me hoped it came to a knock-down, drag-out fight for dominance. I loved the idea of him physically overpowering me, and we'd had so much fun with orgasm denial and edging that trying to keep him off me would only make me wetter for him.

Not that I wasn't already soaked.

I'd been primed and ready to go since the second I stepped into the trees, turning to blow a goodbye kiss at Josh and telling him not to go easy on me just because I made him feel weird in the tummy.

He'd barked a laugh and told me to run, and the sight of his eyes darkening with desire sent me sprinting into the woods.

Initially, I'd wanted to do this at night to really play into the scary vibes, but we'd decided it was too dangerous. The risk of tripping over something and either spraining an ankle or knocking ourselves out just wasn't worth it.

A sound pulled me from my lustful thoughts, and I spent a heart-stopping moment thinking Josh had found me, but it was only a squirrel fleeing up the side of a nearby tree. I refocused my full attention on the narrow path, breathing a sigh of relief as it started to veer away from the ravine and widened enough that I was able to put on more speed.

The trail continued to pitch upward, heading higher into the foothills of the mountains. I crested a small rise and pounded down the other side of it, spooking a deer and her fawn when I reached the bottom.

A brook ran through the center of the gully, and I decided to hurdle it instead of taking the time to find an easier crossing. My toe caught on an exposed root when I landed on the other side, and I nearly went sprawling face-first into the dirt.

I paused for a second to catch my breath and make sure I hadn't pulled anything. When it seemed like I'd escaped unharmed, I took off again, lifting my watch to check the time. I nearly yelped when I saw that I'd been in the woods for a quarter of an hour. The timer officially started when Josh entered, so technically, we were now halfway through the hunt. He'd been on my trail for the past ten minutes, and even though I hadn't seen or heard him, I couldn't shake the thought that he was gaining on me.

The man was huge, and we'd worked out together enough in his apartment's gym that I knew he was fast for his size. I regularly drooled over the sight of him sprint-pushing a three-hundred-pound sled from one end of the gym to the other, and I could only imagine how much faster he'd be without all that weight holding him back.

I strained my ears and started being more careful about where I placed my feet, avoiding as many sticks as possible. Whenever I thought about forests, I always imagined them full of birdsong, but it was eerily quiet so deep in the trees, and it made the sound of my passage all the more obvious. Last year's fallen leaves littered the trail, crunching beneath my heels. Branches rustled as I pushed between them.

The upside was that if I was being loud, someone who outweighed me by nearly a hundred pounds was probably louder, but I'd long since learned my lesson about underestimating my boyfriend, so my senses remained on high alert, waiting for some warning that he was nearby.

I heard nothing but the noises I was making and the occasional nattering squirrel or pissed-off blue jay. The quiet made me paranoid. I imagined hands reaching out of shrubs, ghost steps racing after me. A shiver licked down my spine that made me feel like someone had just breathed on the back of my neck. I whipped my head around, but there was no one in sight.

Good thing we hadn't done this at night because it was unnerving enough in broad daylight. My heart thundered in my chest. Adrenaline pumped through my veins, urging me onward and up over a rockfall where I had to grab on to saplings to pull myself forward.

Why the hell did I have to choose this route? The hunt was becoming less of a run and more of a hike, and while my endurance was great on flat ground, my legs were already starting to burn from exertion. It made me feel even more unbalanced, jumpy, and nervous, like a rabbit with a fox on her heels.

Hoping to spare my aching legs, I took a sharp left near the top of another hill and abandoned the trail to run through the woods along the hill's wide peak. This high up, the old-growth forest was more conifer than broadleaf, and the understory was sparse enough that I could see hundreds of yards ahead. The trunks of pine trees rose around me like matchsticks, clear all the way to the canopy far above. I'd be able to see Josh long before he reached me.

It was perfect.

I slowed to a quick walk, grateful for the soft needles carpeting the forest floor, silencing my steps. The time for speed had passed. Now was the time for stealth. With any luck, I'd be able to hear Josh coming and either hide or take off back down the mountain, letting gravity do most of the work and saving my energy for when I hit flat ground and could sprint again.

I might have been prey, but I was smart prey, and I was going to make my predator work to catch me.

A sharp *snap* echoed through the trees.

I turned around and nearly screamed.

Josh stood less than a hundred feet behind me with a broken stick in his hands. I wasn't proud of it, but he had caught me so off guard that I froze. Where the fuck had he come from?

He stepped toward me out of a cluster of shadows, looking huge and ominous in his dark clothing. Had he gotten *bigger* since we'd been together? His biceps strained against the sleeves of his tee. Corded muscle climbed up his arms. Like me, he wore running pants to protect his legs from getting scratched, and they pulled taut over his tree trunk thighs.

Yeah, he'd definitely gotten bigger. I bought that T-shirt for him two months ago, and from the way it strained across his chest, he'd either gained weight or it had shrunk in the wash.

The son of a bitch wasn't even breathing hard. He'd managed to sneak up on me so soundlessly that he'd intentionally broken a stick to give me a sporting chance. As I watched, he tossed it aside, a victorious grin splitting his handsome face.

It felt like he was mocking me.

Oh, hell fuck no.

Like a shot, I was off, as annoyed as I was afraid. I'd gone through all that trouble to make this good for the both of us, and the bastard had found me the second I stopped running.

His laughter chased me through the forest.

It was too late to hide, too late for strategy. I ran on instinct alone, my arms pumping at my sides as I drained my last reserves. The trees blurred around me. My feet flew over the forest floor. I caught sight of a dense scramble of shrubs and beelined toward it.

"Oh, no, you don't!" Josh called, his feet pounding against the ground as he gave chase.

Despite how hard I was pushing myself, I heard him gaining on me. It was tempting to glance over my shoulder and check how close he was, but I worried that slowing down even half a second to do it would spell my demise. Every step felt like it could be my last. My shoulders stiffened as I braced against being tackled from behind.

Fucking run, bitch, I told myself, pushing through the pain to put on one final bid for freedom.

A masculine growl hit my ears as I approached the scrub brush.

Holy shit, was I going to make it?

My gaze snagged on a barely there game trail bisecting the dense thicket, so narrow it had probably been made by rabbits. It was the only way through I saw, and I didn't have time to look for another route.

Here goes nothing.

I plunged straight into it, ducking to avoid the higher brambles and lifting my arms to protect my face. Briars snagged at my pants. My arms burned as prickers ripped across my skin. A crash sounded behind me, followed by a frustrated yell. It was too narrow for Josh to follow.

Triumph and anticipation coursed through me as I pressed on.

Part of me wanted the chase to last forever, while another part couldn't wait for the fight to start. Dampness coated my panties. My breasts felt full inside my sports bra, longing for Josh's touch. Despite my renewed efforts to win, my body was prepared to lose, turning supple and pliant.

I burst out of the other side of the thicket back into sunlight and angled downhill. The brush hadn't been that deep, but it was wide, and Josh would lose precious seconds circumnavigating it. Seconds that I planned to use to my advantage.

I pushed harder, half running, half sliding down the hill back toward the gully with the stream. Somewhere behind me, Josh had probably rounded the thicket and could see me getting away. He had the advantage of sight, of knowing just how fast he'd have to sprint to reach me. I was forced to move on instinct alone, putting every last ounce of energy into blindly fleeing and hoping it would be enough.

He couldn't catch me. Not yet. It felt like an hour had passed since I'd last looked at my watch, but I knew that was because of the chaos of the chase. I couldn't risk checking it again. All I could do was pray that my legs held out long enough to get me over the finish line.

My hair whipped around me, pulled free by the brambles. I could feel the first burn of blisters forming on my heels. Each breath I took was more ragged than the last. I could do this. If I just held out a little longer, I could win.

A dark shape tore out of the trees to my left, and this time I really did scream as Josh plowed into my side, tackling me around the waist like a goddamn middle linebacker. I'd told him not to go easy on me, and, fuck, did I regret it now. All the air in my lungs burst out of my mouth in a rush as we went down. He managed to turn midair, taking the brunt of the fall when we landed, but it still hurt like a sonofabitch. Rocks bit into my skin. My head bounced off the ground.

"Shit," Josh groaned. "Aly, are you o—"

I slammed my elbow into his stomach.

"Kaaay," he wheezed, his arms loosening around me.

I struggled free from him and scrambled to my feet, trying to bury the regret that threatened. I hoped I hadn't hurt him too badly. The goal was to have fun getting rough; not seriously injure each other.

An iron vise clamped around my ankle, and I had just enough time to realize Josh had grabbed me before a vicious yank pulled my leg out from under me, and I went pinwheeling forward.

Motherfucker.

I slammed into the ground, catching most of my weight on my hands and knees.

Owww.

I didn't let the pain slow me, twisting onto my back as Josh dragged me toward him. He looked both pissed off and turned on, and it sent my pulse ratcheting up another notch.

I had to get away, but, god, the temptation to give in was strong.

Sorry, baby, I thought, lifting my free leg.

Josh's beautiful brown eyes flashed wide when he realized I was about to kick him in the chest. I pistoned my foot down, but he released me and rolled sideways just in time to dodge the blow. I spun the other way and surged to my feet. He must have been one step ahead because he snagged my arm and spun me back around.

I was halfway through breaking his hold when he grabbed the back of my head and hauled me forward, crashing his mouth into mine. It was almost my undoing. My body recognized him as its main supplier of orgasms. Sex hormones rushed into my veins, my hypothalamus giddily triggering the flood. Despite my desire to get away, my lips popped open on instinct, welcoming him inside.

He swirled his tongue against mine, backing me against a tree.

I moaned into his mouth, clawing at his shirt as I pulled him closer.

His erection pressed into my belly, long and hard and—

Shit! What was I doing?

I stomped on his foot.

He swore and hopped backward.

I turned and fled down the hill.

Just like that, the chase was back on.

The forest was thicker here, broadleaves creeping in, their lower branches whipping against me as I fled past. Good thing I had the next week off. I was going to need all that time to heal afterward. I could already feel bruises blossoming over my skin from our brief tussle, and I was sure I had more scrapes on me than the night we'd fled from Brad's house.

No. Don't think of him, I told myself. *Thoughts of him aren't welcome here. This is just for me and Josh.*

The sound of pursuit reached my ears, and . . . was Josh laughing?

I smiled as I stumble-ran down the last few yards of the hill. He was right; this was a fucking blast. I might have been minorly annoyed with him for finding me so quickly, but it only made me want to up my game for next time. Maybe I could find a survival course and learn to slip through the woods like a ghost.

The sound of rushing water told me the stream was just ahead. It came into sight a second later, looking wider than where I'd first crossed it. That was okay. I was moving so fast that I was sure I could vault it again.

Trouble was, Josh was moving even faster. The snap of a stick told me he was only inches away before his fingers snagged the back of my shirt. I twisted, trying to break free, but his momentum carried him into me. His big arms banded around my waist, and we stumbled, feet tangling, and fell.

Straight into the goddamn water.

Cold! Fuck, it was cold!

Though it was barely a foot deep, it felt like I'd been dumped into an arctic lake. The brook must have started high up in the mountains, where white still capped the tallest peaks.

I came up spluttering, my mouth full of water. If I contracted giardia, I was never going to forgive Josh for having such shitty timing.

He grabbed my ankle and hauled me toward him. My ass hit about a dozen river rocks along the way. I tried to kick him, but he snatched my other foot out of the air, fingers clamping down and biceps straining as he fought to keep me still. His show of strength was impressive as hell.

I had to get away, or I was done for.

I stopped fighting him and surged forward instead. He wasn't expecting it. I plowed straight into his chest, knocking him over backward into the water. His hands popped loose, and I started to scramble away, only for him to grab my pant leg and tear a huge hole in it as he dragged me back down.

More splashing ensued as he tried to get ahold of my slippery flesh, and I tried to get the hell away from him. We must have looked ridiculous. Like two lost salmon ineptly flopping around as they attempted to unravel the mystery of which way was upstream. Thank god this section of forest was far enough away from civilization that we were the only humans for miles around, and there was nothing but confused forest creatures to witness our idiocy.

I would have laughed if not for the genuine threat of becoming a guest star in Josh's next video. People online were *mean*. And also a little scary. There was an ongoing discussion in one of his comment sections about where we might live based on the glimpses of the city they'd seen out his windows. We'd stopped filming near them in response, but that didn't mean web sleuths weren't still trying to find us.

If I could avoid giving them more fodder, I would, which was why I needed to get away. Now.

I managed to slip free from Josh long enough to flip onto my front and scramble forward on all fours. I'd barely made it to the muddy edge of the brook before I was tackled again. This time, Josh put all his weight into it, flattening me like a pancake. I floundered beneath him, trying to throw him off, but between the slimy mud and the fact that he was well over two hundred pounds, it was a lost cause.

He managed to grab both my wrists in record time and pin them over my head, holding them in place with one oven-mitt-sized hand.

Shit. I was going to lose.

A dozen jujitsu moves flashed through my head, but each one could cause serious injury, and as much as I wanted to win, I could never bring myself to hurt Josh like that. And nor could he, I realized. Josh was even more skilled than I was in martial arts, but he hadn't used a single move on me either, which was why we'd resorted to slap-fighting like a couple of amateurs.

Still, I wasn't ready to give up, so I bucked my hips sideways, trying to throw him off.

He dug his fingers into the hole in my pants and ripped upward, tearing them to my waist. My underwear got unceremoniously yanked aside, and I had just enough time to realize what was happening before he surged into me with a brutal thrust.

I cried out, both from surprise and relief.

Josh froze behind me, tension in every line of his body. "Are you done fighting, or do you want me to give you another chance?" He ended the question by rocking his hips forward, showing me what I'd be missing if I made the wrong decision.

The sharp sound of an alarm rose around us, our watches beeping in tandem. My time was up. He'd won with seconds to spare, and there'd be no more chances for me.

Instead of answering his question aloud, I turned my alarm off and arched my spine, lifting my hips enough for him to slide in another inch. My pussy clenched around him, trying to drag him deeper. I wanted it hard, rough. He'd run me down like I was prey, and now I wanted him to fuck the last of my resistance out of me.

He groaned, the hand pinning mine loosening but not letting go. "You did so good, baby."

With a snap of his hips, he thrust into me harder, deeper, and even though we'd been doing this for months, I still felt like he was going to split me in half.

"I loved chasing you," he said. "Loved that you were smiling the whole time."

Was I? Even when we'd been fighting? Damn, I really needed to work on my poker face.

Another thrust and Josh was hilt deep. It felt like he was close to hitting the back of my teeth. I loved it. Loved being so filled that I could barely breathe, barely think past the initial sting of discomfort and the way my body had to work to take all of him.

"You're soaked, Aly," he said, his voice rough with lust. "Did you like being hunted?"

"Yes," I moaned.

"You liked getting run down like prey."

It wasn't a question, but I answered him anyway. "Yes."

"Spread those legs for me, then. Show me how much you like getting caught."

"Make me," I told him.

He froze for half a second, but I could tell from the way his dick twitched inside me that he liked the idea. The hand pinning mine pressed down even harder while the other gripped my hip. He yanked me up with him as he repositioned us, and then used his knees to shove mine even wider, one after the other.

And then he was moving, driving into me deeper, harder. The angle made me feel every inch of him thrusting inside. My pussy quivered, a tremor wracking my spine. The way he pinned me left me with almost no leverage. All I could do was angle my pelvis and push back against him as his movements picked up speed.

His hips snapped against my ass. We knelt at the stream's edge, water rushing over our lower legs, mud squelching beneath our knees. The smell of the forest filled my nose, the scent of pine mingled with dirt and fallen leaves. My back heated where the sun beat down on me.

Yes. This was what I wanted. To be pinned like an animal out in the open, with no inhibitions and no thoughts in my head besides how well my boyfriend fucked me.

"Harder," I said.

Josh grabbed my hair and hauled me up by it, his fingers tangled in my strands as his thrusts turned punishing. My mouth fell open as I stared wide-eyed at the woods around us. Sunlight fell in dappled shafts along the gully floor. Moss clung to nearby rocks. The sound of our ragged breathing filled the air.

There was something so primal about it, so *right*.

I thought I wanted this because of things I'd read in paranormal romances involving werewolves, but now I wondered if my desires went deeper than that, were more instinctual. This was how our ancestors fucked, rough and desperate in stolen moments between hunting and being hunted, giving it everything they had because they didn't know if they would live to see the next sunrise.

It made a strange sense that I craved it, and I felt like the luckiest woman in the world to have a boyfriend willing to play into my every fantasy.

"I love you," I said, punching my hips backward.

Josh groaned, his fingers tightening in my hair. "I love you, too, but don't say it again, or I'll come."

I grinned. "I love you."

He thrust into me so hard that I slid an inch forward in the mud. "I'm serious, Aly."

"I love—" Another ruthless thrust had me gasping. Words of praise and devotion started pouring from my mouth as he fucked me closer and closer to the edge. "I love you so much. I love being your prey. I love how easily you overpowered me. I love that your cock is almost too big. I love feeling it get even bigger inside me right before you come."

Josh's thrusts became frenzied. I moaned, almost senseless with need as my pussy spasmed around him. Tremors wracked my whole body. I clawed at the mud, trying to find purchase, desperate to ground myself through the pleasure that was building inside me. Usually, I needed more than this, clitoral stimulation or nipple play to push me over the edge, but Josh was fucking into me so deeply that he was about to trigger my favorite kind of orgasm: the brain-melting, spine-buckling, knees-shaking, titties-bouncing, pussy-soaking cervical orgasm.

And then he yanked my head up higher and bit my neck.

I hadn't been expecting it, and the brief flash of pain paired with the thrill of feeling teeth sink into me sent me to new heights, frantic, needy sounds falling from my lips. My mind blanked. My ears filled with a buzzing noise as I slammed my hips backward. I was coming. I was coming so hard that all I could do was writhe, my pussy clenched so tightly Josh could barely move.

And then he was coming, too, his cock lengthening, stiffening, warmth flooding into me as he unloaded deep inside. The feel of it prolonged my orgasm, or maybe it triggered a second. All I knew was that I'd never felt so good for so long, and I never wanted it to end.

We came down slowly, together, breathing like we were still running. Josh lay draped over my back, his forehead resting against my spine. The sound of his exhalations filled my ears. I felt his heart pounding against my rib cage.

I'd never felt so connected to someone before, never loved someone like I loved him.

"Marry me," I said.

Josh stiffened. "What?"

Panic punched into me, chasing away the afterglow of sex hormones and dumping me straight back into reality. Oh, fuck. Oh, fuck, fuck, fuck.

Josh pulled out of me, the warmth of our climaxes slipping down my thighs. This was why people shouldn't speak right after they came. They overshared or said foolish things their partners weren't ready to hear.

"I'm sorry," I said, scrambling up and trying to tug my ruined pants back into place. My fingers were slick with mud, and I was shaking so badly that I could barely grip the wet fabric.

Josh was quiet behind me.

Shit! What had I done?

I spun toward him, expecting the worst, and found him kneeling on the forest floor. One hand lifted, something in it catching the sunlight and sparkling.

I clapped a hand over my mouth and took a disbelieving step toward him. It was a ring. Josh was holding a ring. A stunning ring with a center ruby that looked like a large drop of blood framed by tiny diamonds. It was perfect.

"Alyssa Cappellucci," he said. "Will you marry me so I can spend the rest of my life chasing you?"

I lowered my hand, grinning, joy replacing panic. "I thought people got married because they wanted to stop chasing someone?"

He shook his head, his expression serious for what felt like the first time in our entire relationship. "Not me."

"Not me either," I said, reaching him in two strides and dropping down to throw my arms around his neck. "Yes, I'll marry you."

■ ■ ■

Ten minutes later, we were cleaned up and heading out of the forest. I'd taken us so far off the beaten path that we had to use GPS to find our Airbnb.

As frenzied as my race through the woods had been, I'd missed a lot of the beauty surrounding me, and as we meandered back to the main trail, I took my time drinking it in. This land was part of a state park that hadn't been logged in at least fifty years. The trees were giant, their limbs spreading far overhead to blot out the blue sky with the canopy they formed. Streams like the one we'd flailed around in dotted the woods, some bare trickles, others deep enough that there were footbridges over them.

I sent a silent prayer of thanks to anyone who might be listening that I got to experience this. That I was free and not behind bars. The police had never come to interview me, though they had asked Erica questions. As Nico promised, Brad sightings continued until a few weeks ago, ending near a private airport outside Quebec. The reigning theory was that the Bluhms had chartered a jet and flown their son to a country that didn't extradite to the US.

They were getting dragged over the coals in the media, and the city's sentiment had long since turned against them, making them little more than prisoners inside their house. I might have felt bad if not for the fact that a) their house was a twenty-thousand square-foot mansion and b) while they might be innocent now, they had covered for plenty of Brad's previous crimes. I considered it their comeuppance for all their past sins.

I didn't think I would ever stop worrying that what we'd done would catch up to us one day, but I no longer let it rule my thoughts. I was free. I was in love. And I was determined to enjoy those things for as long as possible.

Taking a deep breath, I turned my face toward the sky. As stifling as the heat had been during my run, I was grateful for it now because it helped dry our soaking clothes.

"Next time we do this, we should wear backpacks," I said.

Josh cocked his head sideways at me. "For sex toys?"

"For spare clothes and a first aid kit."

He lifted his brows.

I rolled my eyes. "And fine, yes, for sex toys."

He grinned, looking pleased with himself, and threaded his fingers through mine. I didn't miss his glance down at my hand. Or, more specifically, the ring on it. "We should consummate our engagement when we get back."

"I need a shower first," I said. "I have river sand in unmentionable places."

He chuckled. "Same. And you should probably look at this cut. I think it might be serious." He lifted his other arm and curled his fist inward like he was posing. There was a tiny scratch on the inside of his bicep. "See? Right here." He flexed, making his muscles pop. "Do you see it?" He flexed again.

It was my turn to laugh. "Yes. It looks like it might be life-threatening. We better hurry."

He slapped my ass.

I reached out and ran a hand down his crotch.

By the time we made it back to our Airbnb, we were groping each other like a couple of teenagers on their first date. Somehow, in between kisses, Josh managed to get the door unlocked.

I pushed it open and dropped my hands to the hem of my shirt, more than ready to get out of my damp clothes.

We froze at the sight that greeted us.

The cabin was small, just a single, wide-open space with a living room on one side and a mini kitchen on the other. The bathroom was tucked farther back behind a door, and the queen-sized bed that Josh could barely fit on was overhead in the loft.

Someone had toilet-papered the entire place.

What the hell? Was this some sort of prank?

Oh, god.

Josh and I shared a panicked look.

"The cats!" he said, dashing inside.

My pulse skyrocketed as fear slammed into me. If anything had happened to them, I was going to join Josh in killing someone.

He came to a stop in front of me so fast that I bounced off his back. I shook my head to clear the spots from my eyes and glanced around him to see what had pulled him up short. There, sitting in a nest of toilet paper, was Maud, our twelve-week-old problem child. She chirruped in greeting, grabbed a mouthful of paper, and took off toward the bathroom, trailing a long line of it behind her.

I stepped beside Josh, watching her go. "We'll get a little girl kitten, he said. She'll be super cute, he said. Fred needs someone to play with so he doesn't get lonely."

As if summoned, Fred leaped out from behind the bathroom door, paws raised, and tackled Maud. They went rolling and spitting across the floor before Fred took off with her hot on his heels, still trailing toilet paper in her wake.

"You did this to us," I told Josh.

The cabin was so small that there was nowhere for Fred to go but up, and as we watched, he scaled the nearest curtain. I had just enough time to realize that maybe I *had* been overfeeding him before a crack ricocheted throughout the room, and the curtain rod fell to the floor, burying the cats in fabric. Two little bumps popped up beneath it, running in opposite directions as they tried to claw their way free.

"Well," I said. "There goes my five-star guest rating."

Josh wrapped an arm around my shoulders and pulled me close. "If you were really that mad, you'd put a stop to it. Don't lie. You love this."

"I wouldn't go that far," I said.

"Well, I would. Hell, I hope our future clan of children is just as batshit."

I almost choked. "How many kids make a clan?"

"I dunno," he said, rubbing the back of his neck. "Like, eight?"

I knew my vagina couldn't speak, but I swore I heard it let out a low whimper of terror. "How about two?"

"Seven," Josh said.

"This isn't a negotiation."

He dropped his arm from my shoulders and turned to face me. "Okay, six. But that's as low as I'm willing to go."

"Two," I said, fighting back a grin.

He crossed his arms over his chest. "Five. That's my final offer."

"Keep it up, and it'll be zero."

He leaned forward and waggled his brows. "Picture me holding a toddler in one arm and a baby in another."

Uh-oh. No, ovaries. Put down the warpaint.

He leaned closer. "Shirtless."

Fuck. I was totally going to have this man's giant babies.

He must have seen his victory in my expression because he closed the distance between us and scooped me up, kissing me breathless while Fred tried to climb the other curtain and yanked that side of the rod straight out of the drywall.

It was pure chaos.

The absolute best day of my life.

I couldn't wait for a million more of them.

ACKNOWLEDGMENTS

This is the book that was never going to be a book. It was simply an idea that popped into my head while scrolling through social media one night. Without thinking much of it, I stitched a video of a masked man and said, "Okay, hear me out. It's a romance novel." Over one hundred thousand people watched that stitch and demanded I make the idea a reality, and now here we are.

There are so many people I should thank, starting with those early viewers. And especially my Patreon subscribers, who read chapters of *Lights Out* as I wrote them and cheered me on all the way to "The End."

My mom, for her endless support of my writing. She had better never see this because she's been banned from reading this book—for obvious reasons—but Mom, if by some hellish twist you ARE reading this, I'm not paying for your therapy.

My husband, for encouraging me to follow my dreams, whatever they may be, and for being the best romantic partner and friend I could ever ask for. So many of my male leads are inspired by him in at least some small way, and in *Lights Out*, Josh inherited his needling sense of humor. And yes, it is just as hilarious (and, at times, exasperating) in real life as it is in fiction.

My agent, Jill Marr, for being "all in" on this book from our very first Zoom call. She opened my eyes to the possibilities for this book, and hit the ground running as soon as I was ready. Jill, you're a rock-star, and I am so grateful for your advocacy and championing of my books and career.

Lastly, Zando and Slowburn, especially Hayley Wagreich and Sierra Stovall. Thank you for taking a chance on an indie release and seeing its greater potential. Thank you for being so welcoming and helpful and excited about this book. And thank you for bringing more romance into the world with your imprint. It is an honor to be part of the team.

ABOUT THE AUTHOR

NAVESSA ALLEN lives on the shores of Chesapeake Bay with her husband and their spoiled cats. She posts her books in serial format to her website via Patreon. To catch up on her latest work in progress, read exclusive bonus scenes, and feast your eyes on NSFW character art, please visit: patreon.com/navessaallen.